THE ANTEDILUVIANS

BY
ABBY BLACK

ᴄhe Aᴎᴄeᴅiluᴠiaᴎs

To contact the author or publisher:
South Main Media™, A Creative Company of Mindwatering
520 South Main Street, Wake Forest, North Carolina 27587
www.southmainmedia.com, www.mindwatering.com
contact@southmainmedia.com

ACKNOWLEDGEMENTS

Thanks to my Dad, for patiently editing my content.

Thanks to my Grandma, Bide-A-Wee, for enthusiastically
editing my grammar.

Thanks to my Mom, for imaginatively designing my
book cover and websites.

Thanks to both my Mom & Dad, for their love and support,
and for always cultivating a creative environment.

Thanks to my Little Brother Max, because he's my brother,
and he's pretty cool, too.

And thanks to all of you for reading this book,
and being a part of my journey.

TABLE OF CONTENTS

TABLE OF CONTENTS

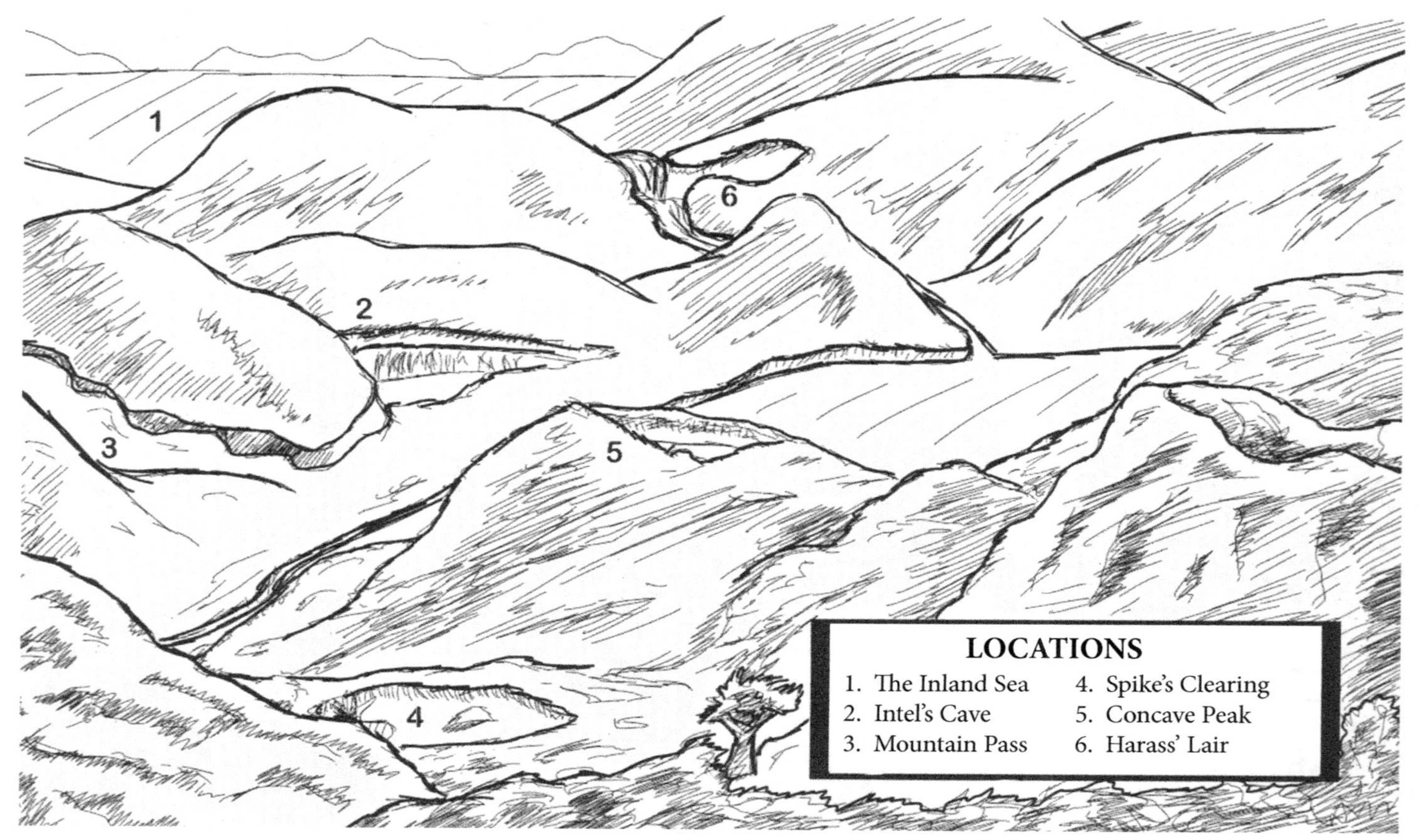

LOCATIONS
1. The Inland Sea
2. Intel's Cave
3. Mountain Pass
4. Spike's Clearing
5. Concave Peak
6. Harass' Lair
1
2
3
4
5
6

There was a whirring and banging. A single missile streaked out and collided, creating a massive fireball of blue and white flames that belied the missile's inauspicious size. A scarlet laser swept across the land, instantly igniting the already charred trees nearby and setting aflame what was left of the foliage. All life with moveable limbs fled, and most were quickly brought down by another small missile. Those that couldn't escape succumbed to the flames and fell incinerated and lifeless, their hides disfigured. The sky was turned black by the smoke of the fires, and the light was red from the same flames.

It was a scene of absolute desolation, and in the midst of it was the perpetrator; a massive, hulking Acrocanthosaurus, 30 feet tall at the shoulder and 50 feet long from nose to tail. He was built like a small mountain, and had the temper of a vicious snake. He roared in victory at the scene around him, his bellow starting at a low rumble and quickly growing to the volume of nearby thunder, as he gazed at the fires. He was now King of the Squamas. His court would be his Tyrants. No other beings would dare approach him, for on his back was a mastery of amazing foreign weapons, the Annihilator, a box filled to capacity with a rationed supply of missiles and a destructive laser. With the Annihilator, he would rule. He prepared to fire another precious missile; there were none to attack him, so why not show his prowess with such a massive demonstration of destruction?

But what was this? Out from a dense sheet of black and red flames leapt a small, young Squama whose hide was a dull yellow ocher in color and oddly lacking in injury, with a defiant expression on its face. He nearly laughed; this little nuisance, a mere mosquito compared to his size, dared to come against him? Why, this skirmish would be nothing more than stepping on the thing. He went to get his feet dirty when he spotted a version of the Annihilator on the defiant bug's shoulders. His laughter died away and was replaced by a growl; this foe was now dangerous. He fired the laser that should slice the tiny irritation cleanly in two, but the young Squama nimbly and quickly leapt aside, and the laser bored a hole in the ground instead.

He growled again; this little tyke was frustratingly agile. So what? A missile should take care of it. He fired, but again, the foe avoided his attack.

He roared in a mixture of frustration and ire. "Stand still!" he snarled, his deep voice sending terrifying bass vibrations through the air. He didn't care to waste his ammunition.

"And be crushed or cooked?" the Squama quipped, the pitch of her voice betraying her youthfulness. "Think again!"

The Acrocanthosaurus was slightly perturbed. Of all the insect Squamas to challenge him, a mere child was the one to do it! "Die, mite!" He fired three missiles in sequence, effectively trapping the foe in a circle of flames. She stood there, stuck, and rose her head to find that she was staring down his glowing and hot missile launcher.

PROLOGUE

Creatures large and small scurried off to hide themselves away, hoping that *they* wouldn't find them. Ever since *they* came, the sun seemed dimmer, the nights longer, and everyone slept uneasily.

A loud, intimidating roar swept over the hills that were illuminated by a glorious setting sun. All creatures within earshot of that dreadful sound cowered and rushed to hide in trees, in holes, anyplace that could fit them and conceal them from sight. The roar was closely followed by a second one; it was shriller, but carried every bit of the menace of the first roar.

A small mammalian beast, violently quaking with absolute terror, dared to peer out from beneath the leaves under which it was buried. Its beady black eyes, full of fright, stared up at two of the largest land carnivores ever to terrorize the earth. Their legs were as thick as grown pine trees and bulged with muscle, their tails dense and capable of toppling a maple. Tiny arms in comparison to the body size gave illusion to being harmless, but those little three-fingered limbs could give nasty gashes if neared. Thick necks led up to oblong heads tipped with gaping maws chock full of sharp serrated teeth. Long ridges ran from the back of their skulls down to the middle of their tails. These terrifying animals were Acrocanthosaurus.

These two diabolical Acrocanthosaurus were known as the King and Queen. Due to a hereditary mutation, the royal family was nearly twice the size of a normal Acrocanthosaurus. The Queen was slightly smaller than the King, and had a Tyrannosaurus rex standing at her hip. The T-rex was carrying a large, ruddy swamp-green egg in its arms. The egg was due to hatch soon, and the hatchling was expected to carry on the reign of terror.

At the thought, the mammalian beast hiding under the leaves shivered even more with insurmountable horror. A Prince or Princess would leave the valley and the neighboring mountains trapped under their tyranny for another generation. This was made worse by the fact that Acrocanthosaurus were notoriously well known for having long life spans; one of them could see 40 White Seasons and still be relatively young.

Its dread was interrupted by the sounds of footfalls in the brush, crushing crackling fallen leaves and loudly snapping twigs. The mammalian looked and saw several dozen Squamas emerging from the forest and moving toward the King and Queen. The newcomers' heads were held low in a gesture of submission as they moved at a brisk trot. What remaining sunlight was left, momentarily highlighted one of them. The mammalian cringed; the newcomers were the King's and Queen's most loyal band of followers called the Tyrants, a band consisting of the most vile and bloodthirsty Squamas in the region. They milled at the Acrocanthosaurus' feet, showering them with praises and flattery.

"Silence!" the King snarled, and his followers cringed as one. The mammalian almost had a heart attack from the volume and sheer tenacity in the tone. "What news do you bear?"

One of them walked forward and swept her head down in a low bow. "Your Excellency, we've handled the uprising at Concave Peak Mountain."

"Did you kill them?" the King prodded, his scarlet eyes gleaming with malice and excitement. He spoke slowly, as if tasting his words as he said them. "Did you make them plead and *beg* for their pitiful lives to continue?"

"Yes, your Lordship," the follower replied, licking her lips.

"Excellent," the King said, drawing out the word as a hiss of pleasure. "We will *not* tolerate *any* rebellion against us."

"Our realm must be secure for the hatch of my child," the Queen added. "Separate and eliminate anyone you find that even *breathes* a word against us." She snapped her jaw to accentuate her demand. The snap from bone meeting bone caused the poor eaves-dropping mammalian's heart to beat ever faster.

"Yes, O' Queen." All of the Tyrants bowed, nearly scraping their heads on the ground, before splitting into three groups and running off.

The mammalian's eyes widened as one of the groups ran its way. There was no way to avoid them without being seen. As it hurriedly mulled over whether to flee or stay, one of the Tyrants accidentally stepped on it's back. It involuntarily squeaked in pain, announcing it's presence. Less than two seconds later, the leaves covering the mammalian were swept away. Then, a hungry and salivating maw grasped the mammalian's sides. A crunch later, and the mammalian yipped in agony before becoming eternally still and silent.

The Albertosaurus' nostrils flared as she inhaled the twilight air. Her strong sense of smell captured many scents borne on the breeze. She identified water from the large lake that adorned the center of her valley home a few miles away, a herd of Ankylosaurus taking a cautious and quick return to their somewhat safe nightly dwelling, and then a sharp, nasty scent that harshly struck her sensitive nose.

"They're back," she murmured under her breath. She whirled around and quickly moved to a clearing. In it was a myriad of species of Squamas, consisting of brave Stygimolochs, Troodons, other Albertosaurus, and several other species that could fare well in a bloody fight.

She weaved through their midst, carefully stepping over the smaller Squamas and sidestepping the rest. She was heading toward the center of the mass, where an Allosaurus going by the name of Grit stood. He was a large brute for his species, but smaller than she. He made up for his lack of size by being brave and voracious. As far as anyone knew, Grit was one of the last of his species; the King's and Queen's ferocious acolytes had managed to slay all of the Allosaurus that hadn't already fled the valley.

She arrived at her destination and showed her respect to Grit by bending her head so that, if the Allosaurus wished, he had an unhindered path to her jugular. "Sir, I have dire news."

"What kind of news?" Grit replied instantly, his fiery orange eyes narrowing in concern.

"The King and Queen," she responded, spitting their names like they were a vile poison on her tongue. "They've returned from their trip to the mountains."

Grit's nose wrinkled, his lips peeling back to show his sharp teeth, in a silent growl. "Then gather together the Defiance band to the east. We *cannot* allow them to continue ruling over our lives with their tyranny."

She nodded and prepared to give the signal, which was a loud, guttural roar and three shorter, shriller ones. But no sooner had she inhaled when the wind carried a faint, shrill screech. All noise in the group immediately silenced, and then they could hear the last echoes of the screech, which was soon followed by four shorter but equally shrill screeches.

Grit hung his head, and he was mimicked by everyone else. The five screeches meant that the Defiance band to the east had fallen. A pact had been made with the pterosaurs in that area: The pterosaurs wouldn't be eaten, and they would notify them of any ill outcomes; in this case, the annihilation of the Defiance band.

"We can't call for them any longer," Grit said, then, snarled and snapped at the air in frustration. He stood and shouted, "Attention! We are now the last standing force of the Defiance of the Tyrants. We cannot wait a moment longer. We must search out the King and Queen, and destroy them in order to free our valley and the surrounding lands. *Their reign ends tonight!* Move out!"

The Troodons stamped their feet and screeched. They were soon joined by other Squamas, and soon there was a strange symphony of earth-shaking thuds and screeching. The sounds rose to the sky and reverberated throughout the earth. It was loud and easily showed their location; so, it only lasted a short while before they stopped abruptly and disappeared into the trees.

On that unforgettable night, the remaining party of the Defiance was executing a final, last-ditch effort against the King and Queen.

The Albertosaurus took the lead, her nose sniffing the air for the sharp, pungent scent of the Acrocanthosaurus. She was joined by three other scent-sensitive scouts who were also using the air to find the King, Queen, and their Tyrants. The group quickly made their way through the dark forest, skirting around trees, but not bothering to avoid flattening the low shrubbery. Any creatures that were not part of their group wisely scurried out of their way.

The Albertosaurus halted suddenly, smelling something new. She raised her muzzle to the sky and inhaled deeply. She recognized the scent; it was one that was a constant smell around hatching grounds and nests during the birthing Green Season.

The group had stopped seconds after she had, and looking around cautiously. One of them stepped forward and asked quietly, "What is it?"

"Do any of you smell that?" she asked at the same volume.

Several of her comrades sniffed the air. "Egg mucus," one remarked.

"Exactly," she said. "It's the middle of the Colors Season. Tell me, whose egg is left to be hatched this far into the Turn?"

An eerie quiet immediately came upon the group as they concurrently came to the same disheartening conclusion.

"It's hatched."

And now their pace quickened. There was no time to waste; they *had* to get rid of the King, Queen, and now their newly hatched offspring before the land had to bear another great many Turns of tyranny.

Bright crimson eyes, glistening with life and promise, gazed up at the new world. It had been so very dark and cramped, but now it was a little brighter and he could finally stretch out. He tried to stand, but his stout little legs were unable to bear his weight quite yet, and he immediately fell onto his chin. He squeaked at the sudden change in perspective.

He realized that he was being watched, and he looked up. The first things he saw were six huge nostrils. Looking further, he saw there were three huge heads hovering over him, watching him with really big red eyes. Frightened, he cringed away. His fear was slightly alleviated when one of the large heads began making a low guttural sound that he could feel in his bones. The noise calmed him, and he crooned. He shuffled closer to the head making the sound.

An instinct reared up from deep within him. The one making the sound was Mother. She would take care of him. He trusted her already, and he hadn't even been out of his shell for two minutes.

And then, suddenly, there were more sounds, sharper ones, louder ones. He curled up into a scared little ball as many large forms burst from the dark around him. The three heads above pulled back, making angry roars at the newcomers.

He keened in fright, unable to speak but more than able to convey what he wanted by noise. *Mother! I need comfort! What's going on? I'm scared!* was the gist of his screams.

No one answered his pleas.

Noise. Screeches of pain. More than once, something dark, warm, and wet was dribbled on him. He was harshly moved around by various bodies via accidental kicks that were always mere inches away from crushing him. And then *pain*. Pain all the way down the right side of his face, just barely under his eye. Something warm was now coming out of it, streaming down his cheek and neck. He screeched, partly in agony and partly for help. What kind of horrible world had he entered into; it hurt! He wanted to be back in his shell, where it was safe!

Suddenly, he was sharply picked up by the scruff of his neck. The skin and membraned spines located there stretched to uncomfortable limits. He writhed and squirmed in the tight grip, fearing more pain. But a soft rumble above him made him look up. One of the three heads, the smallest, was there. It must be carrying him away from the pain, because the horrible sounds were fading away.

No, new roars were growing louder. He heard many fast steps coming after them. They roared at his rescuer's tail. He cringed and curled up as much as he could. Thankfully, his rescuer was faster than their pursuers, and soon the only noise were his rescuer's footfalls.

His rescuer ran throughout the night until sunrise came, and even then they didn't stop until they reached a wall of cascading water. His rescuer carried him through the water and entered a damp and glistening cavern.

As he was put down, he crooned and shrieked. Where was

his mother? He still hurt, but the pain had turned into a throbbing as the light came. He was also getting hungry. Why wasn't his mother answering? He eventually curled up into a ball and put his head under his tail, careful to avoid touching the throbbing side of his face. At least the wound had stopped bleeding. This was a *terrible* world he had come into. He keened and began to cry, large tears sliding down his cheeks and harshly stinging the one.

They were victorious!

The King and Queen laid dead at their feet, nevermore to reign. They were free from tyranny! As one, they reared back their heads and roared a victory cry into the sky.

Grit suddenly stopped roaring as a realization popped into his mind. He looked around. "Wait. . ." he muttered, narrowing his eyes.

"What is it, Grit?" someone next to him said with a huge grin. "We've won!"

Grit turned and inquired quietly, "Then where's the hatchling and the Tyrannosaurus?"

As if he had yelled the question, the jubilant roaring ceased, as the silence spread out from him as if he was the epicenter of an earthquake. A deathly quiet dropped upon the group as they also realized that the hatchling and the T-rex were missing and not among the dead.

"Find them!" Grit yelled in desperation.

The T-Rex and the Prince remained missing for five White Seasons. The Defiance scoured the valley, valiantly searching for any clue as to their whereabouts. They shifted their search when they received a report from a far corner of the valley, where the herbivore population had declined.

Another White Season had come and gone before a Triceratops youngling came dashing from the forest seemingly from nothing but thin air, frantically pushing through the gathered masses of the Defiance, and throwing himself at Grit's feet. Grit looked down at the youngling with concern; the Triceratops was breathing hard and it was painfully obvious that he had been running for some time.

Grit patiently waited for the youngling to catch his breath before inquiring, "What's the matter, little one?"

"Attack!" the youngling whimpered. "Mother and I were at the edge of the herd feeding, and we saw the Tyrannosaurus and the Prince you're after in a thicket! Mother called the alarm, and they started to attack, so Mother told me to run for help. I ran and ran until I found you."

Grit growled, then faced his comrades. "Favor is on our side. Our patience and perseverance have paid off."

"Canter, take care of the youngling. The rest of you, we will hunt them down!" Taking a breath, he roared into the sky.

The other Squamas roared with him, following him into the forest. Grit kept the lead, following the trails at a brisk run that ate up the ground. They made a massive thundering as they went, but Grit didn't mind it this time. They knew where to begin looking for the royal offspring and its guardian, and Grit was determined not to lose them.

When they reached the area that the Triceratops had been, they stopped. It was in the middle of the forest, and it sounded like there was a waterfall not far away. This area was definitely the place the youngling had described, as there were large bloody carcasses of adult Triceratops lying in the midst of trampled ground and broken trees. It was a gruesome sight that made many of the onlookers feel ill; what could possess someone to heartlessly murder an entire herd of Triceratops without even partaking of any of the meat?

Grit lowered his head and sniffed at a vivid print in the dirt, a print that was disturbingly almost twice the size of his own.

His lips retracted enough to show two lines of interlocking canines when he identified the stench that was rising from the print. "We have Tyrannosaurus," he told the others. He plodded to a smaller print and sniffed it. Almost immediately, he recoiled and snorted harshly. "There's no mistaking that miasma. My friends, we have found the royal offspring."

Those with keen noses began sniffing for any sign of the rogues. The trail was soon found, and was followed to a waterfall that emptied into a river. The air was absolutely saturated with fine mist, and any sign of the trail was gone.

"They must've fled into the river and used it to lose us," a Troodon said, peering downstream.

Grit pursed his lips and squinted through the mist. He gingerly stepped into the river, careful not to slip on the slick, damp rocky bed. He tried to tune out the sounds of his comrades and focused on the waterfall. Looking at the heavy sheet of water, he could see where it was bouncing off of rocks. He noted where the water changed color depending on where the stones were behind it.

Then he spotted the discoloration. Taking a step closer to

the oddity, he saw that the water was murky over a tall but rather thin section. He pushed his hand through the water and expected to hit rock, but found nothing but open air behind the water. He retracted his hand, and decided to cautiously poke his head through.

The first thing he saw was that there was a wet cave behind the waterfall. The second thing he noticed was a clawed hand coming straight for his face. Only by reflex did he manage to avoid having an eye gouged out.

"They're behind the waterfall!" he shouted as he dropped into a combat stance. He roared a battle cry and lunged into the waterfall.

With water cascading over his tail and spraying everywhere, he saw that the formerly missing T-rex was waiting for him. The T-rex growled and attacked. Grit easily avoided the slashing teeth and countered with a few kicks and a swipe with a clawed hand. Grit had to retreat several steps when his much larger opponent charged. The T-rex tackled him, knocking them both out of the cave and into the open. Grit was immediately assisted by his comrades, and the T-rex soon realized his mistake. Not a minute after the tackle, the T-rex was pinned to the ground with several large Squamas holding him down.

"Where is the hatchling?" Grit demanded of the T-rex.

"Hiding, just like I taught him to do if a situation like this ever happened," the T-rex replied snappily, his jaw scraping against the rocks on the shore of the river because a Stygimoloch was holding down his head.

"Where is the hatchling?" Grit slowly repeated, narrowing his eyes.

"I'll never tell you," the T-rex growled. "He is the Prince and the future King! I'm loyal to him and him alone. I'll *never* tell you where he is."

Grit snarled and snapped his jaw angrily, and then had a small hunch as to the location of the Prince. With a few steps, he passed through the waterfall. He carefully stepped along the glistening wet stone of the cave, sniffing the air. Amongst the heavy mist and the overwhelming scent of water, he smelled another creature. He peered into dark and shadowed corners, and it wasn't until he reached the very back of the cave did he find his quarry, who had crammed himself into a narrow crack.

The Prince stared up at him with terrified crimson orbs. "Who are you?" he squeaked, trying to make himself impossibly smaller than he already was.

Grit's eyes narrowed as he stepped to the side to effectively block the youngling's way to the exit. The Prince was almost as large as a Stygimoloch, and for a being that was only six Winter Seasons old, Grit had a frightening idea of how large the Prince would be when he was fully grown.

Still cringing, the Prince added, "Are you going to hurt me?"

Grit bared his teeth, and the youngling twitched. "It depends. Now, I'm going to ask you a question, and I want you to answer it honestly. Understand?"

The Prince nodded.

"Good. My question is; If I bare my neck to you, what will your reaction be?" The youngling's life depended on his answer.

After blinking, the Prince said, "I don't know. Isn't baring the neck a sign of submission?"

It was Grit's turn to blink in surprise. "What did the Tyrannosaurus tell you about your parents?"

"He said that I would know next Turn."

Unexpectedly, Grit found himself thinking compassionately. "I believe you," he said, "and for honestly giving me your answer, I won't kill you. Instead, I want you to *run*. Run like a scared rodent who has seen a pterosaur. If you are *ever* seen again in this valley and its surrounding mountains, you are going to be killed." Grit stepped to the side, allowing a clear passage to the exit. "Run, youngling."

The Prince scrambled to his feet and ran for the exit. He burst through the water. Grit followed suit and saw a few Troodons starting to run after the Prince.

"Leave him!" Grit ordered, and the Troodons stopped. "He's been banished; but if he is ever seen again in this valley or the surrounding mountains, he must be immediately killed." Grit snorted harshly, then stalked over to the pinned T-rex. "Why didn't you tell him of his heritage?" Grit demanded to know.

"Would you want some youngling ordering *you* around?" the T-rex huffed in reply. "The kid was asking too many questions about his mother and patriarch. Telling him to wait till his next Turn shut him up nicely."

"You don't seem to care that the Prince to whom you profess your loyalty just ran off with his tail between his legs, *all by himself*, without any protection at all," Grit said, then snorted. "Some loyalty you have for him."

"He can survive for himself. You don't think that I spent all of those six Turns doing all of the hunting, do you?"

Grit snarled at the pinned Squama. "You're a despicable beast." And with that, Grit swept his claws through the T-rex's throat. Less than a minute later, the T-rex had perished.

Rinsing his hand in the river, Grit looked off at the section of trees where the Prince was last seen. "Our valley has been spared of the tyranny of the King and Queen. But was it a mistake for me to merely banish their Prince?"

CHAPTER ONE

If any of the scientists working on their latest representation of middle 21st Century technology warfare knew that one of their greatest weapon creations would end up in the sinister grasp of one of the most terrifying creatures ever to place a step on the Earth, they would've laughed and shrugged it off.

After all, they worked in a private arms development research facility. Their facility included top-notch security at multiple levels.

Saying, "Goodnight," to the armed guards posted near the lab door, the scientists left for the night, leaving their completed prototype in the lab.

In the morning, the scientists returned to find their brainchild had completely vanished. The guards reported that no one had gone through the door. Security was called to review the camera footage to determine what happened.

It turned out that it wasn't a who, but a what, that had made off with the weapon. Long after the scientists had retired for the night, the cameras had displayed the formation of a mysterious hole which appeared near one of the far walls of the laboratory. The hole would've been invisible except that the air around it rippled like disturbed water. Shortly after the hole formed, out of it came an actual *dinosaur*. A lanky, ostrich-like dinosaur had been flung out of the hole, landed on its side with a heavy bump, and skidded to a stop on the smooth metal floor. For a moment, it just laid there, apparently stunned, before it slowly used its forearms to push itself to its feet. It had wobbled for a second, shook its head, before steading.

Initially, it had looked around at the hole, then around the room. The creature made an intrigued sound as its jaw moved and the throat fluxed. There was a simultaneous intake of air amongst the scientists watching the video when the dinosaur focused its attention on the prototype and reached out to touch its shiny surface. After walking around the table a few times, the dinosaur reached out again with both arms and hefted the weapon off of the table. It lowered its head so that it could view the weapon from all angles, and turned back toward the hole.

"No!" one of the scientists pleaded with the video.

The dinosaur, shifting the weapon in its arms to ensure a better grip, walked back to the hole. After poking it with its tail, it stiffened and then disappeared. The hole quivered, then vanished by imploding on itself.

Stunned, the scientists stared at the now empty room

through the cameras. They all looked at each other.

The Struthiomimus had been experimenting with a few selections of rocks, striking them against each other. Pleased, he had recently discovered that some rocks would scratch others but not be scratched themselves, and he wondered why. On a large slab of stone was a rock that he had yet to be able to leave a scratch on. He thought it the prettiest with the way it refracted light, casting rainbows of color on the walls and floor of his cave.

He looked up toward the entrance of his laboratory. The entrance was a long tunnel linking his cave to the outside world. Sniffing the air with his sensitive nose, he searched for any hints of danger. He could never be too careful.

He lived by the saying, "You can't judge the taste of a dragonfly by how it looks." It paid to be cautious, no matter the species.

The light was growing dimmer in his cave. Looking behind him, he saw that the fires keeping the cave from becoming enshrouded by darkness were growing low. Reluctantly, he left his stones and shoved an appropriate amount of wood fuel into the flames. He checked the pipes leading to a crack in the ceiling. The pipes went all the way to the surface, releasing the smoke there. Those pipes were his pride and joy, and it wouldn't do for them to leak the smoke that could fill the cave and suffocate him and. . .

He stopped that thought; he didn't want to admit that he was paranoid. Seeing that the ventilation was working fine, he returned to his stones.

A few of his assistants were out gathering more rock varieties. He made a mental note to make sure that they weren't secretly double-agents intending to assassinate him and sell his findings. *Just in case,* he reminded himself. *My works are pure genius. Many would pay handsome amounts of the finest meat for my work.*

Refocusing his mind on the task at hand, he struck a strange luminescent blue stone against the shiny stone to see if he could finally mar the shiny stone's flawless surface. Bright green sparks soared from the point of contact and flew behind him. He turned to follow their paths, just in case they alit the stockpile of firewood. As the sparks landed on the rocky floor of the cave, the air made a strange snap and crackle noise, and he saw the peculiar sight of the air fluctuating from around a circle of undisturbed air. Despite his paranoia- no, *overzealous sense of self-preservation* shouting in his mind, his curiosity consumed him, and he stuck his head in the hole.

The next thing he knew, the hole had sucked him in. He screeched, more out of surprise than pain, when he felt as if his entire body and mind were being stretched. Briefly, his five senses vanished abruptly, leaving him feeling as if he was suspended in nothing at all. Just as he was thinking, *Is this how the pterosaurs feel?* he was flung into an open space. He tripped on the ground, then fell onto his side. Stunned, he laid still for a moment before he tried to rise to his feet. He wobbled from lack of balance, but quickly recovered his equilibrium by violently shaking his head from side to side.

Finally able to focus, he peered around at his new surroundings. Much to his relief, the hole was behind him and still open, but for how much longer he didn't know, and he didn't want to find out what would happen if it closed before he could go through again. He was apparently in a space similar to his cave, but the walls, floor, and ceiling were astonishingly smooth, shiny, and unmarred. The space was lit by some strange kind of fire, one that hung high on the wall, created a white light, but emitted no semblance of heat. Something glinted in the corner of his vision, and he turned to face the source.

His eyes widened as educated curiosity surged through his mind. "Amazing," he muttered, moving to the object that had caught his attention. It had an extraordinarily shiny surface, even more interesting than the strange stone back in his cave that couldn't be scratched. He reached out with a hand to touch it, careful to not scar the surface with his sharp, pointed talons. It was the smoothest item he had ever felt underneath the thin leathery skin of his fingertips.

Overwhelmed, he walked around the object, viewing it from all angles in order to learn more. It was mainly a rounded rectangular shape with small cylinders sprouting out from the sides. He wondered what it could do, and decided that it would be best to bring it back to the cave for further inspection. Carefully, oh so carefully, he picked it up. It was surprisingly light in weight, and easily handled. He walked over to the hole, then paused, thinking about how he got sucked in the last time. He turned so that he could stick his tail in, as if to test the waters; the tip vanished and he lost all sense of touch, but nothing else happened. Figuring that nothing bad would happen on his trip back, he stepped through the hole.

The numbness returned, along with the stretching sensation. He patiently awaited for his exit from the void, ignoring the quiet panic in the back of his mind. He found himself back in his familiar cave. The hole behind him closed with a final *snap*, and it was as if the anomaly had never been there in the first place.

He exhaled, feeling much better now back in familiar surroundings. He felt the comforting heat from the fire, and smelt the burning wood. With the light from the flames, he looked around.

This was a space to which he was accustomed, and he had no plans of abandoning it.

Placing his new object onto the table, he made a mental note to add some more fuel to the stockpile; his firewood was almost gone again. He wasn't all that comfortable venturing outside, where there were many threats and dangers. That's why he had several Microvenators to do the "dangerous" work, also known as the tedious errands.

Speaking of them, where are they? At his wondering thought, his paranoia supplied a suggestion that they were contacting someone in order to betray him. He strived to ignore it. His Microvenators wouldn't do that. . . *Would they?*

His sensitive hearing picked up the sound of someone pushing aside the vines that hid the entrance to his cave. Immediately, he tensed and took up a defensive position in front of his stones and the object. Hopefully, the combat training he received from a band of friendly Troodons would suffice. He sniffed the air to see who it was.

It turned out to be one of his Microvenators. He relaxed his posture just as she entered. She held several more rocks in her arms, the three fingers on each of her hands keeping the rocks from falling. "Here you are, Sir," the Microvenator said, placing the rocks as best she could on the slab of stone with the others. "I've found different kinds this time." Her crown of spines constantly twitched as she spoke, a trait he found almost twee.

"Thank you, Spines," the Struthiomimus said, gently pushing the shiny object aside to look at the new samples. He peered at them closely.

Spines took a few steps around him so that she could see the object. It was slightly difficult for her to see it because the top of the table was at her head level. "Excuse me, Sir," Spines said, looking the object, "but what's that you have there?"

"This?" the Struthiomimus said, gazing at the object. He thought for a moment before continuing. "I have no idea. A hole appeared in thin air, and I went through it to this most *intriguing* place. This thing was there on an impeccably smooth slab of a material I have never before seen. Since I wanted to learn more about the object, I brought it back here."

"Where's the hole, Sir?" Spines inquired, looking around the cave.

"It closed behind me."

Spines reluctantly stopped looking around and returned to peer at the object. "What does it do?"

The Struthiomimus shrugged, at a loss for an answer. "I have no idea. Perhaps you could go and bring the others, and we could all find out together."

Spines nodded eagerly. "Yes, Sir!" she said before turning and jogging off toward the exit tunnel.

The Struthiomimus turned to the retreating Microvenator. "Spines, be sure to get more oak and locust wood. The cave will plunge into darkness soon when the stockpile expires."

"Yes, Sir!" came the enthusiastic chirping reply that echoed down the tunnel. Yes, she was a twee little thing. He might even consider her his favorite assistant.

The Struthiomimus looked back to the object he had acquired. He tapped it with the rounded part of his talon as to not cause any scratches. He leapt back in surprise when the object hummed softly and quietly, but the sound stopped as suddenly as it began when his talon ceased touching it. Gingerly, he stroked the object again, but this time with the palm of his hand. Surprisingly, nothing happened.

Footsteps could be heard coming back down the tunnel. Instantly sniffing the air, he identified several of his assistants. He turned his head and saw that it was Spines, along with a few other Microvenators. Each of them carried an armful of wood, which they spread among the fading piles, and added the remainder to the stockpile in the corner. The amount of light in the cave, which had been slowly growing dimmer with the lack of fuel, increased greatly; and the Struthiomimus found that he could see much better.

"Spines said that you needed our assistance," said a Microvenator, looking up to him like a child finding a friend.

"Indeed," said the Struthiomimus seriously, looking back down with an expression far from the one being given to him. "But first I must ask you all, Did any of you see anyone following you?"

The Microvenators looked at each other, then shook their heads in unison. "No, Sir," one of them said. "We did our best not to be seen."

"Did you disguise the entrance?" the Struthiomimus pressed.

"Yes," answered another.

"Good." The Struthiomimus faced the object and motioned to it. "This is our new project," he said to his assistants. "Our goal is to find out how it works. I have already discovered that it makes a droning noise when touched a certain way, but I want to know *exactly* how this works."

"Yes, Sir!" his aides said.

They worked on the mysterious object well into the night, only pausing because the wood piles needed to be refueled. As the Struthiomimus had no intention of himself going to get fuel, he chose a Microvenator called Kicker.

The Struthiomimus was beginning to become dismayed. So far, only more questions had risen, and no answers discovered.

In addition, Kicker was absent far longer than expected. The light was rapidly dimming; and the Struthiomimus was becoming edgy at being left in the dark. His senses of hearing and smell were quite great, but his eyesight was limited.

I really need to practice seeing in this low light, he thought as he had to harshly squint in order to see his work. "Where is Kicker?" he finally said, looking around irritably. "My eyes are starting to ache from the strain."

"He hasn't come back yet," said a Microvenator.

"I can tell," the Struthiomimus said with a sigh. "So, where *is* he?" Suddenly, a sharp, metallic scent hit his nostrils. His eyes widened in shock as he identified the scent.

"Sir!" came a panicked shout that echoed down the tunnel.

All heads turned to face the voice coming down the tunnel.

Kicker stumbled into view, greatly favoring his right leg which was leaving bloody footprints on the ground. Blood streamed down his shoulders, legs, and neck. He had two jagged tears in his hide down the side of his face and across where his left eye should be.

"Kicker!" Spines yelped in alarm as the others shied away. "What happened to you?"

"Tyrannosaurus!" Kicker said urgently, wavering unsteadily on his feet. "And Coelurus!" He coughed violently, spraying droplets of blood across the floor. "They followed me back and attacked me!"

"How long do we have?" the Struthiomimus asked, moving to place himself between the object and the tunnel. He could smell them now; the Coelurus had very bitter scents, ones of malicious intents and pasts; the trait seemed to pass from generation to generation, sadly enough. The Coelurus were close. Uncomfortably close.

Kicker started to reply, but suddenly there was a shrill screeching from the tunnel, and Kicker froze in terror, then collapsed in a heap. A dangerously beautiful crimson red and aquamarine blue Coelurus was on his back, one elegantly clawed foot on the now dead Microvenator's neck.

"Intel," the Coelurus said sinisterly, her yellow eyes glinting with vindication. She slowly swung her long, stiff tail from side to side in obvious anticipation and glee. "Give me the object you are hiding, and my master might just let you live."

Intel did not have the inborn skills of a carnivore, but he *had* studied their skills from the Troodons. Hopefully, the training would be enough. "I will *never* let you nor your kind get this," he spat.

Spines and the others had crowded into a corner of the cave, all of them huddled together and shivering in fright. Spines was closest to the Coelurus, and tried to cover her quivering brethren as best as she could with her body.

The Coelurus cackled as she stepped off of Kicker. The crown of bright scarlet horns on her skull gleamed in the diminishing firelight, reminding him of fresh red roses. "Wrong answer," she hissed, then gathered her legs beneath her and lunged.

The Struthiomimus met her in the middle of her leap by twisting his body around and swatting her with his somewhat flexible tail. She grunted as she was knocked aside, stumbling a few steps before regaining her balance and leapt again at his unguarded haunches. This time, Intel had no time to cover his vulnerable side, and the Coelurus latched herself onto his body, her claws drawing blood.

He screeched in pain and writhed, but his movements only made her claws deepen.

Now that the intruder was occupied, the Microvenators took the chance to make a mad dash down the tunnel. Spines brought up the rear, pausing in her flight to look helplessly at Intel before resuming her run, and they all vanished down the tunnel.

"Get off!" Intel snarled, bending his neck around and biting the hide of his tormentor. Keeping his teeth clenched around her shoulders, he twisted his neck around and flung her away. She landed on her back and rolled several paces, only stopping when she struck a wall.

The Coelurus displayed a frightening grin as she rose to her feet. "You will pay for that," she said, growling. She took a deep breath, faced the tunnel, then screeched at the top of her lungs.

Intel growled, pawing at his ears as the shrill noise pierced them. The sound reverberated around the cave and in his head, giving him an acute headache. When the screech finally died a few seconds after it started, his retained his gaze on the Coelurus, his ears still ringing.

Something small slammed into his side from the direction of the tunnel, causing him to stumble. He turned his head to see six more Coelurus emerging from the tunnel, one on his side, and the first still stood on the other side of the cave.

"Get the object," the first Coelurus said to them.

"No!" Intel yelled, quickly throwing the foe on his side away and dashing to get to the object.

But he was too late. Two Coelurus reached it before he, roughly grabbed the object, and carried it off. The rest swarmed him, plaguing him with their talons, claws, and sharp teeth until they took him down. He roared in pain as their lethal talons drove into his skin. His vision started fading, he couldn't tell if it was because of the bits of wood burning out, or if he himself was falling into unconsciousness.

"Leave him!" the female Coelurus said, her voice sounding oddly distant and echoing. "The blood loss will finish him off soon enough. Let's get the object to our master."

The Struthiomimus groaned, then succumbed to the darkness.

Intel's body ached. He moaned softly, shifting his head, and his cheek scraped on the rough stone. He tried to see, but he had either been blinded or the wood piles had burned themselves out. Rolling onto his stomach, he bit back a cry from his tender wounds. He slowly managed to gather his legs beneath him and attempted to rise to his feet. He couldn't; he was too weak.

"Sir!" he heard someone say. Quiet, but quick, footsteps approached him; and he sensed a body next to his.

"Spines?" Intel asked, feeling his knees dangerously shaking. He shifted his weight to steady his body before his knees could give. "What happened?"

"You've lost a lot of blood, Sir, I was worried that you were going to bleed out," Spines said softly. "I managed to stop it. You've been coming in and out of consciousness for *forever*, Sir." He felt small hands on his sides, and winced away from them. "Do you think that you can handle some food?"

"Where's the object?"

"The intruders left with it. I know not where they took it."

"Where are the other Microvenators?"

Spines sighed sadly. "They were ambushed, Sir. The Tyrannosaurus mentioned by Kicker killed them."

"How did you escape their fate?" the Struthiomimus asked. *Yes, how, Spines? Were you spared because of some shady reason?*

"I lagged behind while everyone was running ahead," she said. "They exited the cave before I did; and then I had enough warning. They screamed that there were Tyrannosaurus outside. I managed to stop before I emerged and got into a crack in the wall of the tunnel. I stayed there until they all left. I came back here just before the wood burned out."

So, I am not blind, Intel thought in relief. "How long was I out?"

"Not long. They all left before the light came back, and the moon is coming back out in a bit."

The Struthiomimus narrowed his eyes at the darkness. "We must find another hole. I need to go through it and recover another similar object."

"Can you walk, Sir?" Spines asked.

"No. Continue bringing me food. I will stay here until I can move."

"Yes, Sir."

The darkness of the cave made Intel oblivious to the time of day. He slowly recovered, gathering his strength. Finally, he informed Spines that he was ready.

"Are you sure, Sir?" she asked.

"I believe so," the Struthiomimus said. "Lead me outside."

"Yes, Sir."

Intel felt Spines touch him, and he followed her down the tunnel.

The tunnel gradually grew lighter, and the exit eventually came into view. There was a thick curtain of lush, leafy vines covering up the exit, illuminated from the other side by a pale, gentle blue light of the moon. Spines went ahead and poked her head through the vines.

"All clear, Sir," she called back. "The view's not pleasant, though."

"I will survive the scene," Intel replied.

Spines pulled aside an armful of vines, giving the Struthiomimus a clear exit. Intel limped through, then winced from the sight that greeted him. All of the other Microvenators laid prone on the ground, dead. Only one dead Coelurus was present, and Intel mentally congratulated the one who had killed it.

Intel looked down at Spines, then blinked. "You are injured."

His lone assistant looked at her shoulder and rotated the joint. On her shoulder was a long scrape that had torn her rough skin. It was still tender. "Oh. The crevice was really tight. And terribly jagged."

The Struthiomimus sighed softly.

"Where do you think that we can find another hole, Sir?" Spines asked.

"I don't know," the Struthiomimus replied. He thought back to what he had been doing when the hole had first appeared. "Spines, do you recall where the luminescent blue stone and the shiny stone were found?"

Spines nodded. "Yes, Sir. The shiny one was found in a pit about fifty paces that way, and the luminescent one was found imbedded into the rock just behind you."

Intel turned and peered closely at the rock that surrounded the tunnel. A stream of blue coursed through the rock, and he used another rock to pick at the stream. The rock around the other fell apart ridiculously easy, and he soon held a luminescent blue stone in his hand.

"Take me to the pit," he ordered Spines.

Thankfully, it was a short distance. Intel was relieved that it didn't take very long. The pit was halfway disguised by a bunch of ferns that draped over its rim. Spines led the way to a hidden path, then descended down it. Once they were down at the bottom, Spines scrambled over to a corner of the pit, dug around with her feet, and used her mouth to pick up a rock.

"Here you are, sir," Spines said, carrying the rock to Intel and dropping it into his hand.

The Struthiomimus held the rock up to the sky for the

moonlight to illuminate, then looked at the luminescent blue rock. He racked his mind for how he summoned the hole. He spread his arms, then struck them both together.

From the point of collision sprang green sparks which danced spectacularly through the air before landing on the ground. From where they landed, the air immediately crackled, and behind them appeared another hole. Again, the air rippled and shook around the anomaly.

"Sir?" Spines murmured uneasily as she eyed the hole, which was rippling intensely.

Intel walked toward the hole, placing the two rocks on the ground. "Come, Spines," he said.

"Is it safe, sir?" she asked, edging toward it with sideways steps.

Intel turned to face his last assistant. "I myself went through one of these and came back. Do you see anything wrong with me?"

Spines paused, then slowly shook her head.

"Then come. We should go through and back without incident."

The Microvenator hesitated, but jogged to Intel's side. Together, they stepped into the hole.

CHAPTER TWO

Nicole Nike sighed sadly as she stared into the mirror that adorned one side of her hallway just in front of the door. Staring back at her was a plain woman with lightly tanned skin, dark brown, almost black, straight hair at shoulder length, and light bluish gray eyes. Her eyes appeared sunken and had carefully concealed bags underneath them, by-products of many weeks of almost sleepless nights of work.

Something nudged her shin, and she looked down to see her golden Labrador, Compeer, standing next to her. She patted the area between his floppy ears, and he whined in content.

"I'll be back later, Compeer my boy," she murmured softly as she straightened up again.

Her dog's whine became plaintive, but he made no move to stop her departure.

She turned away from the mirror and began unlocking her door. She sighed again as she undid the chain, the five bolt locks, and inserted three keys. She opened the door, passed through, and did them again, only this time in reverse.

After she finished locking her doors, she travelled down the hall to the elevator. She pressed the button, heard a *whoosh*, then the doors opened. She stepped in. Looking down at her feet, she could easily see the 200+ feet gap through the glass floor. The traditional elevators were on the other side of the building.

The elevator began its controlled fall. Seconds after she had entered, it reached the bottom floor, and she exited once the doors whooshed back open. Several quick steps, and she was at the building's front doors and onto the street.

She looked up at the sky, where dirt red clouds obscured the sun. The clouds were blown over by the wind from the war in the west. There were so many explosions in the battlegrounds that the sun was hardly ever seen anymore, despite the battlegrounds being hundreds upon hundreds of miles away.

Just humanity performing as we always do, Nicole thought grimly as she headed for the metro train subway that would take her to her work building. *We just can't seem to go more than a few years without getting ourselves caught up in war.*

The war had begun a few years back. A new powerful organization determined to unite planet Earth had risen up. At first feigning pacifism, the organization's leaders shifted to forced unity and amassed weapons of mass destruction, coercing neighboring countries to join their cause, and then started waging war for world peace under the name of the Unison Order.

Nicole couldn't help the urge to laugh at the sheer ridiculousness. As if another war could solve Earth's problems. None of the hundreds in the past had, after all, so how could yet another one pull it off?

Pulling her thoughts out of the dismal shadows of war, she found the transit escalator, went underground, through the security, and stood on the crowded platform, waiting for her train.

"Did you hear?" asked a woman to another, poking her digital news site. "There's a rumor of the war intensifying; Europe getting into it."

"Is this going to turn into World War III?" asked her companion with a pale face and wide eyes.

"Looks like it, but I dearly hope not."

Nicole clenched her teeth in frustration. *And I'm making weapons in the hopes that they'll end it before that happens. Why did that freak dinosaur incident have to happen?! Thank God we had the design and machining files with which to work, but we were set back months because the replacement laser optics needed re-fabrication!*

She let out a sigh as she thought. Her company was smaller than most and competing with some of the most powerful out there, but unlike other R&D companies, her company's focus was empowering the individual in a military unit rather than the institution. Like the atomic bomb of the 20th century, her mission was to create a weapon to not just end war, but to end this war, and make impractical the current mode of warfare.

Wars were fought more with drones and computers nowadays, leaving the humans safely out of harm's way. How can war end when there is no human toll of life and the fatigue of war? The simple involvement of humanity gave a cause to finish wars because no one wanted their own people to die.

The train arrived with a sleek *whoosh*, then elegantly came to a stop. Nicole barely noticed the Maglev Line design of the train as it arrived with a sleek *whoosh* and elegantly came to a stop. She entered, found her usual seat was taken, and used another. The doors closed just as she was getting seated, so she placed her hand on a railing in preparation for the jolt of acceleration. There it was; her body pressed into the seat as the train leapt forward. The train entered the tunnel, and the only source of light came from the lights in the ceiling.

It was a quick trip to her work, and she stood as the train came to a stop. She was one of the first off, and headed directly for the escalator that led back up to the surface. From there, it was only a two-minute walk to her workplace, a discreet white building. She strode up to the doors and flashed her pass at the security camera. At the beep, she pushed through the doors.

"Good morning, Miss Nike!" the receptionist chirped as she wrote something down on her tablet with a special digital pencil.

"Tell me 'Good morning' again when I've had a good night's sleep," Nicole replied as she approached the elevators.

"Still working all nighters?"

"Do you wish to trade jobs with me?" Nicole replied as she pressed the 'down' button.

"Not in the world. I'm perfectly happy where I am. Aren't you?"

"I'll be happy when the war's over, and I can get a decent night's sleep," Nicole replied sourly.

The elevator doors opened and Nicole stepped inside. She pressed the button that read 'Sub 6.' For a moment, there was no movement, as the elevator verified her identity with her imbedded RFID chip. The doors shut and down she went. When they opened again, she was greeted with the familiar blinding white walls and overhead lights. She squinted as she walked down the halls and to a door that read 'Weapons Development Room 7.'

"Good morning, Miss Nike," said one of the four posted guards standing on either side of the door. "Please show your security pass."

She held up her pass for the guard to see. Once he had nodded, she opened the door as the light above the handle flashed green.

"Guys! Nicole's here!" came an enthusiastic cry from her colleague and good friend, Pete Berg. "We were worried that you wouldn't get here."

Nicole huffed as she hung her overcoat and handbag on a hook and donned a white lab jacket that had handy pockets on the chest, waist, and around the bottom rim. "You know me. I just *can't* keep myself away from work that I've already done. Isn't it just *marvelous* that we somehow lost our prototype to a reptile supposedly long extinct?" She inwardly grimaced at the bite in her voice.

"I must say, you're in a *great* mood," one of her colleagues remarked.

"Let's just finish this," Nicole grunted, walking over to a stainless steel table to overlook the bundle of wires, gears, nuts, bolts, and other things that should turn the mess into a modern work of warfare art.

"Mark, did you go over the specs for the turbines?" a fellow scientist asked.

Mark displayed the specific design file above the table and held out his tablet of notes for review. "The computer models show that the turbines will likely exceed the performance specs."

"Excellent."

"In regards to that," another scientist interjected. "Why did we add that mod in the first place?"

"It's not our fault you decided to take a vacation. Management approved it last week. It was on the revision list, anyway."

"Cut the chit-chat," Nicole grunted as she picked up an automated screwdriver. "I'm wanting to finish this project, and useless babble about the past *isn't* going to make this progress faster. Pete, would you hand me that soldering iron?"

"Only if you pass me the 12.7 millimeter wrench," he lobbed back.

Nicole sighed quietly as she got to work, pondering the dinosaur incident. After the theft, the team had switched development rooms, transferring from Room 13 to Room 7. The forensics teams were still puzzling it out and had locked out Room 13. A private reason was that the scientists were worried that the portal would open again, and they didn't want another prototype stolen by a creature long extinct.

She forced her mind off of the dinosaur and focused on

what her current project. It wouldn't do if she made a stupid mistake merely because her mind was wandering.

Finally, the replacement firearm was given its final touches. Nicole stood back as Pete sealed on the last plates of condensed lutetium and tungsten. The invention was similar in function to the prototype, but vastly different from the prototype in shape; it was sleeker, with a modification that had been added almost as an afterthought; but the mod had integrated well.

"I never liked 'Annihilator.' What are we going to call this? How about something that sounds less like it came from an old sci-fi movie? Anyone have any ideas?"

"Harrier? Tyrannizer?"

"Tyrannizer? That sounds as bad as 'Annihilator.'"

"Terminator!"

"Yeah. . . *no.*"

"Intimidator?"

"Intimidator. At least we're now talking prevention and following our corporate values. Who else likes the name '*Intimidator*'?"

Nicole raised her hand. If they had dubbed it 'Harrier,' she wasn't sure that anyone in a like mind to hers would take the weapon seriously.

"'*Intimidator*' it is! Pete, fasten the last plate!"

Pete had just finished fastening on the final sheet of shiny modified metal when the air suddenly became tense and energized. They froze, then whirled just in time to see a hole appear out of thin air, and the air around it was rippling furiously.

"Not again!" a scientist moaned.

Nicole stood aghast at what she was seeing. It was supposed to be in Room 13! *Why on Earth had it moved to the very place it simply couldn't be by chance alone?!* Surely God had to have it out for her or something. Some vague part of her brain tried to figure out where she had gone wrong.

"Guards!" Mark shouted, running for the door. Keeping his gaze on the hole, he didn't see a colleague and tripped.

Out of the hole came the same tall and slender dinosaur, though this time it looked rather beaten up with the dried blood and the stiff way in which it moved. It owlishly blinked at the scientists, as if in surprise. A second later, a second dinosaur appeared, much smaller than the first, about the size of a rottweiler, and it looked very different as well, and in better condition save for a few scrapes. Nicole narrowed her eyes at the larger one; it had stolen the *Annihilator*!

Helping Mark up off the floor, the scientist asked Pete, "You've studied them. What are they?"

Pete squinted. "Ah, the big one is a Struthiomimus, an omnivore from the Cretaceous. The smaller one is a Microvenator, a carnivore from the Cretaceous."

A scientist coughed nervously. "Carnivore?"

"Insects."

"Wouldn't that make it an insectivore?"

"That's a technicality; the Struthiomimus' supposed to be able to eat fruit, too."

"Omnivorous?"

Behind them, the door was unlocked.

"Would you two be quiet!" Nicole hissed at the two scientists, though she didn't take her eyes off of the two intruders.

Now in the room, the guards leveled their guns at the dinosaurs. Pete hastily motioned for them not to shoot quite yet, which earned him some queer looks, but they complied.

The Struthiomimus took a step forward, simultaneously cutting short the scientists' discussion and partially blocking the Microvenator from their view. The tall dinosaur saw the object on the table and its eyes widened in recognition.

"No!" Nicole yelled frantically, diving to protect the invention. "You're not taking this one, too!"

The Struthiomimus blinked, then narrowed its eyes. It growled, snapping its jaw. The motion earned it the guns pointed straight at its head. The Microvenator by its side looked first at the Struthiomimus, then at the scientists, as if it was unsure.

"Stay away!" Nicole ordered, sounding far braver than she felt. She could feel her heart thudding against her chest at twice the speed it normally went.

The Struthiomimus curled back its lips to reveal its small but sharp teeth. It took a single step forward, but stopped when the scientists moved into defensive positions. Raising an arm, it pointed at the invention, then sharply bobbed its head toward the hole that was still open behind it.

The scientists' jaws dropped. "Is it. . . *communicating* with us?" one of them said incredulously.

The Struthiomimus tried again, pointing first at the invention then at the hole. Its intentions were crystal clear.

The scientist that had researched dinosaurs stepped toward the Struthiomimus. "You can't take the invention," Pete said, using many body motions to better convey his words.

The Struthiomimus shook its head firmly. It pointed to the invention again, but instead of pointing back at the hole, it started hissing and making scratching motions in the air. The scientists and guards tensed, but then the Microvenator pointed with a hand at the wounds on its companion. The Struthiomimus pointed again at the weapon, then made a motion with its shoulders that looked a lot like a shrug.

"What'd it say?" a scientist asked.

"It's amazing!" said Pete. "These dinosaurs are intelligent enough to use body language to convey words! Apparently, the big one got in a fight, and something's happened to the other prototype."

Nicole stared at her comrade. *Is he nuts?! Dinosaurs can't be intelligent enough to convey body language like that. They're prehistoric* animals!

The awed expressions on the her fellows' faces must have shown the Struthiomimus that they understood. It relaxed slightly and pointed at the invention yet again.

Nicole shook her head violently, saying, "No!" Even if they didn't understand English, and if they were as intelligent as Pete believed, they would definitely get the meaning via her tone of voice and expression.

Both dinosaurs slumped, as if they were disappointed. They stayed like that for a moment, then the Struthiomimus looked at the Microvenator and made a series of short growls, grunts, and rumbles. The Microvenator blinked owlishly, then nodded.

The small dinosaur took a few steps forward, looking at the floor, then moved its feet closer together and looked up at the scientists with large round eyes that somehow increased in size. The tail curled around its haunches and the arms tucked in to become flush with the chest. Making a few quiet whimpering sounds, it shifted so that it looked as cute and round as possible. Its crown of spines twitched a few times adorably, like a puppy shifting its ears.

One of the scientists watching the Microvenator nervously laughed. "A dinosaur is giving us the puppy-dog eyes!"

The Microvenator blinked, then lost the cute appearance and made a frustrated growling noise before plodding back to the Struthiomimus.

The Struthiomimus narrowed its eyes. Suddenly it bolted forward and gingerly grabbed up the invention. Before the scientists could retaliate, the dinosaur lunged away and raced for the hole. The guards opened fire, grazing the Struthiomimus as it vanished through the portal. The Microvenator took a last look at the scientists, shrugged, then also disappeared through the hole.

"No!" Nicole shouted, running forward. "I'm *not* going

through this a third time!" Before the others could stop her, she passed through the hole.

Just after she disappeared, the hole quivered, then collapsed with a snap and crackle. The air almost visibly quivered where the hole had been before the air pressure in the room returned to normal.

"Great," Pete said, wilting. "Now what?"

"Incredible! This dinosaur has managed to reopen the portal; and not only, steal the *Intimidator*, but also get one of us go back with it!"

"Are you daft?" Pete said, whirling on the other scientist. "She's gone to only God knows where and when without any preparation whatsoever! I can only hope that she manages to survive in a dinosaur-eat-dinosaur world, if that Struthiomimus and Microvenator are any clue."

". . . How are we going to get her back?"

She wanted to scream, but couldn't even if she had opened her mouth, much less hear if any noise had come from it. Her body felt like it was being stretched like an elastic band, but it didn't hurt; more like tingled, as if her whole body was being given a mild electric current. Through her mild panic of being trapped in a senseless void, she idly wondered how she was going to get back home.

Then she was back in reality. She stumbled across the uneven ground for a few feet before gaining her balance and straightening. Her first reaction was to turn, and she did so just in time to see the portal that she had emerged from vanish with a whip-like snapping sound, and then it was as if it had never existed.

She groaned and let her shoulders slump.

Since there was really nothing else she could do, she looked around at her new surroundings, which appeared to be the bottom of a moderately deep pit, having walls at about fifteen feet high. About a yard away and slightly imbedded in the dirt were two stones, one a luminescent blue, and the other a charcoal grey with a bit of rainbow shine where the black part was absent. A narrow path was inlaid into the wall of the pit, leading up to the surface.

"Is that a diamond?" she uttered in awe, picking up the black and partly shiny rock. She put it in one of her lab coat's pockets. She also picked up the luminescent blue rock, examined it briefly, and let it join the diamond.

She looked down at the ground again, then spotted slight indents in the soil. There were two sets, both with three toes; one was about twice the size of her hand, and another half the size of her hand.

"Now, where am I?" she asked herself as she made her way up the path. "And where are those dinosaurs?"

She reached the surface and looked around. She spotted a smudge of dark brown on her pristine white lab coat, and sighed. Searching for any sign of the dinosaurs, she saw two sets of foot-prints in the soft dirt. She smiled in relief and followed the prints.

It was an arduous task, following the tracks through the thick brush of the forest she seemed to be in. The sun was blister-ingly hot, but was nearing the last leg of its trek across the sky. She soon shed her lab coat, folded it up, and draped it over her arms. The plants scraped and latched onto her clothes and skin, and her shoes seemed to find every possible opportunity to trip on an exposed root or sudden rise or dip in the ground. But she faithfully kept to the trail of footprints, knowing that when the sun set, she would be unable to see them. The ground was very hilly, which seemed to be foothills as there were tall weathered mountains a couple of miles away.

"Wonderful," she said in dismay when she came upon a stream. It was an effervescent little stream, babbling happily and completely oblivious to her irritation at seeing that the prints disappeared into the water. She glared daggers at the stream as she walked along its edge, peering closely at the mud for any signs of the prints reappearing.

Something hissed, and she whirled around with a surprised yelp. On top of a nearby rock was a strange furry beast, glaring at her with beady little black eyes in a rodent-esque skull. It was displaying two impressive rows of needle-thin teeth. Nicole quickly stepped backward, not willing to go near the apparently hostile rodent thing. The creature kept its eyes on her until she rounded a bend of the stream and could no longer see it.

Only when it was out of sight did she turn around and run for what seemed to be a quarter mile. She slowed and sighed in relief at putting a good distance between herself and the animal. Her breath was coming in fast and sharp. She hadn't had such a workout in what seemed to be forever, and she bent over at her waist and propped it up with hands on her knees.

"Hello," she said with a smirk as she spotted two familiar prints in the mud on the far side of the stream.

The stream was too wide to jump over, and she didn't want to leap and risk slipping on the slippery rocks underneath the water. With a grumble, she walked into the water. When she reached the center, the water was up to the middle of her shin, occasional splashes soaked her jeans up to her knees, and the bottom of her lab coat was completely drenched. She almost slipped and fell a few times, but she safely made it across. She paused only to wring out her lab coat and pants before she continued following the prints.

The sun was just starting to sink behind the mountains when she saw movement ahead. She murmured a word of thanks when she spotted ahead of her two familiar forms walking casually through the foliage. "Hey, you two!"

The two dinosaurs froze and their heads whirled around to face her. She came into their full view, then glared at the bigger one, which was still holding the invention. She placed her hands on her hips, looking angry in hopes that they would understand her facial expressions, and thus how she felt about them taking the *Intimidator*.

While they were apparently frozen with surprise, an assumption she got from their wide eyes glued to her form, she looked them over. She began racking her brain for what species of dinosaurs Pete had said they were, along with information that they had studied. They had spent almost three days drowning in dinosaur facts and grown terribly behind schedule on the *Intimidator*'s production, but the sacrifice was starting to become worth it.

The smaller one, the Microvenator, stared at her for a moment before making a moaning noise and fell dramatically onto its side. The bigger one, a Struthiomimus, glared briefly at its companion before looking back to her.

Nicole pointed at the invention with a stiff and demanding index finger. "Give it back! Now." She stomped her foot to emphasize her demand.

The Struthiomimus growled and shook its head, holding the *Intimidator* closer to its body. She winced when the talons got dangerously close to the metal surface.

"Listen, I figure that you're an intelligent animal," she said, using many body movements. "Even if the language gap is pretty big, how about we start of with introductions? I'm Nicole." She tapped on her chest to emphasize her name. "Nicole." *I feel ridiculous.*

The Microvenator, which had gotten to its feet, tilted its head. It chirped at the Struthiomimus, who rumbled back.

"Nicole," she said again, this time breaking up her name into its two syllables, and said it very slowly. *This is stupid. How can I think that I can teach a dinosaur my-*

The Struthiomimus blinked, then made a noise that sounded vaguely like, "Neh-l."

She froze momentarily, startled into freezing in shock. "No, no, no!" she said, shaking her head, then repeated her name.

"Ni-ole" the Struthiomimus repeated.

"Close, but not quite. Ni*cole*."

The Struthiomimus frowned. "Nicole," it finally said. Its voice was rough, tough and raspy.

It actually did it. "Yes! That's my name. Nicole. I'd say that it's nice to meet you, but you stole something that I would like back." By the time she was done speaking, her smile had become a tad wry.

The Struthiomimus looked proud of itself, then made a short growling noise to the Microvenator. The smaller dinosaur used one of its arms to point to its larger companion, then made a strange yelping sound.

That must be what the Struthiomimus is called, Nicole thought, then tried to repeat the noise. She immediately began hacking, as the mixture of a rasp and a growl she tried to mimic made her throat itch. Thankfully, she only coughed for a few seconds.

The Microvenator suddenly made a series of sharp chirping noises while the Struthiomimus' expression twisted into something resembling annoyance. After a moment, the Microvenator made the yelping noise again.

Nicole repeated the yelping sound in her mind before she opened her mouth and mimicked it as best as she could.

This time, the Struthiomimus looked slightly pleased at her attempt, and it nodded approvingly. She smiled, relieved that it had only taken her one try to get its name right, and made a mental note to remember the right vocalization.

The Microvenator excitedly hopped in place, then pointed to itself. It made a noise that sounded like a cross between the purr of a kitten and the screaming of a parrot.

Nicole's brow wrinkled in concentration as she ran over the sound in her mind and attempted to channel it back out of her mouth. She coughed afterward, the sound having hurt her throat slightly.

The small dinosaur hopped again and made pleased chirps. She concluded that she must've gotten its name right on the first try, and she smiled again.

"Nicole," said the Struthiomimus. When she looked at it, it nodded its head toward the brush in front of them and started walking in the direction indicated.

"Oh," she said, then jogged so that she was walking by the Struthiomimus' side.

The Microvenator made a sharp chirrup and ran to catch up. She yelped in surprise when it leapt and landed on her shoulder. Her first reaction was to shake it off, but the small dinosaur purred in a strange, reptilian way, and rubbed its head against hers endearingly.

"Oh, fine," she said, rolling her eyes. "You want a ride, you've got a ride. You know, you're too cute for your own good. Bet you got everything you wanted as a baby."

The queer threesome walked onward. Nicole paid sharp attention to where her feet were stepping while her thoughts were revolving around her newfound company. She used her other senses to watch them. The Struthiomimus' breath steadily hissed out of its nostrils far above her head. Its large feet made solid thuds when they made contact with the ground, and it paid no attention to where it stepped, though it somehow never stumbled over a root or a sudden ditch. When she did look, the hide was bumpy and resembled crocodilian skin, though the Struthiomimus was a murky reddish brown instead of dull greenish brown. The feet from the ankles down and the hands from the wrists down were a light tan. The eyes were a comforting shade of amber and shimmered with intelligence.

The Microvenator's presence was as a constant weight on her shoulder. If she had to guess, it could weigh around 14 pounds.

Out of the corner of her vision, she could see its mouth; a long, pale orange piece of bone filled with tiny, sharp teeth. With every step she took, she could feel it readjusting its balance, as the weight on its feet changed and the grips with the toes either loosened or tightened. The small dinosaur had a ridge of bright blue quills that started at the back of the skull but stopped only halfway down the neck. These slender spines seemed attached to muscles beneath the skin that would flex according to a certain emotion. The hide was almost identical to the Struthiomimus' in appearance, but the scales were rounder and smoother. It was a solid dark brown with lighter brown stripes.

Her observations were interrupted when the Microvenator turned its head and looked at her with large burgundy orbs. It chirped softly, as if asking a question.

"Nothing," Nicole said, and hopped over a root that threatened to trip her.

When the sun was nearing its point behind the leaves of the tall trees, they arrived at a tall cliff that made up one side of a small clearing. In front of most of it was a large, thick blanket of vines. Nicole tilted her head up, and could just make out the top of the cliff in the low clouds.

"That's high," she commented idly. She lowered her gaze, then gasped. "Well, that explains your injuries."

Scattered around the clearing were the manged and lacerated carcasses of two different kinds of dinosaurs. She recognized all but one of them as Microvenators, and there was one that was a bit larger than the Microvenator carcasses. A few of the Microvenators' bodies appeared to have been crushed. The grass was stained brown with dried blood, which she gave a wide berth. A stray breeze brought to her the hideous stench of death, and she gagged and tried not to throw up her breakfast.

The Struthiomimus rumbled at the Microvenator, who chirped, leapt off of her shoulder, and scampered off into the bushes. Once the small dinosaur could no longer be heard nor seen, the Struthiomimus went over to the vines and pushed some aside with its head, revealing a well hidden cave. Nicole backed up at the sight of its dark mouth and the inky blackness beyond. The dinosaur carefully placed the invention on the ground behind the vines, and let the vines cover it up.

Nicole looked back to the spot where the Microvenator had last been seen, then at the Struthiomimus, which was nonchalantly leaning against the cliff, although it was obvious that it was trying not to look at the field.

"So," she said, rubbing her arm awkwardly.

The Struthiomimus blinked, then looked downward, as if in thought. After a moment, it said, "Nicole."

"Hmm?" she replied, looking at it.

The Struthiomimus raised a hand and pointed at the sun. It made a short rumbling noise. When she did nothing, it pointed and made the noise again.

What is it doing? Teaching me its language or something. . . "Oh!" she uttered, realizing what the dinosaur meant. *They have a language?! This is just too much. . . You know what? I'm just going to take this all in stride until I get home. No sense in going insane over how unthinkable this all is.* She repeated the noise in her mind, applied it to the sun, then did her best to vocalize it. When the Struthiomimus made no indication of correcting her, she decided that meant that she had gotten it right. "Okay." She pointed at the sun. "Sun. That is *sun.*"

The Struthiomimus was still, then opened its mouth. "Sun."

"You're good." Nicole nodded in approval. She knelt down and picked up a handful of dirt. "Ground," she said, holding it toward the dinosaur.

After a moment, the Struthiomimus made a noise that sounded vaguely like, "Ground." She had it repeat the word a few more times before it was intelligible. Then the Struthiomimus lightly stomped the ground with its foot and made another sound, which she repeated accurately.

The exchange of languages continued late into the afternoon, and Nicole found her 'dinosaur-ese' expanding dramatically. She thanked God for her natural ability to hear a foreign language and learn it rapidly.

One of the more interesting things she had learned was when the Struthiomimus used a claw to scratch a deep groove into the dirt. The mark was about three feet long. It had used "Walk" to describe it. At first confused, it had taken Nicole several minutes to realize that the mark in the ground was a measurement in length.

Stifling snickers, she had told it that it was called "Feet" in English. The Struthiomimus was very confused.

As the late afternoon wore on, Nicole had the feeling that 'walk' would be the only closest translation she could get to the dinosaur version of length measurement. She could only assume that the real word was something like 'stride,' 'plod,' or anything like that.

After a little while, she was very pleased with what she had accomplished. Though, from what she could tell, she sounded like a two-year-old. The Struthiomimus was slightly slower in comprehending her language, but it was doing quite well.

It was getting dark. The sun had been out of view behind the mountain for a short while now. As the colors became monochromatic, the Microvenator returned carrying an armful of long sticks. It was dropping twigs left and right, and the pile leaned precariously with every step.

"Let me help you with that before you drop it all!" Nicole exclaimed, rushing over to the small dinosaur to take most of its burden. The Microvenator chirped in surprise as Nicole lifted the wood from its arms. She balanced the bundle in the crook of an arm while she grabbed a few falling sticks. Once she had secured them, she held the pile of wood in both arms.

The Struthiomimus walked over to her and bent its head to inspect the wood. It picked one up between two claws, sniffed it, then nodded. It moved to tap her on the shoulder, then motioned toward the cave. "In," it said with a raspy tone.

She looked first at the cave, then back at the dinosaur. "In?" she echoed. "I won't be able to see. No see in cave." She swallowed, then made a few noises that she hoped would be translatable into whatever the language the dinosaurs spoke was called.

The Struthiomimus' mouth twisted into something similar to a frown. It made a few noises that sounded like grunts, then uttered, "In. See." It picked up a stout, somewhat long stick, dipped one end into a pool of strange-looking green mud, then held up two rocks. It held out the muddy stick in an obvious gesture, and she complied with bemusement after she once again balanced the pile of sticks on one arm. It struck the rocks together, sending sparks from the area of collision. A few of those sparks landed on the mud, and the mud burst into luminous green and yellow flames.

"Oh!" Nicole exclaimed, jumping back from the sudden blaze. She looked at the stick, which was now, apparently, a torch. "That's handy. Could you hold aside the vines?" When her companion gave her an empty stare, she sighed. "Vines. Pull." She couldn't remember the proper 'dinosaur-ese' words.

With a sharp nod, the Struthiomimus plodded to the curtain of vines and hooked a bunch behind his taloned hand. He walked a few steps back, revealing the wide doorway into the cave.

"Thanks," Nicole said as she went through. The Struthiomimus followed her, and the vines fell back into place.

The torch shed a strange greenish yellow glow around the cave. She held the torch closer to the ceiling so that she could get a good look at it. Her jaw dropped when she saw what appeared to be thick bamboo stalks fastened together with vines running across the roof, ending at the mouth of the cave, just behind the curtain of foliage, and continuing further into the darkness.

"Did you make that?" she asked in amazement.

The Struthiomimus made a purring noise.

"I'll take that as a yes."

They continued onward. About 10 more feet inside, there was a sharp turn, and a few steps farther, the cave widened into a chamber. The torchlight could barely made it to all the walls, but what it did light up was more than enough for Nicole to almost drop the torch in shock.

"What. . . is this?" she uttered with her jaw feeling like it was laying at her feet.

She went around to the walls where the mounds of charred, ashen wood laid underneath the tightly woven grass chutes that would capture the smoke and carry it up to the bamboo on the ceiling. On one wall laid a large slab of rock with many kinds of smaller rocks on top. Dark stains were on the dusty, rocky floor, ranging from droplet sized to large splatters.

She deposited the wood she held on the floor so that she could kneel and inspect one of the larger dark stains. "What happened here?" she asked, her hand hovering above the stain, just barely touching.

The Struthiomimus made an expression like a grimace. "Fight."

"Fight?" she echoed. "But it was outside. How would some-" She stopped, then jerked her hand away from the stain. She feverishly rubbed her hand against her lab coat. "Oh. It was in here, too."

Twirling around in a circle to get a full panoramic view of the interior of the cave, she saw a small lump on the floor near the tunnel. She walked over to it so that she could see it better, then recoiled once she realized what it actually was. It was a gruesomely wounded Microvenator, one that was bloody, halfway ripped to shreds, and quite dead. She saw a large puncture wound where the neck met the backbone, which she assumed was the killing blow for the poor dinosaur.

A large dark spot on the floor drew Nicole's attention. She went over and kneeled down to get a better look. It seemed to be a burn mark on the rock, the char arranged in a peculiar pattern not unlike a loose swirling. Touching the mark, she felt that the rock was perfectly smooth. Melted.

The Struthiomimus walked over to the rock slab and gingerly deposited the *Intimidator* onto its surface. Then it went over and grasped a small amount of the wood. It carried it over to one of the chutes and set the sticks underneath. It did the same for all of the chutes until the pile had been exhausted. It came over to Nicole and gestured to the torch, which she handed over. The Struthiomimus set to lighting the wood, washing the cavern in a warm yellow glow.

Nicole watched the smoke from the burning piles go up the chutes and into the bamboo on the ceiling, which in turn carried the smoke along the ceiling and outside to be released. "This is absolutely *ingenious*. Whoever said that dinosaurs were dumb or dumber than us are idiots." *I guess that includes me, too.* She inhaled and enjoyed the scent of burning wood.

The Struthiomimus looked like it was preening. She momentarily pondered how it could've understood most of what she had said, since a majority of her words were ones that she hadn't explained to the Struthiomimus yet. She finally decided that it must've taken her tone of voice and her expression as the compliment it was.

Nicole heard the pattering of footsteps in the tunnel, and turned to see who was coming. The Struthiomimus stiffened and shifted its weight. Out of the darkness of the tunnel appeared the Microvenator, carrying another stack of wood in its arms. As the Struthiomimus relaxed, it went around and deposited a certain amount under each chute to refuel the flames.

The Struthiomimus called to the Microvenator, who jogged over. The larger dinosaur made a series of sounds to the smaller dinosaur, who eventually nodded and vanished back into the tunnel. It wasn't too long before it returned; but, instead of it carrying a pile of sticks, it was dragging several large, thick leaves. It gave them to the Struthiomimus, which went over to one of the fires and placed the leaves just far enough away so that they wouldn't catch aflame. The Struthiomimus arranged the leaves so that there were several lying on top of each other, leaving one leaf alone. It looked at Nicole for a long moment before it carefully rolled up the last leaf and placed it at one end of the pile.

"What is it?" Nicole asked, walking over to get a closer look.

"You." The Struthiomimus said, pointing first at her, then at the pile.

She blinked. "You've made a *bed* for me?" She pressed down on the top leaf, and the pile gave a little under her hand. She was pleasantly surprised by how fuzzy the leaf seemed to be. She crawled onto the leaf and spread out, putting her head onto the rolled up leaf. If she curled up, her whole body fit on the leaf. "Thank you."

The Struthiomimus made a purring noise before it walked back to the slab.

Curling up a little, Nicole tried to make herself comfortable on the odd surface. Even though it was warm in the cave, she couldn't help but desire a blanket.

The Microvenator stared at Nicole, tilting its head from side to side. Nicole stared back for a moment before unrolling her pillow and draping it over her body like a blanket. The small dinosaur blinked, then jogged toward a far corner of the cave. It returned dragging a large piece of something.

Nicole took the object when the Microvenator offered it, then sat up so she could examine it better. From what she could tell, it was a pelt taken from some sort of large furry creature. The pelt was surprisingly flexible, giving her the notion that it had been treated in order to function like a blanket.

A blanket. The Microvenator had just given her a blanket!

"Thank you," Nicole said, sending the Microvenator a smile. She laid back down and draped the blanket over her, fur side down. The fur was soft and tickled her skin a little. The pelt was just barely too short to cover her entire body, so she curled up a little.

The Microvenator stood a few feet away, watching her. It shifted its weight from leg to leg as its gaze went from her to the bed. She thought that it looked reluctant and hopeful, but too timid to outright ask.

"You want to come in here?" she asked, lifting up the section of the pelt that covered her shoulders in an invitation. "Come on."

The Microvenator chirped happily as it hopped into the impromptu bed next to her. It settled down on its side and spread out its legs, letting its weight lean on Nicole's chest. She looped her arm around the small dinosaur, pulling it closer and holding it as if it was a stuffed toy. Its head came to rest inches from her nose. She smiled as it chirped once more before closing its eyes. The Microvenator was one of the sweetest animals she had ever known, and it even competed with Compeer.

Oh, no! Compeer! she thought, suddenly remembering her dog that she had left back at her apartment. She fervently hoped that one of her peers had gone over to her home and had taken care of him. She would have to give that dog a huge hug if she got back. *No, it's when,* she mentally corrected herself. When *I get back.*

The small dinosaur beside her snuffled softly as it shifted itself closer to her body. Nicole fell asleep feeling her bed-mate breathing under her arm.

Across the room, the Struthiomimus' mouth curled up into a small smile at the sight of the two. It went out for a few minutes for fuel for the wood fires, then, once it had stocked enough under the chutes to keep them alight for the rest of the night, it laid down next to the rock slab. After grabbing another blanket from the corner, it settled down and fell asleep.

Chapter Three

Something's different.

As she slowly eased herself back into awareness, she wondered if she had returned home from work and had collapsed and fallen asleep on her couch again. *I should really get that thing replaced. The padding's shot.* She felt Compeer beside her, once again spending the night at her side. *Such a sweet dog.* Reaching to stroke him, she thought. *His fur's really rough. . . I need to give this dog a bath.*

She raised a hand to rub away the sleep residue on her eyelashes. She blinked owlishly, trying to make sense of her surroundings.

Why am I in a cave?

She looked down at her chest and saw the tiny brown dinosaur there, nestled up against her chest and snoozing peacefully. That was *not* Compeer.

The memories of the past 24 hours came flooding back in a rush, and then she was wishing that she really *was* back in her apartment with her loyal dog. Nicole, now fully awake, raised her head to locate the Struthiomimus. In the dimmed light of the gradually dying wood fires, she could just make out the large dinosaur stretched out, also sleeping soundly underneath another blanket, on top of the rock slab at the other end of the cave. It was curled protectively around the invention.

She tried not to move the Microvenator beside her as she stretched out her stiff muscles. The pile of leaves had appeared to have sunk and flattened under her weight while they had slept. She could now easily feel the craggy and uneven rock floor beneath her, uncomfortably jutting into her skin. Her pillow was quite squashed as well. She sighed softly in relief when her spine cracked as it shifted back into place.

The Struthiomimus' head rose abruptly as its eyes snapped open. It stared fixedly at the dark tunnel, as if expecting something to come through. After a few seconds, it relaxed and looked her way. Seeing that she was alert, it rose to its feet and hopped down from the rock. Head cocked to one side, it walked toward her.

"Good morning," she yawned, scratching her ribs. "Is it morning? It's hard to tell in here."

The Struthiomimus blinked. It paused for a moment before bending its neck down and gently nosing the Microvenator. The Microvenator made a soft growling noise and feebly kicked out one leg; but, otherwise, did nothing. The Struthiomimus rumbled as it nosed the smaller dinosaur again, this time, a bit harder. The Microvenator opened its eyes. It blinked sleepily a few times, and stretched. The Microvenator lethargically got to its feet, and shook itself like a wet dog. It waved its tail from side to side as it eyed Nicole curiously. It walked a step closer and nudged her with its nose.

"You want me to get up?" she murmured, raising herself rather stiffly onto one elbow. She moaned again as her shoulders made a few snapping noises. She rotated her shoulders blissfully.

She slowly got to her feet, then ran her hands through the tangled mess that was called her hair in an effort to comb it out. She hissed as her fingers got caught in a snarl, and she worked to get it out. A few seconds later, she eventually succeeded, but not without pulling out a few hairs with her fingers. She rubbed at the sore spot.

"Ugh," she grunted, pulling her hand away from her hair and examined her fingers. They were shiny and slick with her body's natural excretion of oil, and she rubbed the tips together. She grimaced from the slippery sensation, then wiped her hands off on her lab coat. She held up a handful of hair in front of her face to examine it; the hair was dark, clumped together, shiny, and heavy. "I need a shower, bad."

She rose to her feet and picked at her clothes. They were dirty and wrinkled, and she could only suppose that they'd look even worse once she was outside and in the sunlight. The Struthiomimus led the way to the exit of the cave, the Microvenator following close behind, and pulled aside the curtain of vines. She walked through the gap.

Outside, it would have been a picture-perfect scene if the carcasses were absent. She wrinkled her nose in disdain at the stench of their rotting flesh, and moved to stay upwind. The two dinosaurs mimicked her, apparently in full agreement with her disdain of the stench.

"Is there a stream nearby?" she asked, then mimed drinking. "Water?"

The dinosaurs looked at each other and seemed to converse for a few seconds, then the Microvenator made a sharp chirp to her. It disappeared into a fern, then reappeared, chirped again, and went back into the fern.

"Coming!" she said. As she chased after the smaller dinosaur, she spared a quick glance over her shoulder. The Struthiomimus was going back into the cave. The vines closed behind it with a gentle rustle.

She ran after the Microvenator as it dodged plant life. The further she followed the dinosaur, she could eventually start to hear the sounds of water flowing over rocks. She soon overtook the Microvenator, following her ears instead, and soon came upon a wide river of crystal clear water. Nicole squealed in excitement as she pulled off her upper layers of clothes and waded into the river. The small dinosaur watched from the shore as she began splashing herself with surprisingly lukewarm water.

"This must be heated by an underground source," she mused thoughtfully, fingering the water. *Like a volcanic vent or something.* She dunked her head and upper torso under the water, then quickly straightened up. Her wet hair was flung over her head and slapped wetly against her back as she wiped water from her nose and eyes.

Nicole made sure that her body was sufficiently washed, albeit without any kind of soap at all, before wading back to the shore to her clothes and the Microvenator. The small dinosaur chirped happily at her as she picked up her clothes and took them onto a rock that was bathed in the warm morning sun. She spread herself and her clothes over the rock's surface and basked in the sunlight, letting its warmth and the gentle breeze dry them. She closed her eyes, smiling slightly.

Once she was dry, she redressed and looked over the water. Her brow crinkled as she thought about what she was supposed to do now that she was trapped in a world full of dinosaurs. She had yet to see anything animal or human that she recognized. She hadn't eaten since the morning before, and she couldn't exactly use her scientific tools stowed in her lab coat's pockets to survive with. She needed weapons to hunt for food.

As if to mock her thoughts, she saw a school of rather large and rather tasty-looking fish swim by. They appeared to be some sort of trout.

She narrowed her eyes as a thought came to her, and she began to jog back to the clearing. The Microvenator squeaked and ran after her.

Nicole reached the carcasses and slowed. She compared a Microvenator to the Coelurus, then found that the Coelurus had bigger talons. Holding her breath as not to pass out from the horrible stench, she bent down over the body and jerked a claw from its place in the foot. She examined the claw, then carried it over to the river to wash it. Once it was cleaned to her approval, she found a very stout and short stick. She rounded out an end of the stick so that the claw would fit snugly with the claw itself, then tied the stick to the bone with a vine. She appraised her finished knife, then made a few swiping motions in the air to find the balance.

"Not bad," Nicole hummed, fingering the sharp tip of the bone. "Not bad at all, since I have no idea what I'm doing."

The Microvenator climbed up onto a sunny rock and made itself comfortable. It watched her with observing eyes.

She bounced her new knife in her hand a few times and looked at a nearby tree. It was a thick, old pine with rough and craggy bark. She rearranged her grip on the knife and then threw it at the tree. It spun around a few times, then collided with the tree. Unfortunately, it had hit with the butt of the hilt and not the claw itself. The knife bounced off of the wood and landed in the dirt.

She frowned and fetched it. "I apparently can't throw," she grumbled. She wiped off any dirt that had gotten on the knife. Then she slashed at the same tree to see how sharp the claw was. She stood back to look at her handiwork, which turned out to be a long deep gash in the bark and wood. She hummed.

Looking at her knife again, she went back to the Coelurus. She picked out another claw, cleaned it, then found a long, straight, and thick stick. She scooped out the end, then attached the claw in the same way she had done with the knife. She hefted her newest weapon, a spear. After stowing her knife in one of her lab coat's pockets, she gave a few experimental stabs in the air, then threw it at the abused pine tree. The curved claw caused the entire spear to spin. It wobbled through the air like a toddler taking the first step, then, with a sudden *thwack*, struck the tree like straw blown with hurricane-force winds. However, the wobble had completely thrown the spear off kilter, and the spear fell in almost the identical fashion the knife had.

Nicole sighed, then fetched it. *It seems that having a claw as a spearhead isn't suitable for throwing purposes. I can settle with simple slashing, though I'm not so keen on fighting dinosaurs at close quarters.*

After fetching the spear, she twirled it like a baton for a

few seconds, then held it leisurely in her hand. After taking a few steps away, she preformed several swipes through the air. Then she slashed the claw at the tree, which ended up with a neat cut that showed the green wood behind the bark. Nicole preformed the exercise several more times, striving to make her aim impeccable and her swipe strong. She also experimented with various grasps; moving her hand closer to either the butt end or the clawed end.

Her stomach growled again, but she shoved it aside so that she could hone her skills. She needed to survive in this prehistoric land, and she wouldn't stay alive long if she didn't have any survival abilities.

A sharp yelp made her jump, and she whirled around. The Struthiomimus was halfway out of the cave, with the vines covering its back half. It was staring at her with wide eyes and the jaw was slack and slightly ajar.

"Hey, there," Nicole said as she went to pull the spear from its place in the mutilated tree. "I've been perfecting some defense and hunting tools." She held up the spear for the Struthiomimus to see. "What do you think?"

The Struthiomimus slowly came closer, walking slightly sideways. When it was close enough, it narrowed its eyes at the spear. After a few seconds of looking it over, it looked at her. After a lengthy moment, it said, "Me?"

It took a moment for her to understand. "What? No!" Nicole quickly shook her head. "It's just for food. Hunting. And maybe self-defense. Why, finally having a guilty conscience?"

The Microvenator hopped off of the rock it had been sun-bathing on and chirruped at the Struthiomimus. The larger dino-saur, eyes flaring wide, made the yelping noise again, then looked at the pocket where Nicole kept the knife. She followed its gaze, then pulled out her second weapon. The Struthiomimus looked it over for several seconds before turning away and striding back into the cave.

Nicole hummed thoughtfully, then rearranged her grip on the spear. She whirled around and threw it at the pine tree. The talon lodged in the dead center of the tree. She smiled and pulled it out.

I'm getting better, she thought happily. *Now, let's see if I can put this new skill to use. But first, I'll need a fire.*

She found a bunch of sticks, then cleared out an area of ground. After she plucked out all of the grass, she arranged the sticks she had found in a teepee shape. As the fire ate at the inner sticks, the outer ones would fall in and continue to feed it.

With the Microvenator following, she traveled down a trail until she reached the stream. Leaning over the water, she could see the fish swimming just under the surface. She took a few slow steps into the water so she could reach the deeper section better, then held her spear at the ready.

And she waited. Insects with wingspans wider than her head buzzed by. Off in the distance and barely visible through the trees was a herd of Ankylosaurus. She had an itch on her leg. She scratched it, her nails leaving pinkish white streaks that soon turned back into the healthy pale tan hue of her skin.

Then she caught sight of a few trout coming by. She waited until they were closer, then thrust. She growled when she missed and the trout bolted away. She raised her spear from the water and began to wait again. Only about 30 seconds had passed before she saw another trout, a large one. It swam closer, and she thrust in the spot where she thought it would be when her spear entered the water.

"Yes!" she crowed as she felt resistance on the spear. She flipped it out of the water. The fish had been impaled in the tail and was flailing. She grinned, and set her fish on the shore.

Looking around, she saw a nice flat rock nearby. After rinsing the rock, she placed the fish on it and proceeded to clean the fish. She cut the fish's head off just behind the gills. Next, she flipped the fish over so that its belly and pectoral fins faced her. She made a cut from the anus to the front. Using her fingers, she removed everything from the now open cavity. She rinsed both rock and prepared fish with water.

The Microvenator rumbled, then stalked over to the trash heap. It prodded at the entrails with its muzzle, then cautiously nibbled at one. It closed its eyes and licked its lips for a moment before crooning and eating the entrails.

"Glad you like it," Nicole said. "I had no idea what to do with that garbage, anyway."

She returned with the fish. Using the two stones, she lit her fire. After the fire settled down, she placed her rock in the embers to the cook the fish. The Microvenator appeared beside her. It sniffled the air around the fire and fish, then crooned, tilting its head to the side.

"That's fish," Nicole supplied. She pointed to the meat. "Fish."

A few minutes later, the Struthiomimus emerged from the cave and gave a sharp yelp and rumble. The Microvenator looked over and trilled. The Struthiomimus sniffed the air, then walked over. Nicole felt a little intimated and vulnerable, as she was sitting Indian-style, with the dinosaur towering overhead. The Struthiomimus sniffed the meat, then rumbled in distaste.

She pointed to the meat. "Fish," she said.

The Struthiomimus dutifully repeated her, then supplied its own translations, which she mimicked and applied to memory as best as she could. The Struthiomimus walked behind her and laid down on its stomach.

She leaned back onto its side and wriggled a little to get comfortable. The Struthiomimus froze for a few seconds, but slowly relaxed.

In a short time, she decided that the fish was done and used a stick to remove it. Using a leaf as a plate, she took a bite and chewed it thoughtfully. "Not bad," she muttered after she swallowed, and took another bite, careful not to burn her mouth.

When she finished her meal, she doused the fire in dirt to put it out. After all, she didn't want to cause a forest fire.

By the time she finished, the sun was going down. With the Microvenator's help, she gathered more cushioning leaves and carried them into the cave. Nicole arranged the leaves to her liking while the Microvenator went out again for wood to stock the fires.

She laid down on her new bed to test it and moved around a little so she could get comfortable. She couldn't feel the floor, for which she was glad, and hoped that she would fall asleep before the crags started to make their existence known again.

Something in the far corner of the cave caught her attention. Rising from her bed, she strode over. Just under the edge of the wood pile were a few obsidian arrowheads.

"How'd these get here?" she puzzled.

The Struthiomimus hissed suddenly.

The curious arrowheads leaving her mind, she looked up to see it standing in front of the *Intimidator*, looking as if it was guarding it. Its head was down, hiding the neck, and the tail was swishing around restlessly.

"What's going on?" she asked.

The Struthiomimus made a slight noise similar to "Shh," then motioned toward the tunnel.

Nicole listened carefully, tuning out the crackling of the wood fires and the slow breathing of herself and the dinosaur. Noises from outside drifted down the tunnel; noises that made her hairs stand on end and a shiver go down her spine.

Soft thuds were coming from the outside, accompanied by sniffing and quiet growling. Grabbing her knife and spear, she tiptoed down the tunnel to better listen. She reached the curtain of vines and slowly, ever so slowly, pushed a few just far enough aside so that she could get a peek through a very thin gap.

She held in a sharp gasp. Several dinosaurs were emerging from the tree line, intently gazing at the rotting carcasses in the clearing. She recognized the dinosaurs as Deinonychus. They were about 10 feet in length, and their heads would be held two feet below hers. She couldn't help but stare at their enormous toe claws, made only for easily slicing through flesh. The pack of Deinonychus huddled around one of the dead Microvenators. The largest Deinonychus, which she assumed was the leader, took the first taste.

She looked away from the gruesome scene. She grimaced from the sounds of rendering flesh, chewing, and excited growls as she retreated back into the cave. The Struthiomimus made a noise that sounded like it was reprimanding her.

"We humans have a saying," she muttered. "Curiosity killed the cat."

Over the next about half hour, she and the Struthiomimus waited and tensely watched the passageway. Nicole eventually walked back to the vines. Hearing little, she peeked out and saw that the Deinonychus were dragging a few carcasses away.

Returning back to the chamber, she looked toward the *Intimidator*, that was still lying on the rock table. "We seem to be stuck in here, so I might as well check it over," she said, gently picking up the *Intimidator* and carrying it over to where there was more light. Pulling out some tools from her lab coat, she began tinkering with it.

She altered a few things here and there, pulling away a few metal panels to view the circuitry underneath, and verify its power supply was functioning.

"Ah," she said as the *Intimidator* hummed softly, running a self-test. The dinosaur behind her backed away a few steps as a rather small glass orb imbedded in the front of the invention lit up with a pleasant jade light. The rotors on the inside of the two cylinders on the sides of the invention began to spin, while an indigo glow appeared inside the cylinders.

"All's green," she murmured as she switched the invention back off.

Next, she checked the mounting system. Flipping the invention over, she manually opened the plates on the bottom. Several gears and objects that looked like they belonged in a hospital room were carefully positioned inside. Satisfied that the *Intimidator* was ready for use, she refastened the plates.

She turned to the Struthiomimus, who had been looking over her shoulder with intense interest. "This is a weapon that my company's been working on that was intended to revolutionize the playing field back in my time," she told it.

The Struthiomimus blinked, then nodded. "Do what?" it asked.

"Well, we, the scientists I mean, nicknamed it the *Intimidator*, but it's actually a Neural-Linking Mounted Weapons System. In short, it latches onto your spine and taps into your nervous system. Through this link, the bearer can mentally command its functions." She paused to pat the top of the invention. "This system is equipped with fifteen missiles, a fully charged laser, and has a full tank of jet fuel. The first one we made was called the *Annihilator*."

The Struthiomimus looked contemplative.

Nicole realized something. "Hold the phone," she said, frowning. "Didn't you say that the first one you took was stolen from you?" *Oh, please say no. Please tell me you hid it.*

The Struthiomimus looked down at the ground as it nodded slowly.

"Great," she bemoaned, dramatically throwing her head back. "Just great. If those dinosaurs that stole it manage to figure out how to mount the *Annihilator*, we could have an *armed dinosaur* skulking around. As if you guys aren't dangerous enough already." She looked at the Struthiomimus directly in the eye. "I can't bear the *Intimidator*; I had an accident when I was a kid and now I'm incompatible. Look, we need to get it back!"

The Struthiomimus growled softly, nodding firmly. "Wait sun," it said.

Nicole was puzzled for a moment, then realized that it wanted to wait until morning. "All right, then," she said, walking to her bed. She curled up on the leaves as she pulled the blanket over her body.

A familiar clicking came from the tunnel, drawing Nicole's and the Struthiomimus' attention. A moment later, the Microvenator ran into view, chirping and growling up a storm. Nicole's relief at seeing the little dinosaur alive and well was stifled with concern when the Struthiomimus launched itself at the smaller dinosaur. With equal fervor, what seemed to be a verbal dispute engaged. Nicole watched, bemused, until the two dinosaurs seemed to come to an agreement.

Chirping lightly in the Struthiomimus' direction, the Microvenator strode over to where Nicole laid. She obligingly let it in and snuggle up against her.

Nicole soon fell asleep in the warmth of the cave, the body heat of the Microvenator, and the sound of crackling fire.

CHAPTER FOUR

Nicole was roused from her sleep by a sudden push on her spine. She yelped as she rolled onto her stomach over the Microvenator, who also suddenly awakened. Nicole yelped again when the spiny quills on the back of the Microvenator's head dug into her clothes and skin. Nicole quickly rolled back onto her side and checked for puncture wounds.

The Microvenator leapt to its feet and hissed at the Struthiomimus. The spines on its head bristled and quivered slightly. The larger dinosaur growled back before stalking away.

"What a wake-up call," Nicole also grumbled. "Ugh. Spines." She looked up at the Struthiomimus, and decided that she might as well teach it a new word. "Spines," she spat, pointing to them.

The Struthiomimus blinked, then began to bark loudly. Its body was shaking heavily as it barked, and it took her a moment to realize that the dinosaur was laughing. When it stopped laughing, it made the translation.

Nicole frowned thoughtfully as she recognized the series of guttural noises. "Wait. That's the Microvenator's *name!*" She turned to the small dinosaur, who looked as amused as the Struthiomimus. "Your name's Spines!"

The Struthiomimus walked away, still chuckling.

Nicole arose from the leaf bed, which, once again, had collapsed overnight, and stretched. She felt her joints crack as they slid back into place, and then she went outside to take a quick dip in the stream. She returned as clean as possible, munching on a peach she had plucked from a tree by the water.

What a fortunate find, she thought as peach juices flowed down her chin. She swiped her arm across her mouth, staining the lab coat's sleeve. *Great. But will I really want to wear this coat again when I get back home? It's probably going to get worse.*

The Struthiomimus was by the entranceway when she entered the cave. "Time," it said.

"Time to go?" she replied.

The Struthiomimus nodded, then made a move to pick up the *Intimidator*.

Already near the table, Nicole made a protesting noise and retrieved the weapon. "*I'll* carry that." Picking up the *Intimidator*, she turned toward the passageway and waited for the Struthiomimus to take the lead.

Grumbling, the Struthiomimus rumbled to Spines, who trotted down the tunnel. A moment later, it returned and trilled. The Struthiomimus hurried to catch up, with Nicole behind.

They emerged from the cave. Nicole stopped and squinted. When her eyes adjusted, the Struthiomimus and Spines were fast disappearing into the trees. She had to once again jog to catch up with them.

A few minutes into the trek, she asked, "Where are we going?"

The Struthiomimus stopped, then exhaled softly. It turned to look at her and shook its head gently.

"You can't say it in my language?" she asked, a little dismayed.

The Struthiomimus shook its head again, then resumed walking.

Nicole frowned.

While they were walking, she decided to look around at the pristine prehistoric forest environment. Most of the trees and shrubbery looked remarkably similar to the landscape that existed in her time. There were tall leafy trees, large ferns, and many, if not all, of the bushes she saw were flowering in vibrant colors. The sky was a perfect blue, and spotted with small fluffy white clouds. Insects buzzed from all angles. Every so often, she could see a dragonfly the size of her hand go by. The sunlight shined through the leaves of the trees, tinting the light a yellowish green.

Looking through the trunks of the trees, she could see a small lake with large herbivorous dinosaurs drinking the water.

Along the shore, there were several more dinosaurs eating the shrubbery. Along the path in varying places, the plants were trampled by crossing animals. She looked ahead up the path, and saw that it was leading them toward the lake.

After a few more minutes of walking, they exited the trees; and the lake was in full view. Nicole moved so that the Struthiomimus was in between her and the much larger dinosaurs, but kept a clear view of her surroundings. A herd of Triceratops were lined up at the water line, drinking. Further out in the water, a few Brachiosaurus were slowly wading along. The water was at their stomachs, which led Nicole to assume that the water where they were was well over a dozen feet deep. A herd of Ankylosaurus were grazing on the brush a short distance away from the Triceratops herd. About an eighth of a mile away, she spotted a band of Appalachiosaurus exiting the forest and making their way toward the herbivorous dinosaurs.

She balked at the sight of the Appalachiosaurus, and moved so that the Struthiomimus was between her and them. She had no idea how her knife and spear could be against carnivores that she could tell already were almost four times her size. She shifted her grip on her spear, just in case.

A Brachiosaurus in the the water made a loud bellowing sound in such a deep base tone it made her bones vibrate, and the heads of all of the other dinosaurs rose from their drinking or eating. They all looked toward the band of Appalachiosaurus approaching. The band stopped, and the leading Appalachiosaurus took a step forward and screeched. The Triceratops moved so that their heads were facing the Utahraptors, but the Ankylosaurus returned to eating.

The Struthiomimus and Nicole looked between the two dinosaur species, wondering if there was going to be a fight.

The Appalachiosaurus that had screeched walked forward toward the Triceratops herd. When the others began to follow the Appalachiosaurus, it waved its tail at them and hissed. The Appalachiosaurus continued on while the others lingered behind. When the single Appalachiosaurus arrived within a short distance of the Triceratops herd, the largest Triceratops moved forward. The Triceratops grunted and waved its head around, showing off its large head spikes. The Appalachiosaurus hissed, turning so that its flank was vulnerable. When the Triceratops hesitated, the Appalachiosaurus rumbled loudly. After a second's more hesitation, the Triceratops rumbled back. The Triceratops herd resumed drinking, and the Appalachiosaurus band approached. The lead Appalachiosaurus had the band circle around the Triceratops and they began drinking the water on the other side.

"What just happened?" Nicole wondered aloud.

The Struthiomimus didn't answer her, instead walking toward the band of Appalachiosaurus. Once it was close by them, the Struthiomimus screeched.

"What are you doing?!" she said in alarm, her eyes widening. She could feel her heartbeat begin to accelerate.

The Appalachiosaurus raised their heads and looked toward them. The leader of the band screeched back, then trotted to intercept them. Nicole kept close to the Struthiomimus, in fear for her life, as the Appalachiosaurus towered over her and was undeniably a carnivore.

The Appalachiosaurus stopped in front of them and rumbled. The Struthiomimus rumbled back, and then they began exchanging noises between the two of them. Nicole listened carefully, but couldn't clearly distinguish any words. After a few minutes, she clearly heard the Struthiomimus say "Human." Nicole stifled a cry when the Appalachiosaurus took a few quick steps around the Struthiomimus, and she found herself face-to-muzzle with the large carnivorous dinosaur.

Seeing that the large dinosaur was only inches in front of her, she couldn't help but take it in. The hide was a burnt umber, similar in texture to the Struthiomimus', but much looser and showed some bones along the back and ribs. On the back of its head, shoulders, and the end of the tail there were bunches of thin spines. There were a few scars on the face and sides. The eyes were a dark yellow with a wide black slit as a pupil which was focused on her. The teeth were the size of her index finer and twice as thick. She couldn't look away from those teeth.

"Please don't eat me," she pleaded quietly as the Appalachiosaurus sniffed her. She racked her brain for a translation into dinosaur-ese, but came up with only "No" and "Eat." She quickly said those in dinosaur-ese.

The Appalachiosaurus snorted suddenly, leaping back several steps away from her. It blinked at her with its ocher eyes a few times, then hissed at the Struthiomimus.

The Struthiomimus made a few soft barking sounds. It was chuckling.

The Appalachiosaurus looked like it was about to reply when they heard a loud roar. All heads rose as one to face the trees. Another roar was heard, this one shriller, and then a gigantic bipedal dinosaur, a T-rex, emerged from the forest. Milling around at its feet were several dozen smaller dinosaurs, Coelurus, which Nicole recognized as the only other breed that was amongst the Microvenator carcasses at the cave.

The Struthiomimus and the Microvenator stiffened. Nicole

was gaping in terror at the T-rex. *And I thought that the* Appalachiosaurus *was big!*

The herbivorous dinosaurs, upon seeing the newcomers, panicked. The Triceratops herd rushed to the water, which splashed in gigantic waves around their bodies as they swam out to join the Brachiosaurus. The Ankylosaurus herd stampeded into the trees, soon vanishing into the shrubbery.

While this was happening, the two new dinosaur species approached at a full run. The Struthiomimus screeched at the Appalachiosaurus, who ran off.

The Struthiomimus turned and grabbed the *Intimidator* before it and Spines turned tail and ran off into the forest. Nicole followed as fast as she could, leaping over roots and ditches, and using her foot to bounce off of trees in order to make sudden corners faster. She risked looking over her shoulder to see if there were any Coelurus or T-rex following, and promptly tripped over a root that she hadn't seen.

"Never look back, Nicole!" she grumbled at herself as she quickly pushed herself back onto her feet. She had seen a few Coelurus running after them, but they were a ways off. "It's a rule! Whenever you're about to get eaten, never look over your shoulder, or else you'll trip. *Never* fails!"

The Struthiomimus and Spines were farther up ahead, and they had gained distance since she had tripped. Since they had longer legs in proportion to their bodies, they were faster. Nicole assumed that it would be nearly impossible for her to catch up, pretty probable that she would be caught by the Coelurus, and thus, she reckoned that it was time to hide.

As she ran, she looked for any suitable places. She considered a hole and a dense thicket a few times, but wondered how powerful her pursuers' sense of smell was, and discarded those options. And then she saw a tree up ahead with lots of branches. However, the lowest was barely going to be within her reach, and that was *if* she put all of the strength she could into her legs and timed the jump exactly right. Not letting herself second-guess, she threw her spear to the side and leapt up to the closest branch. Her fingers wrapped around the wood and tightened as the rest of her body swung. She almost slipped because of her own momentum. She swung her legs from side to side, caught the branch with one leg, then hoisted herself up onto the branch. Once she was up, she quickly ascended about a dozen more feet before she stopped.

She realized that she was hyperventilating loudly, and she buried her lower face in her coat. Then feeling dizzy from stopping quickly, she roughly shook her head to clear it.

She waited.

Footsteps. She looked down through the leaves just in time to see three Coelurus run by. One sniffed the air as it ran past, and slowed. The other two slowed as well, and then all three came to a stop. The one that had sniffed growled at the other two, and then all three sniffed. One lunged into a some bushes that were next to Nicole's tree. It emerged from the bushes carrying a long stick. The other two growled, then ran on. The Coelurus with the stick snapped it between its jaws and ran to catch up.

Nicole looked down. That stick had been her spear. If their sense of smell was so powerful that they could sense her scent on her *spear*, then she was extremely relieved that she hadn't stayed on the ground. She was doubly pleased that they hadn't looked up, either. She didn't want to go down yet, just in case they were still in the area. So, she made herself comfortable on the branch she was on.

After a short while, she tensed again at the sound of footfalls. She looked toward the source and saw the Struthiomimus and Spines come from the underbrush. Both of them looked tired and were still panting. They were looking around. Spines saw the spear, and then hissed to the Struthiomimus. The Struthiomimus saw it also and hung its head.

She watched them, bemused. *Are they lamenting over me?* When they didn't move from their positions next to her spear, she realized that they were. *They must think that I'm dead.* "Hello! I'm up here!"

Both of them looked up sharply, and their expressions immediately improved. She smiled back at them as she descended from the tree. She dropped from the last branch, landed on her feet, and bent down to pick up her spear. She winced when she saw the teeth marks in the wood. That was a close call.

The Struthiomimus sighed, then began walking toward the nearest mountain without another glance toward Nicole.

"What? That's it?" Nicole said indignantly as the ostrich-like dinosaur walked off. "Hey, let's have a moment of silence for the human. Hey, look! She's alive! Let's not even check to see if she's injured herself, get going." She rolled her eyes.

The Microvenator leapt up to Nicole's shoulder and rubbed its head against hers. Nicole stroked its head in a gesture of comfort.

"Lovely to see that someone cares," Nicole muttered as she set off after the Struthiomimus.

Spines chirruped.

The Struthiomimus seemed to be constantly on the look-out for danger as it led the way to a new trail that curved toward the mountains. Nicole used what was left of her spear as a walking stick, and she began using it more as she grew tired. The large omnivore seemed to have endless endurance, and was always going at a slow jog. Of course, it was a slow jog to it; for Nicole it was a slow *run*. Also, she was carrying a dinosaur on her shoulder as if it was an overgrown and featherless parrot. The Struthiomimus either didn't care or didn't notice about her lack of any endurance, since it didn't let off on the pace.

I hate running, Nicole mentally grumbled as she panted. *No, check that, I hate running for long distances. I'm a sprinter! I don't do long distances!*

Eventually, they came across a lively mountain stream. Nicole almost immediately found a warm rock to collapse upon. With her chest heaving like billows, she watched the Struthiomimus stop in its tracks and look at her over its shoulder with what appeared to be an irritated look.

She shot back at it an identical look. "I don't care. I'm tired. I'm hungry. Leave me alone until I'm ready to go on."

The Struthiomimus narrowed its eyes at her, but when she did nothing, it sighed and walked back. It went to a large bed of moss under a tree and laid down on the moss. The Microvenator, being completely rested from taking the journey doing nothing more than keeping its balance on Nicole's shoulder, apparently decided to play in the stream.

Nicole saw movement in the water, away from Spines' antics. It was a fish. She was really hungry, but wasn't quite willing to move to catch it. And then she had to clean it, and cook it, which involved building another fire. . . *Too much work,* she decided. She looked around for a fruit tree. She was in the mood for an apple. *Mm, apples.*

As if placed by providence, she saw an apple tree not twenty feet away, on the other side of the stream. It was in the peak of productivity, and the apples on it were large, red, and looked extremely juicy and tasty. She wondered how many of them could fit in her lab coat's pockets.

Why use pockets? she thought, recalling pictures of people carrying their belongings with them via bags tied to a stick. She had a spear, she could use it as the stick. And the temperature was moderately warm; she could do fine without the extra layer of fabric.

Having decided what to do, she took off her lab coat and carried it over to the apple tree. She spread out the coat inside up over the grass. She then reached for the nearest apple and plucked it loose. In a few minutes, she had a fairly large pile of ripe apples laying on her coat. Not wanting to make the load too heavy, she reluctantly stopped picking the fruit and tied up her coat, then slid the bundle onto her spear. She hefted it over her shoulder to test the weight; not bad. It was a little top-heavy and wanted to slide down her shoulder, so she put the stick closer to her neck and slid the bundle closer to her body. That was much better.

Thankful, she put her bundle on the ground and plucked another apple from the tree. She ate it with a pleased smile. To rinse down the apple, she drank the stream water. The water tasted pure, but had a hint of nasty grit.

As soon as she threw away the apple core, the Struthiomimus rose to its feet and rumbled at her. Nicole picked up her apple bundle on a stick, then grabbed a second apple from the tree for the road. Spines came out from the water and skipped to the Struthiomimus' side.

And the trek continued. Nicole was dismayed at the pace, once again a slow run for her, but she could take out her annoyance on the apple. Sharply, she bit into it.

The sun was going down when the Struthiomimus stopped. Nicole didn't care about the state of her clothes anymore (they were destined for the garbage bin when she got back home), and she fell first to her knees, and then to her face. She ignored the dirt that got itself onto her skin. It wasn't like she was capable of being impeccably clean right now. She was confident that the first thing she would do when she got back would be spending half of the day in a tub of steaming hot water, and the last half of the day sleeping on a real bed. *Maybe in reverse. Nah!*

She pulled her face from the ground to see the Struthiomimus. It was walking toward a large rock, one the size of a two-story building. It was a craggy boulder, full of ledges that appeared climbable. She wondered what the view from the top looked like, but she was far too tired to try and climb it.

The Struthiomimus apparently wasn't tired at all despite the distance they had gone. Having sat down the *Intimidator*, it started climbing the rock. It leapt from ledge to ledge like a mountain goat. Once it was at the top, it faced a certain mountain in the distance. It was silent for a second, then let out a loud, shrill roar. The roar echoed through the trees until she could no longer hear it. Several seconds later, she heard another roar, this one being deeper and faint. It came from the mountain. The Struthiomimus roared once more before descending down the rock.

"What was that?" Nicole asked as she picked herself up from the dirt. "And where are we sleeping tonight?"

The Struthiomimus landed on the ground, then motioned to a hole at the base of the rock. She looked at the hole, then went closer to get a better look. It was a good sized hole, big enough that the Struthiomimus would wriggle itself through, and apparently that was where they were staying for the night.

What's a little more dirt? she thought as she and Spines entered the hole.

She looked around, but there wasn't much to see. It was almost pitch black inside. The only light came from the hole's entrance, which was now gone thanks to the Struthiomimus entering behind them. She scrambled out of its way against the back wall.

Nicole felt around for a flat area, but found none, so she settled for finding an apple to munch upon for dinner. She plucked out two more for her companions, who accepted them. While they chewed, she leaned back. With the small amount of light coming in, she could see that there were tree roots dangling over and around her head. If she used a little bit of imagination, the roots became grotesque long fingers trying to grab her. She violently shoved that mental image out of her mind.

I hope that it doesn't rain, she thought, noticing how the hole sloped downward. *Rainwater probably carved out the hole in the first place.*

Once they finished the apples, the cores were thrown outside. She yawned and closed her eyes. The Microvenator was settling in beside her as she drifted off to sleep.

CHAPTER FIVE

Nicole awoke to the ground vibrating. She slowly opened her eyes, wondering, *Why is the ground vibrating?* The Struthiomimus was already awake, and it was peering out through the hole's entrance. She groggily pushed herself upright and joined the Struthiomimus to look outside.

Her sleepiness fled when she saw a herd of Corythosaurus passing by the rock. They were a myriad of neutral colors, ranging from primarily black to white, with every combination of brown and gray in between. Each had a splash of bright color on their domed crests, with the males having larger crests in more vibrant crests in hues of red and yellow. There seemed to be about a dozen adults, and another half dozen youth dancing around their feet. The largest were the size of the Appalachiosaurus. Their forelegs were about half the size of their back ones. The forelegs served as arms when going slowly, and as legs when running. The herd had stopped nearby the rock to graze on the lush shrubbery.

"Cool," Nicole murmured, watching the young Corythosaurus play. "They're so cute!" She crawled over the Struthiomimus and emerged from the hole to get a better look.

Once of the closest adults saw her and made a loud trumpet noise that stopped Nicole in her tracks. She quickly assumed a passive body stance, turning her head so that she wasn't looking at them directly. The trumpeting adult lowered to all fours and walked closer to her. She held completely still as the Corythosaurus sniffed her. After a few seconds, the Corythosaurus snorted and brayed. Nicole looked at it out of the corners of her wide eyes, having no idea what the dinosaur was going to do next. The Corythosaurus was in no way a predator, but it could seriously harm her simply with its blunt teeth or weight.

Nicole quickly ran through her dinosaur-ese. "I not harm you," she said in that language, hoping that she got the grunts, rumbles, and other sounds right.

The Corythosaurus snorted again, and turned its head to the side. Nicole leaned back as almost a quarter of her vision was taken over by a large amber eye with a pupil similar to her own. The eye stared at her for another few seconds, then the Corythosaurus huffed and walked away.

Nicole stared at the swaying haunches as it walked away. *What just happened?* she wondered.

Suddenly, she was almost knocked over by several young Corythosaurus. The tallest reared back on its hind legs and she found herself seeing eye-to-eye with it. It planted its forelegs upon her chest, and she suddenly had to bear some of its weight. It nuzzled her neck. The other young Corythosaurus milled around her, sniffing. The one leaning on her got down and joined its buddies.

"I'm very popular," Nicole mused, patting a few heads. They crooned happily, and she soon realized that they loved having their little crests scratched. She tried to tell their genders by the color of their crests, but the colors were dull and almost the same color as their hides, making nearly impossible to determine.

Nicole began a dinosaur version of chase. She was having the time of her life; she hadn't played like this in ages!

She was abruptly jumped and tumbled onto her stomach. She quickly rolled over just in time to have several noses nuzzle her face. She squealed and playfully batted them away; but they were stronger, and her bats did little against them. One of them found the ticklish spot on her abdomen, and she burst into a fit of giggles. The young Corythosaurus around her squealed happily.

And then the Struthiomimus appeared next to her. It snorted a few times at the young Corythosaurus, who made pitiful whining noises in return. A strong rumble from the larger omnivore caused them to whine again, but they went back to the adults.

"Aw," Nicole whined up at the Struthiomimus. "Why'd you have to send them away? We were having so much fun!"

The Struthiomimus shook its head at her and motioned to the sun. She looked up and saw that it had moved a great amount since she had awakened. She estimated that a few hours had passed.

Wow, was I really playing that long? she thought in amazement. "All right. I guess that it's time to get up." She picked herself up from the ground and brushed off the loose dirt on her clothes.

The Struthiomimus nodded, then began walking. Spines came from seemingly nowhere, dragging across the ground her bundle of apples. The Microvenator held them out to Nicole, who took them with thanks. Nicole took out an apple and ate it.

The Struthiomimus continued on the path that led to the mountains. As they made their way along it, Nicole noticed that the landscape was becoming more hilly and uneven, and from what she could see through the trees up ahead, it only became steeper. Fortunately, the path wasn't going straight up the mountainside, but along it, gently sloping uphill.

When the sun was just passing its zenith, Nicole spotted a small band of Appalachiosaurus tailing them. She at first thought that it was the same band as back by the lake, but a few of their markings were different. When she pointed them out, the Struthiomimus froze, then gave a quick screech. The leading Appalachiosaurus gave a return screech, then it and its comrades veered off and vanished in the trees.

"What was that about?" Nicole asked.

"Eat," the Struthiomimus said.

She felt her heart skip a beat. "They were going to *eat us?*"

The Struthiomimus shook its head. "No. You."

Nicole gulped. "I was going to be eaten? It's because I'm small, vulnerable, and squishy, isn't it?"

The Struthiomimus nodded.

She looked over her shoulder at the last place she had seen the Appalachiosaurus. *Thank you, God, that I was able to point them out!*

A little further on, and they reached a small clearing in the trees. It was a steep clearing, but lush with grasses and scattered with a few rocks. She looked behind them and was able to see the valley below. She could see the lake and the cliff (where the cave was). On the lake's shores, she could just make out the dots of the dinosaurs. There were a few flying creatures, but she couldn't tell if they were birds or pterosaurs.

The Struthiomimus grumbled at her. She turned and ran to catch up.

As they were exiting the clearing, she spotted a pear tree. She saw that most of them were half eaten, but there were a few almost ripe ones that hadn't been attacked by fruit eaters. She put the untouched pears in her bag.

Clouds were covering the sun as the Struthiomimus stopped at an ancient tree. She looked it up and down, wondering why the dinosaur had called a halt at the tree. The tree was withered, the bark was pale and crumbling, and the whole tree was full of knots and bent in gruesome ways. It was a very thick tree, having a radius of a half-grown Californian redwood. It was only when the Struthiomimus disappeared into it did she notice a thin rip in the wood. She found the gap and went through it as well. Inside, the tree was completely hollow, and the roof of the partially hollow tree was where there was still healthy and living wood. The floor was made of a very dark dirt scattered with wood chips.

"Comfy," Nicole remarked. "Now, why'd we stop here? There's still about an hour of daylight."

Before the Struthiomimus could answer, a distant rumble of thunder answered for him. She peeked outside to see the darkening sky. The amount of light had drastically diminished with the cloud cover, and it might as well have been twilight.

Nicole ducked back inside the tree's cover when a drop of rainwater landed on her nose. She backed up to the far side of the tree and made herself comfortable on the dirt. Sitting Indian-style, she pulled another apple from her bag and began munching on it. It was steadily raining by the time she had eaten it to the core, and she threw it outside.

The Struthiomimus laid down on the dirt and began inspecting the walls of the tree. It occasionally bit at the wood, and she realized that it was eating the insects on the wood. Spines didn't seem to be hungry, as it walked over to her and laid down beside her. Nicole kept a respective distance from the spines as she stroked its back.

Nicole didn't know when she had fallen asleep. She only realized so when the Struthiomimus nosed her back to wakefulness.

Realizing that she was still muttering nonsensically, she cleared her head and looked around. The Struthiomimus was walking away toward the exit, and Spines was still sleeping with its head on her thigh. Sometime during the night it had stopped raining. The morning sunlight caused the wetness on the landscape to coruscate.

The Struthiomimus exited the tree, so Nicole quickly picked herself off of the dirt floor to follow. Her movements awakened the Microvenator, and Spines trotted after them.

Nicole had to be very careful not to slip on the wet ground. The path was mostly barren of any grasses, and was little more than a wide strip of slippery mud, roots, and rocks.

She almost fell once from a misstep, and grabbed onto the nearest object to keep herself from falling. The object she grabbed onto ended up being the Struthiomimus' tail. It was jerked out of her grasp, causing her to almost fall again. The Struthiomimus whirled around and hissed at her through bared teeth, waving its tail wildly behind it, as if shaking off a phantom touch. She recoiled and held up her hands.

"I get it. No touching the tail."

The Struthiomimus growled once more before turning around and continuing on. Nicole groaned as she saw that it was going a bit faster now. It was enacting a petty revenge by straining her legs and raising the risk of falling face first in the mud. To make things worse, the Struthiomimus was kicking up mud with every step it took, and her clothes were getting splattered with the wet dirt.

Although her endurance had risen drastically since she had first come through the portal, she wasn't going to able to sustain this brisk pace for long.

Eventually, she couldn't take any more and veered off toward a large rock that had been already been dried by the sun. The Struthiomimus stopped when she left the trail.

"I don't care what you say," she said in between gasps for air when the Struthiomimus growled at her. "I'm not moving from this spot until I catch my breath." She threw herself down onto the rock and flipped over so that she was lying on her back.

The Struthiomimus hissed, then walked on. She watched in surprise as it continued down the path. Though with obvious reluctance, Spines went with it.

Is it serious? Nicole laid her head down and stared at the sky. "I'll catch up with it, as long as it keeps on walking." She hummed a song that sprang into her mind when she said 'walking.'

The sun's radiance was very warm, and so was the rock. Even after she recovered her breath, she was becoming more and more reluctant to rise from her spot. Her eyelids were also becoming heavy. She blinked for longer and longer periods.

A branch snapped.

Her eyes darted open and she quickly raised her head to look around. The sun had traveled, indicating that she had fallen asleep and had slept for about an hour, maybe even two. The ground vibrated with a heavy footsteps, and she heard more branches breaking and falling to the ground.

Something big was coming. She felt another step, and a few seconds later, another one. It was bipedal. Bipedal and big didn't create a very promising mental image. She began looking for an escape route, and saw a hill close by. If she could scale it, she could possibly lose whatever it was on the other side. She rose from the rock.

And then she saw it. It was big, colored a murky green, and it was looking directly at her. With a pang of terror, she recognized it as a T-rex. She choked down a scream, grabbed her spear-with-coat sack, and fled.

The T-rex roared and chased after her.

Run run run run. . . was her prayer as she did exactly that. She scrambled up the hill on all fours so that her hands were helping her along. She crested the top. The ground was slippery and was still wet, and she had barely made it a few steps down the other side when her foot slid out from under her and she tumbled down. She rolled uncontrollably down the moderately steep slope, head over heels. She held her spear out to the side, to avoid impaling herself. She could feel the hilt of her knife, stuck into a belt loop, painfully dig into her ribs with every rotation of her body.

She wasn't able to stop her tumble until she crashed through some underbrush and landed with her back against a large root of a tree. For a moment, she laid there with her feet pointing toward the sky, recovering, until she saw the T-rex crest the hill. She quickly grabbed her bundle, clambered to her feet, and resumed running for her life.

Employing the tactics that she had used when running from the Coelurus, she took to a zig-zag course. Since the T-rex was much, much larger than she, she hypothesized that it would have a bit of trouble taking sharp turns. It did, but its legs were strong and ate up the ground. Whatever ground she gained with the tactic was lost.

She began looking for help, but it seemed that the forest was suddenly completely void of any other life. Finally, she spotted large herbivores in the distance. She immediately altered her course and aimed for them. Her feet pounded against the dirt while a choppy *Hallelujah* chorus stanza went through her head. She doubted that she had ever run so fast in her life. As she grew closer to the herbivores, she saw that they were Ankylosaurus, the heavily armored quadrupeds with clubbed tails.

"Help!" she screeched in dinosaur-ese. Several heads rose from grazing and turned her way. She entered their midst and hid behind a rather large one. "Help me!" she added.

The T-rex slowed, then stopped. It growled at the herd as it looked them over. She was watching it from under the Ankylosaurus' stomach. It didn't seem to see her.

And then the Ankylosaurus she was hiding behind moved. It turned to face the T-rex and bellowed loudly. Several more Ankylosaurus did the same, challenging the predator to come any closer. Tails that ended in bony clubs swung from side to side, accentuating the challenge.

The carnivore growled, sniffing the air. It lowered its head and glared at Nicole. It growled out a single word in dinosaur-ese; "Mine."

"No," the Ankylosaurus that Nicole was hiding behind replied defiantly, narrowing its eyes. It pulled its clubbed tail up in the air, then slammed it down on the ground with such a force that the ground shook. Dust rose up from the point of impact before blowing away in a breeze.

Nicole stared at the crater the club had formed in the earth. Such a powerful strike surely could easily break the T-rex's legs.

The carnivore growled wordlessly, seeming to be thinking over its attack plan. Apparently deciding that the clubbed tail wouldn't be worth the trouble, the T-rex stalked off, moving like an angered brat. She watched it leave until the swinging tail could no longer be seen.

The Ankylosaurus that she had hid behind turned around and faced her. She backed up a few steps and held her hands away from her body. Its nostrils flexed as it sniffed her.

Nicole racked her brain for any dinosaur-ese that could convey to the Ankylosaurus that she meant no harm. "Me no hurt you."

The Ankylosaurus reared back its head a little and eyed her with suspicion.

She quickly added that she was with the Struthiomimus. She coughed when she said its name.

To her surprise, the Ankylosaurus' eyes widened, then it nodded. It rumbled something, and it took her a moment to realize that it had said something along the lines of "Come, I will take you." She knew that she was missing a few words in translation, but she understood the gist of it. The Ankylosaurus motioned to its back, and she used the stout spikes to hoist herself up. The back was rough and plated, and only in the exact middle of its back was she able to sit in relative comfort.

Once she was situated, the Ankylosaurus rumbled to the others. It led the way through the trees, moving at a slow walk.

Since there was nothing to do but hold on, Nicole observed her ride. The armor was a bright sky blue and evenly distributed along the back. Parts of the armored tail were dark gray bone, ranging in shape from flat plates to sharp points and varying in size from about a half-meter down to about 10 centimeters. When the Ankylosaurus walked, it swayed like a small boat on a calm sea.

The Ankylosaurus demonstrated that they were herbivores to stay away from. More than once, she spotted predators creeping closer through the trees; the Ankylosaurus on the outskirts of the herd only had to wave and pound their clubs a few times before the predators would disappear back into the trees.

She heard strange sounds, like a cross between a chicken clucking and a robin singing. Following the noise, she looked down and two young Ankylosaurus playing among the adults. One had dark green armor, and the other bright red. Entertained, she watched as they played with each other until they moved out of sight.

Her stomach rumbled, so she reached into her bundle and pulled out an apple. Deciding to take inventory on her food supply, there were six apples left and four unripe pears in her coat. She made a mental note to watch for more food.

The herd reached a steep hill, and she leaned forward to balance herself. She hooked her knees around two large spikes on the Ankylosaurus' shoulders. She noticed that it was placing each foot very carefully. The four claws on each foot dug into the damp earth, but they weren't always enough to keep from slipping down. Whenever it began to slide, it would lock its joints until it stopped. The entire herd endured and eventually reached the top of the hill.

She looked around, and realized that the hill they had crested was actually one side of a mountain. From their mostly treeless peak, she could see the valley below. Looking forward again, she saw mountains to her left and right and a few smaller ones directly ahead with a huge body of water that stretched to the horizon. She could just make out the start of a very distance mountain range behind the water.

From the inland sea, she could make out streams snaking down the mountainsides to the valley. The mountain peaks were snow-capped and glistened in the sun. *If only I had a camera,* she thought.

The Ankylosaurus rumbled, drawing her attention to it. It had turned its head to the side so that it could see her. It nodded its head toward a nearby mountain, one that was large and oddly shaped, as its peak was concave, like the inside of an eroded volcano. At its lowest point was a small lake, and she could just make out dinosaurs gathered at its shores.

"Is that where we're heading?" she wondered aloud.

Even though she knew that her mount wouldn't understand a single word of English, it must've read her tone of voice, as it nodded. It bellowed at the rest of the herd, and then they began moving again, this time toward the mountain with the concave peak.

Before they started down the mountain, Nicole spotted an unusual, smoky cloud. She followed it to the source; a mountain peak on the other side of the valley behind her. Smoke was ascending from its rocky peak in a steady but thin stream.

Nicole shivered; *Whoa, an active volcano!* She looked closer, could not detect any telltale bulge or other signs of it erupting soon. *Well, there haven't been any earthquakes.* She was also relieved to see that the lower half of the volcano's slopes were completely covered with plant life; a sign that made her feel better.

The sun set, yet the herd continued on. As night fell, she looked up at the stars, amazed at how many there were. This was her first time seeing the unobstructed expanse of the night sky. She was in awe. The Struthiomimus had kept them inside during the nights. She recognized a few constellations, but the stars that made them were slightly out of alignment. Since she was in the far distant past, she knew that the stars she had known were in different positions because of their movement. She leaned back as far she dared so that she could watch the sky without having to crane her neck.

When was the last time I could see the night sky like this? she thought in a mix of awe and sadness. Between the city lights and the almost constant cloud cover of war, she couldn't remember the last time she had actually seen the stars so pristine and clear.

She found herself waxing philosophically; contrasting and comparing man' and dinosaurian overwhelming injustices. *Clouds of destruction loom over two worlds,* she thought, *yet I have experienced an unexpected act of kindness like the one below me. Let's hope that this act of kindness leads me to the weapons and home.*

CHAPTER SIX

The Ankylosaurus' rocking was lulling her to sleep, but her head repeatedly smacking against the armor kept knocking her awake each time she nodded off.

When the dinosaur finally stopped, she looked around and saw that the herd had stopped at the edge of the trees that fringed a lake in the concave mountain peak. Out in the open was a band of carnivores that she recognized as Utahraptors. She was wary of them, as they were watching the Ankylosaurus and appeared to be waiting for something or someone.

And then, out from the middle of the band, emerged a familiar Struthiomimus and Microvenator.

Relieved, Nicole squealed like a school girl as she slid off the Ankylosaurus' back and dashed to the Struthiomimus. It froze as she hugged its neck, and then she picked up Spines and hugged it to her chest. "You have no idea how much I've missed you two!" Then her joyous mood crashed and burned, and she glared at the Struthiomimus. "You *left me!*" she growled.

The Struthiomimus blinked, apparently taken aback at her sudden mood change. It made a mild croon that sounded both dismissive and meek.

"Do *not* give me the 'Oh, I didn't mean to' sound!" she shouted, dropping Spines, who squeaked at the sudden release. "You went and left me behind! Do you have any *idea* what I've been through?! I was chased by the mother or father of all carnivores all over the forest, and it's only by the grace of God I found the herd. If one of them hadn't protected me, I'd be dead! Do you hear me? I'd be *dinosaur chow!* Nicole sirloin, nice and rare!"

The Struthiomimus had the dignity to look away and down.

She kept glaring at it for a very long moment. She had no idea if it had caught all of what she had said, but she dearly hoped that her tone of voice and the irate signals her body language was emitting took care of what was lost in translation.

She took a breath to calm herself down before she strode back to the Ankylosaurus herd. She went up to the blue-armored one and hugged its armored head. It closed its eyes and rumbled as it pressed into the hug.

"Thank you," she said after relinquishing her grasp around its head.

The Ankylosaurus seemed to smile at her before it bellowed

to the others. They turned around and began making their way back the way they came.

Nicole went back to the Struthiomimus, then looked at the Utahraptors. They were quite large, though smaller than the Appalachiosaurus. There was one that caught her eye; it was dark brown in color with a light azure fringe that ran from the back of the skull to the middle of the neck. It was heavily scarred, with lighter brown marks on nearly every portion of its body, with more scars grouped together on the face, sides, and legs. She looked down at its feet and saw that it had a large curved claw the length of her hand on the inside of each foot.

The Struthiomimus rumbled to the scarred Utahraptor, and it strode over. Its orange eyes were narrowed at her, and the top spines of the fringe seemed to have moved to become more erect. The Utahraptor shot the Struthiomimus a humored look (which the Struthiomimus returned as a mild glare) and looked her over from head to toe.

"Hi," Nicole said, not looking away from its fairly large teeth.

The Struthiomimus hissed softly to draw hers and the Utahraptor's attention. "Nicole," it said, then motioned to the Utahraptor and made a noise.

The noise was the Utahraptor's name. She nodded and copied it as best as she could. When the Utahraptor made an approving sound, she supposed that she had gotten close enough.

Nicole turned to the Struthiomimus. "Where's the *Intimidator*?"

The Struthiomimus made a few growling sounds to the

Utahraptor, who nodded and jogged away. As the Utahraptor moved away, the rest of the band followed. Nicole ran after them, assuming that the dark brown Utahraptor was going to take her to the *Intimidator*.

A sudden loud booming roar pierced the peaceful air. Nicole realized that she wasn't the only one who jumped in surprise. The band of Utahraptors froze. The roar had long ended, but its echo reverberated around the lake. When the echo finally died, it was followed up by another, this time originating much closer.

Nicole quickly dumped her bundle of food from the remainder of her spear. She saw movement within the trees. Branches snapped and fell as large bodies moved through them. Seconds later, three large T-rex emerged from the tree line. At their huge feet milled more than a dozen excited Coelurus.

The Coelurus screeched and charged forward. Likewise, the Utahraptors swept past her to meet the Coelurus. The Utahraptors were much bigger than the Coelurus, and she hung back, assuming that they could handle the lethal little savages much better than she could with her handmade spear and knife.

The three T-rex followed after the Coelurus, shaking the ground with each step. Nicole darted toward the much larger dinosaurs, planning on using her smaller size and limberness against them. She was joined by the heavily scarred Utahraptor, a few more of its band, the Struthiomimus, and Spines.

Nicole picked out the smallest T-rex, still more than twice the mass of an African bull elephant. The Utahraptors swarmed a second T-rex, and Struthiomimus and Spines tormented the third.

She avoid its teeth as it snapped at her, then skipped sideways beneath its stomach. She jabbed up with her spear at its stomach as it passed over her head. The T-rex growled and stepped to the side so that she would no longer be under it. More nimbly, she moved with it, continuing to jab at its stomach and legs. It wasn't long before the T-rex's legs were heavily wounded and it was limping. So far, she had managed to avoid any injuries to herself.

Finally, the T-rex's right leg crumpled. Nicole quickly ran out from beneath and avoided getting crushed. The carnivore groaned as it fell, then landed on its stomach and lower jaw with a ground-quaking *thud*. It was still very much alive, however, and she dared not get anywhere close to the snapping teeth. Since it was trying to rise again, she looked for help. She gave a call, and an Utahraptor appeared. It dashed past her and leapt upon the T-rex's back. It trotted along the neck until it reached the head. The Utahraptor finished off the T-rex as Nicole spun around, looking for her next opponent.

Holding her weapons out in a ready posture, she scanned the scene. The Coelurus and most of the Utahraptors were occupied fighting each other. Many of the Coelurus were down, injured and dying, along with several mortally wounded Utahraptors.

The T-rex currently being attacked by the Utahraptors appeared well on its way to joining its dead comrade. Sure enough, it fell to the ground and was killed. The Utahraptors then went to assist the Struthiomimus and Spines.

Until now, the last T-rex was faring well, as neither omnivore had any real weapons. All they were really doing was avoiding the T-rex's teeth and clawed feet.

Just as she was moving forward to assist, Nicole spotted something coming at her out of the corner of her eye, and whirled around. Reflexes kicked in, and she just barely managed to avoid becoming eviscerated by a Coelurus. The Coelurus hissed at her, the crown of spines on its skull rattling like a rattlesnake tail.

Still fueled by adrenaline, Nicole challenged it through gritted teeth; "Come on." She waved her knife in invitation as she shifted her grip on the spear.

Emitting a screeching and hissing noise, the Coelurus took the bait and leapt at her. She dodged, simultaneously swinging her knife. The knife found a target, slicing into the Coelurus' neck, but it wasn't a lethal cut. Giving the Coelurus no time to recover, Nicole rushed in, jabbing and swiping with her spear. Because of blood loss from its neck and a slice in its leg, it had slowed drastically and was limping heavily. Again she lunged for the neck and finished off the Coelurus by imbedding the entirety of her knife just below the skull. The Coelurus dropped immediately.

She grunted as she retrieved her knife. Her mind suddenly ground to a halt as she stared down at the new corpse. *Did. . . did I just* kill *a dinosaur? By myself?*

A screech from the Struthiomimus quickly turned her attention back to the fight. It was battling against two final Coelurus, one of which had just given the Struthiomimus a lengthy cut down its back. Bolting forward, Nicole yelled at the second Coelurus.

Their eyes momentarily locked as both warded off their individual Coelurus attacks.

"You left. . . me. . . behind," she said in between her dodges and strikes, "I'm. . ." She swung her spear around, effectively creating a gash in a Coelurus' face. ". . . not going to let a couple of runts kill you as a cheap payback," she continued as it wailed and staggered away, blinded.

Several more Coelurus emerged from the trees. Nicole and

the Struthiomimus disengaged from their Coelurus and ran, as they realized that they wouldn't last long against fresh attackers. As the Struthiomimus was much faster than she, Nicole grabbed its tail and used it to help her keep up. She looked over to see Spines right beside her.

Behind them, she heard a Coelurus yowl and realized that a small group of Utahraptors had split off from the T-rex and ambushed the Coelurus.

Nicole saw that they were running toward the lake before they splashed into it and began to swim. She hoped that Coelurus had an aversion to water. She swam underwater, as it was faster. She squinted through the watery haze as she swam as powerfully as she could. In front of her, she saw the Microvenator scramble out of the water and presumably onto the Struthiomimus' back.

Nicole rose for air, and to see how far out she had gone. The Coelurus had stopped at the water's edge and appeared unwilling to go any farther, confirming her hope. She and her two comrades were a good distance away from the shore, but the distance would be no match for the T-rex, that was fending off the Utahraptors and slowly making its way toward the lake. She resumed swimming beside the Struthiomimus, who was heading toward the deeper water. Once again, she grabbed onto its tail so that it was partially pulling her.

Thankfully, the Struthiomimus' aversion to touch is secondary to life.

Having kicked away its assailants, the T-rex arrived at the edge of the water. The Coelurus milled around, shrieking at the top of their lungs. The T-rex growled as it stepped into the water.

"Hurry!" Nicole screeched in fright to the Struthiomimus.

The Struthiomimus glanced behind them, then began swimming faster. Nicole could feel the water swelling as the T-rex approached. With only a few gigantic steps, it had reached them. She screamed as its head lowered.

The Struthiomimus flipped over, simultaneously dumping Spines and kicking Nicole. The T-rex opened its maw, then closed it around the Struthiomimus' back. The Struthiomimus shrieked loudly as it was pulled from the water. Nicole watched in horror as the T-rex walked back to shore with the Struthiomimus still trapped in its mouth.

Once out of the water, the T-rex heartlessly dropped the Struthiomimus on the shore. Nicole tread water as she watched the Struthiomimus become swarmed by the Coelurus that weren't fending off the Utahraptors. The Struthiomimus was bleeding heavily from the T-rex's bite. One of the Coelurus circled around the Struthiomimus, then nodded at the T-rex. The T-rex picked up the Struthiomimus with its mouth again, and Nicole could see it position the Struthiomimus on its tongue and away from the teeth; an unusual consideration that made her dread the reason. The T-rex walked away. The remaining Coelurus split off to join their comrades, and they all vanished back into the trees.

Nicole and Spines swam back to shore. Nicole stared in dismay at the spot where the dinosaurs had disappeared, hoping that the Struthiomimus would fare well. The Microvenator made a sniffling noise, then keened loudly. It kicked at the muddy ground, sending up a spray of wet dirt.

The scarred dark brown Utahraptor approached them, hanging its head. She couldn't help but notice that it was going to gain several more scars. Behind it, the rest of the Utahraptors tended to their wounds. She saw her food bundle still intact.

Suddenly, six Coelurus emerged from the forest, running at full speed toward them. Nicole shrieked in terror, turning and running as fast as she could. The Microvenator seemed to have the same idea. She didn't even need to look over her shoulder to know that the Coelurus were rapidly nearing.

A Coelurus appeared, soaring through the air with a roar before landing on Spine's back. Nicole gave a shout as she rushed to the Microvenator's assistance, ruthlessly stabbed the Coelurus off. Spines whined pitifully as it tried to get to its feet, but fell back down. Nicole quickly picked it up and immediately jumped away from a lunging Coelurus.

Nicole ran as fast as she could, her speed hampered by Spines, whom she was cradling in her arms. She heard a few Utahraptors roaring, engaging in the new fight.

She made the mistake of shifting her grip on Spines, which made her stumble. Not a second later, Nicole was abruptly knocked down. She screamed in pain as sharp claws and talons dug into her backside. Rolling in an effort as not to squash Spines, Nicole inadvertently exposed her burden.

The Microvenator scrambled out of Nicole's arms and hissed at the Coelurus, then dodged an attack. Nicole struggled beneath her tormentor, then managed to flip over. She lifted her legs and kicked the Coelurus off balance.

"Spines!" Nicole shouted. "Get out of here! You're no match against them!"

The Microvenator screeched in Nicole's face, then bit a Coelurus' ankle as it passed too closely.

The heavily scarred Utahraptor approached. It roared at

Spines, who screeched right back. A second Utahraptor came up from behind Spines and scooped it up in its long arms. The Microvenator shrieked in indignation and anxiety as it was carried off to safety.

Nicole felt as if her entire back was aflame. She writhed weakly on the ground, unable to do anything more. Her mouth was agape in a silent wail as tears streamed down her face. The Utahraptors leapt upon the much smaller Coelurus, valiantly fending them off. The Coelurus hissed angrily at the Utahraptors and retreated, outnumbered.

Slowly and very painfully turning her head, Nicole could see the dark brown Utahraptor leaning over her, eyes glistening with worry. Nicole moaned. She reached for her food bundle, which had fallen by her side. She winced as she pulled out the diamond and the strange blue stone. She held the stones up to the scarred Utahraptor. When the Utahraptor grasped the stones, she painfully clapped her hands together.

The Utahraptor obligingly knocked the stones together, and the sparks flew. Where they landed, the air snapped as a portal appeared in it. The Utahraptor stared in awe at the rippling tear in time.

"Take me through," Nicole said quietly, no longer able to see even where she was pointing.

The Utahraptor rumbled softly in her ear as it picked her up in its arms. She hissed through her teeth as the pain spiked, and she passed out. The Utahraptor rumbled again, and entered the portal.

The open-air marketplace was bustling. Carts chock full of

merchandise lined the buildings. The road was closed off to cars, and people covered the street. The weekend market was one of the most anticipated days of the week, when the city-dwellers could get fresh produce from the farms that spread out over the land beyond the last buildings of the city.

Suddenly, the peaceful and lively scene was broken by the sudden appearance of a rip in the middle of the air. It widened into a large circle.

Screams of surprise and gasps spread through the crowd as people pushed each other away from the anomaly. However, a few daring and curious people took small steps closer to the rippling hole suspended in nothing.

"What is it?"

"Where did it come from?"

"Why did it appear?"

"Hey, there's something coming out- -*get back!*"

Screams burst out as a large bipedal dinosaur emerged from the hole. It was bloody, scarred, and injured. It carried something completely drenched in blood in its arms. It looked around at the area with narrowed eyes before its vision focused on the closest people.

The raptor hissed softly, its long tail widely waving slowly behind it. People stepped even further back, afraid that it was about to attack. But it only lowered the object in its arms to the ground and released it.

"It's a human!" someone said after a moment. "Someone call

911!"

A single brave soul approached the unconscious body and the dinosaur. He kept flicking his gaze between the blood-drenched woman and the less bloody dinosaur. The raptor took a step back as the person came closer. Encouraged by the lack of aggression, he quickened his pace and knelt by the unconscious person's side.

"Call an ambulance!" he yelled over his shoulder. "She needs medical help *now!* Miss, don't worry, help's coming."

The dinosaur took another step backward as the sound of sirens soon drifted over the crowd. A minute later, the crowd parted as a medical team forced their way through. They stumbled in surprise at the sight of the raptor, but quickly refocused their attention on the injured woman.

Policemen burst into sight and aimed their pistols at the raptor. "Don't move!" one of them shouted.

The dinosaur hissed with a gaping maw, its eyes narrowed and the fringe on its neck straightening up as far as it could go. The raptor glanced down at the woman for a moment, then back at the policemen. It opened a fist and dropped two medium sized rocks at the woman's side. It stared intently at the humans as it clapped its hands.

The portal quivered and the circle began to falter in shape. The raptor noticed the change and quickly spun around. It spared one more look at the woman before leaping into the portal and vanishing. The moment the tail disappeared from sight, the portal vanished, and it was as if it was never there.

As the medics brought out a stretcher, a little girl looked up to her mother, who was holding her hand tightly. "Mommy, that was a dinosaur!" the little girl squealed excitedly. Then her face fell. "Why did it have boo-boos?"

"I don't know," her mother replied, keeping her grip on her daughter as the gravely injured woman was carried away. "But let's hope that it never comes back."

"Aww," the little girl said with a sad frown. "Dinosaurs are cool."

Intel was dropped onto the dirt from the T-rex's mouth. He hissed in pain as his numerous wounds and his body in general protested against the impact. He was about to try and sit up when the T-rex placed a foot on top of him, rendering him immobile.

"Get off of me!" Intel grunted as he squirmed to free himself.

"Be quiet and hold still," the T-rex growled, displaying his sharp teeth. "Our master is coming."

Intel glared, but complied. Letting his neck go limp, he dropped his head back onto the dirt. He could do nothing, and looked around.

He was by a massive waterfall, emptying into a river. Since he was at its bottom, the area around him was shrouded in mist. Through the gaps in the branches, he could see the water falling from the top and cascading down. The T-rex had dropped him onto a flat area of barren ground. There was no grass or any other shrubbery besides those that hugged the tree trunks. The dirt was covered with deep tracks belonging to massive carnivores. The lower branches of the surrounding trees had been long broken off.

He could hear someone coming. More than a someone, actually, as there was more than a single set of steps. He could hear splashing, telling him that they were wading through the river. As the steps grew closer, he could feel the ground shaking beneath him. He could feel one set of steps feeling slower and heavier than the others'.

A shiver of dread went down his spine. *It couldn't be,* he thought. *Not* him. *He was banished!*

Four T-rex arrived, moving so that they were standing next to the T-rex that had carried him here. After a moment, another Squama emerged from the trees. Intel looked for the next T-rex's face, but instead found a pair of thick, wrinkled knees. His gaze only went up from there, up and up, until he found the head at last.

"Harass," Intel hissed in disdain, spitting the name out with as much venom as he could muster. He hid his terror. "How *dare* you return here."

The Acrocanthosaurus raised his head loftily, and angled it just enough so that Intel could just make out his eye. "I dare because I have grown," Harass snarled nastily. "You will regret casting me from this valley. I was but a youngling and didn't even know of my heritage!" Harass shouted, his red eyes wide and shining with barely contained fury. "Be glad that I have rediscovered my heritage and have come back to rescue you from the pathetic lives you lead. You all have no direction, no purpose. You merely walk where your legs take you and achieve nothing." With a sniff of disdain, he continued, "You need someone to rule you all."

"It is our way of life!" Intel protested. "We need no ruler to survive and thrive."

Harass snarled as he bent down. Intel fought against the

urge to flinch away as the long, razor-sharp serrated teeth stopped only inches from his own head. "I volunteer for the position, and I won't back down."

"We'll fight back," the Struthiomimus growled. "And we won't stop until you're gone, this time forever."

Harass straightened up and looked over his shoulder. "Bring out the object!" he roared.

After what seemed like forever, yet another T-rex emerged from the trees, carrying in its arms a dingy silver object. Intel recognized it as the *Annihilator*, and he winced at its state.

Harass gazed at the *Annihilator* with desire. "Tell me what this is," he ordered Intel. "My Coelurus pack found this in your cute little cave. It must be of great importance to you."

Intel said nothing.

Upon a look from Harass, the T-rex applied additional pressure.

Properly motivated, Intel spat through gritted teeth, "It's called the *Annihilator*."

"What does it do?" Harass pressed. "You and I both know that you know more than that."

"I refuse to tell you any more," Intel growled.

Harass growled back, snapping his teeth only inches away from Intel. This time, the Struthiomimus couldn't help but cringe.

"Give me what I want to know."

Intel hissed his defiance.

Harass turned to the T-rex. "Press down until he begs for mercy."

Intel could feel his body compressing. He gritted his teeth as the agony increased. He couldn't help it; he began moaning with what breath he could catch.

At the point where he was sure that the weight would quite literally crush him flat, he blacked out.

The next thing he knew, cold water jolted him back to awareness. Sputtering, he opened his eyes to see a T-rex walking away with its mouth still dripping water.

"Now that you're awake again," Harass said, smiling sinisterly, "we can continue. If you talk quickly, I promise that your death will be as quick."

All Intel could do was glare.

Harass' smile bled away. "Very well. You can watch us pull it from your two friends."

Intel's gaze sharpened.

The smile came back. "Yes, we have them. Your scaleless friend seems to be a fun person to get information out of."

Intel curled back his lips.

"Very well. Assuming you survive your injuries, you have just exchanged your life for your companions." Harass turned to a Coelurus. "Go and get the human."

A Coelurus grinned and trotted off.

Intel's will collapsed along with his resolve. Shuddering uncontrollably, he pleaded, "If you don't hurt her, I'll speak."

Harass' grin grew ever larger. "Continue."

Intel sighed. "The *Annihilator* is mounted on the spine. Place it there, and it'll automatically attach itself to you." Immediately after he said this, he felt a tidal wave of deep shame.

Harass leaned back, eying Intel. "You are implying that this *Annihilator* will be a permanent addition to my back?"

"Yes," Intel said dejectedly, wallowing in his ignominy.

Harass faced the T-rex that held the *Annihilator*. "Place it on my back, just behind my neck," he told the T-rex. Harass knelt down. The T-rex walked over and placed the silver object at his shoulders. The *Annihilator* whirred, and then several clicking noises could be heard from its underside. Harass froze, then roared in pain. Intel winced in surprise.

Suddenly, Harass stopped roaring. He fell silent, and his eyes glazed over, as if he was staring into space. Momentarily, he blinked and stood. He rolled his shoulders and tossed his entire back from side to side.

"What does it do?" Harass demanded, looking pointedly at Intel.

"I don't know," Intel grunted, looking away.

Harass huffed, his nostrils flaring. "Very well. Then I am done with you." He glared at Intel venomously.

Without warning, a Coelurus burst into their presence. "My Lord! King Harass!"

Harass roared in surprise and whirled to face the Coelurus. "How many times do I need to tell you minute pests!" he growled. "Do *not* interrupt me while I am conducting an interrogation! The penalty is *death!*"

The Coelurus' eyes widened, and it began to slink away. "My Lord, I-"

Harass hissed. Suddenly, the *Annihilator* whirred to life. A fraction of a second later, a dark object darted from the cylinder and streaked toward the Coelurus. The Coelurus barely had enough time to summon air for a terrified shriek before the dark object hit it. Intel flinched away from the explosion of flames. When the fire died away, all that remained where the Coelurus had stood was a small crater and smoldering dirt.

Harass stood taller. "Impressive," he said. "Apparently, this device requires the desire to kill in order to work." He looked at Intel, then sniffed haughtily. "We have no more need of him," he said to the T-rex present. "You know what to do."

"But-" Intel wheezed weakly.

"Thank you, Struthiomimus, you have finally served me well."

Forgive me. . . Intel thought to no one and everyone.

CHAPTER SEVEN

Spike emerged from the portal. He looked at his reddened hands and claws, and grimaced. His own blood he was used to seeing, but to have his hands soaked in another's. . . as he carried the human back to its world, most likely to die. . .

"What happened?" Grapple, Spike's closest friend, asked.

"It was extraordinary," Spike said, walking slowly toward the lake so that he could wash his hands. "There were more humans, but they were all much cleaner. Then more came, holding short black sticks and yelling. I left the one I was holding in their care."

"What about Intel?" another one of his tribe inquired. "Can we save him? If we gather together enough worthy fighters, we can track them and save Intel!"

"Foolishness!" Spike exclaimed, startling most of his companions. "Do *any* of us have any clue on how many Tyrannosaurus and Coelurus there are? We can't just rush in blindly, and we don't know if they have installed the *Annihilator.* Our only chance lies back at the nesting ground."

"With the object Intel gave us?" Grapple said.

Spike nodded. "The *Intimidator,* I believe is what he called it. That object is our sole chance of fending off whoever will use the *Annihilator.*"

The members of his hunting party looked at each other with uneasiness. The idea of having only one way to protect themselves, a way that could be easily stolen, did not lie well with any of them.

With a quiet growl, Spike set off toward the nesting grounds that he called home. His comrades followed immediately, falling into step behind him. They skillfully trekked through the trees, forgoing the usual and worn paths to blaze their own trail. They went downhill, down the side of Concave Peak that faced away from the lake at the bottom of the valley.

After a lengthy walk, they emerged from the trees and entered a small clearing surrounding an equally small pond. Next to the pond was an ancient tree whose bark was pale, twisted, and wrinkled, the trunk was bent into beautifully gnarled curves, and the leafy branches extended in a thick curtain over the water. Its roots resembled miniature mountains, and the tiny ranges stretched in all directions around the base of the tree. Scattered around the clearing were nests, most of which contained at least two speckled brown eggs, and standing close by the nests were female Utahraptors. The females looked up, hearing their approach.

"Spike," the nearest said, her deep purple fringe nearly upright in her obvious happiness of seeing him return. "Welcome home."

Spike nodded back to her. "It is pleasurable to be back," he said, then turned to his hunting party. "Grapple, where do you have the object that Intel gave to me?"

The Utahraptor dashed off to one of the bushes scattered around the clearing and reached into its dense, leafy depths. After gently pulling out the silver object, he returned. Handing it to Spike, he asked, "What does it do?"

"It is called *Intimidator*," Spike responded, saying the word in the foreign way that Intel had said it. "But I don't know what it does. He thinks that the name might be translatable to 'frighten.' He added that the Tyrants have a similar one, called an *Annihilator*, which he says could be translatable to 'kill.'"

"What are we to do with the *Intimidator*?" asked one of his comrades.

"He wanted me to bestow it upon one of us that is worthy to combat the Tyrants," Spike claimed. "Sadly, none of us are worthy."

"Worthy?" Grapple repeated, confused.

Spike looked ahead. "Right and wrong. Kindness and mercy. A heart of courage and fortitude. Humility. *Those* are the concepts that must be in the Worthy One."

"You just described *you*," an Utahraptor stated.

"No!" Spike exclaimed. "I am not the Worthy One. You may think that I have all those attributes, but I have lived too long, have seen too much, have *experienced* too much. No, I cannot bear it. And none of you can, either."

An Utahraptor huffed. "None of us? There are three dozen of us here. How could *none* of us be worthy?"

Spike shook his head. "Intel said that I would know who is worthy. And I know that none of you, the females, or the younglings are. Our hope lies with the unhatched."

The Utahraptor begrudgingly nodded.

Spike looked at the tree that stood by the water. Its roots were thick and spread out like the strands in a spider's web. "I want a hole dug between the roots of that tree, next to the base," he said to a Utahraptor, motioning toward the tree with his head. "I want it deep enough to bury this *Intimidator* until a worthy Utahraptor is found."

Grapple nodded firmly. "I'll gather the others and have them help dig it."

"No, not now," Spike said firmly. "We need to wait until the cover of night, and when all of the others are asleep. We shall do it tonight."

And so it was. Long after the sun had set and the waxing crescent moon shined a dim pale blue light across the valley, Grapple awakened Spike and those he trusted with his life. They moved silently to the tree.

As quietly as they could, they used their powerful legs to dig up the dirt. When Spike deemed the hole suitable, he had them place flat stones along the bottom and sides of the hole. Afterward, Grapple carefully lowered the *Intimidator* into the hole. Once complete, they placed a large flat stone on top, creating a container. The dirt was pushed back into place, and then the ground was smoothed. The dirt that wasn't able to fit was shoved aside and scattered. Leaves and other organic matter were spread back over the area until even Spike and Grapple had difficulty recognizing where the *Intimidator* was buried.

"Remember!" Spike whispered to those with him. "Until the one is found worthy of bearing the *Intimidator*, it shall be buried beneath this tree. You shall tell *no one* of its presence here, even under the weight of death."

"We won't tell a soul," Grapple declared quietly, his expression serious. The others nodded in affirmation.

They quietly cleaned the dirt from their claws and went to their preferred places of rest.

She tried to uncurl, but there was no room. She was hungry; her supply of nutrients had run out. Her hunger didn't help her mounting irritability. Frustrated at her inability to become anything close to comfortable, she kicked her legs out at the walls that surrounded her. At the sound of a crack and feeling the wall give, her excitement fueled new energy. She kicked at the wall once; twice; three times. After her fourth kick, she felt her foot go through the wall.

Cold air blew in. She shivered. Now that freedom from her cramped prison was within sight, she began using her entire body to battle against the walls. Rearing her head back as far as the confining space would allow, she butted the wall. She felt it crack under the impact, so she butted it again. That time, her head broke through.

A sudden surge of light seared her eyes. A thin piece of her confinement teetered on top of her head. She shook her head in an effort to clear it, and the piece flew off. It was short work after that to dislodge herself from the remainder of her shell.

At long last, she lay on her stomach on the ground, stretching her body in her newfound freedom. After her cramps had faded away, the pangs of hunger returned. She chirruped for attention.

A giant form silhouetted by the sun bent down, and its shadow enveloped her like a blanket. With a squeal, she tried to move away, but her limbs would only flail uselessly. Stuck, she gazed up in awe. A deep instinct came up from the innermost depths of her body, that had her imprint on this being and call it 'Mother.' Fear now gone, she chirped at Mother and opened her mouth wide, showing its bright red interior and tiny pink gums.

Her mother dropped something dark red in front of her, which jiggled upon landing. She looked down at it, then sniffed it. It smelled fresh and made her mouth water. She licked it experimentally, decided that she liked the taste, and then swallowed it. It was mushy, wet, and tasted absolutely delicious. She chirped for more, and another piece of the red mushy stuff was given to her by her mother.

Satisfied, she rolled over onto her back and playfully kicked her legs around in the air.

The light was seemed to come from directly above her, and it was warm. She tried to look at the source of the light; but it hurt her eyes dreadfully, and she had to avert them. After the strange black spots faded away, she looked around with curiosity. She appeared to be in a nest of sticks and covered with soft, green, moss that gave under her weight.

She batted some of the moss with a pudgy, three-fingered hand. It bounced a little before stilling. Trilling with childish laughter, she continued batting at it.

Hearing another chirping sound, her attention turned away from the moss. She saw three others that looked almost identical to herself. One had a dark brown spot over both of his eyes and a deep green frill, and the rest of his body was a light tan with an almost white underbelly. Another had black feet, a dark yellow hide, and a crimson frill. The last one had a light brown forehead and an almost colorless face, a hide of burnt umber, a tan underbelly, and a light blue frill.

Mother was hovering over the one with the green frill, dropping more of that red stuff in front of their faces. Two were climbing over the spotted one in an effort to nab the red stuff first. She watched with fascination them fight as the fight transformed from who could get it first to whom it belonged.

Seeing that they weren't going to be taking ownership of the food anytime soon, she moved her arms and legs under her and flung one arm forward. She placed her weight on it, but it wasn't strong enough, and collapsed. A short grunt came past her lips as her chin met the ground. She scowled at her arm, an expression that would be considered by others to be completely adorable. With the food still available, she tried again, more carefully. Even though her arm was shaking, she lifted her opposite arm and one leg. Then her chin met the ground again as she fell over sideways.

After much practice and frustration, she toddled forward and won the food. The other three were still oblivious as she clumsily dragged her prize back to her side of the nest and began devouring it with relish.

Once she had consumed the entire mass, she crawled over

to the wall and back onto the moss. Feeling tired from her new experiences, she closed her eyes. Even though it had hardly been 10 minutes since hatching, she immediately fell asleep.

As the days, and then the weeks, passed, she learned many things. One of those things was that her mother kept calling her a peculiar combination of sounds. Eventually, she came to realize that whenever she heard the sound 'Scope,' her mother was calling for her. The others in her nest were given sounds to answer which they should; the one with the green frill was Abject, the one with the white face was Pallor; and the one with the dark feet was Benign. They were her siblings; two brothers and a sister. The foursome had a sort of love/hate relationship among themselves; each of them found cheap amusement picking on another, but none of them could imagine life without the other three. They had complications with teamwork, but would band together if challenged. Deep down, Scope adored her siblings with a passion.

Their mother was a beautiful creature. Her skull was smoothly rounded from the crown to the tip of the nose, and her deep jade frill always seemed lush. Their patriarch, their sire, was handsome as well, with sharp angles that were placed just right as to inspire respect. His ultramarine frill was spiky. She always looked forward to his return and felt safest in his and her mother's shadow.

Their mother was always busy taking care them. Abject liked to practice at being an escape artist, as he enjoyed sneaking out of the nest behind their mother's or patriarch's back. Benign had a flair for dramatics, often making a minor situation a calamity. Pallor just wouldn't stop talking. Scope liked to believe that she was perfect.

Like a worm to earth, she found that she was a natural at

language. The Squama language was divided into two categories, vocalization and body language, and it was a delicate balance between the two. When she was first beginning to speak, she learned by watching and listening to her elders. As she was learning to talk, her body often betrayed her; and she said the wrong thing. It was usually in this way that she often accidentally began fights. However, it didn't take her long to become wise in speech.

She was one of many new members of a tribe of Utahraptors, with the leader being the strongest and largest. . . Spike. Spike was the wonder of every hatchling in the tribe, and it wasn't hard to see why. Every inch of the tribe leader screamed respect and leadership. His multitude of scars told everyone who looked his way that he had seen more than his fair share of severe fights.

But Spike was more than just a leader that kept the tribe together. He was also a family beast, often playing with the hatchlings and younglings if he wasn't otherwise occupied. He was always available for a question. Every time the moon was full, Spike would gather all of the others her age and tell them the tale of a very special dinosaur; a Struthiomimus called Intel and *Nicole* the rare, mammalian-like creature known as a human.

Scope was intrigued by Intel, who had been an avid discoverer. Spike spoke of him highly. As the story went, the Struthiomimus had discovered a way to open a portal in time. Intel had gone through the portal, and had brought back with him a strange device. When Spike would reach the part where the Coelurus had stormed Intel's cave, murdered all but one of his Microvenator assistants, and stolen the device, the other Utahraptor juveniles her age would huddle together and whimper. She did not cringe and curl up, but instead quelled her fear and listened as Spike continued. Spike would always end the story when Intel had given to him the second device.

"He gave me the object and requested of me one single thing," Spike would always end with. "He told me to bequeath the device to one of our tribe that was worthy to bear it." At that, he would lean forward and whisper, as if he was telling a great secret, "Perhaps, the Worthy One is *one of you*."

No matter how many times he said it, his words spurred deep thought. Almost everyone would look down at the ground, their sight unfocused. And after the story was over, Scope's parents would herd her and her siblings back to the nest.

"I want to be the Worthy One!" Pallor would say.

"Maybe I am," Benign would interject hopefully.

"No, it's me!" Abject would protest.

And then bickering would break out between the threesome over who was the more worthy.

Scope would say nothing, but her mind would be heavily laden with thoughts.

CHAPTER EIGHT

Golden eyes narrowed. Scope tensed her muscles, preparing to pounce. Her prey was casually walking closer. Just a few more steps. . . With a roar, Scope leapt from hiding, her claws and talons outstretched.

She shrieked as her sight was filled with teeth. Taken unaware, she fumbled in her landing and fell onto her side.

Her prey closed his mouth and chuckled, shaking his head. "Nice try," he said, walking away.

Growling in frustration, Scope got to her feet and shook any dirt from her body. Staring after her former prey, she contemplated where she had gone wrong.

She moved to hide again, but found that a peer had stolen her most recent hiding spot. "This is *my* ambush spot!" she said, lowering her fringe.

"You weren't in it," the youngling retorted. "Fair game. Go find somewhere else to hide."

Scope scowled and stalked off, looking around the clearing. She knew that the best ambush spots were already claimed by other younglings and hatchlings practicing ambush attacks. Every couple of minutes, a roar could be heard. Occasionally, so would a yelp.

A quick look-over of the clearing confirmed Scope's suspicion. The only hiding spots left was the occasional boulder or tree, and those made terrible hiding places; it was nearly impossible to hide one's body completely without the tail poking out.

She glanced at the forest. There had to be some *wonderful* hiding places in there! But the forest was strictly off-limits to everyone except the adults. If she hid in there, she would get in huge trouble.

Scope set her jaw. It was time to do a search for a new ambush spot, unknown to everyone but her. Over the next day and a half, she could be seen scouring the clearing.

The pond was one of the first spots she considered. It was deep enough to completely submerge her, but she had the one inevitable problem with having an underwater hiding spot - lungs. Every so often she would need to come up for air and completely ruin her ambush. She scrapped the idea of using the pond.

The next spot she considered was the withered, ancient tree. It was almost impossibly thick in girth and could completely hide her body, and there were few flying predators big enough to seriously harm Squamas her size, so why would anyone bother to look up? Her only problem was that she was afraid of heights, and going any higher than the third branch (which was about two paces off of the ground) would cause her to freeze with fear. Jumping off of a branch and ambushing prey from above? Forget it.

After the tree, she found a rather dense bush. It was a nicely large bush, thick enough with leaves so that it was hard to see in. She wriggled her way in, slightly scratching up her hide, until she reached the stem. Once she reached the stem, she took note of her position and surroundings. She was in a loose crouch in order to stay below the majority of the branches above, but the position was perfect for leaping. Around her, there were thick leafy branches. Through the leaves, she could see slivers of the outside world. The sunlight streamed in from above, speckling her hide and the ground. She was humored to notice that her ocher hide blended in with the grassless dirt under the bush so well.

It was decided; the bush was to be her favorite hiding place. To make it more comfortable, she used her teeth to break off some of the lower branches in order to make more room for her body. She made herself a little hole in the bush for her to reside in, but left enough branches to keep her suitably hidden from the outside.

Now, to pick a prey. She laid in wait, silent as a caterpillar, and watched through the leaves. Utahraptors of all ages passed by without a single glance her way. She quietly snickered.

There was an Utahraptor coming. Scope grinned when she recognized him as the prey from the day before. She eagerly waited for him to come close enough.

The Utahraptor adult screeched, his eyes widening, as Scope leapt from hiding. Little more than a yellow blur with teeth and claws, she landed in front of the adult. The other Utahraptors stiffened and looked their way, but deemed the situation unimportant; just another ambush from an aspiring hatchling.

Scope looked up to the adult, who was just beginning to recover from his scare. His brilliant sunflower-yellow fringe, standing upright from shock, was slowly beginning to relax. He looked down at her approvingly.

"I commend you, little one," he said, chuckling. "That's a very good hiding place."

"Don't tell anyone!" Scope said, narrowing her eyes at him. She didn't want anyone to steal it, or for them to know where she lurked.

The Utahraptor smiled at her as he began walking off. "I won't. I promise. But I won't be caught like that again so easily!"

She laughed happily before running off to her nest. She didn't go back to her bush, just in case someone had seen her frighten her elder but not see where she had come from.

"Where have you been all day?" her mother inquired as she dumped a hunk of raw meat in front of Scope's siblings.

"Out practicing my ambush skills," Scope replied, trotting over to the meat so that she could get her fair share. She growled at Benign when her sister tried to hog the food.

Her mother chuckled. "Yes, I heard your latest victim. I take it that it went well?"

Benign snorted. "What do you think? She thinks that she's the best at ambush attacks."

"I am!" Scope retorted indignantly. "I'm going to be the *best* ambush attacker in the tribe."

"Keep dreaming," Benign said, biting a sliver of meat a tad harder than necessary.

Scope growled at her sibling, taking a step closer. "I *can* be the best!"

"Now now, you two," their mother interjected, using her muzzle to gently nudge Scope and Benign further apart. "Calm down. This is your last meal today, and I don't want you two going to sleep hungry."

Benign growled once more before returning to eating.

Scope glared, feeling her magenta fringe lowering to become flush with the top of her neck. She bit into her portion of meat with fervor, hoping that she could let out some of her anger on her meat. With a jerk of her head, she ripped her bite away from the rest, then used her tongue to pull in what was dangling outside of her mouth. She bit down hard a few times to chew it, then swallowed.

When the meat was completely devoured, Scope walked over to the pond to wash her throat with a drink of water. She lifted her muzzle from the water, then looked down into it. When the ripples cleared, she could clearly see her reflection. She stared at her reflection for a bit before returning to the nest.

"Where'd you go?" Abject asked, blinking his goldenrod eyes at Scope curiously.

"To get a drink of water," Scope replied. "Why would you want to know that?"

"I *do* like knowing where my siblings are," Abject said, narrowing his eyes. "Have a problem with that?"

Scope snorted hard. "I should have some privacy. Don't expect me to tell you *everything* that I do. Now, if you don't mind, I'm going to finish my meat."

When Scope finished eating, she stalked out of the nest and back to her bush. As she settled in the bush's branches, she thought, *I'm going to be* the *best ambush attacker ever.*

One day, Scope noticed that the younglings a Turn older than she were being herded to Spike. She tried to venture closer to see what was going on, but her mother appeared from seemingly nowhere and herded her away from them.

"Mother!" Scope whined, trying to get past her but failing.

"Not now, my dear," her mother said softly, nudging Scope toward the nest.

Scope groaned. When she got there, her mother was distracted by one of Scope's siblings. Scope laid down and rested her head on the rim of the nest. She kept her gaze upon the older younglings and Spike. After a while, the younglings cheered, then trotted to the nearest forest edge. They stopped just before entering the trees. Spike barked something, and then they raced into the forest.

Scope stared incredulously, glancing between the forest and the tribe leader. It was a strict taboo for a youngling to go *near* the trees, and the younglings had gone in with Spike watching, and he hadn't done a thing! With curiosity overwhelming her, she sought out her mother.

"Where are they going?" Scope asked once she had found her.

Her mother gazed somberly at the trees before kneeling down so that she was on Scope's level. "They are on their Initiation Hunt," she replied.

"What is an Initiation Hunt?" Scope inquired, stumbling briefly over the longer words.

"It is when all of our younglings need to earn their place in the tribe," her mother replied. "They can only return when they have made their first kill. They must bring back a sign that they were successful, such as a few bones."

Scope made an awed noise. "How long will that take?"

"Depends, sometimes it takes a few days, or very many," her mother said, then sighed. "You will be going on an Initiation Hunt on your next Turn. You are growing up far to quickly, my hatchling."

Scope looked at the trees where the group had vanished. She felt excitement to the time when she would take the Initiation Hunt. Desperate to get a taste of being separated from the tribe and spurred by excitement, she began to creep away. Her mother was distracted by one of Scope's siblings and thus didn't notice as Scope took several large and silent steps backward, then turned and quietly trotted away.

She paused at the tree line. Looking up, she could see the thick brown trunks rise high over her head, and split into dozens of branches that sported thousands of leaves. She lowered her gaze to look into the shadowed dimness of the forest floor. She took a few deep breaths, steeling herself for her first advance into the foreboding trees.

"Never go into the forest." Voices echoed around in her mind; orders from the elders of the tribe. *"You are too young. You can easily get lost if you go in too deep. There are Squamas in there that are bigger than you and could hurt you."*

"I'll just keep within sight of the clearing," she said to herself as she took her first steps into the forest. "I'll be fine."

The shadows from the trees' branches spilled over her, small spots of sunlight coming in through the gaps. Suddenly feeling small next to the tall vegetation, she took a deep breath. Something moved in her peripheral vision, and she whirled around to face it with a growl. She felt rather silly when she watched a small mammal scurry up a tree and vanish into the branches.

She growled at the animal nonetheless. Snorting, she moved to stalk away when one of her toes caught on a root and she fell head over heels down an incline. Even after she reached the bottom of the hill, she didn't move for a long moment. When she did move to stand, she grunted as her hip muscles twinged. She glanced up the hill, contemplating whether to climb it. She decided not to and walked along the bottom of the hill.

A shift in the change of scenery caught her attention. It was a fallen tree, suspended at an odd angle by a few other trees. Only able to assume that it had fallen in the past and had been caught by the other trees, she plodded over to its splintered stump. It gave her a decent stepping block as she hopped onto the gently angled trunk. She gasped in surprise when her foot slipped off the side and she stumbled. She waved her long tail behind her, using it to stabilize her balance. After a few seconds, she regained her footing, and resumed walking on top of the tree. It slowly ascended, and soon she was several paces above the ground. A few more paces further, and she knew that if she slipped and fell now, she would be guaranteed an injury of some kind.

"Don't look down," was her mantra. "Don't look down."

The trunk of the tree narrowed the further she went, making her balance harder to keep. The bark was dead and falling off, causing her footing to be treacherous in some places. Glancing ahead, she saw that the tree was soon going to fork and turn into a tangle of dry, leafless branches that would not be able to support her weight.

She decided to stop. Since she was at a height that she had never been able to reach before, she observed the area. The brush around her was thick and lush. A flowering vine was climbing up the trunk of a nearby tree, and she could smell the sweet scent of its flowers. Off in the trees, she could just make out a herd of large bipedal herbivores, perhaps Triceratops, traveling. She watched them until they vanished from sight. A breeze wafted through the forest, stirring up the leaves. The leaves on the bushes and trees brushed against each other, creating a soft symphony. Insects buzzed and flitted through the air, creating their own music.

After a few more minutes enjoying the peace, she began to descend back down the tree. She made sure that she kept note that the clearing was on top of the hill. Hopping down from the tree, she landed slightly roughly and stumbled a bit, but stayed on her feet.

She ascended the hill. Keeping the clearing in the corner of her eye, she weaved through the trees. She saw movement coming toward her from the clearing, and she darted underneath a thick bush. The bush's branches painfully scratched and grabbed at her hide as she dived under it. She could feel the uncontrollable urge to hyperventilate, but the newcomer was coming closer, so she forced herself to hold her breath. Her lungs protested painfully, but she dared not to give into their demand for air. It was only made worse when she recognized the Utahraptor as Spike.

She frantically shoved herself farther under the bush and curled her tail as close to herself as she could. *Please don't look into this bush,* she thought frantically.

Through the leaves, she could see Spike take several large steps into the forest. One of his closest friends, Grapple, was a pace behind him.

"What's the matter, Spike?" Grapple asked.

Spike raised his head and inhaled sharply several times. She could see his nostrils flare. Spike's fringe became slightly more erect.

"Someone is here," he said quietly. He angled his head in several different positions, sniffing. "This way," he added after a few seconds, then stalked away.

Scope watched as he and Grapple retreated into the trees. Once they were out of sight, she listened until their footsteps were barely audible before darting from her hiding place. She tripped as she stood, stumbled several paces, then recovered and fled back to the clearing. She emerged into the open area, away from the main body of the tribe. Stealing back into their midst, she tried to act as if she had never left.

She was walking toward her nest when she heard someone clear their throat behind her. Whirling around, she saw Spike and Grapple standing behind her. Spike had a disappointed expression, while Grapple's was emotionless.

"Yes, sirs?" she asked weakly, knowing why they were standing there. She could feel her fringe lowering to become flush with the curve of her neck.

Spike exhaled slowly. "Come with us," he demanded, then turned and walked toward the old tree, not looking back, as he obviously fully expected her to obey.

She did, her head and tail hanging low. Grapple moved to follow behind, sandwiching her in the middle. They stopped at the shore of the pond, under the thick curtain of the branches of the ancient warped tree. Scope stood sullenly as Spike turned and raised his torso higher by lowering his back half of his body. The tip of his tail tapped the surface of the pond, sending ripples from the point of impact.

"Scope," Spike said, his voice void of inflections.

"Yes, sir?" she replied, preferring to gaze at her feet rather than at him.

"Look at me," he ordered gently.

Scope sighed, hesitated, then very slowly raised her eyes. She stopped just short of his neck and stared at his strong, muscular chest and equally muscular arms, both heavily scarred.

"All the way, Scope."

She unhurriedly trailed her gaze up his neck and to his face. She briefly made eye contact, then lowered her eyes just enough so that she was watching his chin. She dimly knew that her own reluctance to look at him was a clear sign of the guilt he most likely suspected her of.

"What have you done so far today?" Spike asked casually, as if he was only starting up a friendly conversation. But to Scope, his query sounded like the beginning of a terrible interrogation.

"Ah. . ." she started. She paused, cleared her throat in an effort to gain time to think up a believable lie, but decided that it would be best to tell the truth. After all, there was no telling how much the tribe leader had actually noticed, and she had no intention on getting into even more trouble. "I saw the Initiation Hunt group set off. I was curious to what was actually in the woods, sir, so I went in."

"I know." Spike frowned. "I smelled you. You were hiding under the bush, but I went away so that you could escape and find time to think up a lie." He paused, then cocked his head to the side. "Why didn't you lie to me? I have caught the other younglings sneaking into the forest, and they have all lied to me."

She swallowed. "I decided not to lie, sir."

"You decided not to lie?" Spike echoed, his tone of voice slightly altered by skepticism.

"Yes, sir," Scope replied. "Lying would only get me in more trouble, especially since you actually *did* notice me."

Spike exhaled slowly, then lowered his torso so that he was on her level. "Scope, do you know why I made the law that no hatchling or youngling is to enter the forest?"

"To protect us, sir," Scope immediately replied, the answer rolling off of her tongue fluidly and clearly. The law had been burned into her mind very early on in her life, and there was no way she could possibly forget it.

"From what?" Spike pressed.

"From the dangers that lurk beyond the clearing."

Spike nodded. "Correct." He hesitated, then said, "Scope, I would like to tell you something very, very important."

She instantly gave him her full attention, having heard the underlying urgency in his tone. "Yes, sir?"

"There is a new danger amassing," Spike said, his voice firm and somber. "This is a danger unlike any other that you or I have ever seen, and probably ever will see. This newest Initiation Hunt was set off with my blessing, and I dearly hope that even a few of them will return."

Her eyes widened. "You mean that they're in peril?" She squeaked, staring at the trees with new respect. Suddenly, the friendly, gentle shadows seemed dark and sinister.

"Yes." Spike nodded. "The new danger are called the Tyrants. They are a deadly gang consisting of Tyrannosaurus and Coelurus, and led by a horrendous monster of a Acrocanthosaurus. Just before you hatched, I lost a dear friend of mine to the monster."

She looked down. "I'm sorry, sir, about your friend."

"I have mourned and continued on with my life," Spike stated. "It is useless to dwell over what has already happened. I do miss him, though. Now, little one, where are your parents?"

She saw the hidden order in his reply. "Yes sir, thank you, sir."

"Very good." Spike rose to his full height and looked down

at her with a pleasant expression. "Go to your nest. It is getting late, and you have had an eventful day."

Scope smiled back at her tribe's leader. "Yes, sir," she replied, then trotted off.

CHAPTER NINE

"Hey, Scope!"

Scope looked up from her half-eaten lunch; a dead bird her mother had caught. She swallowed what was in her mouth, then said, "Hi, Pallor." She was slightly annoyed at the interruption of her meal, but hid it from her talkative sibling.

Pallor impatiently shifted his weight from one leg to the other. "Benign and Abject want to play this new game we made up. You're supposed to hit one of those big nuts with your tail around, and the first one to let the nut hit the ground loses! It's great fun, you should join in!"

"That sounds interesting," Scope replied slowly, thinking it over. "I'll come and join in after I'm finished eating."

"Hurry up!" Pallor whined. "They're waiting for us over at the pond. I promised that I'd be back soon. If I don't keep my promise, then they won't trust me to keep promises, and then they won't trust me at all, and then. . ."

She half listened to her brother babble on about his reputation as she resumed eating. Pallor had always been quite a talker. Most of the tribe found his constant dialogue an annoyance. She somewhat agreed, but deep down, she thought her brother's tendency to babble on and on without stopping was also endearing.

"Are you done yet?" Pallor asked again as she licked the last of the meat from a bone. "Because it's been quite a while, and I'm sure that they're worried by now. Let's not keep them waiting for much longer! Hurry, hurry, hurry!"

She licked the final ribbon of red from the pale gray of the bone, and then stood up. "I'm finished now, Pallor. Let's play."

Pallor squealed in delight and dashed off. Scope trotted leisurely after him.

After a minute, they arrived at the area where Benign and Abject were waiting. Abject grinned with glee when he saw them arrive, while Benign simply stood there, her eyes halfway covered.

"You're here!" Abject said cheerfully.

"Took you long enough," Benign droned, sighing. "I was beginning to think that you'd never arrive."

"Well, we're here now," Scope said. "Who has the nut?"

"I do!" Pallor said, picking up a large, spherical, brown nut from the ground. He was standing beneath a tree that bore several more nuts. He threw it up in the air. "Think fast!" he shouted, and swatted the falling nut with his tail.

The nut soared higher into the air. Scope quickly tracked its path, and assumed that it would be falling just above Abject. "Abject!" she yelled. "It's coming toward you!"

"I see it," Abject replied, then maneuvered his body into position. He swatted the nut with his tail at exactly the right moment, and the nut rocketed back through the air.

Scope yelped, seeing that the nut was heading directly at her face. She ducked. Her rising haunches deflected the nut in Benign's direction.

Benign cowered, twisting her body into a ball. The nut gently bounced off of her back and landed with a soft plop near the edge of the pond. It vanished under the water for a second, then reappeared on the surface, slowly spinning as it bobbed away.

"I knew that this would happen!" Benign wailed miserably, staying in her curled up state. "I told you all that something bad would happen. This nut is a horrid projectile! Look what happened. It hit me, and it'll bruise, I know it."

"It won't bruise, Benign," Scope sighed. "It only tapped you. Blaming an inanimate object won't do anything." She twisted her neck around to look at the area of impact. She twitched the muscles there, which twinged a little in protest.

"Does it hurt?" Pallor asked Benign. "Does it? Huh? If it did hurt, then I'm sorry that I made you play! It'll be an ugly bruise, all purple and black and blue and all those wonderful nasty colors. . ."

"Pallor, she's fine," Scope said calmly. "Don't fret about it. Your hide's going to be perfectly fine, Benign." Scope sighed in slight exasperation.

Jumping into the fray, Abject interjected, "Stop whining, Benign. It was just a gentle bounce."

"You're not the one who was struck!" Benign continued. "I'm hurting, I tell you!"

Scope leaned over and whispered, "Thanks, Abject. She was just settling down."

"Someone has to say something," Abject replied. "If no one does now, she'll be an even higher high-maintenance bother later."

Scope sighed. *Yes, but your delivery and execution need some work.* However, she said, "Abject, would you help me get the nut?"

They jumped in, retrieved the nut, and carried it back to land. After she and her brother shook the water from their hides, they trotted over to the others.

"We've got the nut!" Abject said, smiling. "Let's play!"

"Leave me out of this!" Benign exclaimed, finally uncurling and running behind the nut tree.

Abject tossed the nut into the air and batted it with his tail. It sailed through the air in Scope's direction. She twirled on the balls of her feet and swatted the ball with her tail. It headed in Pallor's direction, and he repeated the action. The pattern repeated a few times, and then Abject gave the nut a particularly hard cuff toward the ground. The nut struck a rock and immediately broke. Translucent white liquid splashed all over the dirt.

"Well, now you've done it," Benign said, looking at the mess. "You've broken the nut."

"Oops," Abject remarked.

Scope looked at the remains of the nut, then at the ground under the nut tree. "I don't see any more fallen nuts. I guess that the game's over."

"Aw," Pallor said, sighing. "That was a fun game. We'd better keep an eye out for any more fallen nuts."

Benign crept forward and sniffed at the remains of the nut. She licked at some of the liquid, rolled her tongue around her mouth for a moment, then hummed and lapped up the rest. Her imagined agony was apparently forgotten.

"That is gross!" Pallor said, wrinkling his nose as his fringe became vertical. "What does that stuff taste like, since it was on the ground?"

"Like water," Benign replied, licked her chops, then added, "but with more twang."

As Pallor bent down to taste, Scope vented and trotted off to hide in her bush.

Scope was sleeping soundly when she heard something that roused her. She raised her head and checked the position of the sun. It was close to setting, and long shadows were being cast over the clearing. The dense trees made the shadows on the forest floor seem 10 times as dark.

She blinked, then concentrated on what had woken her. It had been a sharp, quick sound, like a branch breaking.

Snap.

Like that. Her head whipped toward the trees. She narrowed her eyes at the forest, trying to see into the dark shadows. She shifted to a more upright position, having been sleeping on her side, so that she could see better. Sniffing the air, she searched for any scents that she didn't recognize. Her sensitive nose filtered through the regular smells and singled out two new scents. The new smells were sharp, tangy, and held some underlying odor that sent a small shiver down her back.

"Who's there?" she called out into the trees, looking for any moving shadows. She rose to her feet and took a step toward them.

She heard a few sharp hisses, and then two shadows split from the rest. Her mind was sending her frantic warning signals, but her curiosity of the strange shadow-beasts overwhelmed her urges to flee.

As the shadow-beasts took several steps closer to the tree line, she was able to get decent looks at them. They were both the same size, about two times hers but nowhere near to the size of an adult Utahraptor. Their hides seemed completely black, but upon closer inspection she spotted dark grey stripes on their thighs, forearms, and noses. Both of them had a crown of spikes adorning the back of their skulls. One had deep scarlet eyes and the other had bright yellow eyes.

"What are you?" she asked, moving so that she was slightly walking sideways. She glanced at the area around her, realizing that most of the tribe were out hunting, and the remaining adults and the younglings were gathered near the pond. "You're very dark," she added, narrowing her eyes in an effort to see them better.

"Yes, we are," agreed a shadow-beast, ignoring her question. "Now, where is your tribe leader?" He licked his chops and shifted his weight from one leg to the other, clearly anticipating something.

His query made Scope uneasy. To her, it seemed. . . off, like how they were eyeing her like she would look at a piece of fresh meat. Even though Spike was out hunting, she nodded in affirmation. "He's over by the pond. I can get him."

The shadow-beasts looked at each other, then back at her. "No, don't get him," one said, narrowing his eyes.

Scope cocked her head to the side. "Why not?"

"Because. . . because we want to surprise him." After another look at each other, the other shadow-beast nodded. "Yes. We'll bring some friends, too. It'll be a party."

"Okay," Scope said.

"Don't tell anyone that you saw us. It would ruin the surprise."

"Okay," she responded again.

The shadow-beasts hissed softly through their teeth, then backed up a few steps back into the deep shadows. It was then that Scope lost sight of them.

She could feel her heartbeat pounding in her ears. Standing still, she tried to hear if the shadow-beasts were leaving, but they were silent. She took several deep breaths before turning and walking back to her nest. She desperately wanted to run, but fear that the shadow-beasts were watching leaded her feet.

She buried her muzzle in her tail and covered her head with a hind leg. Those two shadow-beasts had amassed a large amount of suppressed fear within her. She shivered violently as she let it out. There had been something very, very *wrong* about them. She longed to see Spike.

It was nighttime when she heard the hunting parties returning. She raised her head and saw all of them entering the clearing. They were carrying a large amount of meat. Combined, she assumed that they had caught at least two large herbivores. She urgently looked among them for Spike. When she saw the royal blue fringe, she leapt up and ran as fast as she could to him.

"Scope," Spike said in mild surprise when she skidded to a stop in front of him. "What is the matter?"

"Shadow-beasts," she replied, panting from her sprint.

Spike immediately became wary. "Where?" he asked firmly as he gave his heap of meat to another Utahraptor.

"At the trees," she replied. "I didn't go in. They were in there, didn't come out from the trees. Gone now."

"What did they look like?" Spike coaxed in a calming voice.

"They were all black, bigger than me but smaller than you. They had a crown of spikes on their skulls."

Scope cringed slightly when Spike narrowed his eyes. "Coelurus," he hissed, then spat to the side. She fought against the instinct to show timid submission when he suddenly gazed at her with hardened eyes. "Did you talk to them?" When she nodded, he added, "What did they say?"

"They said that they wanted to meet you. I lied and said that you were at the pond. They said that they would come back later with friends, to surprise you."

Spike tensed. "Did they say when?"

Scope quickly shook her head.

Spike rumbled deep in his throat, his fringe having long lowered to become flush with his neck. He bowed his head, then roared into the sky. Everyone around them jumped and whirled to face the tribe leader.

"We have an incoming Tyrant attack!" Spike declared loudly, lowering his hindquarters so that he was taller. "All younglings are to be gathered in the center of the clearing. There will be Utahraptors posted as guards throughout the day and night."

As Spike stomped away, still shouting instructions for preparation, Scope sighed in relief that she had told him.

"Scope!" She turned and saw her mother trotting toward her with her siblings in tow.

"Mother!" Scope called back.

"Quickly now," her mother said, nudging Scope toward the center of the clearing. "We need to claim a spot."

The center of the clearing was elevated above the rest, and had a large rock in one part of it. A Utahraptor was on the rock, clearly acting as a sentry as he kept looking around with keen raptor eyes. Scope's mother led her to a empty spot near the base of the rock.

Scope looked around at the new nesting spot in dismay, which she thought was quite a bit lacking in the comforts she was used to, such as moss cushioning and decent little dips that she could fit just right in. Here, there was nothing but dirt.

"Go on," her mother said to her. "I know that it's not the same as our nest, but we're going to be staying here until the threat goes away."

Scope wrinkled her nose as she stepped into the nest. "But it doesn't have any moss. I want moss!"

Her mother sighed.

"I can sleep without moss," Abject said, sauntering into the nest and laying down in one spot. "Unlike *some* Utahraptors I know."

Scope glared at her brother, her fringe laying flat against her neck to show her irritation. "I just like the moss. It's comfy. I *can* sleep without it, you know."

"Oh, really?" Abject scoffed. "Prove it."

"Really!" Scope responded. She stomped down to the far side of the nest from him and settled down in one of the shallow dips. She hid a grimace at how the dip felt too small for her and felt her legs being forced to stay at uncomfortable angles. She hid her discomfort and shot a superior look at Abject.

Her brother rolled his eyes.

As their mother began convincing Benign and Pallor that

the new nest would be more than fine until they could return to their regular nest, Scope looked up at the sentry that stood on the rock. He was completely motionless unless he was rotating his head to look around, and even that motion would be sharp and quick. The sentry practically radiated attention.

That has to be so boring, Scope thought, looking in the same direction as the sentry, a section of trees. She didn't think that the sentry had to be *that* diligent at staring at a bunch of trees.

Spike walked across her vision, catching her attention. Her eyes followed him as he walked toward the pond. He paused at the roots of the wizened tree and looked down at the dirt. After a long moment, he resumed walking.

Scope still looked at the spot at the tree's roots. What had he been looking at? All she could see was exposed wood and dirt. Curious, she stood up and climbed out of the nest. She weaved through other Utahraptors on her way to the tree. When she reached the ancient tree, she stopped at the roots. She looked at the empty dirt, then sniffed to see if something had been there. There was something off about the smell, but she had no idea what. She cocked her head to the side, perplexed.

"What are you looking at?"

Scope turned her head to see Spike standing behind her. Now that she had seen him, Spike took a few steps forward so that she didn't have to turn so far to look at him.

"I was wondering what you were looking at," she replied, glancing down at the dirt before her.

Spike blinked slowly, then also glanced down at the earth. "I was in thought, young one."

"Oh," Scope said, slightly frowning.

"Go back to your nest, Scope," Spike said gently. "You need to be close to your parents when the Coelurus return."

"I can fight!" Scope remarked indignantly. "They'll never see me coming!"

Spike chuckled. "Ambush attacks don't count. What will you do after you scare them? Now, little one, go back to your nest."

Scope scowled and hung her head as she plodded back to the nest. She collapsed in her dubbed spot in the nest and glared at the earth in front of her face. Snorting, she watched her breath stir up some dust and swirl in the air.

"What'd the dirt do to you?" Pallor asked. "Did you trip and fall or something? You could set it on fire if you could, but you don't have any lightning to do that, and can dirt catch on fire anyway? That makes me wonder whether. . ."

Scope's eyes suddenly shifted to look at Pallor. She slowly rose to her feet and fell into a crouch. Pallor recognized her predatory stance and fell silent.

"Scope?" he said hesitantly. "What're you doing?"

With a roar, Scope launched herself at him. Her feet landed on his side, sending him to the ground. She placed one foot on his neck and tapped her long toe claw on his neck. "Yield," she ordered. "You're dead."

"No, I'm not," Pallor said, confused.

"This is combat practice, you dummy," Scope said, stepping

off of him. After she moved back to her original spot, she added, "Prepare."

Pallor tried to dodge her next lunge, but she managed to land on his tail and pin it. He fell onto his stomach and chin, and Scope wasted no time in stepping onto his neck and tapping it with her toe claw again.

"Yield. You're dead."

"No fair!" Pallor complained. "I wasn't ready!"

"Would you be ready for an ambush attack?" Scope retorted. "I even gave you a warning. Seriously, you're not helping my combat practice."

There was a roar, and Scope was suddenly struck from the side. She hit the ground hard with a heavy weight on her side. She looked up to see Abject on her. Before he could pin her neck, she thrust up her midsection, successfully tossing her brother from her. She rushed to her feet and leapt at him. Abject managed to dodge, and Scope landed roughly on her side, stumbling but managed not to fall. Abject didn't let her recover from her stumble, and her legs crumpled when a heavy weight was suddenly dropped on her back. Scope grunted when her neck was pinned.

"Yield," Abject said, tapping her neck with his toe claw. "You're dead."

He hopped off of her and she scrambled to her feet. They both moved to the far sides of the nest from each other. They eyed each other warily, waiting for the other to make the first move.

I can be the best fighter ever, Scope thought in determination, then lunged forward.

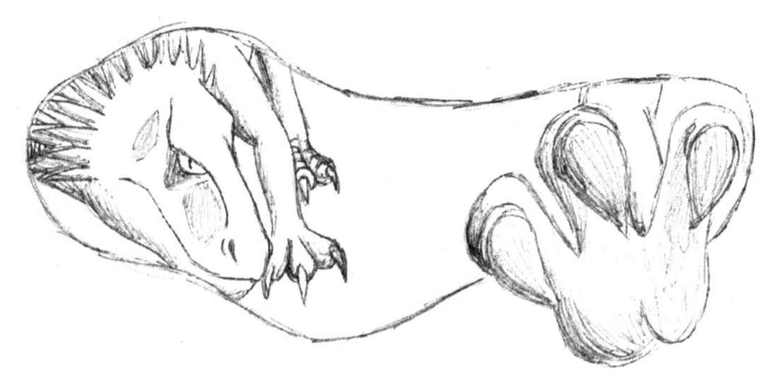

CHAPCER CEN

Scope sharply cocked her head to the side and heard her neck crack. Now that it was looser, she looked around at the trees.

It had been almost five days since she had seen the Coelurus. The entire tribe was seemingly perpetually tense, as there hadn't been a single sign of any Tyrants. Scope had spent her time sparring with anyone who would spend the time. Her favorite opponents were her siblings, and she had even tried to pick a fight with Spike, but Spike had simply swept her feet out from under her and 'killed' her in one smooth move.

Scope stamped her feet on the dirt, then looked at her prints. Next to her were her patriarch's prints, and she scowled at how hers were so much smaller than his. Her patriarch was so much stronger than she was, and she reckoned that if she was stronger, she could use that same trick Spike had used on her.

She looked up and around for Spike. She spotted him patrolling along the forest edge. With a grunt of determination, she strode his way. She sneaked up behind him, plotting her attack. She took a breath, then raced forward. She ran into his legs, hoping that her weight would knock them out from under him, but it felt like she had just run into a rock. She fell to the ground and groaned.

Spike calmly looked down at her. "Do you want something?"

"I want you to teach me that trick," Scope grunted as she got up to her feet.

Without warning, Spike swept his leg through both of hers, knocking her onto her back. "That one?"

"You are sneaky," Scope said, scowling, as she got back to her feet.

"I'm hurt," Spike replied, putting on a facetious pouty face.

"I was being sarcastic," Scope responded dryly. "Now, are you going to teach me that trick or not?"

"You're not large enough to succeed," the tribe leader replied gently. "Now, if you were about twice your size or if I was half of mine, it might work."

Scope was about to reply when there was a loud screech from the Utahraptor sentry on the rock. All heads turned to him, and he roared at one section of trees. The adult Utahraptors immediately rushed to that section, leaving only a few guarding the back.

Scope was picked up by the scruff by Spike's mouth and carried back to the center of the clearing. She was dumped on the ground and Spike rushed off.

Scope clambered onto a small ledge on the rock so that she could see over their heads and at the trees. She saw shadowed beings moving through the forest floor toward the clearing. They moved too quickly for her to see how many there were.

And then, in a fine display of intimidation, came the Coelurus from the trees. They formed a line and screeched at the Utahraptors facing them. Then they lunged into action, and the fighting began. Scope had a hard time discerning one Coelurus from another, despite them being different colors; they were using hit and run tactics and were moving so fast it was hard to keep track of any particular one.

Despite her inability to see how many there were, Scope felt that there were far too few to pose an overwhelming force against larger predators such as Utahraptors. Feeling a bad sensation in her gut, she turned to face the other side, where the adult Utahraptors were few and her peers were.

She wasn't wrong. There were many more Coelurus coming through the trees, using the fight as a distraction. And from what she could see, no one else had noticed. She looked up at the top of the rock, but the sentry was gone.

No one would notice the flank attack until it was too late. With that in mind, she quickly scaled the boulder, took a deep breath, and let out the loudest warning screech she could muster. When those that weren't already occupied looked her way, she roared equally loudly at the hiding Coelurus.

Since their cover was blown, the Coelurus raced out from

the trees. Scope dropped down from the rock and faced the oncoming foes. She fervently hoped that the fighting skills she had learned over the last couple days would keep her alive.

"What are you doing?" Benign growled incredulously at her from inside their nest.

"What does it look like?" Scope hissed back, not looking away from the Coelurus.

"You're going to get killed!" her sister said.

"Not if I have anything to say about it."

The fighting on the other side of the clearing became more frantic and rapid as Utahraptors rushed to kill Coelurus so that they could dash over and ward off the failed ambush attack.

At an unheard cue, Scope and the others ran forward to meet the Coelurus. Scope ducked in between the their legs, using her teeth and sharp little claws on them. She was pleased to note that her small but painful gashes were slowing them down. Her heartbeat was pounding in her ears as she ducked and rolled and leapt and bound. It wasn't long before she was taken notice of and a Coelurus began chasing her. Scope took a sharp turn and ran at the Coelurus' legs, hoping that Spike's ascertains were right. She beamed with accomplishment as she knocked the Coelurus' legs out from under it, and it fell to the ground. An adult Utahraptor leapt at the fallen foe as Scope ran on.

Scope soon found out that more Coelurus were following her. She tried to use the same tactic that had toppled over the other one, but they dodged her attempts. She screeched in pain as one of their jaws connected, scraping her side and tearing into her hide. Trying not to limp from the agonizing pain, she dashed for cover. She ran to the rock and tried to scale it, but her feet and hands slipped and she tumbled back down to the ground.

"Now we've got you," one of the Coelurus snarled.

Scope cowered against the rock, cornered by three Coelurus. If she ran, she would run into jaws. Against her will, a scared whimper leaked through her lips.

"Isn't this the pipsqueak that alerted the others?" said one.

"I think so. Her little warning ruined our ambush. Shall we teach her a lesson?"

"Yes, a lesson," another hissed gleefully.

Mustering up any bravery, Scope growled and snapped her jaws at them, sticking up her fringe so that she looked bigger. "Don't come any closer, or. . . or I'll attack!" She tried not to show what she thought of her outright *pathetic* threat.

They laughed at her, nonplussed at her meager warning. They took a step closer.

A quick glance around told her that there was a deep hole that went under the rock. The opening was just large enough for her to enter. She looked back at the Coelurus, then dashed for the hole. Her tail was only a hairbreadth from being nipped when she entered. She pushed herself against the far side of the hole. A Coelurus peered in, then tried to swipe at her with its arm, but the it fell just short of getting her.

The Coelurus persisted in trying to reach her, eventually getting the idea to dig at the hole so that they could fit their heads in. Scope fervently hoped that someone would rescue her before they dug it out enough, for she knew that they could easily reach her that way.

Just before they succeeded in sufficiently widening the hole, Scope saw one of them struck down by someone she couldn't see. The other two Coelurus turned away from the hole to face the new threat. Scope watched as they were taken down, and then the last one's jugular was sliced open by a large toe claw.

Then she saw a familiar face appear. "You're safe now, come out," Spike said.

Scope climbed out of the hole and tapped his chin with her muzzle in thanks.

"You're welcome," Spike said. "Now, I must see how many we lost to this attack."

"Is it over?" Scope asked, only then noticing the silence.

"Yes."

Scope found some niches for her to use to climb up to the top of the rock, and then she looked around. There was carnage everywhere, thankfully mostly Coelurus, but she could see several Utahraptors lying motionless among them. The dirt and grass were stained red. Scope couldn't look anymore, feeling sick, so she hopped down to the ground and retreated to her nest.

"Where's Mother?" Pallor asked, craning his neck as he looked around. "And Patriarch?"

"They're around here somewhere," Abject said. "After all, they're two of the best fighters! They wouldn't die from a simple Coelurus fight."

Scope wasn't so sure. She knew that if she had made even one mistake, just one false move, she would've died. Not even Spike was exempt from her reasoning.

"Why'd they attack us?" Benign asked meekly, blinking owlishly. "The tribe's done nothing wrong."

"How would I know?" Abject responded sharply.

Scope noticed a Utahraptor rushing their way, and smiled. "Patriarch!" she called.

"Little ones!" their patriarch exclaimed in relief, nuzzling them. His ultramarine fringe fluxed between almost being flush with his neck and fully upright. "You're all all right." Then he noticed her injury. "Scope, your hip!"

She bent her neck to look at her wound, which was throbbing and gave her agonizing pain if she turned her body wrong. It was bleeding and raw. "I'll be fine eventually. I fought the Coelurus."

"You fought the Coelurus?" her patriarch said in awe. "Scope, it's a miracle that you're still alive! My brave, brave daughter! That'll be your first scar."

"Where's Mother?" Benign whined. "I want Mother!"

Their patriarch straightened and looked around. "I don't see her. . . Stay here, little ones, I'll be right back." He trotted off, still looking around.

Scope laid down in her spot in the nest, then rested her head on her arms. As she wrapped her tail around one side of her body, she tried not to whimper as her wounded hide stretched.

She could just see the raw injury on her left hip. It was going to undoubtedly scar. She had always wanted a scar; after all, the more scars one had, the more respected one was. She just didn't realize that it was going to hurt so much. She could only imagine how much pain Spike had gone through in order to have all of *his* scars.

She tried to nap, but noises from around her kept her awake. She could hear Utahraptors moving around and dragging the dead away, tending to the injured and dying, and the occasional lamenting keens of someone discovering a deceased loved one. Scope was relieved that her patriarch was alive and well, albeit a little wounded, but she didn't know at all where her mother was. The last time she had seen her was the night before, when her mother had laid down in the nest with them.

Benign was still whining for attention. Scope held back an annoyed growl as the whining grated on her ears; she knew that her sister was only relieving her tension. On the other hand, Pallor was unusually silent. Scope cracked open an eyelid and saw that he was blindly staring at the pebble-laden ground outside the nest. Abject was lying half in and half out of the nest, idly batting a few blades of trampled grass on the nest's rim.

Scope let out a heavy breath. Normally, she disliked waiting. However, in this case, it wasn't the waiting more than the fear that her mother was *gone*. Patriarch was taking a long time just to find her. . .

A breeze wafted over the nest. Scope wrinkled her nose as her stomach did flip-flops. The scents on the breeze were of little more than the stench of death and blood. But she was a carnivore. There was no reason for her suddenly becoming sick from the death smell. She swallowed some bile and spat out the saliva left behind, as she still tasted the acid.

It was near the end of the day when Scope saw their patriarch return. One look at him sent a shiver of dread through her; his head was lowered, his fringe drooped, and his feet practically dragged along the ground with every step.

Her chest squeezed painfully as he approached.

"Where's Mother?" Pallor timidly asked. Scope could tell he already knew the answer, like she did. But like him, she held onto a string of hope.

Their patriarch's gaze met Pallor's. "She fell to the Coelurus, Pallor."

Instantly, Benign keened. Her wail of mourning rose into the air, echoing eerily around the clearing.

Abject was gritting his teeth, then surged to his feet. "They killed Mother! The next time I see a Coelurus, I'm going to kill it as heartlessly as they killed her! I swear it." Their patriarch went to calm him down, but Abject was already out of the nest and stalking away in a fury.

Abject didn't go far, just to the pond. He collapsed at the shore, his chin just short of the water. Their patriarch walked over and laid down beside him, and they started to talk softly.

Scope felt like her feet had been swept out from underneath her, despite that she was lying down. *No,* she thought numbly, her eyes wide and staring at nothing. *Not Mother. I. . . I never even got to say good-bye, or tell her that I loved her one last time.*

Having returned to the nest, their patriarch and Abject laid down at the center. Scope wasn't the only one who shuffled up next to their patriarch. She wedged herself in the space where his arm connected to the body. Lying so that she could hear his heartbeat, it took her a while to fall asleep.

CHAPTER ELEVEN

The days and nights were steadily growing colder, much to Scope's discomfort. During the day, she began spending more and more time sunning herself on rocks. Being one to stretch out while sleeping, she now had to curl up into a tight ball and share body heat with her patriarch and siblings.

Scope scowled as another violent shiver rocked her body, starting from her head and traveling all the way down to her tail like a wave. To make things worse, a frigid breeze drafted over her, making her shiver again.

Frankly, she was amazed that none of her siblings or her patriarch had awakened yet due to her muscles' incessant spasms. She clutched her hide blanket closer to her body in an effort to cocoon herself.

She looked up toward the sky as she scooted further into the tight crevice between her patriarch's armpit and his body. Unfortunately, she had moved beyond the spot on the ground that had been warmed by her body heat, and now she had to wait for the hard frigid ground beneath her to warm up. She shivered again and tried to curl up tighter.

Not for the first time, and most certainly nowhere near the last, she wished that her mother was still alive. Not only did she miss her greatly, but her mother would provide another source of heat other than her blanket.

A pointed glare of envy was directed at her siblings. Pallor was sleeping soundly beneath their patriarch's chin. Abject was a small distance away from their patriarch and was actually *splayed* out over the ground, leading her to believe that her brother possessed a Hot Season sun somewhere inside his body. Benign was nestled in a gap between their patriarch's knee and body. And their patriarch was sleeping like a rock.

A crunching sound of feet drew her gaze to an Utahraptor that was acting as one of the two sentries. Barely able to distinguish the Utahraptor's identity in the darkness, she watched at it traveled up to the tall rock and scaled it. The pebbles that were dislodged from the rock seemed excessively loud as they tumbled down to the ground.

Scope looked up at the dark sky. Scattered across it were scintillating pinpricks of stars surrounding a pale curved sliver that was all that was left of the luna before it vanished for a few nights. On one side of the clearing she could see that the stars were being completely blocked out, and she could only assume that there were clouds over there.

The stars above her were being blocked out by a few large shapes. Scope recognized the shape of the nocturnal predator and immediately tried to cram as much of her body out of sight as she could. The eagles flying above her usually looked for fish and, as Spike had told her, hunted in the lake not far from the clearing. But the eagles weren't restricted to strictly a marine diet. She had heard a few stories from her elders where the eagles would sometimes swoop down and snatch up a hatchling or a small youngling for dinner. Scope had no intention of being bird food despite that she could very well be too large by now to be carried off.

The eagles eventually flew away, and Scope had finally shifted enough times to discover *the* warmest and most comfortable spot. She rested her head on the ground and let her eyes drift closed while a discreet shiver shook her. Sleep was coming, she could feel her body becoming heavier and her sense of self draining away. . .

Her eyes snapped open again when something *freezing* and wet splashed on her nose. She shook her head and looked up at the sky just in time to have another drop land on her face. The stars were completely covered now, and freezing rain was starting to fall. Scope pulled her tail closer in to keep it from getting wet and rested her head on the tip.

Her patriarch didn't provide much shelter, but since a majority of her body was shielded from the downpour, she managed to fall asleep.

Her warmth was leaving her. Why was her warmth leaving her? Her warmth was *never* supposed to leave her! As Scope opened her eyes only a sliver and prepared to growl, she thought, *When I find out who took my warmth. . . oh.* Her half-asleep mind woke up completely when she saw that the source of her heat, her patriarch, was awake and standing up.

"Did you sleep well, Scope?" her patriarch asked in a voice far too cheery for morning.

Scope closed her eyes and curled up, almost disappearing under her soaked blanket. "Come back down here and we'll talk when I wake up again," she grumbled.

Her patriarch chuckled warmly and nosed her in the back, careful to avoid jostling the almost-healed scar. "You're going to want to see what happened overnight."

"It rained. Everything's wet. I'm *cold*!" Scope whined without opening her eyes at all.

"It didn't *just* rain," her patriarch stated, nudging her again. "Get up and help me wake up your siblings."

Scope grumbled disgruntled gibberish as she hefted herself to her feet and rubbed her eyes open, careful not to accidentally gouge them out with her claws. She blinked a few times, and then her eyes widened in surprise.

"Why is everything white?" she asked in awe.

It covered *everything*. The Utahraptors that weren't up and about were little more than large mounds of white fluff. Where her patriarch had been laying was a bare spot surrounded by the white stuff. When she took a step into it, she sank up to her ankle. It was cold and wet. When she took a bite of it to see how it tasted, it melted in her mouth and turned to water. She squeaked in surprise as she swallowed.

"It's called snow," her patriarch replied, taking a step to a small white mound. He snorted, and the snow blew off to reveal Abject, who was still soundly sleeping.

While her patriarch roused her siblings, Scope moved off to explore the new substance called snow. She exaggeratedly stepped around, lifting her legs higher than necessary, getting used to watching it fall onto the tops of her feet and then cascade off when she moved them. It was still cold, but she was too distracted to care. She hopped up and down a few times, listening to the snow crunch underfoot.

Without warning, her vision became smothered in white. Scope yelped as she shook her head and the snow slid off. She looked behind her to see Pallor waving his tail around excitedly with a large gouge in the snow beneath him.

Scope smirked as she lowered her hindquarters and swept her tail through the snow. The disturbed snow soared toward her brother, who also yelped and turned away. Satisfyingly, the snow struck his side and he shivered violently.

Scope started to laugh, but then there was a cold *splat* against her chest and neck. She sucked in a breath of frigid air in shock, then coughed a few times as she turned to see who had swatted her with snow. Abject was on her other side and cackling.

"Leave me out of this!" Benign yipped as she ducked under an onslaught of snow, courtesy of Pallor. She ran behind their patriarch's leg for cover.

After thinking up a quick plan, Scope smirked as she bent down and scooped up a pile of snow in her hands. She quickly molded it into a vaguely round shape and tried to chuck it at Abject, but her body structure wouldn't allow the movement and her sloppy snowball fell far short of its target.

Abject started laughing at her pitiful attempt, but he abruptly stopped when Scope tackled him to the ground. Scope landed on his stomach and leapt off before he could kick her off.

Scope could hear her brother leaping up from the snow, so she ran. Her feet crunched and left tracks behind. An escape plan was streaming through her mind with surprising quality, but the snow revealed her path. If she could somehow find a place that was bare of the snow, perhaps she could lose Abject. She looked around frantically, and the nearest bare spot was the place where her patriarch had laid down. Since she had no better options, she headed right for it.

She put on a burst of speed and entered the bare spot. A quick glance over her shoulder showed that her brother was still close behind her. With a grunt of effort, she took a sharp turn and reentered the snow. Her legs ate up the ground as she rounded the base of a small rock. She leapt up onto the rock, quickly scaled it to its top, then realized that she had too much momentum to stop.

She needed a place to jump to, and fast. A quick glance showed that her patriarch was watching her and Abject in amusement and was standing just within jumping distance. She planted her feet on the very edge. Vaguely feeling her tensing muscles, she leapt off of the rock. There was a moment of weightlessness, and then a sharp jar as she landed on her patriarch's back. He grunted as she lost her balance and had to dig her claws into his hide to keep from falling to the ground. However, she had been going too fast, as she slid off and then tripped headfirst into a snowdrift.

Her momentum sent her deep into the snowdrift, leaving a hole behind. However, the lack of stability collapsed the hole, and she was effectively buried. Holding her breath in order to conserve air despite how much her body craved it, she gingerly used her muzzle to punch out a small hole to the open air. Now that she had air to breathe, she stopped holding her breath.

"Where'd she go?" she heard Abject ask, panting heavily.

"If you want to hone your hunting skills, you're going to have to find her yourself," their patriarch said with a chuckle.

Scope exhaled and relaxed. Hopefully, the caved in snow tunnel had efficiently covered up her path. She could hear her brother walking around, occasionally sniffing. She could also hear other members of the tribe rising from slumber. She held very still, wondering if anyone would be able to spot her before accidentally stepping on her. She didn't want to be trod upon.

After waiting a few minutes and Abject still hadn't found her, Scope decided to emerge from her hiding spot. She wriggled her way out of her hole and shook off the snow that had fallen onto her back. Looking around, she saw that Abject was nowhere to be seen.

Pallor came bounding up to her, taking hops instead of walking. "It's so white, Scope! It's fluffy and cold. Why is it wet? When it melts it looks like water! Is the snow actually water? Why is it white, then?"

"Excited, are you?" Scope queried casually, shaking some snow from her tail. It fell with a *plop*.

"Yeah!" Pallor said. "And you can see where I've been! I've been to the pond. It's hard! I can't sink anymore!"

Scope eyed her brother. "The pond's hard? Really?" she asked with skepticism.

Pallor nodded rapidly. "Come see, come see!" He bounded

away, using both legs to hop at once instead of simply leaping.

Scope followed along behind him, jumping over any drifts that proved to be too deep for her to cross. When she finally reached the pond, she had to actually search where land ended and the pond began. Snow had covered everything, and it was only when her feet suddenly slid out from under her she knew that land had ended.

"What happened to the water?" she said, gaping with astonishment, as she struggled to her feet on the slippery surface of what used to be water. Where the snow was swept away, she could see the hard surface of the clear water. It was like she was standing on the water itself.

"I don't know," Pallor said, sliding a little as he slowly walked further out on the pond. "But this is amazing! How long will this last?"

Scope finally stood up, then almost fell as she overcompensated for the lack of traction. Careful to keep her center of balance in the same place, she raised her head. Moving only her eyes, she looked around. Some of her peers were venturing out of their nests, having varying reactions to the fluff that had appeared over the night.

"This stuff is great!" Pallor's exclamation drew her attention back to him, and her eyes darted as far as they could go to see him, not daring to move anything else. Pallor was sliding along the surface of the pond, balancing on one leg with the other tucked up to his stomach.

Scope's eyes widened and her bottom jaw slackened as she watched him skate. *How is he* balancing *like that?* she wondered incredulously.

She peeled her eyes away from his form and focused on making her way back to land. She was only a pace or so away, so how hard could it be to walk there? She cautiously lifted up a foot with the intention to start walking, but the foot that was still on the ground suddenly slid out from under her and her chin got reintroduced to the hard water. She gritted her teeth and struggled back to her feet.

"Scope!"

She looked up and saw her patriarch standing not far away. "Little busy!" she said, trying to keep her feet under her.

He chuckled. "Have you forgotten about the assets on your feet called claws?" He walked away.

Immediately feeling like a fool, Scope dug her claws into the ice. She could immediately feel the traction difference, and quickly made her way to shore. Once there, she fled toward her nest.

On her way back, she saw Spike walking along with Grapple by his side. She looked at them with curiosity; Spike looked slightly distressed. Wandering closer, Scope could overhear their conversation. About a minute later, she had heard enough to tell that there had been some strange footprints in the forest, several dozen paces from the field. The snow had preserved the prints, and Spike was presuming that the prints had belonged to a trio of small, bipedal Squamas.

Scope's mind jumped to the Coelurus to whom she had talked, and the ensuing skirmish that had claimed her mother's life. She fervently hoped that the Coelurus hadn't returned. Her scar tingled, reminding her of its presence.

She made it the rest of the way back to her nest. Her patriarch wasn't there, and neither were any of her siblings. It made sense, since the entire tribe was active, with her peers exploring the snow. Scope followed a pair of younglings her age with her eyes as they bounded past her, one chasing the other with the intent to mock fight. Seemingly out of nowhere, a small group of five joined the pair, with six now chasing the one. The one being chased squeaked as he looked over his shoulder and saw how his pursuer had suddenly multiplied. They soon left her line of sight when they went behind the rock.

Scope huffed, her breath gusting out in a cloud of steam. Her eyes crossed briefly as she watched her breath float away and eventually evaporate and vanish. She laid down on the bare ground where her Patriarch had laid, hoping that some of his body heat had lingered. She was mildly disappointed when the ground was just as cold as the snow. She crumpled herself up into a ball to get warm as she looked for her blanket.

"Watch out!"

She yelped as she was suddenly tripped over, a toe claw coming dangerously close to her face as she toppled onto her side. The youngling that had tripped over her landed on the ground behind her with a thud and a squeak.

"Would you watch where you're going?" Scope snapped at the youngling, righting herself.

The youngling narrowed his eyes at her as he scrambled back up to his feet. "Well, excuse me, I didn't see you! Now, I'd better be going before Froth catches up to me!"

"Who's Froth?" Scope asked, but the youngling was already off.

"Whoa! Watch out!"

Scope had just enough time to look behind her before half a dozen younglings slammed into her. She squeaked as she was suddenly at the bottom of a pile of living bodies. Though the weight was great, the warmth that suddenly enveloped her was welcomed. However, she didn't have much time to bask when the younglings slid off of each other and she was exposed the cold air.

"Sorry 'bout that." Scope looked up at the speaker, who helped her to her feet. "Didn't see you in time."

Scope hummed as she looked the youngling over. He was slighter bigger than herself, with a light yellow fringe and a dark tan body with a tan underbelly. The other younglings were standing up behind him. "Apology accepted," she replied. "Were you chasing someone?"

The youngling's eyes lit up as he nodded. "Yeah. Did you see him?"

Scope pointed. "He ran off, not long before you and your buddies bumped into me. Why are you chasing him?"

The youngling nodded his thanks, then gestured to his fellows before all of them ran off. None of them answered her query.

With a grunt, Scope settled back down in the nest. Where was her blanket? It took a few minutes before she found it partially covered by a layer of snow. She grabbed it, shook it clean, and draped it over her body. It was bone-chillingly cold at first, but it didn't take long before her body heat began to warm it.

She had just gotten comfortable beneath her blanket when she heard another shout. Popping open an eyelid, she tiredly glared at Benign.

"Sleeping already?" Benign asked as she lowered her heard to Scope's level. "But the sun is hardly at its peak yet!"

"Well, I've been chased, knocked down twice, and I've banged my chin on the pond more times than I wish to recount," Scope replied drily. "Let's not forget how *cold* it is."

Benign gave her a sympathetic wince. "Sorry that your day was kind of bad," she murmured. "So, not planning to leave the nest?"

"Nope." Scope hid her face under a fold of her blanket, signaling that the conversation was over.

She heard Benign walk away.

Once Benign was gone, Scope peeked out. The light reflected off of the snow and into her eyes, partially blinding her. She closed her eyes and opted for listening instead. She heard laughter, snow crunching underfoot, and thuds of someone falling. The air simply radiated with festive emotions.

Scope sighed heavily as the positiveness around her began to tear away the depressed state she was in.

"Hey, you!"

She cocked her head to the side. The sound came from just out of her line of sight, coming toward her. However, she had no idea if the speaker was talking to her.

Her dilemma was solved when someone nudged her thigh. "You! I'm talking to you!"

Scope looked over her shoulder to see the yellow-fringed youngling from earlier. "Do you need something?" she asked him.

The youngling gestured over his shoulder. "My buddies and I were wondering if you'd like to play with us."

"Play?" Scope said. "Play what?"

The youngling shot her a grin as he replied, "Well, we were playing chase before. That's when Kilt over there. . ." he paused to nod toward the youngling that had bumped into her first. ". . . collided with you."

Scope tossed the offer over in her mind. After a few moments of considering it, she stood up and stretched her leg muscles. "I have five words to say to that, but first I want to know your name."

"I'm Froth," the yellowed-fringed youngling said, raising his chin proudly, smirking slightly as he did so.

Scope nodded her acknowledgement of his name, then said, "Catch me if you can!" before taking off at a dead run.

A breathless giggle escaped her throat as she ran. Her feet thudded and crunched, and the ice-cold air stung her lungs. Behind her, Froth growled something she couldn't quite hear before she heard his footsteps engaging pursuit.

She strived to make the chase as difficult as she could for her chasers. Creating a mental map of her surroundings, she weaved through other Utahraptors, ducking under legs and bodies if she could. She took sudden turns around rocks, and even braved the frozen pond by miraculously keeping her balance as she slid at high speeds across its frozen surface.

She leapt back onto solid ground and bee-lined for her favorite bush. She was pleased to see that the snow on it had been disturbed enough so that it wouldn't be obvious that she was hiding there. A quick glance over her shoulder showed that Froth and his buddies were a good distance behind her. She put the ancient tree between her and them, effectively blocking herself from their line of sight. She had only a few seconds, she threw herself at the bush. She skidded to a stop at its base.

Since her heavy breathing was blowing the snow in front of her nose, she tried as best she could to slow it. She peeked through the leaves of the bush, staying very still. Her tan body blended well with the ground, but snow had even gotten into the bush. Hopefully, she would just be mistaken as a large bare spot.

Froth slowed, his companions doing so as well. They slowed to a stop and began looking around. Scope recalled that they were in one of the spots that would give them a pretty good clear view of the clearing. If they didn't see her, then they had to think that she was hiding nearby.

"Does anyone see her?" Froth asked the others. When they shook their heads, he said, "I don't see her either. She's hiding. Let's look around."

Scope watched through the bush's branches as they started peering around the area. She kept as motionless as possible, and was hoping that the sounds of enjoyment from the others members of the tribe were covering up the noise of her breathing. *I'm just a little bare ground patch, nothing to look at, keep on going. . .*

One of Froth's friends had found her footprints. "Froth! I've found her tracks!"

"How would you know if they're hers?" Froth questioned,

walking over.

"They're the only ones around here that are spread this far apart. The other tracks are just regular running speed. She was going full kilter. See the amount of space between that track and the next?"

He might become a tracker when he gets older, Scope mused. *He's got the talent.*

Froth bent his head closer to the ground. "All these tracks look the same. How can you tell which ones are hers?"

"I just can," the potential tracker youngling said slowly, as if he was being talked out of his confidence.

Definitely going to be a tracker, she amended.

"Do you know where she went then?" Froth asked.

The tracker youngling followed her footprints closer to her hiding place. Scope held her breath as he said, "She ran this way. . . and here's a place where her prints are deeper; she must've jumped over this bush." He rounded the bush. The only thing moving on Scope's body were her eyes. The youngling stopped and peered at the messy snow on the other side of the bush.

"Well?" Froth prodded.

"It's kind of hard to tell," the tracker youngling admitted meekly. "A lot of Utahraptors messed around over here. I can't tell which tracks are hers."

"Then we split up," Froth declared. "Each of us follow a different trail. Off we go!"

Scope waited until they were a fair distance away before scrambling out from the bush. She glanced their way before vacating the area by jogging away.

"That was impressive."

She yelped and whirled around, looking for the owner of the voice that had spoken. Spike was behind her, leaning against a small rock. "Spike!" she said, then forced herself to calm down. "I didn't see you, Sir. What was impressive?"

"How you managed to hide so well from them," the tribe leader said. "I see some potential in you, little one. Not only are you a very fast runner, you know how to use the land around you for your advantage, and then use a false trail to lead your pursuers away from your hiding place."

"The trail thing was kind of a fluke," Scope said, looking down at the snow sheepishly. "I was just trying to confuse them."

"You did a very good job, no matter how it is put," Spike reassured her with a smile. "You'll be quite prepared for the Initiation Hunt coming up this coming Green Season."

Scope's eyes widened in excitement, and she was vaguely aware that her magenta fringe had sprung up and her tail was wagging. "You mean that I get to *go* this Turn?" she almost squealed.

Spike chuckled at her enthusiasm. "Yes, you and your peers."

With a squeal of excitement, Scope began to bound away, almost forgetting to thank Spike for his input. After she had done so, she pranced back toward her nest.

"Hey, there you are!"

Scope was jerked from her excited mood by Froth's shout. She turned to see him standing not far away, eyeing her with amused annoyance. "Froth!" she greeted him.

"Nice trick you used," he said with a smirk. "We couldn't find you at all. Where were you?"

"My secret," Scope purred mischievously. "I *might* tell you some time in the future."

"Scope! Pallor! Benign! Abject!"

She cocked her head and craned her neck. Her patriarch was calling her. From what she could tell, he had a decent-sized hunk of raw meat, still on a thigh bone, sitting at his feet. "Sorry to leave, but Patriarch's calling for me," she said to Froth.

"It's okay," the youngling with the yellow fringe said with a dismissive wave. "I think that I hear my mother calling for me, too. Catch up with you later!" He jogged away.

"See you!" Scope called after him. She spotted her siblings bee-lining for the meat at their patriarch's feet. Not wanting them to get all the good tidbits, she raced after them.

CHAPTER TWELVE

"It's time for your Initiation Hunt."

Looking back, Scope would later think that the instant the last word was said she was on her feet faster than she had ever been before. She stood so quickly that the motion caused her head to spin. When she recovered from the brief dizziness, she stared at her patriarch in excitement. "Really?" she asked with an excited squeal.

Her patriarch laughed at Scope's obvious excitement. "Yes. Now, Spike is giving your final briefing to the other younglings. Your siblings are already there."

Scope trilled and ran to join the other younglings gathered around Spike at the ancient tree. She reached the outskirts of the group and took a seat.

". . . be many dangers out there," Spike was saying, looking around at them with a very serious expression. "This Turn may be the most dangerous I have ever seen. All of you will need to constantly be on your guard."

"I can deal with any Squama!" Froth disrespectfully crowed, his fringe erecting with assurance in his talents. "*We* can. After all, strength in numbers. Besides, you've been training us," he added.

A glare from Spike quickly silenced Froth and any younglings that loudly agreed with him. "So sure of your and your comrades' abilities, are you, Froth, that all of you could face a Tyrannosaurus and survive?"

"Sure we can!" shouted a youngling.

Spike's glare became heavier. "That is thinking that can easily cause your deaths! Tyrannosaurus are one of the most deadly of Squamas, and they are out there in large numbers. *Two* of you could fit underneath just one of their feet. Who can tell me what the proper course of action is when you see a Tyrannosaurus?"

"Run?" asked a youngling.

"No," Spike said, shaking his head firmly. "To turn tail and run would result in a chase that will almost certainly result in your death."

Scope swallowed nervously. "Hide and wait until it goes away?" she piped up, her voice a little more than a scared squeak.

To her relief, Spike gave her a small nod. "That is the best course of action. Well done, Scope. To hide and wait for it to leave would not be a sure way to survive an encounter, but it's the best one that you could have." He paused and took a breath. "Now, I will tell you the Squamas you will need to avoid. Tyrannosaurus are, of course, one of the species. Coelurus you already know about, thanks to their attack this last Colors Season. Appalachiosaurus are scavengers but will hunt if they think that the prey is vulnerable enough, aka *you*."

Scope listened carefully as Spike laboriously went through a list of dangerous Squamas. She could recall when she had been a mere hatchling, and her world had been nothing but play and fun, nothing was wrong and all was perfect. Of course, that was before the Coelurus attack.

"Please list the species I just warned you about," Spike said once he had finished. Over the next minute, younglings supplied the species. He said, "Good. Any questions?"

"What are we supposed to be doing on the Hunt exactly?" a youngling piped up.

"Very good question, Pace," Spike said with an approving smile. "All of you need to contribute to the Utahraptor tribe, and the Hunt gives you first-hand experience. Now, in the Initiation Hunt, you won't be bringing back food, but you must bring back at least five bones of the kill you make. It can only be one kill, and it must be a large one. I don't want slackers bringing back heaps of mammals. Hunting nothing but mammals drastically cuts down on their population and it could take Turns, or maybe even never, for them to recover their numbers. Thus, your kill *cannot* be mammalian in any form or number. It must be an elderly herbivore."

"What kind of kill, then?" Pace added.

"The younglings before you have hunted Corythosaurus,

Ankylosaurus, and other large herbivores," Spike replied. "Now, are there any more questions?"

Scope didn't have any, and she looked around at her peers. From their own glances and expressions, they didn't either.

"Very well, then," Spike said. "Now, off with you all! Remember to return with your prey's bones."

Scope rose to her feet and began trotting toward the trees. She was at the front of the pack, leading the way to the border of unfamiliar and unknown territory. Behind her, she could hear her peers' breaths, their feet landing on the ground. She could smell the excitement and anticipation in the air, both of them electric!

She hesitated as she came within paces of the trees. The scents of excitement and anticipation slowly bled away to nervousness. She demanded bravery from within herself, took a deep breath, and entered the trees.

She growled as she reminded herself, *I've gone through Patriarch's and Spike's drills. I know how to fight. And I've been into the forest before.*

"Come on, you hatchlings!" Froth yelled, surging ahead at a fast jog. He skipped sideways so that he could look at the other younglings behind him. "We're going to get ourselves a kill and become full members of our tribe!"

A meek shout of "Hurrah!" sounded. Scope scoffed; She found the lack of confidence disturbing. *How can we get our first kill if we're all so timid?*

"Is that the best you can do?" Froth scorned them, snapping his jaw in disapproval. "What are you, tiny mammals that scurry for shelter when a big bad new-hatchling comes along?"

She was pleased to note that Froth's reprimand was productive, as the next "Hurrah!" was much stronger this time.

Froth looked pleased at what he had accomplished. "Let's move out!"

Scope grinned, showing her narrow, sharp teeth as she increased her speed to match Froth's.

The sun had just passed its zenith when Froth motioned for a halt. Scope slowly came to a stop, letting her momentum die gradually. She looked at Froth, wondering why he had had them stop.

"What's the deal, Froth?" a youngling asked, coincidentally voicing Scope's thoughts. "Why'd we stop?"

"We need to find a scent," Froth responded, motioning with his tail toward a large rock that had a peak that came to just below the treetops. "Who has the best sniffer?"

A second passed before a dark gray youngling with a burgundy fringe started climbing the rock. Scope watched the youngling ascend, reach the top, then begin sniffing deeply. The youngling soon started favoring one side of the rock.

"I smell herbivores!" the youngling called down. "A large herd, I think, the closest herd to us. I can't recognize the specific species."

"It doesn't matter," Froth said. "Did you smell any danger?"

"Lots of it in the direction of the valley," the youngling answered as he began descending the rock. "But that's the direction of the herd."

Scope frowned. She didn't like the idea of risking an encounter with Coelurus or other deadly Squamas just for a simple kill. She'd rather go further. She decided to voice her comment.

Froth looked at her with a dubious expression. "You seriously want to lengthen this out? The faster we make the kill, the better we can impress Spike that it won't take us days to make a kill!"

"This is our very first hunting trip. We're amateurs!" Scope retorted, feeling her fringe lower in her annoyance. "We don't need glory. We just need to come back alive and bring the bones. We need to make plans of attack, not rush in blindly."

Froth rolled his eyes in irritation. "You need to relax. If we go to the closest herd, we can use them as a deterrent for the dangers."

"I don't follow your logic," Scope said slowly, narrowing one eye.

"If we see any Tyrannosaurs or the like, we can persuade the herd that we mean them no harm and they can help protect us until the threat leaves," Froth said slowly, as if he was speaking to mentally deficient beasts. "Safety in numbers."

Scope narrowed both of her eyes. "And once the threat leaves, we turn on the herd. That's what I'm understanding."

"Right," Froth said with a sharp nod.

He took a wary step back when Scope growled harshly. Scope could feel boldness born from her wronged conscience arising inside of her; otherwise she would be leaving the planning to Froth, no matter how bad his ideas seemed. "Are you *mad*, Froth?" she spat. "Becoming liars to the herbivores will earn us a very, very bad reputation, not only for us, but for the *entire tribe*. We'll all be labeled as liars and untrustworthy. Our promises will mean little more than dirt. *I'm* not willing to take a risk like that, especially with deadly Squamas close by your wanted destination." Scope looked to the youngling that had sniffed the air. "Joint, come over, please."

"Yes?" The youngling seemed startled at being singled out in the middle of a command argument.

"How far away is the next closest herd?"

"Hold on just a moment here!" Froth interjected, frowning heavily. "Scope, you're undermining my authority!"

"Who made you the pack leader?" Scope snarled. "You're a liability to our health and reputation if you stay in command. Joint, please answer my question."

Joint idly scraped a foot along the ground as he thought. "Well, the herd Froth wanted to go to is the closest, but it smells like Tyrants, too. Much fainter is another herd." Nodding over one shoulder, he added, "I don't know what's that way, it's downwind from us."

"How far to the faint herd?" Scope asked.

"I don't know, it's not like I've tracked anything further than the clearing. It could be a day's travel, maybe more."

"It'll take *forever* to travel that far," Benign whined, sinking to the ground.

"Don't be such a hatchling, Benign, and think of your morals," Scope said with a frown to her sister. "We're going to the herd that is farther away. The sooner we leave, the sooner we'll get there. Let's move out!"

Scope started trotting in the direction Joint had pointed out and didn't look back. She was pleased to hear multiple feet follow after her. She slowed down so that Joint could move ahead of her. A quick glance over her shoulder showed her that all of them had moved to follow. Froth was at the back of the pack, looking disgruntled.

"I need scouts!" Scope called as she moved. "Those with a keen eye, come up to me so that I can give you orders."

A few seconds later, four younglings moved to up to trot by her side.

"Four of you," Scope mused. "You two, look for any danger up ahead, like Coelurus and the like, and keep an eye out for hiding places to keep us safe. When darkness comes, you need to find us a secure place to rest for the night. You other two, guard our tail ends. Go upwind and stay within warning distance. Keep us in sight. Oh, and watch out for water."

They nodded and moved off.

Scope felt good. She felt important, knowing that she was responsible for the entire pack. Adrenaline flowed through her veins, giving her a feeling of energy and a sense that she could do anything. She held her head high and her fringe flew erect. What a big job for her to do, keeping the pack safe!

What a *big* job. . .

Can I do this? she thought, feeling the boldness from her confrontation with Froth beginning to bleed away. She thought of the four younglings she had just made into scouts. *Have I sent them to their deaths, sending them off?* She glanced behind her. *They're counting on* me *for getting us the kill we need to succeed. Why did I confront Froth? I should've kept my big mouth shut.*

She shoved these thoughts out of her mind. *I do* not *need to be constantly second-guessing myself. Jeopardizing this pack and an entire herd just for a moment of glory isn't right. My plan will take longer, sure, but I'm proud of who we are.*

Almost simultaneously, she and Joint picked up a strong scent and slowed. She raised her head higher to smell better. There was water up ahead, and a lot of it from the scent. As they came closer to the source, she picked up the sounds of crashing water.

A river came into sight a minute later. Scope came to a slow stop, hearing the others do the same. Scope walked a few steps until she could see the rushing water, then paused in awe.

Churning and frothing, the river was a raging beast flowing down the mountain. The din caused by the river drowned out nearly everything else. The rocks were covered in slippery algae and lichen.

"Now what?" a youngling asked.

Scope swallowed uneasily, wondering how they would be able to ford such a furious river. *We'd be swept away in a moment.* Looking downstream, she saw that the river was much wider. Sometime in the past, it appeared that something had scooped out huge chunks out of the banks. Happily, she noticed that this area was more shallow and much slower.

With a hum of relief, Scope said, "Look downriver. It's slower there. We might be able to cross there."

She took a sharp turn and began trotting downhill. She kept her distance from the edge, having no idea how strong the edge of the ground was. Her eyes scanned the surface of the river for protruding stones.

A streak of motion upriver caught her attention. It was the lead scouts she had sent up ahead. They ran to her.

"We've found a place to cross upriver," one of them said, panting slightly. "We've already leapt across and back."

"Lead us there, then," Scope replied, nodding firmly.

It was a five minute walk to the place the scouts had found. When they got there, Scope wondered how on earth they had managed to summon courage to cross; the narrow river channel raged like a wild beast. If any misjudged the distance, death would be certain.

She immediately decided that her scouts were nuts.

She looked over at the far side of the river. With a sigh of determination, Scope turned to face the others behind her. "We cross here."

"We'll drown!" someone exclaimed fearfully, voice quivering slightly.

"Only if you time it wrong," Scope replied as calmly as she could. "They made it across just fine. If it'll make any of you feel better, I'll go first."

She moved as close to the edge as she dared and estimated the distance between her side of the river and the far side. It seemed to be about a three or four paces gap. Given enough speed, she could leap over with ease. She retreated several paces into the trees to create the distance she needed, then turned to face the water. The other younglings had given her a wide path to the shore. After taking a deep breath, she dug her claws into the ground and sprang into a sprint. Her strides ate up the ground and before she knew it, it was time to jump. She grunted and placed her feet on the very edge of the ground. She felt it crumble slightly under her weight as she bent her legs and leapt.

For just a moment, she was weightless, seemingly hovering in the air without any indication of wings. *Would this be what it'd be like to fly?*

And then she landed. The sudden solidity of the earth after being suspended in midair was a jolt to her muscles, and she stumbled heavily, almost falling onto her face. It took her a few steps to recover and a few more to disperse her momentum.

"Who's next?" she called over the river's noise to the younglings on the other side.

There was some initial hesitation, but one by one the younglings leapt over the river. Most of them landed heavily but managed to stay on their feet while a few completely tumbled. The bank edge crumpled and fell away as the last youngling leapt.

Scope's eyes widened. *She'll never make it!* she thought and ran forward.

The youngling came down just a few inches too early, her

chest landing on the bank but her hindquarters swinging in midair. Falling backward, she grasped the grass of the bank and screeched for help.

"I'm coming!" Scope shouted. She lunged and wrapped her jaw around the youngling's fringe. The youngling screeched again, this time in pain. Scope pulled backward and tugged the youngling fully onto the ground. When she was completely safe, Scope let go and spat pieces of fringe from her mouth.

"That hurt!" the youngling whined, her cracking voice split between pain and relief. Her fringe was mangled but otherwise fine. There was no blood.

"Well, it was either hurt your neck or let you drown in the river," Scope shot back, slightly irritated.

The youngling sighed, looked down at the ground. "Sorry." Looking back up, "Thank you."

"Forgiven. Just glad you made it."

Scope took stock, then had the scouts run ahead again.

Scope sighed as she found a clear path through the trees and decided to follow it. The path was wide, which seemed to indicate that large herbivores often took this way through the forest. Logic dictated that to follow the path would lead them to the herd for which they were looking.

Or Tyrants? She shuddered and cleared her mind.

After a while, the sun began to set behind the mountains. Scope kept a close eye out for the scouts, hoping to see them soon so that they could tell her if they had managed to find a place for them to sleep for the night. It was when the colors around her had faded to monochrome the two scouts came back.

"Did you find a place for us to rest?" Scope asked.

One of them nodded. "It's not far. Just a little ahead and off the path."

Scope nodded. The scouts led the way to the resting area, which was an array of boulders.

"This is it?" Scope said, looking around as they neared the rocks.

"It was the best place we could find," a scout said with a shrug.

Scope hummed as she took a careful scan of the surroundings. The boulders were large, the biggest almost emerging above the treetops. They were splayed out in an erratic pattern, some close together, some further apart. The area had a gentle slope. Scope decided that the area would do nicely.

"We'll stay here for the night," she said. "Now, with the danger, I'll need some of you to volunteer for guard watch."

"For the entire night?" a youngling behind her said incredulously.

"Of course not," Scope said. "There'll be at least four guards over the course of the night. One guard will begin when we all fall asleep. When the luna reaches that point right there, he or she will be replaced. And so on until daylight, each guard getting a fair amount of guard time. Does anyone disagree with me?"

"What's for dinner?"

"I'll take that as a no," Scope said with a sigh. "Well, I guess that dinner is just whatever we can find. Return before the luna comes within view. Make sure that you stay in twos and threes."

The pack dispersed. Scope watched them leave, then walked into the maze of ground between the rocks. She wasn't hungry. She had assumed that the stress of the day had killed her appetite.

Using what was left of the light, she walked around until she saw a medium sized ledge on one of the rocks. It was too high to directly leap upon, so she used much smaller ledges to get there. The ledge was large enough for her to lie upon comfortably. She curled up on her stomach and rested her chin on her tail.

Not wanting to go asleep yet, she laid awake and watched the dusk fade away. Younglings trickled back, and she kept a tab on what was being said. After a while, she managed to gather enough knowledge to know that everyone had returned safely, although a few hadn't found a meal.

A movement in the luna's light drew her attention. It was the first guard of the night, leaping from rock to rock until he reached the tallest one. He scaled it to its peak then sat down. He stayed perfectly still save for the stiff motions of his head and the occasional sniffing.

Scope closed her eyes and squirmed a little into the rock. However, her desire to sleep was left unfulfilled. There were simply too many negative emotions in the air for her to rest. She could sense anxiety, nervousness, and hints of fear. Sounds of soft scraping told her that younglings were shifting uneasily as they tried to sleep.

She understood why her comrades were feeling in such a way; this was their first night without being under the watchful eyes of their tribe. Their first night sleeping somewhere other than in a nest. If they ran into trouble, there were no adult Utahraptors to protect them.

It was blatantly obvious that the Initiation Hunt not only weeded out those who couldn't stand the trials of hunting, but also taught bravery, independence, and self-confidence.

It was very late when she finally drifted off into the realm of slumber.

Chapter Thirteen

Scope awakened to the sounds of rustling. She opened her eyes to see, in the early morning light, the younglings rousing from slumber.

She stretched out her body before dropping from her ledge. Landing slightly heavily, she shook herself from nose to tail to further loosen herself up.

A quick look around told her that everyone up. Scope made a wordless yelp to get their attention.

"Before we really set off, we'll go ahead and find breakfast," Scope called. "Split into the groups you made last night and rendezvous here when the sun reaches that point in the sky." She pointed to a spot in the sky.

Scope accompanied a group of two into the woods. They looked surprised that the pack leader was with them. She gestured and off they went. It wasn't long before they heard the rustling of mammals in the underbrush. Scope and her comrades quickly stopped and hid. Scope watched from beneath a bush at the spot and waited.

It was a patience game that she had long mastered from her games with the adults. She minded her tail from slowly waving from side to side and disturbing the leaves.

Fur. She resisted the urge to leap and kept waiting, although it was harder. After a painfully long stretch of time, two large mammals slowly emerged from the bushes. They sniffed the air warily, their beady brown eyes looking around. Another second later, a smaller mammal came out.

The rustle of leaves was the only warning the mammals received before one of the younglings lunged. Scope leapt at another as it tried to scurry away, her foot landing on its spine. She bent down and broke its neck before it could escape and run away. Once she was sure that it was dead, she looked to see how her comrades had done. Both had caught the other two.

"These look good," one of them purred, licking her catch.

"Really plump," the second said, drooling in anticipation. "They've been eating well."

"And now we will, too," Scope added with a grin.

It was indeed a delicious mammal, as Scope tore off a section of meat from its side. It *had* been eating well. She could taste hints of the mammal's diet, mostly berries and bugs. She herself normally didn't eat such things, but the overtones of the meat was delightful.

They finished their breakfasts several minutes later and trotted back to the rocks. Scope saw that many of the other younglings had arrived before them. Much to her pleasure, she thought that she saw hints of a meal on each one of them. None of them had gone hungry this morning, which meant it wouldn't distract them from tracking.

When the last stragglers had returned, Scope sent out the scouts again. An earlier test of the air had come back with the result that the herd was closer, probably close enough to reach by this evening or the next morning.

She could hear chatter behind her as she trod along the path at a lively trot. It mostly consisted of excitement over encountering the herd, singling out one of them, then killing it, eating it, then bringing the bones back home. A few had dreamt up fantastic fantasies of taking the herbivore down using some ridiculous move.

Scope chuckled to herself when she related to one of the fantasies. Pallor had conjured up the idea that he would approach one of the herbivores and manage to talk it to death. Abject had replied something that went along the lines of "For you, I don't think that that's completely impossible!" Pallor didn't know whether to take offense or preen.

The day passed surprisingly quickly and without incident. There was no sign or scent of danger anywhere. Birds were singing and flitting from branch to branch. It was as if there were no T-rex, Coelurus, or Appalachiosaurus in the area.

As if on cue, she heard someone comment, "Do you think that those warnings Spike gave us was all just a bunch of wasted air?"

Scope's chest tightened uncomfortably. Such a comment meant that someone had gotten the notion that all was going to be perfectly fine.

It's only been a day since we've left, she thought, frowning. *It's far too early to lose caution now!*

Worse yet, the comments started to multiply from then on. It wasn't long before Scope was actually *hoping* to catch a whiff of danger, just to prove that what Spike warns is *important* and he doesn't say things just to scare others.

But as the sun tracked toward the horizon, there was still no smell or sign of danger. The scouts had also seen and smelled nothing upwind. They were making good time and everyone except Scope was in high spirits.

Scope swallowed nervously. She cast a glance into the trees, looking for any large forms hiding within the shadows. Thankfully, the shadows were empty. The only movement she could see were birds and the occasional mammal. Insects buzzed and sang their unique symphonies. She had been told that when everything was quiet and still was when there was danger about. In contrast, the forest seemed completely carefree and noisy.

Froth came up by her side. He was smirking, which meant that he had something cooking in that head of his.

"What do you want, Froth?" she asked warily, narrowing an eye at him.

"You look nervous," he replied cooly, holding his head up with his chin sharply dipped. At the speed they were going, it was going to hurt his pace and body if he held that pose much longer. He was showing off his confidence.

"What makes you think that?" she said, looking away from him so that she could jump over a fallen tree.

"Well, it's your expression for one thing. For another, you're being hesitant." She could almost *hear* the smirk he was wearing. "Is the stress of being the pack leader too much for you?"

"I'm doing quite well without you coming up to me and trying to make me feel insecure," she said snappily. "Besides, if we had gone with your plan. . ."

"We'd be already back at the clearing," he interrupted her.

"Excuse me?" Scope huffed, mildly glaring at him. "But this way, we've been safer."

"You're scared to take risks," Froth said with a roll of his eyes. "Look, I'm just trying to help. I've been leading my friends for over a Turn. You'd barely gone out of the nest before I talked you into playing Chase with us in the snow! You're a rookie. You need to learn from someone with more experience."

Scope felt herself bristle. "Go away, Froth. I *can* do this. Besides, no better time to learn than on the job."

"Whatever you say," Froth said, his smirk gone and his eyes narrowed. He slowed his pace and dropped back.

She exhaled sharply and forced her body to shiver violently. *I've got this,* she repeated to herself. *I can do this. No problem.*

The whispers of doubt still in her mind didn't help.

"Why are we guarding?"

Scope blinked at the youngling. "We need watchers to keep an eye on the area. Anything could sneak up on us under the cover of night."

"Is there anything out there at all?"

"It'd be better to be safe than sorry. Will you be up in that tree by nightfall?"

The youngling shrugged nonchalantly. "Sure, I guess."

Scope frowned, nodded, then walked away. She wondered how hard the younglings that were supposed to be guarding the pack would watch the forest. For all of their sakes, she hoped that there wouldn't be an attack.

It was nearing sunset. The scouts had found a patch of trees where the ground had been worn away, revealing the root systems of the trees. The roots created little caves under the trees themselves. Scope hadn't been crazy about the notion of being trapped in a cage of wood, but the only other option was an open grassy field that she was even less crazy about.

With a sigh, Scope went a short way off into the trees. She smelled a mammal nearby and she was hungry. It didn't her long to flush it out and kill it. Instead of eating it where she had killed it, she picked it up with her mouth and carried it back to the place where the trees-with-the-exposed-roots were. She found an empty tree and crawled into the space. Her tail stuck out into the air, so she pulled it in and curled it around her body as best as she could.

She dropped the mammal onto the ground. Its carcass almost bounced upon landing. She sniffed the fur, sneezed from the dust she breathed in, then dug into the meat. She ate until there was nothing left but the gray bones, then she licked the bones clean and shoved the remains into the open.

A quick look toward the sky told her that the sun was almost gone. In the dim twilight, she saw the first guard of the night approach a tree. The tree was tall with many branches, some of which came very close to the ground. The guard hopped onto the first branch, balanced, then leapt to the next highest one. Scope watched the guard's progress until the guard reached the last branch that would stand its weight.

Scope laid her chin on the dirt and looked around at the pack. Most of them were already in their root cavities, some sharing the space with two or more younglings. The rest were just now getting to their own chosen place of sleep. A youngling found an empty root cavity, turned around, then shimmied backward through a gap in the roots. She shivered once, as the temperature was getting cooler, which was a little strange, since it was the early Green Season and White Season was over.

Scope hummed and squirmed a little so that she could get a little more comfortable. She wasn't tired. Too many insecurities planted by Froth coursed through her mind; she was too stressed over the duty of being a leader.

Was Froth right in that she would collapse under the weight of her job?

Sleep didn't come to her until the third guard had taken up post.

CHAPTER FOURTEEN

Scope peered out through the thick branches of the bush under which she was hiding at the herd of Edmontonia. The midday sun shined down on the large herd, reflecting off of their healthily glistening armor as they grazed on brush and grass.

She and the others had finally reached the herd they had been tracking for two days. Scope had sneaked closer and had gotten a good look at their target before returning and telling everyone what to do.

Edmontonia had heavy armor, like Ankylosaurus, but they lacked the heavy club at the end of the tail. One less defense to watch out for. However, they would need to be wary of the dangerous long and thick spikes lining the shoulders and sides. The underbelly and legs were the only vulnerable parts, and those were the places they needed to attack.

With the plan confirmed, Scope had the call for when they would burst from hiding. She looked around to pick out a target. The hatchlings, younglings, and young adults were out of the question as they still had a full life ahead of them and it would be unfair to kill one of them in their childhood or prime. Her pack considered it unethical to kill a peer.

There were some elderly Edmontonia on the outskirts of the herd. She could tell that they were aged because of how much duller and muted the color their armor was. One of *them* would do.

She roared out the signal and leapt out from under the brush. The Edmontonia looked up in alarm as over a dozen youngling Utahraptors approached them with obvious intent. The adult Edmontonia moved their younglings and hatchlings closer to themselves in an effort to protect them.

Scope saw this and quickly said, "We are not here to kill your hatchlings, younglings, or adults in their prime. We've been tracking you for two days, and we need a kill so that we can pass our Initiation Hunt."

The elderly Edmontonia looked sadly at the others before stepping forward. "We're the ones you will want," one of them said, voice cracking with age.

Scope looked the elderly herbivores over. There were three of them, all ranging in size. The smallest was three times as big as a fully grown Utahraptor. She knew that the bigger the bones were, the harder it would be to bring them home.

"You, Edmontonia," she said, singling out the smallest one.

She instinctively knew that her comrades, upon hearing her words, moved to stare at the smallest Edmontonia. The herd beat a fast retreat into the trees, leaving all three elders behind.

"Why are you still here?" Abject asked them.

An elder snorted. "Well, since you deem one of us so worthless, then what are *three* of us to you?"

"Why not?" another responded. "We're 'old' and 'no longer useful,' according to you. But by my nose, young snips, our lives are for naught."

The original Edmontonia snorted at the Utahraptors and pawed at the ground with a thick foreleg. "I won't go down easy, younglings," it warned, narrowing its eyes at the pack.

"Good," Froth spoke, lowering his torso. "We wouldn't want you to make this *too* easy for us."

Scope cut off the pre-fight banter by screeching, "Attack!" She lunged forward toward the Edmontonia. She saw a few of her comrades aiming for the prey's legs. The Edmontonia reared up slightly, nowhere near enough for an Utahraptor to duck underneath, and batted at the younglings as they approached. The younglings moved away in order to avoid being struck.

Scope circled the Edmontonias, keeping an eye on their swinging tails. The other two were defending their target, using their tails to whack at the younglings. A few younglings were caught by the tails and went flying. She thought that, if they could avoid the tails, they would still bring down their prey.

She waited until she was in all three's blind spots before darting into the fray. Ducking under a batting tail, she took a passing bite at the smallest Edmontonia's right hind leg, causing several deep punctures. The herbivore bellowed with pain and violently waved its tail. Scope dodged the appendage and ran to a safe distance.

When Scope turned back, she saw one of the younglings run toward the prey's side. Scope's eyes widened as she estimated the trajectory and goal of the youngling; to slice the abdomen. The youngling jumped. The Edmontonia saw the youngling coming and lowered its body. Trapped in midair with no way to alter course, the youngling screeched as it impaled itself on the shoulder spikes of the Edmontonia. The youngling pulled itself away with two very deep wounds in its chest area.

Scope winced in sympathy as the youngling stumbled away from the fight, collapsing on the ground a short distance away. Two other younglings ran from the fight and to the fallen one, bending down above it.

Siblings. Her imagination immediately summoned up the image of one of her own siblings lying on the ground, likely not to live for much longer. She shoved the image from her mind and went to focus on the prey again.

The Edmontonia was wounded in a few places; the back legs, one of the front legs, and there was a sizable scrape running down the length of the tail. It was limping slightly but still full of fight. The other two stood near it, their tails waving powerfully.

The pack wasn't without their own wounds. Besides the critical nature of the impaled youngling, there were a few younglings that were limping from blows given by the Edmontonias' legs and tails. Several were still recovering from their impromptu flight lesson. A few had nasty bite wounds. The Edmontonia had no teeth, but that bony beak could inflict serious injury.

Scope crept closer to the prey, keeping a safe distance from the other two. She couldn't go for the sides, as they were effectively protected by the spikes, unless the prey was sufficiently distracted. The only way to take it down would be by getting to the jugular (which was nearly impossible to reach thanks to the low-slung nature of the head), slashing open the guarded sides, or managing to get the Edmontonia to topple over by wounding the pair of legs on one side of the body.

Getting to the underbelly via the legs was the best bet. Scope screeched to the other younglings, calling them to her. The Edmontonia stood still, recovering, as the younglings came.

"What is it?" Froth huffed, irritated. "We're on a roll!"

"I've thought of a way we can take this prey down," Scope said, shooting a brief look at Froth. "If we keep darting in erratically and unplanned like we've been doing, we'll keep getting hurt.

. ." She paused to look at the gravely injured youngling lying not far away. "Now, the jugular and the sides are almost impossible to reach. We'll need to take out the legs on one side of the Edmontonia's body to knock it over. Then we can reach the underbelly. Does everyone understand?"

Heads bobbed in the affirmative. "What side?" someone asked.

"From the injured side, the right. Go!"

Scope stayed behind, moving at a slow trot as everyone else darted forward. She circled the Edmontonia as they turned to greet them head on. The attacks began, the pack splitting into thirds. Two parts went to distract the other Edmontonias while the others went to attack the prey.

Scope got closer, moving around the back. She ducked under a tail as it swung her way, then took a quick bite at the prey's left right leg. The Edmontonia would've moved in retribution, but it had to defend itself from a different attack.

With their coordinated effort, it wasn't long before the right legs had taken their toll. The Edmontonia was limping heavily, and knew it couldn't take much more abuse before going down.

A youngling moved in, and a second later the Edmontonia toppled. It bellowed in pain as Scope and the others moved in for the kill. The underbelly was wide open for direct attack. The prey had moments left to live.

Moving to the Edmontonia's head, Scope looked down. "You gave us a good fight. Thank you."

The Edmontonia sniffed. "I may be old and look like the

more righteous kill," it said, its voice raspy and pained, "but my mind is still sharp and I know that you're not the biggest threat here."

"What?" Scope said, disturbed.

"I suggest that you kill me quickly, as we all shall die."

Before Scope could ask for clarification, Froth darted in and slit the jugular.

The Edmontonia let out a raspy noise before going limp and lifeless.

Scope joined her comrades in roaring into the sky to declare their victory. The only thing left to do was to carry some bones back to the clearing. Their Initiation Hunt was almost over.

The other two Edmontonia backed away as the younglings approached. "You only needed one of us," one said.

"But Spike will be surprised to see that we managed to kill *three* Edmontonia!" a youngling exclaimed.

"*I* will be surprised if we survive."

"That's the spirit!" Froth crowed. "Accept your doom!"

Scope cocked her head to the side as she felt the ground slightly tremble under her feet. It stopped, then happened again. It occurred four more times in a steady beat.

Steps. Scope looked frantically around, sniffing the air hard, sucking in as much as she could. The scent of the dead Edmontonia was almost overwhelming, but through it she could smell trees, leaf decay, and something rotten. She sucked in another breath, but this time it wasn't to taste the air. It was because she recognized the rotten smell as the stench that the Coelurus had carried. Evil smelled rotten.

"You knew," she said in shock to the Edmontonia. "You *knew*!"

One of the two nodded solemnly.

Movement in the trees. Her head swiveled so quickly her neck twanged. She squinted into the forest. She saw more movement, high off the ground and colored a dull greenish gray.

Danger. It suddenly filled her nostrils with a pungent and nasty scent. Scope's heart skipped a beat as she experienced the inundating urge to run away as fast as she could.

"SOMETHING'S COMING! RUN, EVERYONE, RUN!" Scope screamed as loud as she could, taking several large hopping steps backward.

The younglings snapped their heads around to stare at her and then at the trees she was looking at with an expression of terror. A few of them sniffed the air, and then their own expressions twisted into fear.

Tree branches broke with loud cracking *snaps* as something big charged through them. Scope choked on a scream as five T-rex emerged from the forest. The huge carnivores towered over them and glared at the younglings with piercing red eyes. One of the T-rex roared.

Scope wasn't the only one who began to run as soon as it opened its maw. She could feel the air vibrate with the baritone volume of the T-rex's roar.

The T-rex charged forward, their steps covering the ground quickly. One of their steps was equal to fifteen of the younglings'. Scope screeched and dodged as one of the T-rex moved to step on her. She stumbled as the ground shook from the force the T-rex had used when it had moved to stomp her flat.

"Hold still, mite!" it gutturally growled at her.

"Why are you chasing us?" Scope yelped as she jumped to avoid its teeth when it snapped at her.

"Our food," was the reply.

"We killed it! It's ours by right!"

"Our food," the T-rex rumbled again.

Scope bee-lined for the trees, hoping that she could lose the T-rex in the forest. As she exited the open space where the Edmontonia carcass laid, she saw that there were only a few younglings running away. The rest were unmoving, flattened. One of the T-rex had pursued and dispatched one of the two remaining Edmontonia, and the third was nowhere to be seen.

She took a tight turn to the right, moving so sharply she skidded a little. The T-rex was too big to make the turn as quickly as she did, so it had to stumble several steps the wrong way before it could resume chasing her. She had gained ground and time, but the T-rex's huge strides drastically reduced what she had gained.

Looking frantically around for a place to lose her pursuer, Scope saw a tight grouping of trees up ahead. She dove into them and squeezed her body through the tight gaps in between the trunks. Clearing the trees, she glanced behind her in hopes that the T-rex had been dissuaded by the trees.

Unfortunately, it continued charging forward. Lowering its head so that the top faced forward, the T-rex broke the trees themselves, sending splinters of wood ranging from tiny to the size of Scope herself flying.

Scope began running again as the T-rex stumbled, apparently a little dazed from charging headfirst through several fully grown trees. She found a large flat rock that leaned against another, creating a small gap underneath. She bolted into the dark hole and stayed completely still.

She tried to calm her erratic breathing as the T-rex growled. It slowly walked around the area, sniffing. It roared angrily, the volume causing Scope to tremble, before stomping away.

Her gaze darted to the side as she heard something big coming from a different direction. *Another Tyrannosaurus?* she thought in worry. *Please, not another one.*

Something small burst from a thicket; a youngling. Scope squirmed to the side as she spotted the youngling coming straight for her hiding place. The ground quaked with heavy steps as the youngling slid into the hole beside her.

The moment after the youngling's tail had moved inside the hole, a second T-rex appeared. It slowed to a stop and looked around with narrowed eyes. The first T-rex rumbled angrily at the newcomer who snapped its maw in reply.

Scope looked at the gasping youngling beside her. "Pallor?" she uttered under her breath.

Pallor twisted to look at her. His terror-filled eyes widened in shock and relief as they connected with hers. "Scope!" he replied at the same volume. As quietly as he could, he moved to lean against her. "Thought you were dead."

Scope wrapped her neck around Pallor's in a gesture of comfort. *I'm here,* she said without speaking.

Both T-rex growled in frustration before moving off beyond their range of vision. Scope felt the vibration of the ground start to get more distant as they moved away.

"Where are the others?" Scope asked her brother quietly, looking him in the eye.

Pallor looked down at the ground as a violent shiver racked his entire body. "I don't know, Scope. All of them. Abject, Benign, *gone.* Squished or snapped. Dead. Everyone's dead!" He finished with a scared whimper and blinked as tears began to come to his eyes.

Scope gave a sympathetic whimper and nudged Pallor. "We'll get out of this," she told him, sounding more determined and sure than she felt. "Alive. We'll get back to the clearing all right."

"Promise?" he asked her meekly, gazing at her with glistening eyes.

Her reply caught in her throat. She wanted to reply *I promise* so badly it hurt, but she couldn't promise. She wasn't in control of the situation; far from it. "I'll do my best," she admitted instead.

Pallor sniffled and gave her a small smile.

The ground shook again. That was the only warning before

a gigantic maw lowered to their hole. Scope had a full view of two jaws chock full of teeth that put her own to blistering shame. The T-rex's nostrils flared as it inhaled the air that bore their scents, and it growled menacingly.

We were too loud.

The maw moved away, then the rock shook. Dust and tiny grains began raining down on the two younglings. Scope looked up to see tiny cracks snaking through the rock. The rock trembled again from the force of a mighty stomp. More dust and larger chunks of rock fell.

"He's breaking the rock!" Scope yelped. "Run, Pallor!"

They burst from hiding side by side. Scope tripped as she attempted to get up to speed and Pallor turned and began to assist.

"No, run!" Scope screamed as she clumsily dodged a massive foot. "Don't worry about me. Run, Pallor, run!"

Pallor nodded and turned. He vanished into the thicket.

Scope got to her feet and hissed at the T-rex trying to flatten her. She couldn't tell if it had been the one that had chased her or the one that had chased Pallor, but she was going to give her brother the opportunity to escape if it killed her.

As the predator lunged to snap her in two with its mouth, she stepped to the side and used her teeth to rake its lips. The T-rex jerked away, a thin line of blood beginning to trickle down into its mouth. It snarled at her.

Scope snarled back, her voice sounding downright pathetic compared to the guttural vocals of the T-rex. She was *not* going to go down without a fight. Her death was imminent, she knew. Pallor needed to live. She was going to make sure that he stayed alive.

"Well, you big lug?" she spat at the T-rex. "What are you waiting for? Oh, has this little baby Utahraptor put up an unexpected fight? *Ha!*"

The T-rex emitted a cross between an irate growl and an enraged roar as it lunged. She dodged its mouth again and leapt upon its nose before it moved its head too high. She raked her toe claws through the tender muzzle before running down the length of the head toward the neck. The T-rex violently shook its head, but she was already on the neck.

Scope compared running along the back of the massive predator to running across a sliding log. She slipped a few times as she crossed the back but used her toe claws to regain traction. Sliding down the tail, she fell several paces to the ground. She fell onto her stomach, but was up again in a flash and running in the direction Pallor had gone.

She hadn't gone a dozen paces before a second T-rex moved into her path. She yelped in surprise and ducked in between its legs, emerging out the other side and kept running.

She saw rocky ground up ahead. She hoped that the craggy boulders would hurt the T-rex's feet as it ran across them in an effort to catch her. She jumped across a wide gap in between rocks, stumbling a little upon the landing.

The two T-rex roared. Scope glanced behind her at their coming forms and began to run again.

How long had she been running? She glanced up at the dark sky that she could just see through the trees. Her feet ached from abuse. She was bruised from her narrow escapes. Her muscles were cramping, her lungs strained, and her eyes burned from wind and tears.

She could hear the T-rex still coming after her. Once or twice she had heard them roar into the sky. The roar had been wordless, but from how they did it she knew that they had called for assistance.

They needed assistance. That meant that she was leading them on a merry chase and they couldn't catch her. A small burst of pride had coursed through her when she had thought of that. She wouldn't be going down easily.

She desperately needed to rest. She stumbled over nothing, almost falling flat on her chin. She began forcefully lifting her legs higher so that her toes didn't scrape on the ground.

The ground shook, more severely than usual. They were getting closer because she was slowing down. *Don't they need a break, too?* she wondered. Even her thought words were parted by pants. *Don't they get tired? We've been running all day.*

In the darkness, she spotted the trees the pack had slept under the night before. She darted that way and huddled beneath one of the trees. The roots were lower so she was better hidden. She collapsed on the dirt, panting as quietly as she could. She could feel her chest heaving with her gulps of air.

Large bipedal bodies moved through the trees. She could hear the two T-rex talking, but she couldn't discern their words. They milled around for a few minutes, looking around and occasionally sniffing the air.

Scope's eyelids began to droop with weariness. She tried to fight off the urge to sleep, but her body began to overwhelm her efforts.

The forest floor began to rustle with many feet. She cracked open a heavy eyelid to see several small forms about her size milling around the T-rex' feet. Coelurus.

She now had even greater incentive to stay awake, but she couldn't fight off sleep any longer.

CHAPTER FIFTEEN

Spike sensed that something was wrong. He didn't know what, but something had gone very, very wrong.

"Spike?" Grapple said, his voice conveying his concern.

"Hmm?" Spike said, realizing that he had been absentmindedly staring at the forest. "Oh. I'm sorry. My mind was elsewhere."

Grapple narrowed his eyes. "You've been distant ever since you sent off that last Initiation Hunt. What's eating at you?"

"Nothing," Spike said with a brief shake of his head.

Spike's closest friend snorted in disbelief. "Yes. Nothing.

And I'm an Appalachiosaurus. Spike, how long have we known each other?"

"Not again with your whole 'We've known each other since we've been hatchlings and you trust me so much that I'm your trusted secret-holder,'" Spike said with a slightly amused sigh. "Fine. I've been having this really bad feeling about the younglings. By I Am, I can't help but think that we're never going to be seeing them again."

"They're dead?" Grapple gasped, his eyes wide.

Spike didn't answer, and instead shook his body in an effort to shake off his negative thoughts.

Grapple looked off to an area behind Spike. "Here comes another hatchling. Looks like the little tyke wants a word with you."

Spike turned around and looked down. The hatchling was still unsteady on her feet, wobbling ever so slightly as she walked toward him. He could feel a fond smile etching itself onto his lips at the irresistible cuteness that belonged to the babies of almost every species.

"Horn, sir?" the hatchling said, looking up at him with over-sized amber eyes.

"Spike, little one," Spike corrected. "I am called *Spike*."

"Spike," the hatchling said, "I feeling bad."

Spike cocked his head to the side. "What's wrong? Did you eat something bad? Take too big of a bite?"

The hatchling violently shook her head, almost knocking off

her equilibrium and falling over. "No tummy. In head. Sort of. Not there but can feel it."

Spike narrowed his eyes in concern. "What does this feeling feel like?"

The hatchling's eyes were wide with fear of something she could only sense. "Bad. Lots of bad."

Spike felt his own ill-boding feeling surge back to the forefront of his mind. Hiding his discomfort, he forced a smile to the hatchling. "It'll pass eventually, little one. Everything will be all right."

With a slightly relieved expression, the hatchling nodded and toddled away.

Grapple looked worried. "What was that about?"

"Hatchlings are more innocent than we adults," Spike mused. "We adults can double-guess ourselves and convince ourselves of something. Hatchlings are too young to know how to do that."

"So something bad *is* going to happen?" Grapple replied with more than a hint of apprehension.

"Or just did," Spike replied.

Scope was ready to collapse, but she couldn't stop yet. Her body was betraying her, she was so tired; her eyes kept on closing so she was running blind. Legs feeling like twigs while her lungs burned, she struggled to remain awake, much less not execute a spectacular face-plant/tumble onto the ground.

She had been leading her pursuers on a merry chase through random parts of the valley. She had forded the same river no less than eight times, darted across multiple random clearings, and had lost the Tyrants for a short while by mingling with a large herd of Triceratops.

She had awakened before the sun had risen. There had been no trace of T-rex or Coelurus near her tree, though their scents still lingered in the air. She had wasted no time in resuming her escape.

The river was coming up again. She jumped over it for the ninth time, easily clearing it thanks to the amount of momentum she had, and darted to the side.

It felt as if eyes were upon her, though she couldn't hear her pursuers at all. She wondered if the Coelurus had arrived and were noiselessly railing her. It was a very disconcerting feeling.

Darkness suddenly descended, and it took a moment for her sluggish mind to realize that her eyes had closed again. Growling in frustration, she opened them. She yelped and leapt to avoid running directly into a pine tree. Her knees trembled threateningly beneath her as she took another turn.

A roar from behind unleashed another gush of fear-induced adrenaline, fueling her enough so that she could put on a massive burst of speed. It wasn't until she was clearing over three paces with each step that she realized that she had previously slowed down to barely a weary trot.

The only sounds she could hear was the clamor of her own steps. The birds and insects were silent, and there wasn't the telltale rustling of a mammal browsing for food. It was as if the entire forest had frozen into silence. When something was coming, everything hid and stayed very quiet.

I'm not out of danger yet, she thought.

Spotting a clearing up ahead, she aimed directly for it. The flat area would offer her another burst of speed as there wouldn't be any obstacles.

Not a second after she had exited the trees did she slam into a large form and crash onto the dirt and grass.

So much for no obstacles, she thought as she struggled to get her exhausted legs back under her. But her legs were simply too weak.

"Scope?"

Her mental processes screeched to a halt. She looked beside her, where a very familiar Utahraptor laid. "Spike!" she exclaimed in shock. *I'm home? Oh, no no no no no. . .*

"Scope," Spike said, his eyes wide. "Where are the others?"

"No time, run!" she replied hurriedly, fright managing to get her back to her feet. She began to stumble away, but Spike was faster and planted himself in her path.

"Calm down, Scope. Where are those who were with you?"

"Gone!" she said breathlessly. "Please move, I've gotta go. Tyrants after me, need to run!" she added deliriously.

"What!" Spike ejaculated.

A booming roar interrupted them. Eyes widening, she looked back the way she had come. Crashing sounds were coming from the trees and drawing closer.

I led them here! she realized in horror. *What have I done?!* Looking back, she rationalized that in trying to find a safe place to hide until the threat left, her subconscious had taken her to the place she felt safest, despite her random flight path.

Spike stared past her and at the trees before turning and shouting to the others, "Gather the hatchlings and keep them in the center of the clearing! Tyrants are coming! I repeat, Tyrants are coming!"

No sooner had panic begun did another loud roar split the air. Scope yelped and jumped closer to the nearest adult, which was Spike.

"Tyrannosaurs," Spike hissed in hate. "They're coming!" he yelled. "Everyone prepare!"

Everyone backed away from the trees. The hatchlings were crying, gathered together in the middle of the clearing by the tall rock. Scope looked for her patriarch and spotted him helping to herd the last of the hatchlings.

Trees were cracking and breaking loudly. The ground was shaking. Scope moved closer to Spike, subconsciously wanting a sense of protection from an adult. She sighed slightly when she felt Spike's tail drape over her hindquarters and loosely wrap around her own.

Scope sucked in a terrified breath when she saw no less than seven T-rex burst into the clearing, tree remains falling to the ground around them. After them appeared what seemed to be dozens of Coelurus. The Tyrants surveyed the clearing with their obvious malice.

She felt Spike tense, and then his chest quaked with the rumble of a deep and guttural growl. She mimicked him as best as she could, though hers sounded hollow.

The largest T-rex spotted her and shot her a sadistic smile. "Thank you, little one," he thundered. "You led us here quite nicely. We will dine well today."

Scope hissed; only her patriarch and Spike called her 'little one', and the T-rex made her shiver in distaste when he said it. "Don't call me that," she spat.

The T-rex barked out a laugh, then boomed, "Attack!"

"Stay behind me," Spike hissed softly to Scope before he lunged forward. He clashed almost immediately with a Coelurus. Spike found an open spot and wrapped his jaws around the Coelurus' neck. The Coelurus managed to shriek once before Spike jerked his head. There was a loud *crack* and the Coelurus fell limply to the ground.

Scope squeaked as she dodged a lunging Coelurus. The Coelurus sailed over her head with an angry screech. Before it could land, Scope snapped her taloned fingers up and clawed several deep gashes in the Coelurus' underside. The Coelurus fell to the ground and tried to get up again, but Scope quickly rendered it immobile via stomping on its legs and breaking them.

Catching movement out of the corner of her eye, Scope whirled around just in time to see several Coelurus ganging up on her. Scope noticed for the first time that, instead of being half their size, they were now equal. She was only outnumbered instead of outweighed.

One of the Coelurus leapt. Scope ducked and copied the same move she had done on the last Coelurus. With one down, she focused on the others. One of them went for her legs while the others went for her neck. She barely managed to avoid all of them and dashed out of the area. Running was considered a cowardly move, but she didn't care about how her valor looked at the moment. Cowards survived, but she wasn't planning on abandoning the fight at all.

The hatchlings screamed. Scope joined them in their screaming as a T-rex charged onto the ground near the hatchlings. A few steps later, two-thirds of the hatchlings were flattened.

Scope saw red. She screeched her fury as she bolted toward the murderous T-rex. Vaguely aware that she wasn't the only one that had seen the blatant massacre, Scope used her toe claws and raked them against the T-rex's legs, leaving long bloody rips. The T-rex stumbled as she headed for the next leg. She ripped that one up as well, then charged at the first leg. She body-slammed it in an effort to knock it over, but the T-rex's weight was too great.

Scope caught the eyes of several other attacking Utahraptors. They had obviously seen her attempt. With one nod, she managed to convey the desire for collaboration. They all backed up several paces. Before the T-rex could turn around to face them, they ran forward toward a single leg. Scope grunted as she slammed against it.

The T-rex bellowed as it began to tumble. Scope quickly moved so that it wouldn't fall on her. When the T-rex fell to the ground, she saw an Utahraptor go for the jugular. She decided that the T-rex was dead, so she went to chase off some Coelurus that were attacking the hatchlings.

Her patriarch was there. "Scope!" he said as he eviscerated a Coelurus.

"Patriarch!" she replied, dodging a Coelurus' bite.

Together, they began to simultaneously keep the remaining hatchlings behind them and ward off Coelurus. Her eyes narrowed to the point where they were almost closed, she sliced a Coelurus' jugular and then knocked down another one by jumping on it.

More Utahraptors joined her and her patriarch, so Scope retreated to the rock to rest and recover her breath. She gulped in air as she evaluated the clearing which had turned into a battlefield. There were three T-rex, a third of the Coelurus, and her extended family already dead.

Scope scaled back down the rock and met an oncoming Coelurus. She jumped and knocked it down. A quick slice with her toe claw to the neck, and the Coelurus was rapidly moving toward death's door.

It became an erratic pattern as her vision narrowed and sharpened with adrenaline pulsing through her veins. Instincts began to take over her movements. Slice. Duck. Leap. Move out of the way. Bite. Slice. Bite again. Run if needed. Slice. Duck.

"Scope!"

She saw Spike charging toward her. She yelped as he violently bumped her aside. A giant murky green foot slammed down in the very spot where she had been standing. The T-rex she hadn't seen coming growled.

Spike ran to fight the T-rex before she could thank him. She decided that she'd get to do that later, and, then, attacked yet another Coelurus.

Hatchling screams were suddenly cut off.

Scope's head snapped around. "*NO!*" she screeched.

The T-rex carelessly scraped its feet along the ground, looking very pleased with itself. Not a single hatchling survived.

That had been the next generation, now all dead. If any Utahraptor remained after this attack, they would have to wait a full Turn before the generations could begin again. The actions of the Tyrants were absolutely *inexcusable*. Scope roared, then charged.

The T-rex's pleased look fell away when it was leapt upon by more than a dozen *very* irate Utahraptors. They sliced at its legs, snapped at its jaw, and tried to leap upon its back. The T-rex managed to stomp and eat a few more, but a collective smash against one of its more injured legs sent it toppling. The Utahraptors then came after its neck with deadly intention.

Scope limped away from the dead T-rex. While it had been stomping Utahraptors, one of its claws had just caught the skin of her thigh. A thin but long bloody line went down her leg. Luckily for her, the wound wasn't deep, but it would scar.

"Scope!"

She quickly jumped, then checked behind her. Not seeing a T-rex trying to flatten her, she looked around. Spike and her patriarch ran to her.

"What is it?" she asked, panting slightly.

"Follow," her patriarch said before he and Spike ran off.

Scope obeyed. Spike and her patriarch called to every Utahraptor they ran past. Scope soon saw that she was in a group of seven. As they ran toward the forest, Scope saw that the clearing was almost completely stained red. Corpses were *everywhere*.

There were only a few Utahraptors left, and they were fighting against two T-rex and about a dozen Coelurus. Grapple was leading the assault. If those Utahraptors stayed and fought against those horrific odds, they would die. But Spike never once shouted out to them.

One of the lingerers glanced away from a fallen Coelurus and watched the group flee. Scope recognized the Utahraptor as Grapple. *What's he doing? Come on, Grapple!*

They had reached the trees. Scope paused and watched with horrified, wide eyes.

Grapple made no move to follow them, instead leaping at a T-rex's leg. The T-rex roared and shook Grapple off, sending him flying. As he landed on the ground, Grapple's expression was resigned, as if he knew that he was going to die and was ready for death. Coelurus screeched in glee as they swarmed him before he could rise back to his feet. He screeched in agony as the Coelurus ripped into him.

"Scope!" Someone grabbed her arm and pulled her away from the clearing. Scope tore herself away from the sight and ran after the group.

As they dashed through the forest, Spike called over his shoulder, "Don't look back. Everyone, don't look back! Don't shout, just run. Follow me and run! Stop and die!"

Scope choked on tears of fear and pain as she increased her

speed so that she was running alongside her patriarch. "Where are we going?" she asked.

"I don't know," he replied quietly.

CHAPTER SIXTEEN

They were still fleeing after nightfall had come. They hadn't stopped to rest, drink, or eat, though Spike had allowed them to slow to a trot so that they could recover their energy.

Scope barely saw where she was going, merely copying what those alongside her were doing. Tears blurred her vision, rendering her almost blind in the darkness of night. Her mind kept running over the events of the day, torturing her with images she'd rather not experience ever again.

I led them right to the clearing. Stupid. Stupid. Stupid. I've killed everyone. Everyone's dead because of me.

"Scope."

She blinked hard so that she could force some of the tears out, then looked at the speaker. "Spike, sir," she replied glumly.

Spike sighed at seeing her expression. "Don't be so hard on yourself, little one. It wasn't your fault."

"*Not* my fault?" Scope repeated incredulously. "This is completely my fault! I led them to the clearing." She looked away and violently shook her head. "I should've noticed the territory and led them away."

"Scope, it's not your fault because there was no way you could've known that the Tyrannosaurs were going to appear and pursue," Spike pressed, his voice level and calm.

Scope huffed. "I still ended up killing the tribe. And *why* did they chase me? They got our kill."

Spike frowned. "You didn't kill the tribe."

"I did!" she protested, feeling angry tears coming up. "I led them there! That means that I led their deaths! It's all *my fault!*"

Spike shook his head but said nothing more.

Scope's patriarch looked over at Scope. "Honey. . ."

"Don't *honey* me!" Scope snapped. "I don't deserve it." To keep them from speaking to her, she dropped back so that she was trailing behind the group.

Now that there wasn't anyone to copy, she had to keep blinking her eyes so that she could see. Water streamed down her cheeks.

I did this. I killed them. Scope, how idiotic can you get? How can Patriarch still look at me? I'm as bad as the Tyrants. Yeah. Scope, the first Utahraptor Tyrant. I should leave the group. They're probably livid at me. Why would they want a traitor moving with them? I'm a Tyrant magnet. I should leave.

"Let's stop."

Scope plodded a few steps, slowing down, then came to a stop. Her head still hung abnormally low, as if she was still running. She just didn't have the willpower to raise it to a more comfortable position.

Spike walked around in a loose circle, looking at the ground. The ground was mossy and even in the darkness she could tell that it was a lush green. "We'll rest here for the night," Spike continued. "The moss will help insulate us. It would best for us to sleep as close together as possible."

Scope shivered, noticing how sharply the temperature had dropped since the sun had gone down. There was a cold wind blowing as well, and clouds blocked out the sky.

She watched as the other Utahraptors began to lay down on an especially thick carpet of moss, and took notice of them. Besides Spike, her patriarch, and herself, there were four other adults. Of the four, one appeared to be only a Turn older than herself, and had probably gone on last Turn's Initiation Hunt.

Scope felt another swell of guilt wash over her. All of the younglings had returned from that Hunt, albeit some of them injured or barely able to walk. They hadn't had such a horrendous failure.

"Scope." She looked up to see her patriarch looking at her.

Everyone was already laying down, huddled next to each other. One of the Utahraptors apparently had had the presence of mind to snatch a few blankets from the clearing before they left, and was spreading them out. "Come."

She shook her head and moved to lay down a short distance away. She didn't deserve to mingle in their company.

Curling up into a tight ball, she violently shivered. The injury on her thigh ached, throbbing in sync with her pulse. She focused on the vague pain, partially glad for a distraction from her depressed thoughts and the freezing cold air.

Something cold landed on her nose. She extended her tongue and licked the spot. Water. Another landed on her neck, then on her back, tail, and then another on her head. It was raining. She thought back to early last Winter Season, the night before she had experienced her first snow. She had been small enough to huddle next to her Patriarch for warmth.

She was too big to huddle in his armpit now, and she wasn't about to go over to the others and request warmth from the freezing rain. Why would those who probably blamed her for what happened want to offer her comfort?

A small whimper escaped her throat before she was conscious that she was making the noise. She stifled the last part and buried her head under her tail. She swallowed a pitiful whine that tried to follow the whimper. However, she couldn't stop the hot tears that started dripping from her eyes.

The rain quickly became heavier and turned into a downpour. Scope couldn't get her body to stop shivering so violently that it looked like she was experiencing a personal earthquake. She was curled up so tightly only her back and part of her neck were visible.

As she grew colder and colder, she stopped trying to keep track of how long it had been raining. She let her mind become empty and thoughtless, simply waiting until the rain showed signs of letting up. Sometime in the late night, the rain began to become mixed with tiny ice pellets.

Sleet, she thought in dismay as she felt the ice bounce off of her hide. Despite her very tough skin that had a layer of small scales, the ice felt like a horde of bees were trying to sting her.

The temperature continued to drop, and the sleet eventually turned into thick sheets of snow, blowing and swirling in the wind. It seemed only a few minutes before there was a layer of white coating the ground, it was coming down so heavily. She could only see about a pace in front of her muzzle.

The snow on the ground was about ankle-deep when Scope realized that she had stopped shivering. Running a mental check, she noticed that most of her body had gone numb. She definitely couldn't feel her toes, fingers, or part of her tail. Now that she had stopped shivering and shaking off the snow, the downpour began to collect on her body.

Tiredness began to creep upon the edges of her mind and slowly seeped further in. She yawned, her mouth expending as much as it could in the little space she had it in. Frigid air surged into her body, causing her to cough and shiver once.

She was so *tired.* Even thinking was becoming a chore. She let out a slow breath and settled into the hardening moss. She vaguely felt the numbness increase.

"Scope, wake up!"

Huh? What? She opened her eyes and blinked heavily. Her

head felt like it was a lump of rock on a neck as weak as a hatchling. She forced herself to raise her head to look at who had spoken to her. She blinked a haze from her eyes.

Spike had his head raised and looking at her. "Come over here, Scope," he said.

She squinted through the falling snow at him with half-lidded eyes. She felt as if she should be replying, but her mind felt as frozen as her body.

"Quickly, Scope!"

She might as well. After all, she couldn't think of a reason not to. Her limbs were stiff and weak as she slowly rose to her feet. She stumbled through the snow, leaving deep trenches. Barely able to lift her legs, she moved into the midst of the others. Spike scooted to the side, creating an open spot.

Scope laid down in the open spot. Spike shifted so that his neck, arms, and tail were draped over her body. He bit the edge of the blanket that covered his own body and moved it so that it was draped over her as well. The reptilian hide was stiff and slightly scratchy, but it did keep the warmth in. Scope sighed as she felt heat begin to return to her body. Her extremities tingled as she fell into slumber.

Scope gradually moved into wakefulness. She yawned; and, then, wheezed as air far colder than she would've preferred entered her lungs. The shock fully awakened her, and she opened her eyes.

"Good morning," her patriarch said, nosing her gently.

She shivered, then tried to stretch. When her body was stopped, she realized that she was surrounded by the others. "When did I get here?" she asked, shivering again.

"Spike probably knows," her patriarch replied, nodding to their slumbering leader. "I woke up and you were here."

Scope nodded, then leaned into her patriarch for warmth. There was still snow coming down, heavy and thick. The flakes were large and quickly adding to the moderately deep layer already on the ground.

"I thought that White Season had ended," Scope remarked, shivering from the low temperature and wind chill.

"Must be a late snowstorm," her patriarch answered, looking around.

Spike began to stir, then blinked. He shook his head a little before raising it. "Scope," he said with a pleased and rather relieved expression.

"Sir?" she asked.

Spike sighed at her. "You almost froze last night, Scope."

She blinked. "I did?"

"You stopped shivering. Did you happen to feel very tired afterward?"

Nodding, she replied, "Yes. So I almost froze to death last night?"

"You did. I'm glad that you decided to come into the huddle

and recover your warmth."

She looked down at the snowy ground. *I almost died. . .*

Spike rose to his feet and shook his body, dislodging any snowflakes that had landed on his hide. "Everyone up!" he said loudly. "We need to keep moving."

The others began to grumble sleepily as they shuffled themselves into wakefulness. The ones at the edge of the huddle were noticeably slower to open their eyes and much stiffer in their movements.

"It's still snowin', Spike," the adult a Turn older than Scope whined, his voice laced with the slur of sleep. "Can't we sleep for a li'l while longer?"

"We need to move out," Spike pressed, squinting into the snow. "The further we get from our clearing, the better."

"Surely they're gone by now," another Utahraptor said, slowly getting to his feet.

"We don't know for sure," Spike replied, taking a few steps into the falling blanket of white. His form immediately became muted. "Get up and follow me. The sooner we leave, the sooner the snow can fill our tracks. The Tyrants could be looking for us."

Scope kept by her patriarch's side as the others began standing up. They shook their bodies before trotting to join Spike.

Spike looked them all over, and began moving. The others had to keep close to each other, lest they become separated and lose sight of each other. Scope noticed that any sounds they made were absorbed into the snow. Their breaths came from their noses and mouths in large, thick clouds that were almost instantly borne away on the biting wind.

The amount of sunlight that managed to pierce the clouds and the thick snow just barely managed to light up the forest. Scope estimated the time of day to be early afternoon, although she had no idea of the real time. Several hours after Spike had awakened them, the wind suddenly gained strength and blasted even more snow in their faces.

Scope blinked hard, trying to clear her eyes. She dimly heard Spike shout for a halt through the howling wind. Her neck felt unusually heavy, so she shook it. She saw heaps of snow fall, so she assumed that snow had accumulated in her fringe.

"I can't see!" someone said. Scope knew that whoever had said that was screaming, as she presumed from the tone, but she could barely hear whoever it was over the wind. She had to agree; the snow was falling so hard she could barely see her patriarch and Spike, both of whom she could touch if she extended her nose.

She shivered as she felt the temperature take a nosedive. Surely the Tyrants would have trouble tracking them in this freak blizzard! She screamed her thought at Spike, hoping that her voice would reach him over the wind's din.

Spike was silent for a moment, then nodded. "I agree! We'll rest here until the wind relents!"

Scope yelped as someone bumped into her tail. She twisted her head to look behind her and saw one of the others laying down. Spike was circling the ground, rounding them all up and having them lay down in a huddle so that body heat could be exchanged. The blankets were spread again.

She ended up in the middle of the huddle again, though she couldn't complain. Heat, no matter how meager it was, surrounded her on all sides. Spike waited until everyone had laid down before moving to the edge of the huddle. Scope's patriarch and a few others protested, shoving and biting at Spike until he relented and laid down next to Scope in the middle.

It was a long time before the wind died down and the snow thinned out. By the time Scope could see a pace ahead of her muzzle, darkness was falling and it was no longer seemed worth the effort to continue moving.

"Are we going to keep moving, sir?" Scope asked Spike for clarification on her observation.

Spike looked up at the unseen sky, squinting to keep snow-flakes out of his eyes. "No. We're staying here until daylight comes again."

Scope curled up, but before she laid her head down she looked for her patriarch. She just barely made him out, lying at the rim of the huddle. He was leaning into someone else for warmth and curled up into so tight a ball it seemed physically improbable.

A quiet squabble came up, and she glanced toward it out of curiosity. It was a few Utahraptors, including her patriarch, arguing with Spike.

"Get in the inside," Spike ordered them, fixedly standing at the outer rim of the huddle.

"No," one of the Utahraptors stated firmly. "We're sleeping on the outside."

The others nodded their heads in full agreement. Spike

relented and moved to the center of the huddle, right next to Scope. The protestors settled down at the rim, clutching their blankets as tightly against their hides as possible.

With a gusting sigh that formed a thick cloud in front of her muzzle, she put her head beneath her tail and closed her eyes.

"Get up! We're moving!"

Scope groaned as Spike's demand intruded on her sleep. She squirmed a bit before stiffly rising to her feet. Blinking her eyes to rid them of the remains of sleep, she looked around and saw that a couple Utahraptors weren't moving.

Spike trod over to one of them and gently kicked the snow-covered form. "Get up, we're moving. Up and at 'em."

Scope took a few steps closer, trying to identify who was still sleeping. "Patriarch," she said. "Come on, we need to go."

With a troubled frown, Spike leaned down and sniffed her patriarch. His frown deepened, then became sad as he moved to the other unmoving Utahraptors. After sniffing them as well, he straightened and slowly shook his head.

A scrap of anxiety bit at Scope as she moved to nose her patriarch. "Come on. Get up."

"He won't be doing so, Scope."

Her head whirled around to stare at the tribe leader. "What?" she squeaked.

"He's frozen to death, Scope," Spike said sadly. He pointed to the other still Utahraptors. "And they have as well."

Four dead, frozen in their sleep, including the last of her family. Scope choked on a half sob, half cry. "Patriarch's dead?" she whimpered.

Spike nodded. "Come, we need to move."

"No!" Scope exclaimed, leaning down to nudge her Patriarch again. "Patriarch! Wake up! *Please, wake up!*" Sobs broke her voice as she continued to plea, but her patriarch remained lifeless.

"Come." Spike's voice was gentle, sympathetic, and laced with sadness.

She stared at her patriarch for a long moment, hoping beyond hope that his eyelids would flutter open, that his chest would rise and fall with breath. But he did no such thing. Tears beginning to roll down her cheeks, Scope took the blanket that covered him and clutched it in her arms. She draped it over her shoulders and tied two of the ends under her neck.

It was only then that she moved to follow Spike. The white scene of cold seemed to match her emotional pain inside.

CHAPCER SEVENCEEN

Her stomach clenched as the icy water entered. Scope grimaced and continued to drink slowly.

Spike had stomped a hole in the ice of the river. The blizzard had died a little over a day ago; so, the wind was almost nonexistent, although the snowfall was still rather dense.

Scope barely noticed that she had stopped drinking as she thought back to the day she had doomed the tribe. *Has it really been almost a week?* she thought dismally.

"Hey, I want to drink, too! Could you move?"

She saw that the adult a Turn older than herself, a neon-blue-fringed male called Blur, had spoken to her. She obligingly stepped back and gave him room to drink.

The snow's depth was enough to reach her knees, making it well over a pace deep. Everyone had to leap in order to go anywhere, and jumping took up their energy far faster than anyone would like. Food was hard to find; the herbivores had somehow managed to make themselves scarce. A few days ago, they had stumbled across a half-frozen carcass of a Corythosaurus, apparently having died in its sleep from the cold. They had gorged themselves before moving on.

They were wandering without a sense of direction. It was difficult to see more than a half dozen paces ahead. The days were cold and the nights far colder. Four nights ago, they had lost another Utahraptor to the frigidity.

She ran a mental tally. They had left the clearing with seven, including herself. Her patriarch and two others had frozen to death on the second night; then four were left. With the fourth lost, the group now included herself, Spike, and Blur. Only three Utahraptors left alive out of a tribe of dozens.

Her patriarch's blanket was tied around her neck. She could still detect his scent on the hide, but it was slowly becoming overridden by her own. She dreaded the day his scent vanished completely.

Turning around, she saw that Spike was standing a short distance away. Since he was motionless, snow was collecting on the top of his body. His fringe was so filled with snow, it was hard to see the light azure color.

"Where now?" Blur asked their leader.

Spike sighed, a cloud flying from his nostrils. "We go back."

"Back where?" Blur asked, cocking his head to the side.

"The clearing."

Scope's brow pinched. "But you said that we can't go back there! The Tyrants. . ."

"Are probably gone by now," Spike interrupted her. "There aren't any herbivores who would go anywhere near a place that reeks of death. They must have moved on by now. It'll take us at least a few days to return, so we should leave now. Finish drinking."

Scope looked at the direction from which they had come. The snow had already almost filled in the trenches that were their tracks. "How will we find our way back?" she asked.

"We follow our noses," Spike replied smoothly. "Are you two done drinking? Good; we move." He sniffed the air, sneezed, then began moving in a certain direction.

Scope leapt into his trench so that she could save energy by not having to plow through the snow. Positioning herself at Spike's tail, she saw that Blur had had the same idea. The group of three moved in a single file.

"Why are we going back?" Blur asked. "There's nothing left for us there."

"Yes, there is," Spike said firmly. "Liberation."

Scope was about to ask for clarification when a loud roar was suddenly heard through the descending snow. The group froze in place. Scope sniffed the air, but she could smell little more than the wet fluff that surrounded them on all sides.

"What was that?" she whispered.

Spike stiffened. "They've found us."

Scope cringed and knelt down so that she looked as small as possible. On the contrary, Blur puffed himself up and stood taller, although his eyes held the same fear she felt. Blur took a step closer to her, placing a foot over her hindquarters so he was partially standing over her.

She appreciated the protection, no matter how useless it would be.

A large shape appeared behind the curtain of snow and drew closer, more forming behind it. She whimpered when she saw that a group of T-rex were coming their way.

"You gave us quite a chase," the largest T-rex, a huge muddy red brute, said. "Luckily for us, you managed to run right into our territory."

How far did we run? Scope wondered.

"Your territory?" Spike said, his voice flat and his expression one of apprehension.

"Yes," the red T-rex said, his lips curling up into a shark's smile. "Now, all three of you are going to come with us."

"And if we refuse?" Blur said.

"You can use your own feet or you can travel in our mouths," the T-rex snarled.

"We will walk," Spike said, shooting a look at Blur. "How far away is our destination?"

"Just up the river," the T-rex said as he moved to turn around. His tail collided with several trees and created a veritable waterfall of snow from the branches. "Follow us."

Spike treaded after the T-rex, having to leap in order to keep up with their long strides. Scope kept as close to Spike as she could, unconsciously seeking comfort from the danger that hung in the air so thickly it was almost palatable.

The T-rex led them back to the river, then they followed it upriver. It wasn't a very long trek to a frozen waterfall and then to a small clearing next to it. Scope saw many other T-rex milling around, some of them coming from a different direction. One of the other incoming groups carried pieces of a large herbivore in their mouths. Coelurus hissed at the Utahraptors, their spiny crowns rattling noisily.

Scope quickly took in their surroundings. The immediate area of ground was almost completely barren of snow, most likely because of the frequent foot traffic. There were Tyrants milling everywhere, eyeing the Utahraptors hungrily. In contrast, not far away was a large pile of dead herbivores that had yet to be devoured.

A few paces from the herbivores was a single body about the size of an adult Utahraptor, half rotten yet showed no signs of even being nibbled on. It was lanky, and appeared to have once been some brown color. It had a small head on an unnaturally bent neck.

She noticed Spike looking at her, then following her gaze. He almost froze in the middle of a step as he stared at the carcass. Scope saw recognition, then an immense sadness in his eyes. A growl from a T-rex sent him moving again.

A much, much deeper growl brought Spike, Scope, and Blur to a dead stop. Scope looked into the clearing and saw a form standing half-masked by the falling snow. The veiled form nearly dwarfed the largest T-rex. The absolutely humongous beast stepped forward, and the details became clearer; it was an Acrocanthosaurus.

Spike choked. He was very quiet, nearly silent, but Scope's eyes widened at her leader. She had *never* heard him make such a sound, not even when the hatchlings had been killed. If *Spike* was actually *scared,* then they were doomed.

"What is this that you've brought me?" the monstrous being purred dangerously, lowering his head closer to the ground. Scope couldn't help but stare at his teeth, the smallest of them being as long as her arm. "Three snacks? How thoughtful, but I dearly hope that you brought me something more than this. I'm *very* hungry."

"Your Highness," the red T-rex said reverently, lowering his head so much his chin almost scraped the ground. "These three are the last Utahraptors from the tribe that used to reside in the mountaintop clearing."

"I was told that the entire population had been decimated," the colossus creature growled, narrowing his crimson eyes at the T-rex.

Scope blinked as she caught a glimpse at the Acrocanthosaurus' back. Nestled at the base of his neck, where the spiny crest that went down the entirety of his back sank into the skin, was a strange dull silver object. It was dirty and water stained, and she was sure that without all of the scratches that marred its surface it would've been likely to be perfectly smooth.

"There will be no more once these three have been eliminated," the T-rex said quickly. The Acrocanthosaurus shifted so that his back was no longer visible, and the object was lost to Scope's sight.

The massive beast rumbled deep in his gullet, then glared down at the threesome. "I hope that you three know exactly to whom you're speaking, or have my minions been neglectful?"

Spike growled. "Harass."

"It's *King* Harass to you!" the mammoth being snarled, biting at the air just in front of Spike's nose. To his credit, Spike only blinked at the close proximity. "Now, I know that Intel gave you the only other device that could possibly end my reign. I want to know where it is, immediately."

"I will *never* tell you where it's hidden," Spike spat.

Scope cowered as the T-rex and Coelurus began closing in. Harass' rumble turned into a deep growl. Her instincts *screamed* for her to run as fast as she could. Adrenaline was beginning to flow through her veins, making her jittery.

Spike stayed silent. Blur shifted his weight from foot to foot, eyeing the much larger carnivores warily.

I need to do something! she thought. "Run, guys," she said under her voice, hoping that the T-rex, Coelurus, and Harass wouldn't hear her. "I'll hold them off. Run."

Spike glanced at her, then gave a minute nod. He swatted Blur with his tail and stamped his feet. Scope prepared to dodge and duck.

"Go!" she screamed, running one way while Spike and Blur went in another. She yelped as a T-rex planted its foot right in her path. She leapt onto the foot and used it as a jumping platform. As chaos broke out, she saw Spike and Blur evading the efforts of Coelurus. The Coelurus, however, were nearly useless since the snow's surface was almost to their heads.

"Pests!" Harass roared. "My minions, kill the two little ones but spare the eldest!"

Scope dodged a foot that meant to flatten her. She tumbled a bit in the snow and frantically moved to get her feet under her again. *I need to get to a place that has less snow,* she thought. *The river! There's hardly any snow on the ice.*

She changed directions and bounded toward the river as fast as she could. Her energy was being sapped with every leap she made and the T-rex were gaining. She made it to the river before her pursuers reached her. She yelped as she stepped on the ice and promptly slid. Her momentum carried her across the slick surface on her stomach. When she slid to a stop, she hurried to her feet and dug in her claws to keep them from sliding out from under her.

The T-rex paused at the shoreline. One of them took a step forward, but the second it put enough weight on its foot it broke the ice and fell through. The T-rex rumbled darkly as it quickly pulled its foot and and shook off the water.

Scope sighed in relief; the T-rex were too heavy to reach her. She turned and began to jog across the ice, carefully placing her feet so that she didn't go out of control. She headed out toward the center of the river, heading for the other side. The T-rex trailed along the shoreline after her, roaring threats.

She didn't see the thinner patch of ice and didn't notice how the ice stopped a few dozen paces on and revealed freezing water. She gasped as she fell through the ice and into the water. The shock of the temperature caused her to involuntarily stiffen and cease moving, and she began to sink. Regaining control, she kicked herself up to the surface. She breached it with a gasp and clawed at a stray block of ice. The river's current began carrying her downriver.

The water was cold. *Oh so COLD.* Scope struggled to reach the shoreline. She could already feel her muscles stiffening, her breath was becoming short and shallow, and her energy was draining away in frightening rapidity.

She sank beneath the water as her legs became too weak to keep her afloat. She desperately summoned her strength and kicked harder, managing to breach the surface again. "Help!" she cried out as loudly as she could before she sank under again. Kicking hard, she came up once more. "Help me! Help!"

Something was moving in the forest, beyond the shore she was trying very hard to reach before she drowned. She called for help again, then went under. She tried kicking, but she had exhausted her energy. Her shuddering sigh of defeat came out as nothing more than large bubbles as she closed her eyes and tried to hold her breath as long as possible. Anything to prolong the time of her imminent death.

I'm so sorry, she thought, thinking of her tribe. Everyone she had ever known. Had Spike and Blur escaped? *I'm so, so sorry.*

Her lungs were burning. Against her will, she felt her airway begin to open. Her lungs would get nothing but water and not the blessed air they needed so badly.

She sucked in a surprised breath when something bit her tail. River water, cold as ice, rushed into her body. Her sight was rapidly darkening as her drowning reached the final stages.

As she began to succumb to the darkness, she was pulled from the water and dragged onto the shore. She gagged, then coughed up all of the water she had swallowed. The water burst from her mouth in a small river.

"Are you okay?" said a voice.

She squinted up at the blurry form hovering above her. She couldn't make out much more than a dark shape against a gray sky.

"Stay back!" the someone hissed at someone else who was out of the range of her vision. "It could be dangerous."

"Half drowned?" the thing beyond her vision replied. "It can't even lift its head. Besides, we heard it yell for help."

Scope was so tired. She needed to rest. Her eyes drifted shut.

"We need to help it," echoed in her ears as she fell asleep.

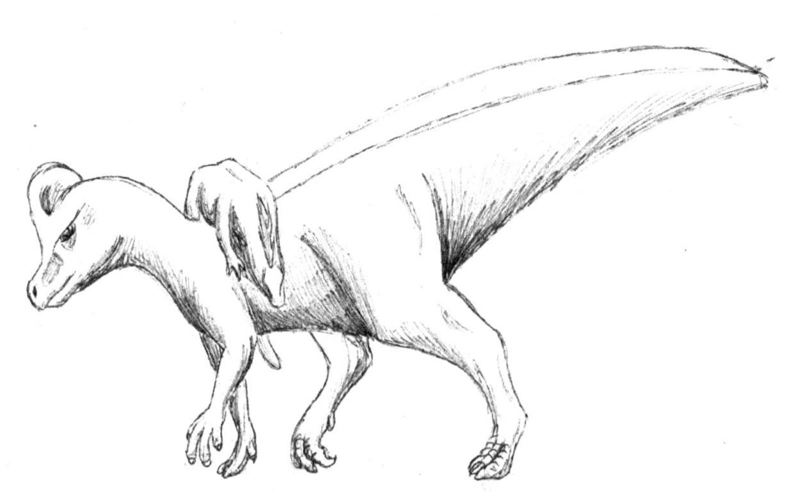

Chapter Eighteen

Why am I swaying? Is the ground moving? As Scope shifted toward consciousness, she wondered if she was feeling the gentlest earthquake to ever exist. In order to see if she was right, she cracked open an eyelid. The sudden glare of nothing but bright white seared her eye and she groaned as she squished it shut again.

"Hey, I think it's awake. It moved."

Who was talking? Was it talking about her? She opened her eyes, this time slowly so they had time to adjust. She saw that she was lying on her stomach, draped over the shoulders of a Corythosaurus. Raising her head, she noticed that the Corythosaurus she was riding on was only one in a large herd of what seemed to be more or less a few dozen.

"Oh, it *is* awake. Hello there, stranger!"

She swiveled her head around to face the speaker. It was a small Corythosaurus, maybe her own age. It had a large dome-shaped, green-colored crest adorning its head. It pranced alongside the Corythosaurus she was on.

"Who are you?" she asked, then looked around again. The herd was traveling through a forest that consisted of only two colors; the grayish brown of the tree trunks, and the white of the snow. The forest seemed endless in all directions, and it seemed that the herd was moving up a slope. "Where am I?"

"I'm Scratcher," the small Corythosaurus said, then thumped his thick tail against the Corythosaurus she was riding. "My big brother Hoot is carrying you. We found you by the river! There were some really big carnivores stuck on the other side. They looked *really* mad when Hoot and me took you to our herd."

Scope looked at Hoot. The Corythosaurus twisted his neck around so that he could see her, then gave her a brief nod. Hoot had a jade blue crest.

"So, Hoot, you rescued me from the river?" she asked.

Hoot nodded again, but said nothing.

Scope furrowed her brow at him, silently wondering why he wasn't speaking.

"Oh, don't mind his quiet," Scratcher said, making a face. "He's not too talkative around newcomers. Anyway, he's the one that saw you drowning; he swam after you. I hope your tail don't hurt, he bit it kind of hard when he towed you back."

She glanced at her tail, checking it for bite marks. There were a few scrapes on either side near the middle of the appendage, though they were nothing major. They should heal in a few days.

"Hey, what are you?"

She looked back to Scratcher. "What?"

"What are you?" he asked again, looking up at her inquisitively.

"I'm an Utahraptor," she replied.

Hoot suddenly stopped dead in his tracks and bucked. With a yelp, Scope tumbled off of his back and landed on the ground in a heap. She scrambled to her feet when Hoot whirled around with a speed that belied his size and faced her, pawing the ground. Hoot's tail swept Scratcher behind him.

"What did I say?" she said in alarm, backing away as fast as she could in the deep snow.

"Utahraptors kill us," Hoot growled, his eyes narrowed at her. "Carnivore! Trap, so that others can follow you and find the herd!"

"No!" Scope said, her own eyes wide. "There's no trap at all! My tribe's been killed off by Tyrants. I might be the last one. There's no one else."

Scratcher peered around Hoot's hind leg at her. "Your entire tribe died?"

Scope nodded sadly. "I was on the run from Tyrants so that they wouldn't kill me next. I fell through the river ice while I was escaping."

"Were the Tyrants those big carnivores roaring at us?" Scratcher asked.

She nodded again. "Probably."

Hoot snorted, then stared at Scope for a very long moment.

"Hoot! Scratcher!" Scope traced the voice and spotted a large Corythosaurus, standing and facing them while the herd walked on. "You're falling behind!"

Hoot looked at the speaker, then back at her. "No place to go?"

She shook her head. "They're guarding the clearing I used to call my home, waiting for any escapees trying to come back. If I go anywhere, I die."

The larger Corythosaurus huffed out a huge cloud of air. "Fine. Get back on my back, you'll never keep up with those short legs."

"I'm coming with you?" she asked as Scratcher also asked, "She's coming with us?"

"Hurry up, carnivore," Hoot said, turning around so that he was ready to catch up to the herd.

She wasted no time. Making sure not to cause deep scratches, she scrabbled onto his shoulders and made herself comfortable between his neck and shoulder blades. "Thank you," she murmured.

"Don't make me regret it," Hoot rumbled threateningly before trotting to catch up to the herd.

"This is great!" Scratcher said, bounding after them in excitement. "You're coming with us. . . hey, I never got your name."

"Oh. I'm Scope. Could you two keep an eye out for any dead creatures along the herd's path? I can't eat grass like you two do."

"No problem," Scratcher said with a wink and a nod.

Scope chuckled under her breath as she watched Scratcher prance in circles around the herd, peering off into the trees. The lively youngling Corythosaurus was taking his job of finding her a corpse very seriously. Hoot wasn't galloping around, but he was often turning his head and looking.

She snorted as a thought hit her. *I'd be vigilant, too, if I was prey harboring a predator. Rule number one; don't let the predator get hungry.*

Some snow had collected on her nose, and she quickly shook it off. The blizzard had receded to a light snowfall and the wind was almost undetectable. The temperature had raised considerably from bone-numbing freezing to shiver-a-lot. It was *almost* warm enough for the two-pace-deep layer of snow on the ground to start melting.

The Corythosaurus herd was large enough to plow through the snow, leaving very deep trenches behind them. Those at the front of the herd, parting the snow, were constantly being switched out with a different Corythosaurus that was fresh, letting the formerly plowing one rest. Excepting Scratcher, the younglings were hanging out in the middle of the herd, mostly demolishing any snowdrifts left over.

It was a very peaceful scene; a lone herd of Corythosaurus moving in a snowy forest. But she did wonder why the others hadn't raised the alarm at her appearance. It was more than obvious that she was a carnivore and regularly ate their kind. Despite the wary glances shot at her, none of them seemed overly worried.

Is it because I'm alone? she wondered. *No single Utahraptor can take out a Corythosaurus all by itself. Maybe that's why.*

A movement from one of the largest Corythosaurus drew her gaze. It was blatantly male, with a large dual-colored crest in both scarlet and fiery orange. Hoot jumped a little when the male drew alongside him.

The male eyed Scope with a sharp gaze. "Who are you?" he grunted.

"Scope. I'm an Utahraptor."

"I know what you are," the male said. "What I want to know is why you're here. You should scurry back to the tribe you belong to."

"I can't. The Tyrants killed my tribe. I think that I'm the last one."

This seemed to catch the male off guard. "The last one?" he hummed thoughtfully. "Why are you with this herd?"

"Hoot and Scratcher saved my life. I fell in the river and almost drowned. I don't have anywhere else to go."

"How can I know that when you get hungry, you won't jump

the younglings?" the male queried warily.

"Scratcher volunteered to keep an eye out for any carcasses," she replied. "I'm a little hungry now, but I can last a few more days before I desperately need food. I'll avoid the younglings, if that makes you feel better."

The male snorted a cloud of warm air. "Hmm. Hoot."

Hoot jumped slightly. "Yes, sir?"

"Keep a very close eye on her." The male increased his speed so that he was near the front of the herd and in the position he had had before falling back to speak.

Scope frowned, thinking. "Who was that?"

"Vole," Hoot replied. "He's the herd's alpha male."

"Alpha male?" she echoed. "Is that like a tribe leader?"

"The terminology's different, but yes."

Scope sighed. "He doesn't trust me."

"Not many of our kind trust carnivores." Hoot trailed off and fell silent.

She had the feeling that he wouldn't be talking to her again for a while, so she settled down in her spot on his back.

When the sun went down and darkness fell, Vole called for a halt for the night. Scope slid off of Hoot's back so that he could lie down. The snow crunched loudly as she fell into it. She shivered violently as some of it brushed against her soft underbelly.

Scratcher moved up to her, taking great bounding leaps in the deep snow. "Sorry, Scope," he said with a lamenting sigh, looking down at the ground. "I didn't see anything you could eat."

"Don't stress about it," she replied with a comforting tone. "I'll be able to hold out for a couple more days."

The young Corythosaurus nodded glumly, then turned around. "See you tomorrow," he said before jumping off.

Scope shook her head. *He's working too hard,* she thought. *I'm not worth this much trouble.*

The snow was beginning to melt in the rising temperatures. As she moved toward one of the nearest trees, she noticed the variations in the snow's depth. It varied greatly between her shins and haunches.

The snow's getting patchy.

When she reached the tree, she moved around it until she found the place that was the shallowest. To make things even better, the tree and the snowdrift against it created a natural wind block.

She used her feet to scrape away the snow until her claws began to create gouges in the frozen dirt. As she laid down in her nest, she bit back a surprised yelp as frozen blades of grass prickled her underside. She shifted until she had either broken up the grass blades or had thawed them.

Around her, she could hear the Corythosaurus herd moving into their chosen resting positions. She craned her neck so that she could see over a snowdrift. Most of the large herbivores were lying huddled together in an effort to share body heat, though there were a few lying by themselves. The younglings were nowhere in sight, which led her to assume that they had been forced into some of the huddles.

She lowered her head and curled her neck so that her chin laid on the ground next to her side. Her feet were being laid upon under her body.

Reaching up to her neck, she fingered open the knot and her patriarch's blanket slid from her shoulders. She flung it so that it covered most of her body.

The snowfall had finally let up, and the silence was peculiar without the constant snow and the blizzard. However, the clouds stayed, keeping the moon and stars from being seen.

She shivered, beginning at her muzzle and ending at her tail. Sighing, she contemplated moving over to one of the Corythosaurus and asking for a bit of warmth. After a few moments, she decided not to; the temperature was merely cold, and not downright *freezing* anymore. With her blanket, she would last the night.

As she was just beginning to doze off, she heard a very distant roar. It was deep, long, and sounded very angry. If it had words in it, she couldn't distinguish them. Her head shot up and faced the direction the roar had come from. She stayed very still for a long moment, blocking out many of the nighttime sounds and focusing on listening for another roar. When another didn't come, she reluctantly laid her head back down.

They're at least a day's travel behind us, she thought. *Hopefully, the water erased my scent and the Corythosaurus herd overwhelmed it when I dried.*

The ground suddenly shook. It wasn't a violent tremor, but it was enough to make her panic. Were the Tyrants closer than she had thought and was the tremor the ground shaking under the weight of their bodies? Her panic subsided when she heard a distant rumble, seeming to come from a very far distance. It was a simple earthquake, not Tyrants.

Despite the fact that there was nothing to fear tonight, it was a while before she managed to fall asleep.

CHAPTER NINETEEN

Scope groaned quietly as she stared up at the sky. Hoot rocked underneath her as he walked, ever so often glancing back at her with a slightly frantic glint in his eye.

It had been nearly three days since she had been found by Scratcher. Six days, at least, since she had eaten that Corythosaurus carcass with Spike and Blur. Because she hadn't eaten in over a week, she was very much feeling her stomach's complaints. It felt like it was clenching, causing terrible cramps that caused her to become breathless and curl up into a ball.

A day ago, she had tried gorging herself on melting snow, but it was only a brief respite. It had worked for a few hours, but then the hunger pangs had returned.

Hoot and Scratcher weren't the only ones actively searching for dead Squamas anymore. Once Scope had told them that she was getting very hungry a few days back, they had alerted the rest of the herd.

It was getting to the point where every Corythosaurus looked like a walking hunk of fresh meat without any skin. She dared not tell anyone that as a warning.

With a grimace, she tried to distract herself from her hunger and focus on something else. Like how much the temperature had warmed up.

The snow had melted quite a bit. A few patches of grass were visible. The lack of snow was a good thing for hungry herbivores. The lack of enough cold to keep the snow there was a bad thing for hungry carnivores who needed to find a starved or deathly frozen body.

She groaned again as her stomach screamed at her. She stared off into space, then blinked when she realized that she was staring at Hoot's back, the flesh so *close*. She was in such a vulnerable place on his back! All that she had to do was give the visible spine a good slice with her talons and thus paralyze her prey. When the herbivore went down as his hind legs were unusable, she would go to his belly and sink her teeth into the soft. . .

Snap out of it, Scope! she shouted at herself. She blinked several times and redirected her gaze back to the sky.

Think about something else. Anything *else! Okay. That's a pretty sky.*

And it was. The clouds had finally left the night before, and the sun was shining down and accelerating the melting snow.

Whenever Hoot moved through a patch of sunlight, she could feel the comforting warmth, a welcome thing after such a long time of cold.

Warm, like freshly killed me. . .

Scope growled viciously as her treacherous mind went off on another dangerous tangent. Hoot jumped and his head snapped around to look at her. She could smell the sudden panic that he was emitting. She knew that he was scared. After all, she was on his back, and he was the closest source of food. If she attacked, he would be the first one.

Fear. It made her mouth water. Fear meant that the prey would be near panic. Panic meant that the prey would be unable to think clearly and thus was easier to kill. As if reacting to the scent, her stomach gave off a sound similar to her former growl of frustration.

She needed to get rid of the fear before her primal instincts overwhelmed her. She shot Hoot an apologetic look, hoping that it would ease him. Much to her relief, the scent of fear subsided as he looked away.

A strange rustling in the trees drew her attention. She looked toward the sound and saw a small bipedal form approaching at a fast clip. Vole must have seen the form as well, as he called for a halt. All of the Corythosaurus moved to face the newcomer.

Scope slid off of Hoot's back, stumbling a little as she hit the ground. She was weak from hunger. Taking a deep breath, she drew her strength from whatever energy reserves she had left.

It was a Deinonychus. She felt a very bad feeling in her gut when she noticed that it had a dangerous look in its eyes. An assumption was forming in her mind as she noted that it was stumbling slightly, as if it was weak. This was a starving Deinonychus, and judging from the crazed gaze, it had lost all of its higher thinking and was little more than a mindless embodiment of hunger.

This is what she should be like in a few more days. The thought was chilling.

The Deinonychus looked at the herd and licked its chops. "Food," it murmured. The voice told Scope it was male. His spiky black fringe, different from her own only in texture and color, was fully upright.

Scope growled, moving into an offensive position. No carnivore was going to try and kill the herd that had helped her. If need be, she would defend them to the death. "Go away, Deinonychus," she hissed.

The other carnivore looked at her as if she had appeared out of thin air. He said nothing, but she could tell that he was evaluating her to see if she was an easier prey. It must've been so, as the Deinonychus charged forward without a single warning.

Scope dodged the charge and her attacker skidded, trying to stop, as his momentum carried him past her. Before he could recover, she dashed forward and leapt upon his vulnerable backside. As she was larger than he, her weight easily sent him to the ground. He squirmed like a snake beneath her, causing her to lose her balance and have to jump away to avoid falling over. He swiped at her as she left his body, but his claws fell short. By the time she had turned around, he was back on his feet and charging toward her again.

Scope had to dodge once again, but the Deinonychus must've anticipated the movement, as he swiped at her as he ran past. Scope hissed in pain as his claws made three thin gashes on her tail that quickly welled up beads of blood. The Deinonychus made a quick pass for another attempt, but she summoned up her energy and leapt over his head. He was clearly anticipating another dodge, and he tripped and fell when his swipe caused him to lose his balance.

She was upon him before he had a chance to get up. She leapt at him with her toe claws extended, and struck him on the neck. The Deinonychus screeched as his head was smashed to the ground. As she stood on his neck, she quickly pulled out one of her toe claws and dispatched him.

The Deinonychus frantically writhed under her. She stepped off to wipe her toe claws clean on the snow. Taking the opportunity to flee, the Deinonychus stumbled to his feet and made to run away. However, he only made it a few steps before falling as a limp heap onto the mud.

Scope released a breath and the adrenaline from the skirmish bled away. Her legs shook, and she fought to keep them from collapsing on her. Taking large but slow steps, she trod over to the dead Deinonychus and stared down at him.

Food. After long last, she had a food source other than the tempting Corythosaurus herd. Realizing that she had forgotten their presence, she looked back over her shoulder. They were just starting to walk away, though some were still watching her. She thought that she saw some newfound respect in their eyes. She had protected them from the predator.

It was time to dine on her conquest. She sunk her teeth into his flesh.

To her starved tongue, the Deinonychus tasted like the fattest and juiciest herbivore. She ripped off chunks of flesh and swallowed them as fast as she could, as if the dead beast was going to come back alive and run away before she finished.

The Deinonychus was quickly reduced to nothing but a bare skeleton. She licked the bones with her rough tongue in order to remove any remnants of meat. Scope took a step away and licked her maw. Her stomach felt wonderfully full. As a bonus, when she turned around, the Corythosaurus looked normal again.

She sighed happily as she trotted back toward the herd. Vole gave her a small nod as she traveled past him. She nodded back over her shoulder.

"That was amazing!" Scratcher exclaimed as he bounded up to her, jumping around in fits of excitement. "That guy came out and you tackled him! You went ROAR and he was, like, NO! And then you ate him!"

Scope chuckled as she watched the youngling dance around, trying to act out the moves she had made. However, Corythosaurus are quadrupeds and lacking talons; so, most of his attempts to copy her failed spectacularly. It wasn't long before he tripped over his own feet and fell onto his side.

"I don't think that you're able to do *all* of my moves," she said as Scratcher got back to his feet.

"Yeah. I'm not bipedal like you." Scratcher huffed at his shortcoming, but then he brightened. "But when I'm all grown up, I can trample everyone!"

Scope laughed. "You do that, but make sure that it's the bad Squamas you're squishing under your feet."

Scratcher nodded enthusiastically. "Bad guys. Got it."

Hoot walked up to them. "It's time to start moving again. Scope, are you walking or are you going to ride?"

His words caused Scope's smile to slowly drop from her face. She took a deep breath. He was willing to let her stay with them. It was a wonderful offer, but she simply couldn't risk another time when she went without food for a week. If that crazed Deinonychus hadn't come along, she would've soon succumbed.

Not only was the risk great, she was almost positive that the Tyrants were still looking for her. Almost every night since she had joined the herd, she could hear distant roars break the peace of the darkness. It was only a matter of time before they would finally sniff her out. The herd was going to be slaughtered if that happened.

Scope released a small sigh. "I'd love to tag along, but you and the herd don't need the stress of having a carnivore in your company." She didn't add anything about the Tyrants. "It'd probably be best if we parted ways."

"You're leaving?" Scratcher said softly, looking at her with large glistening orbs.

She nodded. "Yes. But we'll probably see each other again. Right, Scratcher?"

The youngling immediately perked up at the idea. "Yeah!"

Hoot gave Scope a small nod. "It was nice meeting you, Scope."

They didn't question her why she wanted to leave, which gave her a small relief. She returned the nod, her fringe somewhere near the halfway point of upright and flattened. "You too, Hoot. Thanks for fishing me out."

The large Corythosaurus lifted up a foreleg and waved it in an 'it was nothing' gesture. "You might as well get going. The day's still young."

Scope smiled, then looked into the trees. She took a last glance at Hoot and Scratcher before taking off at a quick jog. She looked back over her shoulder once, and saw her two Corythosaurus friends moving to catch up to the rest of their herd.

She took a turn at a ridge of rocks, and the herd was lost to her sight. She slowed down, but shook her head and sped up again. The herd would be safer now that she had left.

But she would miss them.

Putting the herd out of her mind, she focused on other things, like her surroundings. The sun was streaming down through the trees, the bare branches creating skeleton shadows on the grass and snow. There were a few leftover clouds that were drifting across the sky via a wind she couldn't feel. Mammals were dashing around, darting into underbrush as she passed by. She paid them no mind; her stomach was full and her appetite was fulfilled.

As she found a beaten path cutting through the forest, she paused at its edge. She looked up and down it. One way took her uphill, up toward the peak of a small mountain. The other way took her down toward the lake in the middle of the valley.

Harass made his lair by a waterfall, and that direction was up. She wanted to put as much distance between him and his lackeys as possible. Therefore, she turned to the path in a downhill direction.

Moving was decidedly easier going downhill; all her legs had to do was stay underneath her. Every so often, she had to slow down, lest her pace overwhelm her legs. The path was uneven and wove through the forest, often taking sudden dips over exposed tree roots and small rocks. Her trek down to mountain was speedy, so she soon found herself nearing the valley.

The afternoon was halfway over when the path led her to a river. She slowed considerably as she approached the water. Before she left the tree cover, she sniffed for anything drinking. Smelling nothing, she ventured further. The path took a sharp turn to the left, staying several paces away from the river's edge. She took a few steps onto the shore and looked along it.

This must be one of the rivers that feeds the valley lake, she rationalized.

She moved back to the path and trotted down it, wondering if it was leading her to a place where she could cross the river. She went a far distance before the path finally led her to a large mass of wood. She stopped in her tracks, taken by surprise by the mass of sticks. The heap of dead trees cut off a large portion of the river, making the extra water move to the side and become stagnant. She looked at the stagnant water and saw a few more wood piles, though they were a good deal smaller and were in the middle of the expanse of water. Once or twice she saw some fat brown mammals with strangely flat tails swimming.

She took a closer look at the huge mass that was choking the river. Now that she was taking a good look at it, she could see that the mound was not only made of sticks, but of mud and soggy grasses.

"It's a dam," she murmured.

The dam was very wide and expanded to link both sides of the river. The top was flattened and more than wide enough for an

Edmontonia to walk across. She could see the path resuming on the other side of the dam.

Suddenly, she heard crashing sounds in the trees behind her. She whirled around, fearing the worst, but only saw about five Appalachiosaurus. She sighed, relieved that it hadn't been Tyrants. She started moving toward the dam with the intention of crossing over it.

The Appalachiosaurus were talking to each other in hushed tones. Scope suddenly got a very bad feeling about the bunch and warily glanced at them from over her shoulder. They had stopped just a few paces from the dam and were talking to each other. What worried her was that they were eyeing her like that Deinonychus had.

Her breath hitched in her throat as she came to the assumption that the Appalachiosaurus hadn't found any food over the blizzard, and were very hungry. Even though they were usually scavengers, they were vicious hunters with some vague Tyrant morals when they did hunt.

The bad feeling in her gut exploded, and she began running as fast as he could, not looking back. She heard the Appalachiosaurus roar, and then heard their steps as they chased after her.

Run, run, run, run!

She was very, very glad that she had a full stomach. She could feel her muscles filling with adrenaline. Her pace increased dramatically and she darted forward.

But the Appalachiosaurus were almost twice her size and one of their steps was three of hers. Despite her adrenaline-fueled body, they were eating up the ground that parted them. If she didn't employ some clever tactics to throw them off her tail, she had only a few minutes left before they overtook her.

I am not *dying today!* she thought forcefully.

She was still running downhill, which was like a blessing to her, but the weight of the Appalachiosaurus only made them faster on the incline. She recalled when the Initiation Hunt had failed and she was being chased by T-rex. She used their huge size and weight against them.

With a growl of determination, she darted to the side. The Appalachiosaurus were wholly taken by surprise and they ran past her. She glanced back and barked out a laugh; they were still running downhill and unable to stop.

She faced ahead again and saw that she coming up to the beginnings of a cliff. On one side, the ground fell sharply, while the other side stayed relatively level. Parting the ground was a line of sheer rock. The top of the cliff lacked trees and was completely covered with snow and grass. If she went along the top of the cliff, she would have no shelter or hiding place if the Appalachiosaurus resumed chasing her.

Down it was. She dashed for the sharply declining ground and didn't see the sudden drop-off. Her foot landed on open air and she yelped as she fell. She tumbled head over tail for a good dozen paces before rolling to a stop at the cliff's base. Even though her body ached and bruises were most likely blooming all over, she got to her feet and started moving again. Her first steps were more like desperate stumbles, but she recovered her motor control and jogged properly.

The cliff side was covered with a sheet of vines. In some parts they were thin and she could see the rock behind them, but in other places it was so thick she couldn't see through. She moved toward the thickest sheet of vines, hoping to wriggle herself behind them and use them as a cover. Hopefully, her tan hide wouldn't stand out too much against gray rock and dull green vines.

She poked her head through the sheet of vines and expected her muzzle to brush against stone. However, there seemed to be nothing but air behind the vines. She gave a curious croon as she moved through the vines and entered a hidden cave. The vines fell back into place as soon as her tail finished following her in, as if she had never gone through.

She looked at the vines for a moment before facing the darkness that the cave held further in. As she took a few wary steps, she found her sensitive eyes growing useless. She resorted to stretching her arms out in front of her and feeling her way along.

By her sense of touch, she found out that the cave took a few turns, weaving through the rock of the cliff. The walls were craggy and scraped the tender flesh of her hands. She realized that she would need a light touch.

"Who's there?"

Scope yipped in surprise, her voice echoing eerily in the darkness. Her eyes first widened, then narrowed as she struggled to see. "Who are you? Where are you?" she asked the pitch black.

"In here. Don't try to find me, there's no light in here and any eyes are useless. Now, you didn't answer my question, and in case you've forgotten it, I'll ask again; who are you?"

Scope frowned a little, thinking that she recognized the voice, but she had never been good at placing voices to faces. But as far as she knew, it didn't belong to any of the Tyrants. "Scope."

There was an audible gasp. "Scope? Is that really you?"

"Yeah," she said slowly. "Who are you?"

"Quickly, back to the entrance. I need to see your face."

Scope complied, carefully turning around in the darkness and placing her other hand on the rock as soon as her hand left. If she lost touch and spun around a few times, she would be completely lost. She carefully made her way back toward the entrance, hearing her companion follow her.

When she could see the sunlight up ahead, she looked back. The Squama following her was still too shrouded in shadows to be able to be identified. It wasn't until she reached the vines did she see who it was.

"Spike!" she cried out, lunging forward to wrap her neck around his. "Oh, Spike!"

"Scope, it really is you," Spike said with a happy sigh. "Do you have any idea how worried I've been about you?"

"Worried about me? What about *you!* I thought that you'd been caught and eaten by the Tyrants."

"Speaking of them, how did you escape from them?"

"I ran to the river, fell through the ice, almost drowned, and I've spent the last week with a herd of Corythosaurus." At Spike's incredulous and slightly shocked expression, she went into elaboration.

Once she was finished, Spike nodded. "You've been more fortunate than Blur and I."

"Where *is* Blur?"

"He didn't make it."

Scope looked down. "Oh. Well, how did *you* escape?"

"I managed to use some clever tactics to throw them off my tail, then I ran until I collapsed by the cliff. I found this cave when I was using the vines to help me get back to my feet. This cave is very well hidden, a magnificent secret hideout." He looked behind them, into the darkness. "I felt around and I think that there's some ash and a large flat rock in the back of the cave. If there was some light, we would be able to tell what's back there."

"But the sunlight doesn't reach back there."

"Unfortunately, yes," Spike said with a sigh.

Scope laid down on the floor and vented. "What are we going to do? The Tyrants will never let us rest. I don't want to be constantly looking over my shoulder."

Spike narrowed his eyes and glared out through the vines. "There's only one way Harass can be stopped, and that's by using a weapon exactly like his own against him."

"There's another one?"

"Yes, Harass was wanting to know where I had hidden it away."

Scope had an epiphany. "It's in the clearing, isn't it?"

Spike gave her a sharp nod. "Yes, and we need to get to it before the Tyrants find us."

She shot to her feet. "Well, what are we waiting for? We need to get back, pronto!"

Spike chuckled. "You have a lot of courage and spirit in you, little one. I like that."

CHAPTER TWENTY

Spike led the way back toward the clearing. He guided them through thickets, the densest tree clusters, and forced her to keep to the shadows as much as possible.

Scope hissed softly as a sharp branch grazed her shoulder. She moved away from the offending branch and almost impaled herself on another.

"Do we *have* to go through these thickets?" she whined, trying to ignore her stinging hide.

"They're our best cover," Spike replied cooly, blazing ahead as if the branches weren't creating angry red lines in his hide.

"I made it down to the cave following a public path," she grunted. "Other than the Appalachiosaurus, I was just fine."

"You were blessed," was the immediate reply.

"*Or* the Tyrants haven't made it down this far."

"Yet. That last word you didn't say was *yet*."

Scope huffed hard. "Why are you being so *paranoid?*"

He chuckled softly. "Have you forgotten your earlier statement about looking over your shoulder? Besides, Harass wants me far more than he wants you," he added in a more serious tone.

Scope swallowed. "Okay, so he really hates you. Why?"

"Not here." Spike looked around. "Follow me." He ducked into an even denser area, the branches closing in his wake. Scope followed closely, not wishing to lose him.

He eventually stopped and began breaking the lower branches of several bushes around him. Scope assisted. It took a bit, but they soon created a tiny clear space beneath the thicket. When they laid down, the branches closed overhead and blocked out the sky.

"Now?" Scope asked quietly.

Spike lowered his head. "A very long time ago, before I was hatched, there were two Acrocanthosaurus that went only by the titles of King and Queen. They ruled the entire valley and the surrounding mountains with their league of Tyrants. No one remembers where the King, Queen, or the Tyrants originated.

"It was a very dark time for many, many Turns. To feed their large army of Tyrants, the King and Queen demanded the meat tribute. It forced Squamas both carnivorous and herbivorous to excessively hunt. It quickly progressed to the point where anyone besides someone in their own tribe or herd was shunned, for fear of being a tribute. In order to preserve their own hides, a few already powerful tribes and herds monopolized on this crisis. They massacred everyone around them. Several Squama breeds went rogue or fled the valley entirely.

"Finally, just before I hatched, an Allosaurus called Grit and others realized the valley's dire situation. The birds and pterosaurs had gone. Mammals and reptiles were scarce; over-hunted. Our Squama population had been nearly decreased by a half."

Scope gaped, horrified.

"Grit gathered together a band of rebels dubbed the Defiance. The Defiance was split into several groups and convened in secret at random times; in this way the Tyrants had a harder time finding them. When one of their scouts caught scent of the King's and Queen's offspring hatching, the Defiance decided that it was time to directly assault them."

"Did they win?" Scope asked eagerly.

"Yes, but with great loss. One Tyrant managed to escape with the hatchling Prince. The Defiance spent six Turns searching for them before Grit found them hiding in a cave hidden behind a waterfall; that cave is the very place Harass now uses as his lair. The Defiance killed the Tyrant, but the Prince was discovered to have been raised ignorant and oblivious to his heritage. Because of his innocence, the Prince was only banished for eternity from the valley."

Scope had a feeling that she knew where this was going. "The Prince came back, didn't he?"

"As Harass," Spike said grimly with a nod. "He didn't make his return public until I was a few Turns into adulthood. He had gathered to him what remained of his Tyrant army."

"How'd he find out about his heritage?"

"I'm not sure, but there are rumors that he stumbled across some Squama beyond the valley that had known of what was going on and told him."

"What's that thing on his back?"

Spike paused, an indescribable expression plastered on his face. If Scope had to define the emotions he was showing, it was a strange mix of anxiety, fear, and regret. He took in a shuddering breath before saying, "That is the *Annihilator.*"

"The what?" she said, frowning.

"The *Annihilator.* It's a word in a foreign language that none other than Intel was able to understand or even speak. He learned it from a human who said that the language was *English.*"

Scope felt completely lost. "A who to the what?"

Spike now looked pained. "A human, a bipedal mammal. There used to be a small number of them here in the valley, but they all died in the massacre. She was smaller than us, wore strange hides on her body, and had no tail, sharp teeth, or claws. She had only one patch of fur, and it was long, stringy, and horribly tangled. She was also very pink. She carried a stick with a talon tied to the end, and a much shorter stick with another talon."

"How'd you meet her?" Scope asked, veritably burning with curiosity.

"Intel had gotten frustrated with how slow, cranky, and otherwise troublesome she was, so when she stopped for a nap he left her behind. When she caught up a day later, I was present. She came riding in the back of an Ankylosaurus. She *exploded* at Intel, scolding him in her own language. . ." Spike had to stop and chuckle. "One of the Ankylosaurus remarked that she had run right into the herd with a Tyrannosaurus on her heels! Intel was taken aback at the speed she was supposed to have displayed; she rivaled a sprinting Troodon."

"That's not it, is it?" Scope asked, holding back a few of her snickers.

"It wasn't long before the Tyrants found us and attacked. The human used her two sticks to do some considerable damage to them. She even took down at least one of the three Tyranno-saurs. Unfortunately, by the end of the fight, Intel was taken and the human was gravely injured. I took her back to her home through a strange hole in the air. I cannot describe what I saw there, but it was simply incredible."

"How long ago was this?" Scope asked.

"Shortly before your hatching."

Scope nodded slowly. "And that thing that you said is like the *Annihilator,* what's it called?"

"The *Intimidator.* Intel gave it to me for safekeeping. I've hidden it away in a place that only myself and a select few had known. You and I are the only ones left. We need to get to it and place it on your back."

"What?" Scope sputtered in shock. "*My* back? Why would it go on my back?"

"Intel managed to learn from the human how the object works. It is a weapon capable of spitting cylinders of fire and a red light capable of slicing items far easier than our toe claws could cut through meat, plus some sort of liquid that fuels a function that was unable to be translated. The *Intimidator* needs to be put on your back, as that's the only way to control it."

"Wait, what happened to *your* back?" Scope said. "Are you saying that I'm the Worthy One?"

Spike gave her a level stare. "Yes. You've displayed great courage by sacrificing yourself to protect Blur and me. Over the Turns, I have found you brave, yet meek, and you have stood up to others without backing down. Scope, you are the Worthy One."

I'm the Worthy One? she kept thinking over and over again. "Spike, I don't think that I deserve it."

Spike shot her a pleased smile. "And that statement is exactly why I think you to be the Worthy One." Standing, he added, "Come along, we need to keep moving."

Scope said not another word on the subject.

It took them two days before Scope began seeing familiar landmarks. She knew that they were close to the clearing, and thus close to the *Intimidator's* hiding place.

Spike was constantly looking around and sniffing the air. Scope didn't need to sniff to know that the area *reeked* of Tyrants.

They had to be keeping a close watch on the clearing, as if they had a hunch that Spike had hidden the *Intimidator* in the area; and he would come back for it.

The Tyrants had left tracks everywhere, including areas where the trees grew close together. Many tree limbs were broken off. Deep T-rex tracks that dwarfed Scope's littered the ground. The Tyrants were definitely present.

When Spike suddenly stopped, Scope turned to him to see what was wrong. He sniffed the air, then looked around. "This way, quickly!" he hissed in a volume just below a whisper. She followed him to a cluster of rocks. Some of them had fallen trees lying on them, many of which seemed to be lying in such a way it suggested that something very big had knocked them over in a single direction. Spike had her scramble underneath one of the larger bunches of fallen trees before scurrying under them himself.

Scope grunted as she shifted, making room for him.

"Quiet," Spike whispered to her. He had turned himself around so that he was looking out the way they had come in.

She nodded and laid as still as she could. While Spike eyed whatever he saw or scented outside, she took a good look at their impromptu hideout. The fallen trees had toppled over in a tight cluster, creating a thick roof. Through the gaps streamed rays of sunlight that could easily be seen thanks to the dust she and Scope had kicked up on their way in. The hideout was just large enough for both of them to hide in comfortably.

After a few minutes of hiding, she heard the sounds of several pairs of feet moving through the dry leaves. A second later, half a dozen Coelurus came into sight. They made no sign that they knew that she and Spike were there, though several of them sniffed and looked around without breaking pace. A moment after they appeared, they vanished into the trees.

Spike waited a long moment before he let out a small sigh. "We'll stay here until nightfall," he said. "The dark will be our cover."

Scope nodded but said nothing. She lowered her head and closed her eyes, intending to nap until Spike woke her up. But she couldn't calm down her nerves enough for her to even doze. There was simply too much stress and the air simply radiated danger. Finally opening her eyes, she decided that the best pastime she could think up would be watching the sun splotches on the ground move as the sun tracked across its path. It was incredibly boring, but she couldn't do much else.

And then the ground started to rhythmically shake. Scope froze, holding her breath. Spike seemed to do the same thing.

As the earth-quaking steps grew closer, Scope prayed, *Oh, please, no! Did they find us? Please, don't let them have found us!*

The steps stopped. Scope moved only her eyes and saw bits and pieces of two T-rex through the wood roof. They were looking directly at their hiding place. One of them leaned down and opened its mouth. Scope bit back a shriek as the T-rex used its maw to lift up a large portion of the trees and throw them aside, revealing the two Utahraptors hiding underneath.

Scope shivered in fear. At the T-rex's feet were the half dozen Coelurus that had passed by earlier. So they *had* been sniffed out, or glimpsed.

"Get up, Utahraptor scum," one of the T-rex bellowed. "King Harass will be very pleased upon your return."

She glanced at Spike, wondering if it was worth it to run or not. Despair was in his eyes as he slowly got to his feet, and she realized that there was no running for now. As they started moving, she knew that they were walking right back to torture and their own deaths.

She had never felt so lost and small.

Chapter Twenty One

The Acrocanthosaurus gazed down at the two Utahraptors with an expression of smugness. "Missed me?" Harass asked in a pleased tone.

Scope and Spike were silent. Spike glared at the giant beast that bore the *Annihilator.*

Harass' smug look faded a little. "Well, I do hope that you had a nice little trip. Managed to make it within a few hundred paces of your darling clearing, so I heard."

Scope had been miserable the entire way back to the water-fall. Every step felt heavier and heavier, and now she could barely lift a toe. The Tyrants that had found them were merciless in the subject of rest; they had walked to the waterfall in only a day and a half because she and Spike were not allowed to sleep or even stop.

Initially, Spike had been downcast and nearly listless, which had scared Scope very much. However, near the end of their trek, he had regained some defiance. His fighting spirit wasn't gone yet.

Harass chuckled, a terrible sound that sent chills down Scope's spine. "Spike, during your impromptu leave of absence, I've come up with the most wonderful idea. If you were Grit himself, I'd have more pleasure, but you're the next best thing. I've decided that I'll give you two a taste of what was given to me."

Scope didn't like the sound of that. Not at all.

"Spike," Harass said with a sinister grin, "you're her guardian, are you not?"

Spike's eyes widened. His fringe, which had been erect in defiance, flattened to become flush with his neck, becoming virtually indistinguishable.

Scope's jaw dropped as tears welled up in her eyes. *No!*

"Don't worry yourself in your last moments, Spike," Harass said, stepping closer. "She'll live. I can't guarantee how long she'll last after she enters the Borderlands, though." He raised a gargantuan foot directly above Spike, casting a terrible dark shadow over the adult Utahraptor. "Any last words?"

Spike whirled around to look at Scope. She felt a few tears fall down her cheeks at the resigned yet urgent expression on his face. "Save them all," Spike said softly, as if he was at peace with dying. "Scope, save them all."

"Good bye," Harass said gleefully, then smashed down his foot.

Scope turned away, but even the sound couldn't be ignored. It was a cacophony of noise that would scar her memory for the rest of her life. She let out a few sobs, refusing to turn around and see what was left of her only fragment of family, friends, and good times past.

"My Coelurus will show you to the mountain pass that will take you into the Borderlands," Harass said. Scope knew that he was speaking to her. "Once you exit the mountains, *never* come back. If your face is ever seen within these mountains again, you shall be killed on sight. Am I understood?"

She didn't trust herself to talk without either screaming at the tyrant king or breaking down into a sobbing mess. She nodded.

Two dozen Coelurus moved forward, one of them roughly bumping against Scope. "Let's get going," it said, hissing. "Too bad we can't kill you unless you come back."

"Maybe you will," the other one said, cackling. "You can give us a lovely little game of chase. How long will you last, I wonder, before you're caught?"

Scope began walking, her head hanging low. She just didn't have the heart or energy to keep it up in a more comfortable position.

It was another arduous walk to the mountain pass that led to the Borderlands. It was well into the night by the time they reached it. The moon was out and at its fullest. By using its light,

Scope could see Tyrants standing on rocky niches that were dotted along the sides of the pass. She couldn't hear them; but by the way their teeth showed, she knew that they were sneering at her.

"You have a ten second head start," one of the Coelurus behind her said. "Then we chase you. If we catch you, you're dead. If you get away. . . well, you're just going to have to find a way to live."

Scope gulped, staring at the path ahead. It was craggy, rocky, and scattered with prickly shrubs. It certainly wasn't the best-looking way to get to the Borderlands. She wondered if the Borderlands would look as inhospitable as the pass.

"Well, what are you waiting for? You have seven seconds left."

With a choking sound, she darted forward. The way was uneven, and she had to bound from one place to another. Her legs hurt, she was exhausted from staying up for more than two days without sleep, and her outlook on life was at an all-time low, so her speed left something to be desired. She counted down the seconds in her head as she worked to put as much distance between herself and the Coelurus as possible.

When she heard the Coelurus give off a loud screech, she was thankful to feel the adrenaline kick in. She grunted as she accelerated, moving from a tired run to a full sprint. Thankfully, the cragginess of the ground only lasted ninety paces before dissipating into forest. As she entered, she picked a random direction and accelerated, weaving through the trees as best as she could. Her breath came in quick pants and her eyes were at their widest so that she could see as much as she could in the nighttime darkness.

At first, she could hear the Coelurus coming after her. They moved noisily, as if they were purposely telling her that they were there. However, their noises started to dwindle and became fainter. Scope would have liked to believe that she was too fast for them, but she had the feeling that they were dropping back so that they didn't become lost. After all, that was surely their intention; to get her so hopelessly lost that she couldn't find her way back so easily.

Even after she could no longer hear the Coelurus, she kept running. It was in her health's better interest to be paranoid and think that they had only quieted down so they could jump her when she stopped.

It was when her legs burned with overexertion that she did slow and stop. Her adrenaline rush had long faded and she was only running on fumes. She was hungry and tired.

With a long sigh, she stumbled over to the nearest tree, her feet tripping on the ground. She collapsed at its base and, too exhausted to even get into a comfortable position, fell asleep.

Bird song and sunlight greeted her the following morning. She groaned softly when she tried to move; she felt as stiff as a birch tree. Her muscles painfully protested as she stood, and once she was on her feet she didn't dare to try and take a step for the fear of her leg buckling.

Her stomach growled at her, and she winced. It had been over three days since she had last eaten. Thankfully, she could smell and hear mammals nearby, so food was only a hunting trip and maybe a sprint or two away.

Now, if only she could get her legs working. . .

She took a cautious baby step, her leg crumpled, and she

ended up on the ground. She huffed, her breath blowing the fallen leaves a little.

Somehow, that one tumble was a breaking of the dam that kept her tears at bay. First she whimpered, then broke out into loud sobs. As she cried, she thought of the times when her world was right, and fantasies that would make it better. Like her mother witnessing her first snow. Her Initiation Hunt came back with a heap of trophies. *Her tribe being alive and well.*

It was all her fault. She spoke to the two Coelurus, that led to the fight in which her mother died. Even though their success over the Edmontonia that drew the Tyrants toward the location of an easy meal wasn't entirely her fault, *she* was the lone survivor that led them to the clearing. Everyone had died because of *her* actions. And not only did she have the newfound responsibility of the Worthy One, she was the sole survivor of a tribe consisting of nearly 50 Utahraptors.

She sniffled, feeling so very alone in a big, hostile world. There was a large area of damp ground beneath her head. Her eyes ached.

What are you going to do, Scope? she asked herself. *Everyone's dead. The only others you do know are herbivores and they could've had anything happen to them by now. I'm banished, shelterless, friendless, and forsaken. What am I going to do?*

She didn't want to die, so that meant that she had to start moving and look for shelter and food. Food was close by, scurrying all over the forest floor. If she could get back to walking, she could hunt one of the mammals, eat it for breakfast, and then start looking for a place to stay.

Sounded like a good plan.

With a growl of determination, she shoved herself to her feet. Her leg muscles protested the weight put upon them, but she ignored them in favor of living. Now that she was on her feet, she didn't go straight for a mammal. Instead, she began walking around the tree she had slept under, getting her legs back under control.

It took longer than she would've liked. Once she felt enough strength, she moved toward a bunch of dense bushes, seeing them as a potential hiding place from which she could ambush. Making herself comfortable in the shrubs, she settled down to wait.

It didn't take long for an oblivious mammal to come walking by. As it ruffled its nose through the fallen leaves in search of food, she quietly licked her lips. The mammal was very plump and she was sure that it was equally juicy. Scope waited until the mammal came closer before lunging. The prey had barely enough time to look up before she landed on its back. It writhed beneath one of her feet, struggling to get free. She didn't give it a chance. She quickly ending its life by grasping it in her mouth and giving it a violent shake to break its neck.

She was right. The mammal was very juicy.

Once she had licked the bones clean, she sighed and looked around. She needed to find shelter. To get a sense of her surroundings, she raised her head and sniffed deeply. The faint breeze carried with it hundreds of scents. She singled a few of them out and identified them: there was a herd of herbivores a far distance away; the mammals running around; and a large source of water not far away. She decided to head toward the water source, as she was going to get thirsty sooner or later. She didn't want to risk going so far from water that she died from dehydration.

Her legs carried her in a brisk trot that was easy to maintain. Her breath came smoothly and rhythmically. The trees passed by as she moved in and out of shadows.

Eventually, she could see the water through the trees up ahead. The forest bled away as she got closer, soon stopping altogether and revealing a long stretch of dull yellow sand. Small waves lapped against the shore. Pterosaurs and water fowl flew over the water, occasionally diving to grab a fish. Scope looked across the expanse of water and could just see the hazy outlines of mountains on the far side.

She approached the water, wondering if it was safe to drink. She slowly bent her head and cautiously lapped at a passing wave. It tasted slightly salty, but was otherwise like the pond that was in her old clearing home. She drank until she felt full, then trotted back to the trees to search for a place to stay.

The sun slowly crept across the sky, and it was her only source of direction until it reached its peak. She traveled all through the morning and rested until the sun reached the point where she could use it as a veritable North Star. If she had to guess, she would think that she covered over five hundred square paces by mid afternoon.

During her wandering, she encountered a few herds of herbivores (Triceratops, Edmontonia, and Brachiosaurus) and came across a rather large Troodon hunting party. She had requested assistance from all of the groups, but the herbivores had shied away and the Troodons said that their band was running short on food and the area didn't need yet another carnivore that was even larger than they were.

Clouds, heavy and dark, started rolling in around noon, accompanied by distant thunder and flashes of light. A cold wind whipped up, ruffling Scope's fringe and causing it to make a constant flapping sound. The clouds came fast and soon covered up the sun. Scope was hurriedly searching for any kind of shelter as she felt the first raindrops fall against her hide.

Then, as if someone had destroyed a dam, the few gentle raindrops became a thick torrent of pelting water. She rushed around half blind as the water ran into her eyes. It was coming down so thickly she could barely see three paces in front of her. All she could hear was rainwater. Her mind kept flashing back to the blizzard, where many of the remainder of the tribe had frozen to death. Thankfully, though, this was only a rain storm and there was no way she could freeze to death.

Drown, maybe, she thought wryly as she continued searching for *any* place that could offer her a decent protection from the rain. *Freeze, no.*

It was dark by the time she gave up and huddled under a thick fir tree. Its many bushy branches kept some of the rain from striking her body, but it would be impossible to become dry again until the storm ended. Thunder was almost a constant noise, and she wondered if she could actually navigate by the following lightning that lit up the night like day.

She yelped as a twirling mass of blinding light struck the very tree under which she was sheltering. There was a wave of sparks, and then she smelled burning wood. Despite the downpour, half of the tree burst into giant red flames. Not wanting to become burned, she dashed back into the rain and didn't look back.

It seemed like forever before the rain stopped, and was a little longer before she saw the first glimmer of sunlight. When the sunlight struck the ground, raindrops glistened like tiny jewels. The entire forest was alit with sparkles, and it was a beautiful picture.

Scope didn't appreciate the beauty. She was everything but

thirsty. The world seemed out to get her.

She sniffed the air to see if there were any mammals around she could hunt. Unfortunately, she couldn't even get a whiff of one. With her stomach growling, she followed the scent of water back to the small inland freshwater sea. Standing at its edge, she peered into the shallows. Silhouettes darted back and forth beneath the surface. She didn't think that she'd ever had anything marine to eat before, but there was a first time for everything. She patiently waited for the school of fish to draw closer to her position. Then she pounced.

The water splashed around her, and the fish in the area quickly swam away. Her feet were surrounded by a cloud of silt and sand that she couldn't see through. She bent her head down toward the water. As her muzzle brushed the surface, she held her breath. Her mouth entered the water and she blindly searched around her feet. As she was running out of air, she felt something wriggling that was pinned beneath her right foot. She tightly bit it and raised her head from the water. Looking cross-eyed at her muzzle, she saw that there was a small fish weakly struggling in her mouth.

Dinner was ready. She walked back to land and dropped the now drowned fish on the sand. Ignoring the tiny grains of crushed rock, she ripped out a section of its side. She nursed her sliver of meat, her face contorting as she tried to decide whether she liked the taste of fish meat or not. She swallowed and figured that a snack was better than nothing.

When she was done eating, she trotted away from the shoreline and back into the forest. She still had to find herself a place to stay. She doubted that the Troodons would let her stay with them and she had massive doubt that any of the herbivores would let her travel with them like Vole had.

I was in a desperate position then, she thought as she moved.

Their consciences wouldn't let me die. Now that I'm somewhat healthy again, why would any herds take the risk of me turning on them?

She let out a long sigh. Scope, the lone Utahraptor and last remnant of a once prosperous tribe, was homeless and needed a home. She looked around actively. She didn't want to suffer through another shelterless night.

Scope was feeling disheartened and depressed; nothing new there.

She had been searching all afternoon, and sundown was approaching fast. Her right flank sported a nasty-looking bite mark, courtesy of a Troodon when she had stumbled upon the woody area they claimed as their home. The bite didn't hurt much, but it was a persistent stinging sensation that was her latest reminder that she still hadn't found a home and was not accepted by the locals.

A sudden clamor overhead caused her to look up, a reflex she had undoubtedly gotten from her experience with the larger Tyrants. It was only a large flock of birds flying in a tight formation. It was the sounds of their chirping and wing beats that had drawn her attention.

Then one of her feet hit thin air. Scope gasped, realizing as she fell that she hadn't stopped walking when she looked up. Fortunately, the pit she appeared to have fallen into wasn't very deep, and she had only fallen a few paces before landing in a shallow pond. She sputtered and coughed as water got into her lungs.

Rising to her feet, she vigorously shook her body to dislodge the water. It flew off of her in shining drops that landed back in the pond with tiny splashes. She coughed a few more times to clear her airways, then swallowed to get rid of the rough feeling left behind.

She took a look around the pit she had fallen into. It wasn't very deep, maybe two or three paces, but it was wide. A fully grown Appalachiosaurus could stretch out comfortably at the pit's widest point. The bottom of the pit had a gentle slope and the pond she was standing in was at the bottom end. There were a few sapling trees scattered around the pit, as well as a couple bushes and dozens of budding flowers. The walls of the pit alternated between sheer rock and dirt. At the upper end of the pit she saw a large hole in the rock, which she wondered was a cave or not.

Deciding to satisfy her curiosity, she emerged from the pond and strode to the hole in the rock. As she came closer, she estimated the hole to be roughly a pace and a half wide and tall. Poking her head into the hole, she let her eyes adjust to the darkness. Then she saw that it was a rather large hole, or a small cave, with a floor of very compact dirt, and large enough to comfortably house her.

She sniffed the dirt and looked around, searching for any signs of other inhabitants. If the pit was already a home to someone else, she didn't want to be caught resting here when it came back. Thankfully, the only footprints in the dirt were her own, and she smelled no traces of any other Squama. *But I* do *smell several species of mammals.*

She moved into the grotto and laid down to test out how it felt. Wriggling around a bit, she decided that it would make a decent place to sleep once she got some leaves and moss to make a nest.

Not getting up from her place in the grotto, she looked out to the rest of the pit. *I can stay here,* she thought. *It's secluded, sheltered, and the hole is at the perfect spot so that there won't be any runoff in here when it rains.*

She laid her head on the ground and hummed thoughtfully. She smelled mammals, a ready water source, and a shelter. There weren't any Tyrants out in the Borderlands beyond the valley mountains, so she didn't have to be constantly looking over her shoulder and jumping at shadows.

Maybe life as a banished Squama wouldn't be so bad.

CHAPTER TWENTY TWO

Scope took a deep breath of the late morning air. She stood upon a very high cliff that overlooked a large portion of the Borderlands that she now called her home. A warm Hot Season breeze drifted by her face, causing her to sigh as it caressed her skin.

It had been over a Turn since her banishment. She almost didn't care anymore about it. There weren't any Tyrants to enforce her status, and there didn't seem to be any at all in the Borderlands. The Tyrants were out of sight and almost always out of mind. The locals didn't even seem to know about their presence in the valley.

The Borderlands was a haven. She had a place to stay and ample amounts of food and water. It had taken her until almost the Colors Season to convince the Troodon tribe that she meant no ill will toward them. The herds were entirely theirs; after all, no Utah-raptor could manage to take down even a Triceratops solo. Once she had convinced the Troodons, they had begun letting her participate in their hunts and have a small percentage of the kill. Even then, 90% of her diet still consisted of small mammals.

She shifted her weight, feeling the muscles in her legs shifting with her. With all of the exercise she was getting daily, her body had filled out. She had grown taller, and estimated that she was almost Spike's height. Her body rippled with sinew and muscle. There was little to no excess fat on her.

The breeze moved so that it was blowing in from the valley's direction. Scope grimaced as she caught the traces of Tyrant stenches. Even though she hadn't gone anywhere near the mountain pass over the past Turn, she instinctively knew that Harass and his followers were steadily overtaking the valley. She could almost sense the proverbial dark cloud that seemed to envelope the entire valley and its mountains like a black veil. If there was to be no resistance to the Acrocanthosaurus, Harass would imprison the entire valley in his tyrannic claws.

"Save them all. Scope, save them all."

Scope growled as Spike's last words echoed in her mind. "How can I do anything, Spike?" she murmured. "Tyrants guard the pass and the clearing. To even try to get to the *Intimidator* is suicide." She looked up to the pristine blue and cloud-speckled sky as if she was searching for her old mentor there. "I'd need help, Spike. I can't do it by myself."

She fell silent, half hoping that a few words of inspiration, hope, that would giver her victory over Harass.

She needed *something* to help her.

Nothing came to her. Part of her wanted to cry. The other part gave the impression of "I've done my best."

With a sigh, she moved away from the edge of the cliff and jogged toward her favorite ambush spot. She was hungry and hoped to snag a mammal for brunch.

When she reached her ambush spot, she hunkered down inside of a large and dense bush. Her tail curled around her body so that it didn't stay out in the open and supply a complete giveaway to her position.

It wasn't long before she heard the telltale rustling of an approaching mammal. She smirked to herself, knowing that in the Hot Season heat, mammals were either napping in the shadows or out foraging. Eat or sleep.

The mammal in question came out from under a bush. It raised its slender muzzle into the air and sniffed. The small black nose twitched, shaking the neighboring whiskers.

Scope was about to pounce when she heard a distant crashing sound, like something recklessly running through the forest. The mammal vanished, spooked into hiding. Knowing that she wouldn't be getting anything to eat while those noises were going on, Scope rose from her bush and warily trotted toward the source of the disturbance.

It seemed to be drawing nearer. Scope moved into a thicket and waited. Less than a minute later, a bipedal carnivore of a species she had never seen before burst into sight. The small carnivore kept looking over its shoulder. As it passed by, Scope tensed as a pursuing T-rex appeared. When the Tyrant passed, Scope waited a moment before coming out of the thicket.

"What's a Tyrant doing here?" she wondered aloud. She pondered the question for a moment before deciding to follow the two.

Despite the speed at which the T-rex and the unknown carnivore were going, Scope managed to catch up to them. She kept the T-rex's tail within sight. As they ran, Scope noticed that they were nearing the top of the cliff. She dropped back, knowing that it was a dead end up there and the smaller carnivore would have to double back.

She lost sight of the them, but she continued until she reached the peak of the cliff. Moving to hide behind a tree, she saw that the T-rex had the smaller carnivore cornered at the cliff edge. The smaller carnivore looked terrified, alternating between looking past its feet at the long drop and the T-rex.

Scope frowned. *That carnivore's going to be that Tyrant's lunch if I don't do something!* Without letting herself have time to second-guess herself, she burst from hiding and ran at the T-rex's feet. She used a toe claw to slash at a leg before skipping away.

The T-rex, expectedly, wasn't injured badly but she *had* attracted its attention. It turned around and growled at her.

"You want a lunch?" Scope yelled at the Tyrant. "Come and get me! I'm tastier."

"Are you crazy?" the smaller carnivore said, eyes wide in shock. It was a female, maybe her own age.

The T-rex chuckled. "If you insist," it said to Scope before moving to bite her.

Scope dodged the gigantic mouth and gave a mad dash

away. "You missed me, you big bully!" she said over her shoulder, hoping that taunting it would cause it to follow her.

With a roar, the T-rex took chase.

Scope smirked as she gave the Tyrant a nice game of chase before doubling back toward the cliff, where the small carnivore still stood. The carnivore dove out of the way as they neared. Scope could feel the ground pounding as the T-rex sped up.

Perfect, Scope thought as she approached the cliff edge. Just before she would run headlong into thin air, she made a tight turn and skidded to a stop.

The T-rex bellowed as it tried to stop, but its weight and momentum carried it over the edge of the cliff. It continued roaring as it fell, which cut off abruptly when it hit the ground.

Scope peered over the edge at the inert body far below. "That always works," she said victoriously. "They always fall for it, too." She moved away from the edge and looked around. *Now, where's the other one?* It was nowhere to be seen.

With a quiet grumble, she looked down at the ground. Imprinted in the soft dirt and tender grass were footprints. The carnivore had run off. Scope began slowly trotting, keeping her gaze focused on the prints. They led her down the slope of the cliff and toward an area where she knew a herd of Triceratops liked to frequent. She slowed to a walk as she neared the place. There was a herd up ahead and the prints to led into a bush that was located quite close to the herbivores.

Scope shook her head. "You'll never be able to kill one of them by yourself," she said. "The Triceratops may seem armorless and easy to kill, but those tails can pack a decent punch; and I wouldn't even go anywhere near the head."

The Triceratops' heads sprang up. They saw her, then galloped away into the trees.

The bush rustled, then the carnivore came out. She was glaring at Scope. "You scared them off!" she said angrily. "I had one of them in my sights!"

"You can't take down one of them solo," Scope retorted.

"I can try." The carnivore paused and narrowed her eyes. "Hey, you're the one that gave the Tyrant a tumble."

Scope nodded. "You're welcome, by the way. They can never maneuver well at high speeds, it'd be best for you to remember that if you ever find yourself chased by another one."

"I don't plan on that."

"Good. Um, what's your name? And your species while you're at it. I've never seen a carnivore like you before."

"I'm Rove, a Dilophosaurus."

Scope looked over Rove with an appraising gaze. The Dilophosaurus was a tad bit larger than herself, with a reddish tan hide, two small crests in the middle of the nose and a thin ridge of tall spines that ran down half of the neck. Rove had long arms that ended in slender, three-fingered hands.

"Nice to meet you, Rove," Scope said with a nod. "I'm Scope. So, what brought you to the Borderlands? There's not many that come here."

Rove snorted. "I'm from the valley, part of the resistance against Harass and his Tyrants."

Scope blinked. "The Defiance is back?"

"How'd you know what we call ourselves?" Rove said slowly, narrowing her eyes.

"I was told the history of the valley. It's what the last uprising against Harass' parents was called."

"Ah. Well, the Defiance group of which I was a member was discovered by Tyrants. They split us up, you know, the whole divide and conquer thing? Well, I, somehow, managed to make it all the way through the pass and here without them catching and killing me."

Scope nodded thoughtfully. "Hey, are you hungry? Let's snag a few mammals, and I can take you to my place so that we can talk with a little more privacy. Follow me, I'll show you the nearest best ambush spot."

A little while later, Scope led Rove to her pit home. Both of them carried a limp mammal in their mouths. Scope was salivating, anticipating the first bite into her plump catch. She led Rove down a small ramp into the pit, then dropped the mammal near the pond.

"Talk while we eat, Rove," Scope insisted, lying down next to her mammal.

Rove complied and tore a large chunk of flesh from her mammal. After she had swallowed, she said, "How long have you been living here in the Borderlands?"

"A little over a Turn," Scope replied.

Rove's eyes widened. "A whole Turn? Is it really as bad here as they say?"

"Depends on what they say."

"There's hardly any food here. The carnivores here are bigger than an Allosaurus. It's rocky and desolate and you'll probably die within a week."

Scope barked out a laugh. "The only rocky and desolate area I've seen is the mountain pass that links the Borderlands and the valley, though that speculation isn't really surprising since bare rocks are all that can be seen from in the pass. I actually did wonder about that before I made it to the trees. And the only carnivores I've seen other than myself are the Troodons, and they're in no way larger than an Allosaurus. *I'm* the largest predator here, probably. And food? Well, mammals frolic all over the place and I've spotted at least a dozen herds with three kinds of herbivores."

"I guess, then, that it was all rumors," Rove said quietly as she looked up at the forest above the pit.

"Quite." Scope took another bite of her meal. "So, can you tell me how the valley fares? I can only glean so much from the pterosaurs that migrate here and there."

Rove's lips became a thin line. "It's not very good at all, I'm afraid. The Tyrants have pretty much taken over the entire valley. The Defiance has come up again and, as much as I've been able to learn from the officers, the Defiance is organized into small, independent groups so that they'll be harder to find and eliminate."

Scope frowned. "Something needs to be done about the Tyrants. Someone needs to take down the head."

"Harass?" Rove exclaimed. "Scope, he's the largest carnivore in the valley and the Borderlands! Not to mention that he has a weapon of mass destruction on his back. He's invulnerable!"

Scope looked down at her half-finished meal, deep in thought. After a moment, she said, "So, where're you from? The lake area? One of the mountains?"

"Actually, none of the above. My tribe's a nomad one. We arrived in the valley a couple Turns ago. I was actually hatched in the Great Desert. I've liked the area around Concave Peak, but no one lives there now. The place is *swarming* with Tyrants."

Scope nodded absently, thinking hard. "Okay. Rove, do you know where the other Defiance groups are?"

"Um, I know of a couple, they might still be in action. But I have no idea of their locations; they're always moving here and there. It's all about keeping the Tyrants on their toes. I know the general area, if that helps."

"It does. You need to take me to one of the groups."

Rove's eyes widened. "Go *back?* Scope, if we go back, we'll die!"

Scope slowly rose to her feet so that she was looking down at the Dilophosaurus. "Now, you're going to lead me to the nearest Defiance group where I can offer my services."

"What? Right now, now?" Rove asked, gaping.

"No, not right now. We need to prepare. Stockpile energy. Get eating. We have half the day left to catch as many mammals as possible." Scope gulped down the rest of her meal and powerfully strode toward the ramp.

"What *are* you talking about?"

Scope paused to look over her shoulder. "There's no telling how much the mammal population has declined in the valley, and I don't want to be constantly hiding *and* hunting at the same time. Finish your meal and follow me. We have a lot to do."

CHAPTER TWENTY THREE

Scope peered around the edge of a tall, craggy rock. She cautiously sniffed the air and immediately caught the scent of Tyrants. Narrowing her eyes, she swept her gaze over the rocky cliffs that lined both sides of the mountain pass.

There, she thought, smiling grimly.

The Tyrant she had spotted was obviously carefully picked to man the post that overlooked the pass; the Coelurus was a dull gray with darker gray splotches all over its body, causing it to blend in quite well with the cliff if it kept perfectly still. Scope had managed to see it only by incorporating her keen vision.

"What do you see?" Rove whispered from behind her.

"A Coelurus," Scope said, barely opening her mouth or even twitching toward the Dilophosaurus behind her. Scope squinted at the still form of the Tyrant. The Coelurus was lying on its stomach. "Looks to be sleeping."

"That's a good thing, right? Let's sneak by before it wakes up!"

"Wait." Scope looked carefully further down the stretch of the pass. It took her a moment, but she found another Coelurus standing watch about forty paces away. It was vigilant in its duties, constantly moving its head and gaze. "I see another one. Awake and watching."

"Rats."

"Tasty, but I'm not hungry."

"You know what I meant."

"Stop talking, they could hear us."

"You're changing the subject."

"*Hush!*"

Scope glanced at a sharp dip in the ground not too far from where she and Rove currently hid. From what she could tell, the dip was deep and wide enough for them to dart within until they could move toward another hiding spot. The dip was directly next to a rock that conveniently blocked the alert Coelurus from seeing the dip.

She moved her attention back to the alert Coelurus, trying to find a set pattern in its surveillance. It took her several minutes, but she managed to notice that they had about three seconds to move before the Coelurus would look their way once more.

"On my mark," Scope murmured just loud enough for Rove to hear. "Get ready."

"Ready."

Scope paused. "Mark." She darted forward, keeping as quiet as possible as she navigated through the rough terrain. When she reached the dip, she slammed her body against the rock and held completely still. Rove followed suit.

After taking several deep breaths in a vain effort to slow down her beating heart, Scope slowly extended her neck so that she could see around the rock. The alert Coelurus was frozen, staring directly at one place. Scope tracked its gaze and found that it was looking straight at their former hiding spot. Scope remained completely still, hoping that the Coelurus wouldn't sound the alarm.

It felt like hours before the Coelurus seemed to huff and resumed its pattern.

Scope released a breath she didn't know that she'd been holding, then looked for the next spot to dart to.

"Are we almost to the end of the pass yet?"

Scope held back a sigh; Rove had already asked that question half a dozen times. "Not quite, but I can see it from here."

There! Scope spotted a series of dense but short rocks. If she and Rove crouched, they could probably remain unnoticed. Scope looked for another sentry other than the Coelurus.

Oh, wonderful, Scope thought sarcastically.

There was a T-rex, one of the largest she'd seen yet, leaning against the side of a cliff. Its eyes were closed, but she couldn't tell whether it was asleep or not. Even if it was awake, the series of rocks was clearly within its eyeshot. She would just have to take a massive risk and hope that it was sleeping.

"Tyrannosaurus dead ahead," Scope whispered. "Be as quiet as possible. On my mark."

She glanced back to the alert Coelurus. In just another moment, it would be looking away. This time, they had about six seconds to not only get past it but past the might-not-be-sleeping T-rex, too.

"Mark."

Scope tried to simultaneously keep the alert Coelurus in her peripheral vision, stay quiet, and make sure that the T-rex wasn't going to surge to life as they passed by. Thankfully, the T-rex remained motionless and they moved behind a rock that placed both the Coelurus and the T-rex out of sight.

Breathing shallowly, Scope could see that they were getting close to the end of the mountain pass. She could almost see the individual leaves on the trees. But they couldn't make a mad dash there now. There was no telling how many Tyrants were hidden in the forest, and she still had to find out if there were any more stationed in the pass.

Yes, there was another Coelurus, sitting down its posted rocky ledge. The head was stiffly upright, but it was motionless. Like all the others in the pass, it had an excellent camouflage. It was the only Tyrant left between them and the end of the pass.

The last Coelurus wasn't moving at all, though she could tell that its eyes were wide open. The only reasons she could think of was that it was daydreaming or thinking. Even if it was otherwise occupied, they would be spotted in an instant.

"What are we waiting for?" Rove whispered.

"Coelurus."

"Can't we run for it?"

Scope fixed Rove with a glare. "Okay, then *you* can end up with Tyrants on your heels."

Rove snorted. "Who twisted your tail?"

"I'm trying to get us to safety. If you want to be chased, go right ahead. If you don't, let me figure out what to do about the Coelurus."

Scope placed her attention back on the unmoving Tyrant. The Coelurus had shifted while she had been arguing with Rove, and now it was lying down. The head was nestled in between the arms.

Is it sleeping now? Scope wondered. She decided that it was a blessing. "Get ready to move again."

She singled out a thick group of trees. Glancing around, she saw that there didn't seem to be any more Tyrants in sight other than the formerly unmoving Coelurus. The Coelurus still seemed to be dozing.

Just before she could call for the next move, a thundering sound appeared in the distance. Scope ducked behind the rock as the Coelurus and the T-rex looked toward the source of the noise.

"What's that?" Rove queried quietly.

Scope shrugged, squinting into the forest.

The thundering grew louder, and then a large herd of Brachiosaurus emerged from the trees. Their necks stuck up in the air like trees as their legs pushed their heavyset bodies forward. Dust was being kicked up from beneath their gigantic feet. Scope pressed herself against the rock as the Brachiosaurus stampeded past. She tried not to sneeze from the airborne dust, but it probably wouldn't have been heard over the booming.

As the Brachiosaurus started to vanish further down the mountain pass, Scope risked a peek. She caught a glimpse of some T-rex snapping at the stragglers' heels, driving them faster. The stragglers all sported multiple light wounds from the abuse. The T-rex broke off, letting the Brachiosaurus herd escape into the Borderlands.

Scope was disturbed by how the Tyrants began to laugh and mock the fleeing herbivores. It wasn't hard to discern that the T-rex had decided to "have a little fun" and spur the herd into running into the mountain pass.

Terrorizing others is nothing but amusement to them, Scope thought in disgust. Looking in the direction the Brachiosaurus had gone, she wished the herbivores a lush life in the Borderlands.

The Tyrants began dispersing, and the guards of the pass relaxed back into their patterns. Scope didn't dare call for a move until she was sure that the guards wouldn't notice them.

"When are we moving?" Rove breathed impatiently.

Scope took in a calculating breath. "Let's go! Follow me."

The ground was eaten up quickly as they made a mad dash toward the trees. Halfway to the trees and nearly completely out of the mountain pass, Scope saw the Coelurus raise its head.

For a split second, it seemed that the Coelurus wouldn't see them. But then its head swiveled around.

"Run!" Scope yelped as a shrill alarm screech rendered the air.

"I'm running! I'm definitely running!"

Scope could hear a loud growl from the T-rex that they had passed. Then, she heard it running after them.

Rove surged forward so that she was running alongside Scope. Scope frantically looked around for either a hiding place where they could lose the T-rex or an escape route.

"I see something!" Rove exclaimed, panting slightly. "Up ahead. See those rocks?"

"Yeah."

"I think we can hide among them!"

Scope nodded, changing her direction. Rove seemed to know where she was going, so Scope kept at her tail. The T-rex bellowed a dire threat to their health as they entered the rocks. As they weaved through the veritable maze, Scope vaguely realized that sometime during their entry she and Rove had been separated. The T-rex slowed as it neared the rocks, then barged into their midst.

When she looked back, Scope couldn't see the T-rex despite the fact that she could very clearly hear it. She spotted a shallow dip at the base of one of the rocks. Before she could pass it, she estimated that it would be just deep enough to hide her from eyes kept several paces above the ground. She darted into the hole and pressed herself against the back of the dip. Her breath came in shallowly and noisily, and she started forcing herself to quiet her breathing.

From the sounds of the T-rex's steps, it had slowed and was looking around. She hoped that Rove had managed to evade the Tyrant. In addition, she wouldn't be able to find the Defiance on her own.

As the Tyrant roamed, it continued spitting out threats, ones that ranged from taking them to Harass, to swallowing them alive so that they had a nice painful death by slow digestion. The threats got worse and more creative as time passed, and Scope knew for certain that she was most likely to have very bad nightmares when she slept again.

The T-rex passed by her hiding place a few times, but fortunately it was ignorant of her position and continued on its way.

Sometime in early afternoon, the T-rex finally gave up the search. After spouting out yet another threat that now sounded empty, it moved off, probably back to its post in the mountain pass.

Scope stayed hidden for a while longer before venturing back out into the open. She kept as quiet as she could, constantly sniffing the air for any scent of Rove. She called out for her comrade in a volume little louder than a stage whisper.

"Scope? Over here!" came a small and quiet call.

She whipped her head around toward the source of Rove's

voice. Scope took a few steps forward and spotted another dip in a boulder. Scope smiled a little as she saw Rove shoving herself against the back wall.

"You can come out," Scope whispered. "I think that the Tyrant left, but we'd better be careful, just in case."

"Thank goodness," Rove grumbled as she came out. "I was starting to think that it would never leave. So, now that we're in the valley again, where do we go?"

"The nearest Defiance group. Lead the way."

Scope squinted at the very dark trees ahead of them. The area they were traveling through was shadowed by a mountain, and the trees grew branches so close together it might as well have been dusk within.

"You're certain that the group is in there?" she asked Rove, gesturing sharply with a jerk of her head.

Rove nodded certainly. "I could swear on it, but they might have moved."

Scope accessed the tight spacing between trees. "I'll guess that this is a very well-defended place, then. Tyrannosaurs and Coelurus would definitely have issues getting through."

"Oh, it's not just those two breeds anymore."

Scope frowned. "What do you mean?"

Rove's lips thinned. "I'll explain as we move. Come on." She entered the trees, and Scope hesitated only a few seconds before following. "The Tyrants have gotten themselves more members. It's not just the Tyrannosaurs and the Coelurus anymore. First, there's the Appalachiosaurus."

"What turned them?" Scope inquired.

"You know the Appalachiosaurus and how they've always been bullies. Why not be even more powerful bullies? They're the regional under-lords that enforce fear of the Tyrants across the valley." Rove rolled her eyes. "Second, there's the Deinonychus. They've always been natural followers. They've become the base of a new worker class. Watch out for anyone in the worker class, 'cause they'd just as soon throw you under the nearest Tyrannosaur's foot just for an extra ration and a 'Good Citizen' scar."

"Scar?"

Rove smiled sinisterly. "If you're really, really good, as in a beautiful foot-licker, they give you a tic scar on your nose. The more you get, the more you're respected."

For the first time, Scope was grateful that Spike wasn't around. "Scars are for bravery, for family. . ."

"Right."

Scope bit her lip. "They raise the odds against the Defiance dramatically."

"You have no idea," Rove nodded solemnly. "Know your place or die."

They fell quiet, and the only sounds that could be heard were the birds, mammals, and their own bodies moving over dead leaves and through shrubs. As they moved further into the dense forest, it grew even denser. Scope eventually had to give up trying to figure out if they were traveling in a straight line.

"You there! Halt!"

Scope and Rove froze, skipping a few steps under their own momentum as they came to a sudden stop. Scope looked around wildly, worrying if they had been caught by some Coelurus.

But the Tyrants usually roar their presence, she realized. "Who's there? Where are you?" she called out.

A few trees rustled, and a Stygimoloch emerged. The numerous horns that crowned his head were interlaced with broken twigs and vines. "What are you two younglings doing here?" he grumbled, having an undertone of worry. "You shouldn't be alone during these times. Go back to your tribes."

"We don't have anywhere else to go," Rove said. "We've just come from the Borderlands, back into the valley."

The Stygimoloch narrowed his eyes a little, a soft growl coming from deep in his throat. It was obvious that he wasn't quite convinced.

"I am an Utahraptor, the last of my tribe," Scope piped up. "Rove is a Dilophosaurus, and was a member of one of the late Defiance groups. We're both looking for one of the surviving groups. We wish to help."

The Stygimoloch clapped his beak a few times in contemplation. There was a long pause, and Scope was scouring her mind for any way she could convince him that they did, in fact, come to help. But before she could say anything, the omnivore said, "Did you come alone? Did you see anyone following you?"

"It's just us, sir," Scope said. "I'm pretty sure that we weren't followed, but I certainly wouldn't bet my life on it."

With a nod, the Stygimoloch said, "Our group is a short distance away. Follow me." He carefully squeezed himself through the trees. Scope and Rove hurried to follow him.

It was a short walk before Scope caught a glimpse of the trees thinning. Then the forest began to look as it normally did, with the trees spaced out with more than enough room for even a T-rex to pass through without scraping the trunks.

Scope took a sharp breath as she saw the many types of Squamas inhabiting the area of thinned forest. From what she could see, there were Troodons that came to no higher than her knees, Albertosaurus, and more Stygimolochs that were just slightly smaller than she, and even some herds of Ankylosaurus and Edmontonia. Pterosaurs, mostly Pterodactylus, large and small, roosted in the trees, cawing and screeching as they flitted from branch to branch. The much, *much* larger Quetzalcoatlus stayed near the middle of the clearing, resting with their wings propping up their chest, neck, and head.

"Welcome to the roaming headquarters of the Defiance," their Stygimoloch stated, moving through the crowd. The Troodons dodged to the sides so that they couldn't be knocked aside, and they gave Scope and Rove curious glances as the newcomers moved by. "I'm taking you to see Kudos, our commander."

"Kudos," Scope repeated, making sure not to forget the name.

The Stygimoloch led them into the midst of several large

carnivores and heavyset omnivores; Allosaurus, Albertosaurus, and Stygimolochs. One of the Stygimolochs, a small one with a bluish brown hide and a deep blue spiked dome, saw them coming and nodded to the others. The other carnivores walked away, leaving Rove, Scope, and their guide.

"Welcome back, Ardent," the bluish brown Stygimoloch said with a stiff nod. He looked up at Scope and Rove, his amber eyes immediately narrowing upon seeing them. "Who are these two younglings? Yet more runaways that want to be heroes and fight the bad guys, yet promptly die by the hands of a few Coelurus?"

Scope bristled at the harsh words and equally rough tone. Beside her, Rove made an almost inaudible growl.

"Commander," their Stygimoloch guide interjected, "from what they told me, they're not runaways. The Utahraptor has lost her tribe. The Dilophosaurus was a member of one of our lost groups."

"Where did you two come from?" Kudos inquired.

"We both came from the Borderlands," Scope said, "but before that, I lived in a clearing at the base of Concave Peak."

"The Borderlands?" Kudos echoed, an eyebrow arching. "The mountain pass is guarded day and night without rest. How did you two sneak by the Tyrants?"

"Very carefully," Rove said with a nearly undetectable smirk.

Scope shot her companion a brief glare, one Rove ignored.

Kudos huffed. "Even if I let you two join this group, what could you two do to help?"

Scope bit her lip for a second before replying, "My late mentor and tribe leader hid an object that could drastically push back the Tyrants and even eliminate Harass himself. It's a duplicate of the object Harass keeps on his own back, and it's called the *Intimidator.*"

Kudos' eyes glinted. "Do you know where this *Intimidator* is?"

"I know the general area."

"Then tell me and I will send a squadron there and fetch it," Kudos declared.

Scope frowned. "I need to be able to trust you, too. You could easily have one of your own soldiers bear it. However, my tribe leader's last wish requires *me* to bear it. And you can't give me a guarantee that you'll get it here without the Tyrants intercepting it."

Kudos' lips thinned. "Very well. When a time comes that we can trust each other, I'll send a squadron with you. But until then, you and your friend can be warning lookouts." He turned to a group of Troodons that were chatting nearby. "Corporal Juts, lead these two recruits to the lookout posts."

One of the Troodons whirled around and nodded sharply. "Yes, Commander!" he declared, then trotted away. "Follow me, you two."

Scope and Rove trailed behind the Troodon as it led them back to the dense trees. The threesome weaved through them until they neared the edge of the tightly squeezed forest. Juts stopped just before they exited at the base of a thick tree. The tree had dozens of branches, all close together and the lowest could be easily mounted.

"Here's your post," Juts said. "At the top, there's a clear view of the surrounding forest. You're to keep a very close tab on the area. There's a few pterosaurs roosting at the top, you can send them to Kudos, but only if there's Tyrants nearby. Kudos does *not* appreciate false alarms. At sundown, a pair of Troodons will be relieving you for the night. Come directly to the headquarters. Understood?"

Scope nodded.

"Yeah," Rove said with a nod.

"'Yes, *sir*,'" Juts corrected sternly. "You're in the hierarchy now. Respect your superiors."

"Yes, sir," Scope said obligingly.

Rove said the same, but hers carried the barest hint of cheekiness.

As Juts jogged away, the Dilophosaurus took a bound onto the lowest branch, which immediately dipped sharply under her weight. Scope watched from the ground as Rove ascended the tree like a natural climber.

Halfway up, Rove glanced down. "What are you waiting for?" she said. "Afraid of heights or something? Get up here, or you'll get us both in trouble."

Scope groaned and leapt onto the tree's trunk. The branch Rove had first used was just slightly too high for her to simply leap onto. Using her claws and talons, Scope worked her way up the trunk toward the branch. She reached up with an arm and pulled herself up onto it. From there, it was simply jumping from branch to branch and refusing to look down. She could hear Rove moving above her.

Scope ascended until the branches began to significantly sag under her weight. She was near the top of the tree. Rove had stopped a little below her on the opposite side.

Scope took a good look around. In the higher branches, there were several Pterodactylus of ranging sizes and colors. They cawed and chatted amongst themselves, not minding her in the least. Her vantage point was just above most of the other treetops, giving her a good view of the forest. She could see well through the canopy to the forest floor, and she well hidden from below.

She settled down and got into a vaguely comfortable position, and then gave herself an anchor to the tree by wrapping her tail around its trunk.

"You want to ask something?" Rove asked.

Scope looked down. "How'd you know?"

Rove rolled her eyes. "I'm not bad at reading expressions. What is it?"

"What's a corporal and a private?"

"Is that it? Well, a corporal is a middle-ranking soldier, better than a private and lower than a sergeant and commander. Privates are what we are; rookies in the army."

"Were you just a private before?"

Something cold glinted in Rove's eyes for a moment before fading away. "Yes, a specialist, and I was in for a promotion before. . . family issues. . . got in the way."

Deciding not to press Rove for more information, Scope returned to keeping watch.

Something caught her eye. Turning to see better, she squinted at a strange nearby mountain. The mountain had a rather bare peak, which she thought was unusual, as the other mountains were completely covered with flora. She noticed a pale gray cloud above its peak. She could feel a strong breeze, and wondered why the cloud wasn't being blown away.

After a a moment, Scope realized she had been staring. She shook her head and redirected her attention to the forest below. It was time to prove her worth and she couldn't spend the remainder of the day staring at an out-of-place mountain peak.

As Juts promised, two Troodon relieved Scope and Rove at sundown. As they descended, Scope did her best to focus her gaze on the branches below her and not directly on the distant ground.

Get over it, Scope, she scolded herself as she hopped down to a branch. It shook under her feet from the shock of her weight, and she immediately wrapped her arms and tail around the trunk. *No! Let go of the tree, Scope. Let go. . .* It was only when the branch steadied did she relinquish her grip and continue down.

"Scared of heights, Scope?" Rove teased once Scope landed on the grass.

Scope only bared her teeth, not deigning to grace that barb at her dignity with a verbal reply.

They made their way back to headquarters, but once they reached the pseudo clearing, both of them stopped, not knowing where to go next. Thankfully, a passing Albertosaurus directed them to the sleeping grounds, where they could rest until daylight came again.

The sleeping grounds were packed. All of the Troodons were up and about, strangely. Scope felt very out of place amongst the multiple groups of Squamas. As far as she could tell, she was the only Utahraptor present.

"Are you going to just stand there or help me find an open spot?" Rove quietly hissed at her.

Scope realized that she had been standing still, and she moved to catch up with Rove. Together, they tiptoed around the sleeping grounds until they found a decent-sized empty area. Scope laid down on her side with her legs and arms stretched out and her neck bent back so that, if she was standing, she would be looking at the sky. In contrast, Rove settled on a stomach position with her legs and arms neatly tucked beneath her and her head ramrod straight in front.

Scope didn't immediately close her eyes. After a while, she glanced over at her comrade and saw that she was asleep, her chest area slowly and steadily rising up and down. Scope shifted a little and vented softly. She closed her eyes.

Her last thoughts of how she could help Kudos followed her into her dreams.

Chapter Twenty Four

"Brawlers, assemble!"

Scope quickly looked up from her lunch, a large mammal, and toward the source of the shout. She couldn't identify who had shouted, but she did notice that the largest carnivores, the Allosaurus and Albertosaurus, were now moving toward the center of headquarters.

"What's going on?" Scope asked Rove, who was nursing her own mammalian lunch. "What does 'Brawlers, assemble' mean?"

With a vaguely bored look, Rove said, "It's a cue for the largest fighters to gather."

"Why?"

"It means that Tyrants have ventured a little too close for comfort. Kudos probably got a pterosaur warning."

Scope frowned. "Shouldn't we get ready to fight, too?"

"Are you as large as an Albertosaurus? No? Then it's not time for us." Rove returned to eating.

Scope began gulping down her mammal, ripping off flesh as fast as she could without choking herself.

"What are you doing?" Rove asked, eyeing her queerly.

"I'm going to tell Kudos that I can help. I may not be the largest Defiance soldier, but I can hold my own against Tyrants."

"He'll never let you go."

"Are you completely certain about that?" Scope swallowed the last shred of her lunch and jogged toward where Kudos always was. She could see him already, speaking to the Brawlers.

She paused before she reached them, waiting for Kudos to send them off. It took a moment, but the second the Brawlers shifted to move away, she trotted forward. "Commander Kudos, sir!"

Kudos turned to face her and frowned a little. "What is it, Private?"

She stopped in front of him, a little thrown off by the tension in his voice. *I've been here for almost a week now!* she thought. *I thought that we were past the wary hostility.* "Commander, sir, I want to go with the Brawlers."

Kudos scoffed. "You'll only get stepped on. Request denied."

"But I can hold my own against the Tyrants!" Scope pressed. "I've fought against Appalachiosaurus, Coelurus, Deinonychus, and Tyrannosaurs. I know how to fight, too. Please, I want to go!"

"I already declined your request," Kudos said firmly. "You're bordering on insubordination."

Scope briefly considered continuing to push, but then thought better of it. "Yes, sir," she said quietly, hanging her head a little. She plodded back to where Rove was.

"Looks like an 'I told you so' is in order," Rove said.

Scope gave Rove a mild glare. "Well, at least I tried."

Rove shrugged; *Whatever.*

With a sigh, Scope trotted over to a small cliff that was near the sleeping grounds. She laid down at the edge of the small cliff, positioning herself on her stomach. From the cliff, she could see a majority of headquarters.

She felt underestimated. *He thinks that I'm a liability if I go with them,* she thought grimly. *He thinks that the Brawlers will be distracted by me underfoot. I can't argue with that. I don't want any soldiers dying.*

She frowned. *The only way to keep them from dying in vain is by getting that* Intimidator *on my back! I need to get to the clearing without the Tyrants spotting me. Rove said that they're constantly present there. I'd have to up the ante on my sneaking abilities.*

But what would I do once I got to the clearing? Spike never said where the Intimidator *was hidden.* She grunted as she thought hard. *Maybe he left me hints. Something that he was doing or said that I didn't pick up at the time. Think, Scope, think!*

"What are you doing?"

Scope looked up at Rove, who appeared to have finished lunch and had wandered over. "I'm thinking."

"Don't hurt yourself."

Scope glared in irritation.

Rove backed up a step. "Hey, that look could kill someone if you're not careful. What's got your tail in a twist?"

"I don't think that I'll tell you right now."

"Oh, that wounds me, right here." Rove dramatically grasped her chest and teetered on her feet, as if she was about to collapse.

"Do you mind? I'm trying to focus."

Rove immediately 'recovered' and stalked away. "Whatever, Scope," she said over her shoulder.

Scope gave the Dilophosaurus a parting glance before returning to straining her brain.

It was a long while later when Scope returned from her musing. The Brawlers were emerging from the trees, all of them battered and bruised. Scope frowned slightly as she mentally tallied them. With a pang of regret, she counted that a fifth of the Brawlers had not come back.

The Brawlers approached Kudos and spoke to him for a few minutes. Kudos finally gave them a sharp nod, and then the Brawlers dispersed.

A movement to her right drew her eye, and she watched Rove walk up and lie down beside her.

"What happened?" Scope asked, having an inkling that her comrade knew what had gone on.

Rove pursed her lips. "Well, the Brawlers managed to kill the Tyrants, but the Tyrants gave them a good fight. At least not more of the Brawlers had died. Some of the Tyrants are dead, and that's what counts." She huffed. "Less for the Defiance to take on."

Scope hadn't known that she had subtly leaned away from Rove until she had to check her balance. Something in Rove's tone made her wary and on edge. *She sounds uncaring, cold. Comrades have died. Why isn't she lamenting them?*

"Scope?" asked a voice in a tone that could only be described as fearfully hopeful.

She turned to face the speaker. Her eyes widened in shock at the sight of Pallor standing only a few paces away. "Pallor?" she murmured.

Pallor let out a cry and leapt forward, wrapping his neck around Scope's as soon as he was close enough. "Scope! You're alive!"

"You are, too!" Scope squealed, pulling away so she could

see her brother more clearly. "I thought you had been killed by the Tyrannosaurs!"

"I found a hiding spot and waited until they were long gone," Pallor said. "It was a tight squeeze, in between two rocks, you know? It took a while to get out of there, and even longer, maybe two days, to get back to the clearing. The clearing! Scope, what happened there? It was *horrible!*"

Scope hung her head in shame. "The Tyrants attacked. I accidentally led them there. Everyone is dead, it seems. Only you and I are left."

"Everyone else?" Pallor breathed.

"Dead. And it's my fault!" Scope blinked back tears, feeling the survivor's guilt coming back with a vengeance.

Pallor wrapped his neck around hers again. "There's nothing we can do now. What's passed is the past, which we can't change."

Scope let out a humorless chuckle. "That sounds something like what Spike had once said. You're both right. I should get over it."

"That's my sister!" Pallor said with a grin. Suddenly, he looked to the side. "Someone's calling me. Hey, meet my sister!"

Scope started to follow Pallor, but Rove asked, "Who was that?"

"My brother," Scope replied.

Rove hummed in a disinterested tone. "Good for you."

Before Scope turned to follow Pallor, Juts trotted up to them. "It's time for your shifts, you two," he said to her and Rove. "Get to your post!"

Scope and Rove were halfway to the dense trees when Scope heard her name called. She turned around and saw Kudos staring at her. Rove paused, then went on while Scope trotted to Kudos.

"Yes, Commander?" Scope said.

Kudos continued staring at her. Scope shifted a little, uncomfortable under the razor sharp gaze. "I got some very interesting intel from my Brawlers," Kudos finally said slowly. "My Brawlers were able to question a dying Tyrant. According to the late Tyrant, your little clearing is under sharp Tyrant attentions. Not only that, but a traitor's given out this group's location."

"Sir?" Scope said questioningly. *Where's he going with this? Why is he talking to* me *about it?* "Are you accusing *me* of being the traitor?"

A low growl began to rumble in Kudos' throat. "I am. There's been other leaks, as well, and they didn't start until you and your friend arrived. You must be planning to betray us to Harass, and you're going to sneak away later and go to the clearing where the hordes of Tyrants are living. It's an ambush! There is no *Intimidator!*"

Scope felt a wave of indignation sweep over her. "I'm not planning any such things!" Kudos only glared, so she continued, "I fight for the freedom of this valley, my *home,* just like you. I'm on *your side!*"

Kudos snarled. "You're to be led to a cave nearby and kept under constant watch by several Troodons for an indefinite amount of time. If at all during your imprisonment the leak stops, you're guilty. If they continue, you're innocent."

Scope snarled at the Troodons who approached, and they backed up a few steps, startled by the animosity she was emitting. Turning to Kudos, Scope said, "Why are you accusing *me* of this?"

"Your Dilophosaurus companion reported that you were acting strangely, and sneaked away a few nights ago. She didn't see you again until the morning."

Scope's jaw dropped, momentarily shocked speechless. "I never sneaked away!" she exclaimed.

Kudos turned to the Troodons. "Take her away."

Scope set her jaw and glared at nothing in particular as she let the Troodons lead her away.

Scope paced back and forth ceaselessly, glaring at the ground ahead of her.

A week, she thought. *It's been a whole week and I'm still stuck in this infernal hole in the ground. This place is cold, wet, and I've been fed scraps. Scraps! I'm not a traitor; they have no proof!*

She stopped pacing merely because she was tired of walking. Laying down, she tried to get comfortable, but the entire cave floor was craggy and uneven with small, sharp protrusions.

A mild glare was directed toward the opening of the cave. Every few seconds, a Troodon would stalk by. The entrance/exit to the cave was extraordinarily small, and Scope had barely been able to squeeze through when she had been forced into the cave a week before. Only Troodons or smaller could fit through the hole comfortably.

Her only visitor had been Pallor. He had given her much needed company, as her guards seemed adamant to ignore her even when she had purposely tried to instigate them into saying *anything*. Pallor had updated her on the happenings within the camp; There had been a close call with a T-rex a few days before, but it had passed by the dense line of trees without a glance inward.

I can't believe that I was stuck with the blame for this, she mentally grumbled. *Rove's behind this. She must be the one who framed me! But I don't have any proof.*

"Hey, Utahraptor!"

Scope looked at the speaker, a Troodon.

"Kudos wants to see you. It's top priority."

She set her jaw and moved to the hole. Her back badly scraped against the top of the hole as she squeezed through it, and she was sure that some of the scrapes had gone deep enough down to draw blood.

The Troodon that had summoned her led the way back to Kudos. Scope felt like there was something heavy in the air that was weighing her down. Each step seemed to take a little more effort.

The sensation was eerily similar to when she and Spike were being marched before Harass.

Finally, she was standing in front of Kudos. He was giving her a stony look. Scope looked sidelong at those surrounding the commander; several Allosaurus and Albertosaurus. Brawlers. All of them weren't giving her any semblance of a friendly look.

Scope quickly glanced around. *Where's Rove?*

"Utahraptor Scope," Kudos began sternly, "you have stayed in the cave for exactly one week. There have been no leaks since your imprisonment."

Of course not. "But I didn't *do it!*" Scope said. "I'm not guilty! The real source of the leak could've simply stopped. This has to be a plot to frame me!"

"Who would have a vendetta against you?" Kudos said with a frown.

"Harass," Scope hissed. "I've already *told* you! He probably thinks that Spike, my mentor, told me the hiding place of the *Intimidator!*"

"And you still stick with your story of a false weapon to give us equally false hope," Kudos stated. "Utahraptor Scope, you have been found of treachery. The punishment is death."

Scope's eyes widened as the Brawlers moved forward. She shot a glance at Kudos, hoping that he caught the emotions carried within it; regret, betrayal, sadness, and hope. Then she burst into a rapid sprint, bee-lining for the trees.

"After her!"

She didn't look back to try and identify the voice. She couldn't risk tripping over a jutting root; to fall at the speed she was going would surely break her neck. She could hear the Brawlers and now the Troodons coming. The amount of weaving she was doing through the dense trees was starting to make her dizzy.

I need to get to the open.

Then she could see the trees thinning up ahead. Taking the deepest breath she could, she sent a surge of energy to her legs.

The Defiance soldiers were left far behind as their quarry darted away with the speed possessed only by the desperate.

CHAPTER TWENTY FIVE

Scope looked back over her shoulder, despite there being no one behind her. She had lost them a while ago, but had kept on running. It was almost sundown, and she was exhausted and, yet again, on her own.

She vented sharply as she idly pawed the stone she was standing on. Her brow furrowed as she pondered.

I need to get to the Intimidator, she thought. *And quickly. But there's Tyrants swarming the area. I'm going to die if I try.*

With a sharp sigh, she glanced around her for any signs of danger. There was the constant stench of Tyrants, but there didn't seem to be any close by.

She shook her head and growled. *I'm just an Utahraptor, barely into adulthood. What was Spike thinking, telling me that I'm the Worthy One?*

Sighing, she looked off into the distance. From her vantage point, she could just see the top of Concave Peak. If she was correct, her home was on the opposite side. It would take a full night to get there.

Spike's voice, a memory, drifted through her head. *"Save them all."* He was entrusting her with the responsibility to rescue the valley and rid everyone of Harass' bloodline once and for all. There was no one else who would be able to stand against the Acrocanthosaurus and his *Annihilator*.

I have to do it. Even if it kills me.

Peering out from the hole she had found, she checked the immediate area for threats. Scenting, hearing, and seeing none in the pre-dawn light, she crawled out of the hole and shook the dirt from her body.

It had been late the previous night when she had found the hole, camouflaged by young apple trees. It was situated directly under a very tall rock. Tree roots invaded the back wall of the hole, and the dirt around the roots was loose and fell onto her whenever she tapped them. The hole had served as a handy hideaway for the night.

She set off again, moving at a brisk trot. Her brief period of sleep had energized her dramatically. It felt like she could take on the world and win.

At least, Harass, and win, came the cheeky thought.

As she trotted along, she could see the morning progress. Ever so slowly, the sun rose over the eastern mountains and cast a reddish orange glow over the valley. Scope watched as the sunlight crept down from the treetops and finally touched the ground. The rays warmed her hide to a comfortable temperature.

Suddenly, a pungent and rotten scent invaded her nostrils. *Tyrants.* Scope quickly looked around for a place to hide, but all she could see were trees. But there was one tree that had a few low branches. It would be a stretch, but she thought that she could get on the lowest and ascend to hiding.

And a view of the distant ground flashed across her vision. *Great. I'm not even* in *the tree yet and my fear of heights is acting up.*

She could hear the Tyrants now. It was either the tree or them.

Disregarding her fear of heights, she dashed for the tree. She barely managed to leap onto the lowest branch, but thankfully there were many close together after that and it was easy work to ascend.

She placed several leafy branches in between her and the ground before stopping. Her breathing threatened to escalate into excited hyperventilation, but she forced herself to breathe slowly and deeply.

The Tyrants came into view, but she could only make out bits and pieces of them through the leaves. From what she could tell, there were a couple Appalachiosaurus, a T-rex, and one other breed of Squama she couldn't identify, though the basic form looked familiar.

Thankfully, they passed by beneath her without seeming to notice her presence. But even when they had long been gone from sight and scent, she stayed in the tree. She wasn't about to risk coming down only to met by a few Tyrants that had doubled back.

Sure enough, an Appalachiosaurus soon stalked past, grumbling under its breath. She could just make out the words, and it seemed that the Tyrant thought that it had been a false alarm and no one was there.

Scope felt like laughing, but she remained quiet until the Tyrant had long left. She hopped down from branch to branch until she reached the ground. She shook herself before continuing on her trek.

It was a miracle. It *had* to be. There was *no way* she could've reached the clearing without being spotted by Tyrants.

Scope was hiding in a large and dense bush, looking out into the clearing she had once called her home. She could hardly believe that she had managed to get all the way to her destination without being discovered.

The clearing looked terrible. There were huge trenches in the ground where it once had been relatively flat. The grass was a weird brownish reddish green color, likely never to return to its natural hue if it hadn't already after an entire Turn. Skeletons, picked bare and bleached white by the sun, were scattered over the entirety of the open area. Sadly, many of them were Utahraptors, and many more had once belonged to younglings. Where there were crushed bones in one area, she knew those had belonged to the hatchlings.

She brutally jerked herself out of a mounting depression

and forced herself to focus. *Okay, I need to find the* Intimidator. *Did Spike ever give me a hint to where it is?* Her gaze raked over the clearing, scanning every particle of dirt, blade of grass, and bush.

She thought back as far as she could, then called up every detail she could remember. Discarding most of the memories, she focused on only the ones that involved Spike.

She drug up again a few key memories. They revolved around Spike looking at somewhere in the middle of a conversation about Harass or the Tyrants, staring at one place for a long while, and other related things.

Scope realized that the *Intimidator* was hidden somewhere by the pond and the ancient tree.

Suddenly, she heard crashing sounds. Holding very still, she watched as Tyrants entered the clearing from the far side. She saw a T-rex, some Appalachiosaurus, and a few Dilophosaurus.

Dilophosaurus? she thought in shock. *They're allied with Harass! But. . . that means that. . .*

And then Rove sauntered into sight. Her head was held high as she swaggered with pride and the air of superiority.

"I can't stay here long, Gnash," Rove stated to the T-rex, sounding as if she was in command. "The Defiance thinks that I'm hunting right now, so let's get to it."

"Watch your tone, youngling," the T-rex, Gnash, snapped. "Or do you wish for a reminder of your place?" When Rove growled but said nothing, it continued, "Do you have the intel from the Utahraptor you pretended to befriend?"

Rove scowled, her nose wrinkling. "Never got the chance. Kudos got suspicious of the leaks I was giving, but luckily I pinned the blame on the Utahraptor. I was planning on visiting her in her prison tomorrow to subtly question her, but Kudos brought her out. He planned on executing her, but she ran off and escaped."

"Why didn't you act sooner?" one of the other Dilophosaurus snarled.

"Keeping up friendly relations without creating suspicion is a delicate balance, Patriarch," Rove snapped back. "I would remember that, but aren't you the main interrogator?"

"Be careful, daughter," the elder Dilophosaurus snarled. "Or else you might find yourself without any place in the Tyrant ranks at all."

Rove pursed her lips and carried on as if the brief spat had never happened. "The Utahraptor would've never told me anything if I questioned her too soon."

"Then we need to keep an eye out for her," an Appalachiosaurus said.

"Agreed," Gnash said with a nod. "Alert the others."

The Tyrants split up. Scope watched them leave with an uncomfortable feeling, silently eyeing Rove as she sped back toward the Defiance group.

This is a good lesson for me, she thought. *Choose comrades carefully.*

She glanced up at the sun and saw that it was nearing the western mountains. Settling down in the bush, she decided that it would be best to wait till the veil of darkness to come out and search for the weapon that would save the valley.

Scope's nose trailed the ground as she sniffed around the pond and the ancient tree. Her mind shifted through the different scents she could detect; dirt, decay, water, etc, searching for something out of the ordinary. After making three loops around the pond, she moved to the tree.

As she was crossing a gap in between two large exposed roots, she faintly smelled something off. She stopped, quadruple-checked for Tyrants, then began using her hands and feet to dig through the dirt. About a third of a pace down, she hit a flat rock. She was about to dig around it when she saw that it shift a little. Hope blooming, she hefted the rock and shoved it aside.

There it was. A shining smooth and flawless surface gleamed in the moonlight, reflecting blueish white rays on her face. She slowly reached down and gently grasped the object, then carefully lifted it out of the hole. She made sure that her talons stayed away from the object's surface.

"You must be the *Intimidator*," she murmured in awe, gazing at the object of liberation. She thought hard about how it could be placed on her body. Recalling Harass and his *Annihilator,* she decided that the space between her shoulders and the base of her neck would be the best place.

She couldn't reach her back, so she tenderly placed the *Intimidator* upside down on the ground. Then she crouched down, positioned herself, then rolled over so that her chosen area of hide was directly over the *Intimidator.*

At first, there was nothing. She laid still, despite the acute uncomfortableness from her awkward position, but she didn't dare to even twitch.

Pain! Horrible pricks sliced into her back, and Scope tried not to screech as something slender and cold punctured her hide. Her vision blurred as she felt her backbone tapped. It hurt *so badly.* The pain was all she could sense.

Then it ended so abruptly she almost didn't notice. A few tingles flitted over her spine as she cautiously rolled around so that she could get her limbs under her. Her legs trembled as she stood, but it was from the shock on her body rather than weakness. She rotated her shoulders, feeling them against the object now affixed to her back. The *Intimidator* wasn't very heavy, but it would take her a little while to adjust to the new top-heaviness. She shook her body to test out how stable it was. It didn't even shift a bit.

She glanced at the hole that the *Intimidator* had been staying in for so many Turns. After a bit of contemplation, she decided that it would be best for her to fill it in and attempt to hide the hole from the Tyrants.

She did, after all, want to see their faces when they saw the *Intimidator* on her back.

After she finished filling in the hole, she stomped the ground so that it resembled the packed dirt around it. She nodded, approving her own work, then jogged into the trees. She wanted to get as far away as possible from the Tyrant-infested area before the sun rose.

After she had run a very good distance from the clearing,

she finally reached an area that didn't reek of Tyrants. She paused there to figure out how the *Intimidator* actually worked. From what she had seen, there wasn't anything that she could push to trigger something, and none of her limbs could bend back far enough anyway. Before she had put it on her back, she'd seen a perfectly smooth and unmarred surface, so there was nothing to push in the first place.

Perhaps the *Intimidator* enhanced her fighting abilities? Scope looked over at a tree. She planned out her attack on the unlucky tree, picturing her hands lashing out and her talons ripping long gashes in the wood. Maybe her talons would slice through the entire tree, backed up with sudden strength.

As soon as she had finished seeing the gashes in her mind's eye, the *Intimidator* made a soft whirring sound. Before she could try and turn her head far enough around to see what was happening, a thin beam of bright red burst past her and moved in a swift arc, seeming to go straight through the tree like it wasn't there.

The beam ended as fast as it had begun. The tree stayed completely motionless for a moment before it began to creak. The top part of the tree began sliding on a perfectly smooth cut along the trunk. It fell off, then toppled over. The branches caught on other trees, so it didn't fall completely.

She blinked a few times, then took a few steps forward to the stump. The rim had a dim red glow that was quickly dimming and going out.

"What was that?" she muttered, her eyes wide.

Her gaze darted toward a small rock. She swallowed nervously, then imagined charging at the rock and body slamming it.

The *Intimidator* whirred again, then there was a soft hissing sound. A moment later, something narrow and black with a fiery back-end streaked from the *Intimidator*. The second it touched the rock, it exploded with a loud boom and a small fireball.

Scope hopped backward and away from the sudden wave of heat. The fireball rose into the sky and dispersed into nothing, leaving a charred crater where the rock had once been. A few seconds later, pebbles only a little bigger than grains of sand fell around her. Several hit her, but they merely bounced off. The *Intimidator* wasn't even scratched by the downpour.

"Is that it?" she said, looking at the *Intimidator* as best as she could. "All I have to do is imagine the attack I want and this thing works?"

As if in answer, the *Intimidator* made a few quiet clicks before whirring down to silence.

She briefly thought of further experimentation with the strange weapons, but she then had the inkling that the beam of red and the black exploding thing may be limited. It would probably be best if she didn't keep on attacking rocks and trees. She knew how to use them now, anyway.

She raised her nose toward the sky and inhaled deeply. The scent of Tyrants was slightly stronger, so she rationalized that they were coming to investigate the explosion. Time to make herself scarce.

She took off at a leisurely run. The Defiance needed her.

chapter twenty six

The dense strip of forest that surrounded the Defiance group was up ahead. She could see it already from her position not far off. The early morning sunlight streamed down through the trees. A light wind made branches shift and wave, causing dark green and black shadows to dance upon her hide.

Scope stared at a single tree amongst the dense strip. It was a watch tree, and she knew that there were Troodons hidden in the branches. If they hadn't seen her yet, they would soon; she was standing in the open in clear view and especially since the sunlight was reflecting off of the *Intimidator*'s surface.

My hide must be blending me in with the ground, she mused as she waited for the alarm to go off. *I'll need to move and draw attention to myself if I don't get spotted soon.*

A moment later, and before she could attract the attention she wanted, she finally saw a Pterodactylus fly from the tree. She smirked a little and shifted her weight from one leg to another. It wouldn't be long now.

Then several Brawlers burst into sight. They wasted no time in moving to surround her and cut off any route of escape. She was undisturbed by their snarls and hostile looks, even sending them a view of her own teeth.

"Why did you come back, traitor?" an Albertosaurus said. "Do you have a death wish?"

Before Scope could reply, an Allosaurus said, "Enough. We're taking her to Commander Kudos. Utahraptor, if you try to run again. . ."

"You will kill me," Scope finished. "I know this song and dance routine already. Just take me to the commander."

When she exited the dense forest on the far side of the strip, she was immediately the subject of many suspicious stares. It took only a cursory look to spot Rove standing a short distance away. Scope made eye contact and gave Rove a knowing look. Rove cleared her face of all expression.

Several gasps erupted in the gathering crowd. Scope could see spots of light reflecting off of the *Intimidator* shining on their bodies. They were staring at the machine on her back in awe.

The single Utahraptor in the crowd caught her attention. Scope smiled at her brother, who looked immensely relieved that she was alive and well.

"Utahraptor!" Kudos growled, snapping Scope's attention away from Pallor. "I should kill you myself! While in your absence, did you sell us out?"

Scope tried not to show the apprehension she was feeling and spoke with a level and strong voice. "I've told you already, sir, that I'm not a traitor. I spent the time away to find the *Intimidator.*"

"Really?" Kudos said, narrowing his eyes.

Is he blind? Scope wondered incredulously. "Yes, Commander," she said smoothly, turning around a little so that her back was in plain sight.

Kudos' eyes widened as his angry demeanor evaporated. His gaze was fixed on the *Intimidator.* "Is that it?" he said.

"Yes, sir," Scope said. "I found the *Intimidator* in the clearing where I used to live. By the mercy of a miracle, I wasn't discovered by the Tyrants. I also found out the identity of your real traitor." Scope looked at Rove out of the corner of her eyes.

"Who?" Kudos said sternly, trying to trace her gaze.

Scope turned to give Rove a full view of her glare. "Rove the Dilophosaurus is the source of the leaks! The Dilophosaurus tribe in this area is aligned with Harass!"

Rove growled. "I deny it!" she shouted. "I have worked for the Defiance for well over a Turn. It is you, Scope, who is the leak!"

"That's not true!" Pallor spoke up. "Scope is my sister, and she would not betray. She only ran away because you were going to kill her."

Kudos exhaled slowly, but said nothing. His gaze flicked to Scope, silently demanding elucidation.

"It was claimed that I was a liar when I spoke of the *Intimidator* and denied that I was the traitor," Scope said. "I obviously haven't lied about the *Intimidator,* and my brother has never been able to lie well."

Kudos turned back to Rove, who was glaring at Pallor. "Brawlers, apprehend that Dilophosaurus," he ordered.

Rove's expressionless face twisted into an ugly one that could give young Squamas nightmares. She hissed at the Brawlers that approached her before making a break for it.

"After her!" Kudos bellowed. "Don't let her last the morning!"

The Brawlers took chase, vanishing into the dense strip of trees.

Kudos glared at the spot where Rove had disappeared for a moment, then turned to Scope. "Utahraptor, I must apologize."

"I understand, Commander," Scope said.

"We need to prepare," Kudos mused aloud. "With your. . . weapon. . . on your back, we can finally go head to head with Harass and his Tyrants! We must vanquish them once and for all and be rid of them!" Kudos summoned a flock of pterosaurs and whispered a few words to them before they flew off in a great rush. "The Defiance will unite," he continued. "This tyrannic oppression will not last the week!"

Scope stood up a little straighter as the soldiers around her began readying for combat. The *Intimidator* simultaneously felt heavier and lighter on her back as boldness and eagerness swept through her.

A brownish yellow Allosaurus came up to her and gave her a respectful nod. "Utahraptor, have you had any combat training?" he asked.

Scope shrugged and shook her head. "Not really, if you don't count what I've learned on the fly over this past Turn."

"I'm Keel. I'm going to instruct you on formal combat, if you want it."

"I have the feeling that I'm going to need all the training I can get," Scope replied with a wry smile. "When do we start?"

"Right away. Come, there's a relatively open area a few paces this way."

Scope followed Keel to a semi-clearing. He turned around to face her and swept an appraising gaze over her from head to feet and tail. "I must warn you; I'm not the gentlest of instructors."

"I've had Tyrannosaurs and Coelurus giving me on-the-job training," Scope said. "They never knew it, of course."

"Good," Keel said with a nod. "That will make my job easier. Now, I want you to try and send me to the ground. Use any means available to you. Go."

Scope instantly decided not to use the *Intimidator* and instead use the good old skills that had kept her alive for over a Turn. She dashed toward Keel, feigned a right, then hopped to the left when he moved to the right to intercept her. His neck was open for attack, but she didn't go for it. Instead, she ducked under his belly while his left arm lashed out.

He was expecting me to go for his neck, she thought. That arm would've given her a few nasty gashes.

Since she was underneath Keel, she slammed her body into his nearest leg. She didn't send him down, but it did cause him to put most of his weight on that one leg. Taking advantage, she jumped up so that her back forcefully collided with his underbelly. Keel's balance broke and he fell over.

Keel blinked up at her as she took a few steps away and strongly waved her tail. "Good," he eventually said, rolling so that he could stand. "I wasn't expecting that."

"My late tribe leader taught me that trick, forcing your opponent's legs out from under them."

"He taught you well. That trick will work on the Appalachiosaurus and Dilophosaurus."

Scope gave a wry grin. "Thank you, sir."

She took a breath and looked around just in time to see the Brawlers return. Many of them had blood on either their mouths, hands, or feet. Scope grimaced and looked down. Even if Rove had only been toying with her, Scope had gotten close to the traitorous Dilophosaurus.

Keel stood to his full height and raised his chin. "Again."

Over the rest of the day, Scope trained with Keel. During a

rest between engagements, Scope looked around the area. Squamas were flooding in, ones of all shapes and sizes, from carnivores to herbivores to pterosaurs. The area was rapidly filling up and beginning to feel claustrophobic. Keel finally called it an evening, as there was no longer enough room to train.

Scope moved to join Kudos. The commander was reviewing and updating battle plans with his lieutenants. Most of the army jargon went over Scope's head; however, she had to hope that he would later explain things to the army as a whole in words she could understand.

The next morning, Scope noticed that she hadn't been given a battery group. She caught Kudos' gaze for a split second and used body language to tell him that she wanted to talk with him.

In another moment, Kudos turned to her and said, "What is it?"

"You haven't given me a battery, sir," she said.

"Of course not!" Kudos exclaimed. "You're the only one that has the *Intimidator*. You're in a battery all your own. I'm planning on having you as a reserve, so that you can give the Tyrants one slammer of a surprise!"

Scope hummed softly as she thought this over. His logic made sense.

"But if you have Harass in your sights, go for him," Kudos added. Then he turned away.

The forest was still. Pale blue moonlight, courtesy of a full moon, streamed through the branches and created thousands of pools of light. Most mammals were in their nests, some pterosaurs roosting, peacefully asleep, in trees. There was the occasional hoot or screech of the nocturnal creatures, but other than them, the night was quiet.

A twig snapped, sounding like an explosion in the stillness of the night.

Scope didn't know whether to chuckle or shake her head at the Troodon ahead of her, who had frozen the second its foot had broken the thin piece of dead wood.

The Defiance was on the move. Kudos had sectioned them all into battalions and then regiments.

It had been a considerable time since they had left, and Scope guessed that there were a few more hours left before the sun would rise again. Kudos had planned to march them through the night and camp out a safe distance away from Harass' lair. There, they would rest, gather their strength, and wage the final battle.

She glanced up at the starry sky. Not long ago, enough pterosaurs and large birds of prey had flown across it to momentarily block out the moon. They were scouting ahead for the campsite, and would report back when they found it.

It was eerie that the Defiance was able to move as a gigantic mass through the forest without creating much noise at all. All she could hear was the hushed rustle of leaves as they were tread through. The larger carnivores were keeping their heads low, as to not bump branches and rattle. Likewise, the Ankylosaurus kept their clubbed tails stiff so the bony ends didn't create loud thuds when they hit tree trunks.

Scope mentally listed the brave Squamas in the Defiance. Unfortunately, most of the Tyrants were almost twice the size as the largest Allosaurus, so the Defiance as a whole was vastly out-weighed.

To occupy herself, she began mentally pairing opponents together. The Ankylosaurus and Edmontonia were the best defended. Despite their lack of speed and prowess in anything resembling an offensive assault, they would do well in standing their ground and using their brute-force weight and spiked armor. They would be best against Appalachiosaurus and anything larger.

Like the quadrupedal herbivores, the Stygimoloch, Allosaurus, and Albertosaurus would do best against Appalachiosaurus and larger, but they would have to keep an eye out for treacherous Coelurus and Deinonychus attempting an underbelly attack.

As the Troodons were about the same size as Coelurus, they would be the main opponents of the Coelurus and Deinonychus. Their only offense against larger Tyrants would be by using underbelly attacks. Like Scope, the Troodons would need to keep an eye out for descending feet.

The pterosaurs and birds of prey were the Defiance's air force. They would use dive-bombing attacks on the larger Tyrants, serving as distractions and could use their sharp beaks and talons to peck the eyes and render blindness. Scope thought that the pterosaurs and birds of prey would have the least amount of casualties, since they could easily fly out of reach.

And herself? Well, she was to stay out of sight and wait for Harass to make his big appearance. Once he did, she would be making an even bigger one against him.

Her mental tallies over, she found her mind wandering to

places she'd much rather not think about. The *Intimidator* suddenly seemed to gain weight as she acutely focused on it. She shook her head; this shiny box thing was supposed to save an entire valley. What if she failed? What if Harass managed to overcome her? She was just an Utahraptor, with only enough battle experience to keep her alive and moving, and she was expected to save everyone from a tyrannical ruler!

Scope gritted her teeth and mentally shoved those thoughts out of her mind. She imagined pushing them over an endless cliff where there was no way to get back up again.

Her breath caught in her throat when she caught movement in her peripheral vision. Head whirling around so fast it cracked, she spotted what seemed to be a dozen Tyrants running at full speed toward them.

"Tyrants!" someone bellowed. She wasn't the only one who had seen them, apparently. "Attack and destroy!"

Scope stayed back as the Defiance changed direction and charged toward the Tyrants, seeming to move as one body and mind. It was almost comical to see the Tyrants' eyes widen in shock and fear as they hurriedly began to back pedal. They didn't have time to run, for the faster Defiance soldiers were upon them.

After that, it was just a swarm of soldiers easily overwhelming the Tyrants. The followers of Harass didn't stand even a fraction of a chance. Before a few minutes had passed, the Tyrants were dead. Not a single follower of Kudos had suffered any debilitating injury.

Without any of the lieutenants saying a thing, the soldiers fell back into line and the Defiance continued on. Even though no one spoke afterward, she could sense that morales had risen a little from the skirmish, despite how minor and insignificant it was.

It was a very long while later when they heard a wordless series of roars. They came from a good distance away, alternating between low pitched to almost screeching. It was blatantly obvious that it was in code.

"It's a warning roar," Kudos soon stated. "They know we're coming. We've been spotted. Hurry, we must make haste."

They picked up the pace, going from a fast walk to a slow trot. Any faster, and the herbivores and Troodons would be too slow and fall behind.

Scope must've missed the pterosaur that gave Kudos directions, because seemingly for no reason they took a sharp turn. No one questioned the course change; there was complete trust in the commander.

Just after sunrise, they reached the peak of a mountain. Uncommonly, the forest was still dense here at the peak, but nowhere as thick as back at the base camp.

"We rest here," Kudos declared. "You all have until dusk to rest and regain your vitality. When the sun touches the western mountains, we wage the attack on Harass."

Chapter Twenty Seven

The Defiance was spread out into a long but thick strand that looped from the river to the peak of the mountain where Harass' lair was located. Scouting pterosaurs had reported that there were hundreds of Tyrants at the waterfall lair. Harass and his acolytes were waiting for the attack.

Not many were worried by the number of Tyrants. There were nearly 800 soldiers in the Defiance.

Scope nervously shifted her weight. Despite her being a reserve battalion all of her own, she was positioned at the front lines and she could just see the Tyrants milling around. Expectedly, Harass was at the back, snarling at the trees. Kudos' advice to attack the moment she saw him would have to be rethought.

Will my beam reach that far? she wondered. If it did, the Defiance was guaranteed a victory. If it didn't, Harass would be alerted to her, and she would be targeted. She decided to stay back and withhold her fire.

The Defiance was silent, and the tension was so thick in the air she could almost see it. Scope compared the situation to the calm before the storm. She had the feeling that this would be a storm that would put the blizzard to ultimate shame, kill it, then consume the remains.

Both forces were awaiting a signal to attack. It would happen at any second, but whoever would sound the battle cry first was unknown.

She looked to her right at her brother. He was tense and his eyes were clenched shut, as if he was readying himself. A small shiver ran through his body.

"We'll be okay," Scope murmured just loud enough for him to hear.

"You can't promise that," he replied just as softly, cracking open an eye. "The last time you said that, the tribe ended up dying."

Scope swallowed the lump that suddenly appeared in her throat. "Pallor, if this gets too much, I want you to run for the mountain pass that leads to the Borderlands. Wait for me at its exit. I need you to promise me this. I *can't* lose the last of my family."

Pallor nodded. "I promise. Try not to die out there."

"The same to you, brother."

Scope took a very deep breath when she heard Kudos roar

first. The commander was out of sight, but she could easily hear him, as his roar was a powerful baritone that made her teeth vibrate and tingle.

She stayed motionless as the Defiance swept past her. The soldiers were bellowing out their own unique war cries as they ran. The disturbed air rushed through Scope's fringe, making it flow and wave. Scope watched as the Tyrants moved forward to meet the Defiance.

They collided like two ocean waves crashing into each other. First there was a clear distinction between the two forces. But as they engaged, chaos reigned supreme. Bodies clashed, clawed, bit and bashed. It was a gruesome ballet, with roars of pain and victory being the symphony; and ducks, dodges, and attacks being the steps and gestures.

Scope paid particular attention to Harass. The huge Acrocanthosaurus seemed to have no battle plan in mind, as he was simply moving in random directions through the cacophony. Harass used every advantage his enormous body gave him; crushing Squamas underfoot, knocking others over with a single sweep of his thick tail, devouring more, gutting even more. Despite the attacks against him, he remained standing and fighting.

It was far too soon to attack the tyrant king. She was one of the smallest Defiance soldiers. It wouldn't take much to kill her before she could make it to Harass' location in the melee. She shifted uneasily in her hiding place, unable to do anything more than watch and wait for an opportunity.

A shuffling noise beside her caused her to whirl around to face it and prepare for an attack. But she frowned when she saw Pallor, who hadn't moved from his starting point.

"I can't go out there," he said, catching her look. "I'll die in seconds! Just look at the Troodons, and they're smaller than us! The Coelurus are dicing them up just like we capture mammals to eat. It's safer back here."

Scope did look, and she winced. "Well, you can be in my battery as my bodyguard. What do you say to hiding in these bushes until I spot an opportunity to attack Harass? Just remember what you promised me."

Pallor nodded, then they both returned to watching the battle.

As time wore on, more of the Defiance's battalions were being taken from the reserve and sent into combat. The area was littered with corpses. Thankfully, the Tyrants seemed to be failing despite their skills in mauling. It was hard to tell which side was winning; there appeared to be just as many Tyrants and Defiance soldiers dead as there were alive.

A screech of "Scope! Watch out!" drew Scope's attention to her right. She barely had enough time to absorb the image of a Deinonychus leaping at her before her reflexes kicked in. She leapt to the side, leaving the Deinonychus to land heavily in the very spot her neck had been an instant before.

Scope quickly glanced around. The Deinonychus that attacked her wasn't alone. It was accompanied by three others. Four against one.

Pallor leapt beside her, snarling at the Deinonychus. Four against two.

The Deinonychus stalked forward, all of them moving to surround her and Pallor. They gnashed their teeth and snarled death threats.

All Scope did was smirk and stifle a barking laugh. While the Deinonychus were caught off guard by her apparent lack of intimidation, she activated the *Intimidator*. The beam of red erupted from it and speedily cut through all four of her attackers. They froze, then fell to the ground in cleanly cut halves.

She turned to see Pallor staring at the bodies. He glanced at her, the *Intimidator,* then back to the Deinonychus. "I'm a terrible bodyguard," he muttered.

"You warned me," she replied. "I could be dead, and the fact that I'm not is what counts. Now, let's go find another bush to hide in"

She spared the bodies a parting glance before they dashed off to find another hiding spot. As they ran, the ground suddenly trembled violently beneath their feet. Her equilibrium failed her and she fell onto her stomach. The earth continued to roll and shake in the most fierce earthquake she had felt yet. Some of the shakes literally sent her airborne.

A thundering rumble started. The late dusk sky was now covered with an ever-growing dark gray cloud, blocking out the first stars and the moon.

The earthquake softened a little, just enough so that she could stay on her feet without falling. Her steps, however, made a hatchling's first steps graceful and professional in comparison to the floundering she had to do just to stay upright. Pallor seemed to be having a better time keeping his balance than she was; she was reminded of the frozen pond back at the clearing.

They made it to a cluster of shrubs and ducked down in

them.

The fighting had quieted down a little bit. Looking over, she saw that the Defiance soldiers had taken advantage of the earthquake and were striking the Tyrants while they were still down. Even Harass was having difficulty standing. With a renewed cohesiveness, the Defiance wasted no time in vanquishing the remaining Tyrants in order to swarm their leader while he was vulnerable.

Scope waited. Her time to act was approaching. She could feel it.

When the last Tyrant fell, dead, there were several dozen Defiance soldiers left. Scope could see Keel among them, but sadly Kudos was missing. A quick look around told her that the several dozen soldiers she saw were all that remained of the Defiance.

She began moving toward Harass. Her help was required. The Defiance imperatively needed her firepower. Her going was slow because of the rolling ground, and she worried that she wouldn't get there in time.

Harass growled at the soldiers, his bloodthirsty eyes narrowed to slits. The Defiance leapt toward him, some of them going for his underbelly, others for his legs, and the rest for his neck. The soldiers were arranged in a line.

Scope's eyes widened, her breath catching in her throat, as she recognized the arrangement for how perilous it was. Just as she feared, a red beam came from Harass' *Annihilator* and sent the Defiance down to the ground in a horrible death with just a single attack.

Harass gazed upon the bloody horror around his feet for a moment before throwing his head back and roaring a victorious bellow into the clouding night sky. When he exhausted his breath, the *Annihilator* whirred and let loose two black cylinders. With a quiet and deadly hiss, they streaked through the air and collided with the forest. Fireballs bloomed with a single bud of blue and white flames. Foliage caught the fire and held it, and soon the trees and shrubs were alight. Scope stalked around him as the light from the fires lit up the night with shades of red, and the black smoke went up to join the massing gray cloud directly above.

Her throat tingled as she let loose a roar that was neither shrill or baritone, but easily conveyed her intent. Overcoming the moving earth, she rushed forward screaming, "HARASS!"

A wind blew a finger of flames into her path, but she jumped through them, her anger numbing her to the searing heat. If she could see herself, it would make a grand picture; a single Utahraptor, scarred and furious, with a backdrop of fire on a battle-marked ground.

Harass slowly turned her way, as if he felt that he had already won and anything more was a mere paltry. His eyes narrowed as he stared down upon her, and his lips curled into a smirk. But the smirk died a few seconds later, and Scope saw his weight shift onto one thick leg, and anticipated the oncoming stomp. But he didn't lift his foot; instead, a section of the *Annihilator* lit up with a scarlet glow. Scope bounded away just before a red beam swept through the spot where she had once been. She had just barely landed before she had to avoid a black exploding thing.

Harass roared, his lips curling up to show the entirety of his teeth. "Stand still!" he snarled, his deep voice sending terrifying bass vibrations through the air.

"And be crushed or cooked?" Scope quipped. "Think again!"

"Die, mite!" He fired three missiles in sequence, effectively trapping the foe in a circle of flames.

Scope glanced around at the fires, cringing away from the searing heat. She looked up at Harass, and saw the *Annihilator* glowing with the light of her demise. As she leapt out of the ring of fire, she frantically imagined one of the black exploding things striking Harass. The heat thankfully diminished as he roared in pain. Her shot had only struck his shoulder just under the *Annihilator*. However, she felt a surge of achievement as she saw that the *Annihilator* was heavily damaged on one side. Small sparks of fire and smoke came from the rent.

Harass roared. "You found it! The *Intimidator!* I should've killed you within the moment I killed your tribe leader!" The red beam came again, but she had moved already and it was a wasted shot.

"One of your last mistakes!" Scope snarled back, firing her own red beam. Harass ducked aside so it merely cut into his haunches.

"I am 10 times your size, runt. Fighting against me is futile. Do you wish to surrender while you still live?"

"Feel free."

Once again, she called for one of the black cylinders. In response, one flew out, colliding with the Acrocanthosaurus' abdomen. He roared in pain as his abdomen burned. The *Annihilator* sputtered ominously as only one cylinder flew at Scope. She tried to dodge but didn't quite get away in time, and the heat from the explosion scalded her tail. She bit back a screech of agony.

She yelped as another black thing exploded in front of her.

Her body screamed in pain as the heat threatened to cook her alive. With a growl, Scope braved the flames as her momentum bore her through. She collapsed on the ground, her body feeling half cooked.

Harass' eyes glinted with triumph as his lips curled into a terrifying crocodile smile. Scope stared down the remaining circular cavity from which the cylinders launched.

She braced herself as the cavity began to ominously glow as before. However, instead of a cylinder, flames shot out as the *Annihilator* made a series of small noises. The flames spread over the *Annihilator* as she noticed the most awful stench she had ever smelled.

Harass roared as Scope scrambled to her feet and ran. Harass took chase, and that was when Scope felt despair. There was no way in the world she could outrun the gargantuan strides the Acrocanthosaurus was taking.

All she could do was run, and run she did. She limped and weaved through the burning forest and skirted the wide and rushing river, heading in no direction in particular.

Behind her, she heard Harass crashing through the forest. Trees snapped into splinters as they fell. She could see the glow from the *Annihilator*'s fire lighting the way, and she realized that he was more stumbling after her than chasing her.

Unfortunately, when she turned back to face ahead, she saw a drop-off mere paces away. She could hear the thunder of water, and realized that she was at the edge of the waterfall. There was a cliff before her, and she quickly peered over the edge. She could see nothing but darkness. Her hard, gasping breaths made the mist swirl before her.

"Ha!"

She spun around. Harass stood before her, somehow managing to keep his balance. He was smiling in the most crazed, horrifying way. Scope gulped as she realized that she had cornered herself on the cliff's edge.

Harass rumbled forward, throwing his torso around. Too fatigued to move, Scope could only stare as his massive tail slung her over the cliff's edge.

Time seemed to slow. As she fell into darkness, Scope took a slow breath and raised her chin. If she was going to die, she wasn't going to be cowering and whimpering. Since she was falling back first, she had a perfect view of the sky. A crimson glow reflected off of black smoke and dark clouds.

The rising mist felt like a balm on her burns. It both stung and relieved the pain at the same time. It began to envelope her like a blanket, blocking out her view of the sky.

She huffed in dry humor as she imagined herself with the wings of a pterosaur and simply flying up and away from her imminent death. *Sorry, Spike. I failed.*

But then *Intimidator* whirred to life. She immediately twisted her neck around in time to see the surface of the *Intimidator* split and reveal two giant cylinders. They moved to the sides of her body, just behind her elbows, and the ends that faced downward began to glow. Around the glow, the air shimmered with heat waves.

Scope was silent from shock as her plummet slowed to a stop, then she screamed in a mixture of surprise and fear as she shot upward. She overtook the cliff and zoomed past a startled

Acrocanthosaurus. Twin jets of blue and white flames were coming from the ends of the cylinders. The force was taking her up into the smoke-choked sky. She felt her old fear of heights returning, and she fervently wished to go down.

The cylinders twisted again so that the glow pointed both down and behind her, and she began to descend forward.

She stopped screaming as her eyes widened. "I can fly?" she uttered in amazement. The cylinders of flame were keeping her aloft. She was flying without wings! "I can fly!"

A wave of sureness swept over her, and she turned around in the air so that she was looking directly down at Harass. He was roaring up at her in a fit of fury. She gritted her teeth and let loose a volley of the black things. They zoomed down and hit Harass. Some missed and hit the ground instead, but all in all they had the desired effect.

Scope imagined more of the black things shooting toward Harass. But nothing happened. She tried again. All she heard were empty clunks. Was she out of them? She used her red beam instead, and it skimmed Harass' leg as he tumbled, but she was horrified to see that her red beam was beginning to dim.

This can't get any worse, she thought.

And, of course and seemingly right on cue, the cylinders that were keeping her in the air began to noisily sputter. Scope immediately flew toward the ground, knowing that whatever powered her flight was also running out and she was *not* wanting to fall from fifty paces in the sky.

She landed roughly. The second her feet touched the ground, the flames on the cylinders died. Then the cylinders retracted back into the hole they had come out of. The surface plates shifted to mostly cover up the hole.

Scope whirled around in a tight circle, looking for Harass' hulking form. She dimly noticed that the ground had ceased rolling.

And then Harass burst through a wall of fire. Flames still licked his body as he lunged toward her. His eyes were crazed with agony and choler.

Wasting no time, she began running again. The fires that were consuming the forest were spreading, widening her range of sight and thus her area of flight. But it was already in vain. The *Intimidator* was now a dead weight on her back, a useless hunk of metal weighing her down. Harass was gaining. She wondered if he was able to catch up to her and squish her flat.

Without knowing sure, Scope continued her flight.

Then grace came. The earthquake came back with a tenfold of power. Scope and Harass tumbled as the ground surged up then fell away, leaving nothing but air under their feet.

Scope knew that trying to stand would be futile, so she merely raised her head and tried to focus on the chaos around her. Harass had been thrown a fair distance away and was trying to stand, but the earth was churning so greatly he would be sent back down before he had a chance to get his feet underneath him.

A bright ruddy yellow glow in the distance caught Scope's attention. The glow was seemingly coming from the peak of the flat-topped mountain that laid across the valley, past Concave Peak and her old clearing.

No, not a mountain, she thought in dread. *A volcano.*

The volcano suddenly exploded, an eruption that put the exploding black things to shame, sending red-hot rocks into the air. A shockwave hit her a moment later, almost immediately followed by a deafening boom. Most of the airborne rocks vanished into the clouds. Even from the distance, she could see a burning thick liquid beginning to run down the sides of the volcano, creating fires the instant it reached the trees. Dark ash flew from the peak.

Rocks began to fall in the valley, sending up plumes of dirt.

Scope's heart skipped a beat as she snapped her head up to look at the clouds. She only had to wait a few seconds before the first glowing rocks plummeted into view. With a scream, she desperately tried to stand. Her panic helped her, and soon she was stumbling across the heaving ground, simultaneously trying to watch the sky and where she was going.

The volcano exploded a second time. The second eruption brutally tore off a large chunk of the volcano itself and sent the dislodged section of mountainside falling down its slope. Smaller rocks and lava were delivered to the sky.

"Insect!"

Scope glanced behind her to see Harass attempting to pursue her. She groaned as she added avoiding the Acrocanthosaurus to her multitasking list, then yelped as a red-hot boulder slammed into the ground paces ahead of her. She used the earthquake's rolling to her advantage and skipped to a new direction.

Looking up, she saw a *massive* boulder falling toward her and Harass. She put on the speed and alternated between looking at the way ahead and the plummeting veritable hill. Harass roared behind her, but she ignored him.

She wished that she had the red beam to break it apart. To her astonishment, a short beam streaked up and sliced a chunk off.

Well, what do you know. It comes back!

The falling boulders came down behind her. The force of the hit made the ground roll again, and Scope was thrown off of her feet. She hit a tree and slid down the trunk. She winced, feeling as if she had been hit by the rock.

The rock! Harass!

She looked behind her and saw the boulders lying in a smoking crater. At the edge of the crater, she could see Harass' remains. Horrifically, his head was still intact, facing directly at her with a frozen expression of intense anger and shock.

Scope let out a breath. Harass was dead. She bowed her head, thankful to I Am. The bloodline of the tyrannical Acrocanthosaurus had ended.

Another rock slammed nearby, shaking her attention. *Whoa, too close!*

She resumed running as fast as she could, avoiding the rainfall of small rocks and trees. The volcano continued to erupt, sending a colossal amount of rock, lava, and ash into the air. Seemingly still under great favor, the earthquake's rolling helped Scope along, heaving at the right moment to send her over a ditch or creek, and tossing her to the side so that a falling tree missed her.

Eventually, she lost all sense of time and was consumed by the living nightmare of surviving an erupting super-volcano.

Sometime during the nightmare, she had managed to make it through what was left of the mountain pass and had returned to the Borderlands. She had collapsed at the exit of the pass and fell into an exhausted and dreamless sleep.

When she awakened again, all was dark. Scope slowly rose to her feet and began hacking. Her muscles screamed at her, but she ignored them. She only knew it was day by how the night lightened.

The sunlight was drastically dimmed, and she couldn't tell if it was morning, noon, or afternoon; all she knew was that it was daytime. The ash cloud had spread to all horizons. Thankfully, the downpour of rocks and the severe earthquakes had ended overnight, but now the ash was descending like foul-tasting snow.

A noise below her alerted her to the fact that she wasn't alone. Quickly looking down, she saw that it was Pallor sliding out from under a large blanket.

She let out a relieved sigh, happy to know that he had managed to survive. Taking a few very stiff and painful steps to him, she nudged him. He let out a deep groan as his eyelids cracked open.

"Scope?" he murmured.

"I'm here," she said. "How'd you fare?"

"Not good," Pallor said with a grunt as he got to his feet. "I received a lot of cuts and scrapes. My right leg really hurts and I can hardly move it, but I can walk. What about you?"

"Pretty much your injuries, plus some burns." Scope winced

as one of the burns on her flank stretched. "Come on, we need to get to my pit." Her first steps were slow and stiff, but she gradually became more limber and could move at a decent walking speed.

Limping after her, Pallor asked, "And Harass?"

She paused and looked back. "Dead."

"Did you kill him?"

"No. A rock fell on him. In a way, I'm sort of glad that I didn't finish him off myself."

Pallor fell silent.

As they walked, a frightened mammal scurried across their path, and she quickly leapt on it. As they were sharing it, the carcass didn't last long.

It was a while more before they reached her pit home. It had been spared destruction by rocks, and it was as she had left it. There was a huge pile of skeletons pushed against one of the pits' walls from when she and Rove had gorged themselves. They descended down the hidden ramp and then went to take a deep draught from the pond. The ash was pooling on its surface in places, and they had to scrape large chunks aside before they could drink.

Despite the water's nastily bitter taste, they had drunk her fill. She looked up at the dark gray sky for a very long moment before her entire body seemed to slump and wilt. Moving as if all of her energy had been drained from her, she plodded over to the cave and collapsed at the back of it.

"Scope?" Pallor asked in a worried tone, peering into the cave. "Are you all right?"

"Not really," she murmured. "I just. . . need some sleep." Her eyes closed and her form became limp. The agony from her burns and injuries consumed her mind as she fell into a deep sleep.

CHAPTER TWENTY EIGHT

It had been too long. Far too long.

Nicole stared at the door to her apartment, her body standing ramrod straight in the empty hall. Her door hadn't changed at all; it was still the boring light tan color and was absolutely undecorated. Her door was really nothing more than a flat slab of plastic designed to look like wood with a whole ton of locks and a peephole.

Did I really expect my apartment door to change? she thought.

Shifting her duffel bag from one arm to the other, she used her freed dominant hand to take her bundle of keys from her jacket pocket. She painstakingly inserted a different key into each lock. When they were all unlocked, she twisted the doorknob and pushed. The door's hinges creaked as it moved. She slipped through the gap and pushed the door closed. She didn't need the keys to engage the locks again.

It was dark in her apartment. She patted the wall beside her, blindly searching for the switches. She found them and flipped them on. She blinked hard a few times to the sudden brightness.

Nothing much had changed in her apartment either. Everything was dusty, of course, and there was a dreadful stink emanating from the kitchen.

"Wonderful," she muttered. "My food's probably all spoiled, too." *Well, everything except the dry and canned stuff, like Compeer's kibble.*

She frowned and glanced around.

Where is *Compeer?* She began to walk around her home, looking for her golden Lab.

When she didn't find him anywhere in the apartment, she began searching for any clues as to where her beloved pet had gone. It took her five minutes to discover the note taped to her apartment's door. She ripped it off and hurriedly read it.

"'Hey, Nikki,'" she read aloud, "'Thought I'd take Compeer back to my place so he didn't starve to death while you're stuck in the ICU department of the hospital. Give me a call when you read this; I'll have my wife bake us all dinner when you pick up Compeer. From Pete.'"

She let out a relieved sigh. "Thank you, God," she uttered,

then plucked her phone from her pocket. She commanded Pete's speed dial and raised the phone to the side of her head.

After it rang a few times, she heard Pete's voice say, *"Hello, you've reached the Berg residence. Leave your name and number after the beep; and if I know you, I'll get back to you as soon as I can. Beep!"*

Nicole rolled her eyes. "Nice attempt, Pete. Try letting it ring a few more times before you try that."

She heard a laugh. *"You're good, Nikki. So, I take it that you've gotten home?"*

"Yes, I've just found your note. Pete, you should've told me while I was in the hospital. I nearly had a heart attack when I realized that I had forgotten my dog!"

"Well, if I'd told you then, you'd be constantly checking up on me. I didn't want you calling me in all hours of the day and night just to know whether I gave him his marshmallow fluff with his dinner. Seriously, I swear dogs shouldn't be eating that stuff. It can't be healthy for them."

"Hmm. I *would* do that, you know. Besides, he's addicted to the fluff, and I don't really mind sharing, plus he's never gotten sick from it. Now, about that dinner. . .?"

"Anita is planning chicken pot pie tonight. Not the frozen junk, the good kind made from scratch. We'll eat at seven. Are you going to come over or decline and eat something there?"

Nicole sniffed the air and grimaced. "I'm coming over."

"We can chat about what didn't happen after you didn't do. . .

that."

". . . Yes. Bye, Pete."

"See you, Nikki."

She hit the 'end call' button, then shoved the phone back into her pocket. Glancing at the wall mounted clock in her living room, she saw that she had about an hour to get ready. It was a 15 minute walk to Pete's apartment building.

Hefting her heavy duffel bag onto her shoulder, she carried it into her bedroom where she unceremoniously dropped it on the bed. It took a quick gesture to unzip it, but her left arm was stretched too much and she bit her lip as the new, tender skin on her back pulled. As the pain dissipated, she flipped the bag over and dumped its contents. Shirts, undergarments, toiletries, and pants fell onto the bed in a messy pile. She chucked most of them into the hamper to be taken to the Laundromat later, then folded the rest neatly and stacked them.

She took a quick shower, then dressed herself in a comfortable tee, jeans, sneakers, and a cute black headband with white imitation rhinestones. A check on the time told her that she still had thirty minutes to kill.

"Ugh," she groaned, plodding in the direction of the kitchen. "I was dreading this."

When she opened the refrigerator door, she was immediately assaulted by the pungent stench. She gagged and ran a few steps away. After taking a few huge gulps of relatively fresh air, she held her breath and began attacking the spoiled mess that was the interior of her fridge.

She pulled out the garbage can from under the sink and began dumping rotten foodstuffs into it. There went the milk, yogurt, and the fast food leftovers. The carrot cake was turning red and green with fuzz; she gave that a mournful look. She had been looking forward to eating that cake. It was supposed to be a self-reward for a job well done on the *Intimidator*. Following the cake went the sausage, and. . . She stared at what she was holding for a moment before throwing it away. She didn't even want to remember what *that* had been.

All that was left in her fridge when she was done were a few cans of soda and some candy. The garbage can was full.

She tied the garbage bag shut, then checked the time again. Time to go. On her way to grab her purse, she snatched a can of air freshener and sprayed a lavish amount into the air. She sniffed the pine scented perfume, then sneezed harshly.

Happily relieving herself of the trash, she pleasantly surprised herself when she managed to walk to Pete's apartment building in only ten minutes. To make things even better, her healing injuries weren't complaining all that much about the exercise. She entered the apartment building and tapped Pete and Anita's apartment's floor number. It was a swift ride in the elevator, and then she counted the door numbers. She rapped her knuckles on the one she wanted.

It took a few seconds before the door was quickly swept open. "Nikki!" Pete said with a wide grin. "So glad you came. Come in, come in."

Nicole gave her co-worker a grateful smile as she slipped past him and entered the living room. She could smell the cooking chicken pot pie, and the scents coming from the kitchen were making her mouth water.

To taste real food after five months of tasteless and bland hospital gunk! She would never be taking a greasy cheeseburger and salty waffle fries for granted ever again after that culinary torture.

Suddenly, a tawny yellow form burst into view. Compeer's body slammed the wall, then bounced off and dashed to Nicole. He reared up into his hind legs and began smothering her face in fond licks.

"Compeer!" Nicole squealed, hugging the dog. "Oh, did I miss you!"

The dog woofed past his lapping tongue, his tail whipping from side to side so fast it was a blur.

"Anita!" Pete shouted. "Nicole's here!"

"Hi, Nicole!" flitted a voice from the kitchen. A pot clattered.

Popping her head around the kitchen's doorway, Nicole said, "Hi, Anita! Thanks *so much* for taking care of Compeer."

Anita shot her a grin as she waved a ladle. "It was no problem at all."

"Need help with anything?"

"Help! Goodness, I forbid it! Get in the living room and sit down!"

Pete seated himself on a black suede easy chair. "So, how've you been doing?" he asked Nicole. "Yes, do take a seat!"

Nicole collapsed on one end of the matching suede sofa. "Depends on what you mean by how I'm doing," she replied, leaning against the sofa arm. She was careful not to pull her skin too much. Compeer jumped up and draped himself over her lap.

"How'd the doctors treat you?" Pete asked.

"Can't complain about the treatments. They fixed me up really well." She rotated her shoulders to prove it, and expertly hid the ensuing wince. "The food there, however, is an entirely different story."

Pete chuckled. "Glad to see you so spry. With the way the news portrayed you when you came back, you were going to die in the ambulance."

"I lived," Nicole said. "Had a ton of blood loss, though."

"I'll bet." Pete leaned forward, his eyes sparkling with interest. "What was on the other side? What happened that made you come back halfway to death's door?"

Nicole winced at the memory of the last attack. "Coelurus are vicious beasts, I'll tell you that. No better than wild boars, but souped up with a full set of canines and some *really* sharp claws."

Pete gave her a sympathetic wince. "Ouch. What happened to the *Intimidator*?"

"From what I understand, the Struthiomimus gave it to an Utahraptor for safe keeping. I didn't see it again."

"Why does an *Utahraptor* have the *Intimidator*?" Pete said incredulously.

"I don't know," Nicole said with a defensive shrug. "I missed it because the Struthiomimus is thoughtless. It left me behind, and I had to hitch a ride with some Ankylosaurus to boot."

Pete snorted. "Speaking of which, we've been on high alert just in case it came back a third time. Do you know what happened to it?"

"The last I saw of it, a T-rex was carrying it away."

Anita poked her flour-dusted head around the corner. "Dinner's ready! You have 10 seconds to get to the table, or else!" She vanished back behind the corner.

As Nicole and Pete got up, Nicole asked, "Or else what?"

Very slowly, Pete turned his head to her and gave her a very serious look. "Or else. . ." Then, as if someone had flipped a switch, a chipper grin was plastered on his face. "I don't know, really. I don't think that she knows, either."

"Huh," was all Nicole said.

When they sat down at the oak dining set, Nicole swept her gaze over the layout. As a centerpiece, there was a large ceramic cooking pot filled almost to the brim with steaming chicken pot pie. In a slightly smaller serving dish was a pile of flaky bread. Then there was a bowl of red grapes, pears, and apples. The scene was making Nicole's mouth salivate so much she was almost drooling.

"Help yourself, Nicole," Anita stated as she seated herself at the foot of the table. "There's more than enough for thirds."

Nicole had to force herself from wolfing down the food as quickly as she could get it on her spoon. The flavors and textures were a warm welcome after so long living on hospital fares.

"Goodness, Nicole," Pete said. "You're eating like you haven't eaten a thing in a week."

Nicole blushed as she realized that, despite her efforts, she was eating at twice the speed manners allowed. She swallowed the mouthful she already had. "Sorry," she said.

"Don't apologize, darling," Anita said. "I'd be going that fast, too."

Nicole made a more conscious attempt to eat normally. Pete and Anita also returned to the meal.

Following dinner, Nicole offered to assist Anita with cleaning up the mess in the kitchen. Anita refused the offer, but Nicole insisted that she had to help. Anita relented, and put Nicole was put on dish duty.

By the time the kitchen was cleaned, it was getting late. Nicole didn't have go get home right away, and they still had to talk about what didn't happen. She told in detail what happened to her in the prehistoric time. It was well past midnight by the time they finished. Nicole bid them goodnight and collected Compeer and his supplies. Before departing, she promised to see Pete later on at work.

Compeer consistently stayed right at her left ankle as they walked. Nicole had Compeer's supplies in one hand and some chicken pot pie leftovers in her other (per Anita's logical assumption that her entire refrigerator had rotted). Her purse was draped over her neck and shoulder and Compeer's leash was looped over her wrist and hand.

The city was bustling and busy, aglow with neon signs, headlights, and street lights. Nicole winced every time a car braked too hard, a horn honked, or at any other sudden noise.

"I miss the forest, Compeer," she stated.

Compeer grunted.

CHAPTER TWENTY NINE

Nicole was abruptly awakened by the harsh blaring of her alarm clock. With a tired groan, she slung her arm and hit the clock. It made a loud noise at the collision as she missed the 'off' button. She groaned again, and she used a little more energy to grab the clock and find the button.

"I miss sleeping in," she muttered as she plodded to her closet to find the day's clothes. "The *one* good thing about being hospitalized. No one's telling you to wake up early. They just don't let you sleep."

After she finished her daily morning ritual, she went into the kitchen and reached for Compeer's dog food. The kibble rattled noisily as it tumbled into the dog dish. She expected to see the golden Lab dash in with his nails skidding on the linoleum, but all she heard was silence.

With a hum of confusion, she walked into the living room, where she kept his dog bed. She spotted him splayed out on the plush pillow, snoring away the morning. She awakened him and took him outside before returning him to the apartment.

Knowing that her dog would be fine for the rest of the day, she moved toward the door. She caught her own eye in the mirror as she went to open the locks.

Quickly checking her watch, she decided that she had just enough time to practice some dinosaur-ese before she had to leave. She hadn't been able to practice in the hospital between being poked from needles, called delusional, etc. She went through all the words that she knew, then tried to string them into proper sentences. Sadly, she didn't have a real dinosaur to rehearse with, so she had no idea whether she was getting it right or slaughtering the language.

Shaking her head at herself, she left the apartment building and took her usual route toward the subway system.

She was halfway there when she heard, "Hey, lady! Got some cash?"

Nicole glanced over her shoulder and saw a scruffy-looking man behind her. In the early morning light, she could tell that he was wearing a worn gray hooded jacket, ratty jeans, dirty sneakers, and a black baseball hat. His hands were deep in the jacket's pockets. Basically, just your usual street bum.

"My apologies," she said. "I don't have any money on me." That was a lie, but she doubted that the guy would want a few quarters and a lone one-dollar bill.

The man frowned. "I'm sure that you've got *something* on you."

"I have a purse and my work bag."

"Wrong answer," the man growled. He pulled his hands from the pockets. In one of them was a five-inch switchback knife. "Give me your purse."

Nicole glanced around. She was near the end of an alley, one that she regularly went through. She and the man were the only ones in the alley. Passerby at the ends were either oblivious or ignoring the mounting robbery from a guy that may or may not have experience with a blade.

I've handled worse, she thought. *And they had knifes built into their fingers.* "I don't think so," she stated.

The man immediately slashed with the knife, aiming toward her bare arm. She sidestepped behind him and kicked the backs of his knees. With a shout, the man went down. The knife fell from his grasp and bounced a foot or two away.

Nicole retrieved the knife. She hid it in a pocket as she exited the alleyway. It wasn't long before she passed by a trash receptacle, and she dropped the knife into it. It landed with a heavy *plunk.* She didn't give a backward glance as she strode on.

Unlocking a safe, she reached in and pulled out the two rocks that the Utahraptor had dropped next to her prone form. Other than being slightly dusty, they appeared to be in the same condition she had last seen them. She was very happy that they had been taken to her place of work after she had been picked up by the paramedics.

Next to where the rocks had laid were a data-disk and tan file. She took out the data-disk and file; then, shut the safe before carrying her load over to her workstation. Booting her computer, she inserted the data-disk and pulled up the recordings that were on it. She put on headphones and dialed up the volume.

The recording started, and Nicole glanced at the time stamp. "Odd," she muttered. According to the recording, her return had occurred a little over one day after she had gone after the Struthiomimus. *But that's improbable! I must've spent half a week in that valley.*

As she watched the data-disk, she noticed that the camera angle seemed to be coming from within a store. She could see the merchandise in the foreground, then a huge window that overlooked a rather busy farmers' market. At first, there appeared to be nothing out of the ordinary.

Then people jumped back as the air in the middle of the road began to fluctuate and ripple like water. A moment later, a very battered and bloody raptor came from the newly formed portal. It was the Utahraptor with all the scars. She watched closely as it hissed at the crowd before gently placing her on the ground.

It must've known how critical my state was, Nicole thought.

One brave person moved forward, yelled for help, and then the paramedics came. A minute later, the portal began to falter and close. The Utahraptor dropped the two rocks before vanishing back through the portal. The only sign that the portal had ever existed was a black burn on the asphalt road.

As Nicole watched herself be carried away on a stretcher, the recording clip ended.

Nicole leaned back in her seat and stared thoughtfully at the monitor. "Thank you, Utahraptor," she murmured.

After ejecting the data-disk, she turned off the monitor and opened the paper file. The first page had the date, time, and place of the street, then a copy of her hospital records and a colorized image of her healthy face, taken before the incident. According to the hospital document, she was suffering from slight dehydration, acute blood loss, and multiple wounds resembling large canine bites and knife slashes.

Moving on, she found a few pages where there were findings from the rocks. One was an uncut diamond valued around $10,000. The other rock was made of a completely unknown element, potentially priceless, and nicknamed 'Portal Ore' until a more suitable name could be found.

She picked up the Portal Ore and held it close to her face. Squinting, she saw that it was riddled with scratches, like something had been repeatedly bashed against it.

"Wait a second. . ." she muttered as a few puzzle pieces fit together in her mind. She quickly reinserted the data-disk and fast-forwarded the recording to when the Utahraptor had dropped the two rocks.

In the video, the Utahraptor released the two rocks, then clapped its hands.

Nicole's eyes widened, then she stared at the diamond and Portal Ore with a new light. Thinking rapidly, she put the rocks in two different pockets in her lab coat. After returning the file and data-disk to the safe, she hurried to Weapons Development Room 7.

Her co-workers exclaimed in a mixture of surprise and recognition as she burst through the door. Dumping her work bag and purse on the floor by the door, she went over to the area of the lab where the portal had appeared. As she had suspected, there was a swirling scorch mark. The metal floor was slightly warped where it was blackened.

"Nikki, what are you doing?" Pete asked.

"I know how the portals are made!" Nicole declared, straightening.

"How?" Pete asked.

"The dinosaurs smash them together," she said excitedly. "Somehow, the Portal Ore's element reacts to the diamond's in such a way that a breakage in time itself is made. That's how the portals appear!"

"Can you repeat it?" Mark asked, his eyes sparkling with interest.

"Not here," she replied. "If I'm right, there's a direct relevance between the place the portal opens on this end and where it opens on the other end. Pete, wasn't the farmers' market about 30 miles from here?"

"Just about," he answered.

"And I estimate that's how far we travelled through the valley," Nicole continued. "The portal that opened in this room emptied into a pit. Now, there's no telling if erosion has filled it in, or anything else, so we should go down to Room 13."

"Do you know where *that* portal empties?" a scientist asked.

She nodded. "The portals leave behind distinctive burn marks. I saw one exactly like this one on the floor here in the Struthiomimus' cave. And since that's the only portal that we don't know where it came from, it's safe to assume that a portal made in Room 13 will take us to the cave."

She strode out of the room, the others following after her. It was a quick walk down to Weapons Development Room 13, which was still guarded by several armed guards. Nicole waved her security card at them, who let her through the door. Inside, the room was empty.

Taking the two rocks from her pockets, Nicole faced the wall where the Struthiomimus had appeared so long ago. Not three feet in front of her was the distinct dark swirl of melted metal. She was aware of the other scientists gathering behind her, watching with curiosity. Taking a deep breath, she collided the two rocks against each other like how a musician would smash cymbals.

Green sparks flew from the point of impact, and landed on the charred floor. The air crackled with electricity before a portal whirled into appearance. They stared at it in awe for a moment before Nicole took a few small steps forward.

"You're not going through that again!" Pete declared.

"I have to," Nicole said. "I need to see if this portal will take me to the Struthiomimus' cave. If that happens, then we know that the portal takes the traveler to another time and not both time and another place. Besides, if it closes before I can come through again, I have the means to reopen it."

"You're *not* going in alone," Pete said, stepping forward. "I'm coming with you."

"You haven't been there before," Nicole replied. "I have."

"I'm not asking." He patted his hip meaningly.

Nicole sighed, then faced the portal. She leapt through with Pete right behind her.

There was the sense of being stretched again. Senseless, she seemed to hang motionless in empty space for a time before she was dumped back into the world.

Nicole coughed as extremely hot air entered her lungs. The air was completely devoid of moisture, and so terribly hot she reckoned that she'd end up getting a nosebleed if she stayed too long. Her clothes were already becoming saturated with sweat. Looking around, she could see that the area she was in was illuminated in a dull red light. The portal was still open behind her. The source of the light seemed to come from a tunnel at the far end of the area.

"Where are we?" Pete asked.

"This is the Struthiomimus' cave," she replied in shock as she recognized the flat table, the bamboo ventilation, and even the withered old leaves she had once used as a bed. "It worked."

Wanting to find out what was causing the nearly unbearable heat, she stalked toward the tunnel. She only made it down a short way, gasping at the steadily rising heat, before she was blocked by a mound of glowing crimson and dark gray.

"Get back!" Pete yelped, grabbing the back of her shirt and yanking her backward. "That's lava!"

"Lava!" she repeated, stepping away from the deadly melted rock. *The volcano went off while I was gone. But when did it?*

They retreated back into the cave, where the temperature was relatively cooler. They turned toward the portal, which was beginning to collapse upon itself already. With a shout, they leapt forward.

When they reappeared, Nicole flopped upon the lab's floor. She gasped at the shock of the cold metal floor against her hot skin and clothes. Beside her, Pete bent double as he gulped in the cool air.

Behind them, the portal winked out of existence.

"Nicole!" Mark exclaimed. "Pete! What happened?"

"It was the Struthiomimus' cave," she said, slowly rising to her feet. "The Struthiomimus let me stay there for about two days before we moved out. The exit tunnel was filled with lava."

"A volcano erupted?" Mark mused.

"That's what I thought. Does anyone know how long it takes lava to cool?"

Pete hummed, standing straight again. "I remember learning something about that in high school. It varies on the thickness of the lava. However, to be safe, we'd better not go back for at least six months."

Nicole deflated. "Six months?" she said with a touch of a desperate and wholly unprofessional whine. "Well, about one day here is half a week there."

"We have plenty of time!" Pete declared.

"Depends. Six months there is three weeks here. Could we prepare in a little less than a month?"

"We can schedule a trip for the first day of next month," Mark said. "That's about three weeks away. We'd need to have supplies, rations, tents, and other things to use for research and collecting samples."

"These are dinosaurs we're going to be dealing with," a scientist said. "We'd need to be well armed, a mandatory defense."

Mark leaned over to him and whispered, "So, what do you have in that end-of-the-world basement that we aren't supposed to know about?"

"I'm heading the expedition," Nicole stated.

"You can't!" Pete exclaimed. "You just got out of the hospital!"

"Can any of you speak dinosaur-ese?" Nicole countered, putting her hands on her hips.

"Dino-what?" Mark said.

"Dinosaur-ese," Nicole replied. "It's their language, and I'm the only one who speaks it. No matter what any of you say, I'm heading the mission."

"That settles it," Pete said, striding toward the wall-mounted phone system. "I'm calling management."

Nicole smiled and faced the others. "Who wants to join me

in shopping?"

A male scientist grinned. "Toys!"

chapter thirty

"I look like some sort of alien from a cheap science fiction flick," Nicole groaned as she put the fireproof helmet over her head. Looking out of the gold-tinted visor at her colleagues, she added, "At least I'm not the only one."

"My suit wasn't tailored right," Pete grunted as he pulled at one of the silver sleeves of his own suit.

Mark adjusted the heavy-duty backpack straps on his shoulders. "Stop complaining. Nicole, do you have the rocks?"

Nicole reached into her satchel and pulled them out. "Got them. Does everyone have everything they could need?"

There were six of them going on the trip: herself; Mark; Pete; and three experts on volcanos, biology, or dinosaurs. Each of them had a personal backpack and satchel, along with a small but large-wheeled cart that carried the heavier and bulky items, such as canned foodstuffs and camping supplies.

Each of the members of the expedition carried at least two different guns; a small but powerful semi-automatic rifle and a pistol. They carried the appropriate ammunition in superfluous amounts.

Behind the departure group, there were some policemen and a few members of the media. The reporters were either recording or scribbling in datapads. Nicole wasn't all that enthusiastic about the media knowing, but she knew that the public wanted an explanation for the Utahraptor suddenly appearing with a heavily injured woman in the middle of the marketplace. They *had* waited over a month already, and deserved the right to know.

Her fellow travelers glanced at each other, then nodded their heads to Nicole.

Taking that as a positive, Nicole faced the wall and smashed the diamond and the Portal Ore together, causing sparks to fly. Where the sparks landed, the air snapped, crackled, then the portal swirled to life. When someone yelled from behind the departing group, Nicole took a look at the media and policemen.

"Miss Nicole!" one of the reporters said, holding out a microphone as far as he could reach. "What are you feeling right now, as you're about to leave through a time portal to a prehistoric land?"

Nicole hid a sigh. The reporters had been asking them flamboyant questions since they had broken the news to them a week ago. Hopefully, this would be the last one she'd have to hear for a while. "Well, how would *you* feel?" she replied before turning around. "Let's go, people!"

They went through the portal.

Nicole came out first. The first thing she noticed was that it was *much* cooler, and she tugged off her helmet. The second thing was that the cave was in complete darkness. As the others came through the portal, she blindly rifled around in her satchel for her powerful penlight. She found it and flicked it on. A few seconds later, her comrades found their own flashlights. The portal was gone.

"That was the *weirdest* feeling ever!" Mikaela said, shuddering. "I lost all of my senses!"

"Watch your heads," Nicole warned as she moved her light upward. "It's less than two meters between the floor and the ceiling."

"So no jumping," Pete said. "Got it."

"Look at this floor," Beatrice murmured, kneeling down so she could touch it. Nicole had to think for a second before she recalled that Beatrice was the volcano expert. Beatrice's fingers skimmed the ripples that were formed in the rock.

Nicole shined her light on the tunnel. The way out was much smaller than before. They would have to kneel in order to move through it.

"I found something!" Mikaela exclaimed. Nicole saw that she had moved toward one of the far ends of the cave and was currently kneeling over something on the floor. Taking a few steps closer, Nicole saw that it was a dead dinosaur. It was very familiar to Nicole.

"That's a Coelurus," Nicole stated, fingering the sharp spines crowning its skull. "These things sent me into the hospital."

"But it's so small," Mikaela said as she pulled a camera from her satchel and began taking pictures of the carcass.

"Get enough of them together, and they're *quite* more than formidable," Nicole cooly replied.

The dead Coelurus seemed to have been dead for a couple of weeks, at most. From what she could see, Nicole reckoned that it had starved to death; the hide around the abdomen was so taut she could define every single rib and spinal bone. It was only slightly harder to define the rest of the bones that made up the skeletal structure. The Coelurus had literally withered away as it starved.

She held no pity or regret for the beast. *Good riddance.*

"Let's move out," Mark said as he moved toward the tunnel. "Be careful; this ceiling's really low."

Mikaela snapped a few more pictures before following them. Samuel resorted to crawling on hands and knees in order to make sure that his head wouldn't bump against the jagged rock above.

Once they exited the tunnel, Nicole nearly took a step back in shock. It looked like a blizzard of already filthy snow had hit the entire valley. The foliage was half drowned in hardened lava, completely leafless, and mere skeletons of what they used to be. The sky was completely covered with dark clouds. The amount of light coming in through the dense clouds was a little more than that of sundown. She couldn't see the sun and she had no idea what time of day it was, so all she knew was that it was daytime. It was as if her vision had been switched to monochrome and she couldn't get the colors back.

"It's so still," Pete remarked softly.

Nicole had to nod. It was like everything still alive had completely abandoned the area. From what she could see through the dead forest and the nearby mountains, the desolation covered the entire valley. She could only imagine how much further the eruption's effects had gone.

"We should get moving," Samuel said as he shrugged his backpack back on. "Nicole, you're the one with the most knowledge of this place. Where do we go?"

"Well, I think that I saw a mountain pass while I was traveling with some Ankylosaurus." She paused as she tried to figure out which mountain she had been on. After a moment, she found it, then projected a memory across her mind's eye. She pointed in an westerly direction. "That way. We need to go that way."

And they walked. Samuel, the biologist, was constantly looking out for any surviving greenery. Whenever they passed a corpse, Mikaela would rush over and examine it. Nicole soon cued up a mental list of all the dead dinosaurs, birds, and mammals they had passed by.

"These are dinosaurs living side by side with birds and mammals," Mikaela stated at one point. "Look, there's a western scrub jay! This *completely* redraws the evolutionary timelines."

"If not throw it out the window," Nicole heard Pete mutter under his breath.

Is Pete an old-fashioned creationist?

As the light of day finally began to recede after several hours of walking, they began searching for a decent place to pitch camp. They settled on a flat area of ground, then spent the rest of the day-light pitching their tents and making a fire pit.

"This wood is definitely dry," Nicole said as she dumped her armload by the fire pit. "I simply touched the branch and it fell off."

"Let's get this fire started," Pete said as he pulled out a box of matches. The firewood was arranged in a teepee form, then Pete threw a lit match onto the wood. It wasn't long before they had a source of warmth.

"Do you think that we can take off these ridiculous fire suits?" Nicole asked as she pulled at hers. "From what I can tell, the temperature's quite cool enough."

"I'm fine with that," Mark said.

In minutes, the fireproof suits were in a large silver heap a couple yards away. Nicole happily sat on a lightweight collapsable stool near the fire, now back in hiking boots, a pair of parachute pants, a tee, and a heavy jacket.

"What's for supper?" Beatrice asked.

Pete reached into a cooler and pulled out some food. "Well, we should eat the perishables first. Who's up for pre-cooked hot dogs on a stick?"

No one had any objections, so Nicole ended up holding a metal stick with a wiener stuck on the end. She held the meat inside the fire near the ashes, where the majority of the heat was. When she estimated it was warmed enough, she pulled it from the fire and took a bite. The juices squirted around in her mouth, and she smiled.

Mikaela suddenly pointed off into the darkness, looking through her camera's telephoto lens. "There's something out there!" she said in a stage whisper.

"How can you tell?" Mark asked, readying his rifle. "It's pitch black out there."

"I saw the fire in its eyes. Like how a cat's eyes glow when you shine a light in them."

Nicole twirled in her seat so she could peer into the dead forest where Mikaela had pointed. "Everyone, be quiet!"

Silence fell, and soon the only sounds that could be heard was the crackling of the fire. Nicole tried to block that sound out and focused on the darkness. She slowly pulled out her own rifle and flicked off the safety.

She just barely heard a branch creak.

"Who there?" Nicole called out in dinosaur-ese, pointing her rifle toward where she thought the sound had originated.

There! The two pinpricks of green orbs. Eyes.

"Come out," she continued, lowering her rifle but keeping it ready. It could be a hungry dinosaur; the forest looked vacant of any other source of food other than themselves. "We no hurt you." She winced, knowing that she had messed something up in her last sentence.

But it seemed like her words had worked, because they heard the soft flaps of wings before something glided into the light. It was a pterosaur, a Pterodactylus, and small for one of its species, yet still slightly larger than a red-tailed hawk. It circled above them a few times before landing on top of one of their tents.

Nicole gave a motion to the others that meant for them to lower their guns. This pterosaur wouldn't be able to kill them even if it wanted to.

"Who spoke?" it hissed in dinosaur-ese, though everyone but Nicole heard a wordless hiss followed by a short grunt.

"I talk," Nicole said, knowing instinctively that she again messed something up, but she knew not what. She resigned herself to the fact that her dinosaur-ese still needed fine-tuning.

The pterosaur looked directly at Nicole. "What are you?"

"I am human," Nicole said. Her last word was in English, as she didn't know the right word.

"Human?" the pterosaur mimicked, causing the others to startle at the unexpected English.

"Yes," Nicole said with a nod. "What. . ." She frowned, trying to find the right word. At a loss, she finally gave a vague gesture to their surroundings.

Fortunately, the pterosaur seemed to understand. "The tree-less mountain exploded. It rained down rocks and. . ." it screeched softly. ". . . for many weeks. The deadly rain stopped a while ago, but the lava continued for what should have been the Colors Season. The mountain still makes the cloud that blocks the sun."

Nicole nodded absent-mindedly as she applied the single screech to what she assumed was 'lava.' Then, something odd that the dinosaur had said stuck out at her.

"What's it saying?" Mikaela asked.

"It looks like there's a weird time distortion between our time and this one," Nicole stated. "It just said that the lava stopped flowing just a few months ago, but this is still fresh rock. Beatrice, you're the volcano expert. What's your estimation?"

Beatrice hummed. "The rock is brand new. Depends on how long this layer of ash took to settle. But you're right, there's a time gap. . ."

"You and Pete went through to here just under three weeks ago," Mark said to Nicole. "The lava was still going then."

"Yep," Pete said. "Time's running faster here than back at home."

"Is that meat?" the pterosaur suddenly blurted, staring at the package of hot dogs.

Nicole glanced at the package. "You want some?" she asked in its language.

The pterosaur nodded eagerly.

Reaching to the package, Nicole plucked out a single wiener and tossed it toward the pterosaur. The moment the morsel of food left Nicole's hand, the pterosaur leapt up from its spot on the tent and caught the meat out of the air. It glided down to the ground and wolfed down the wiener like the world was going to end in the next second.

"Wow, hungry much?" Pete remarked.

"Thank you," the pterosaur said, giving Nicole a curt nod. "Now, why are you here?"

"I come here big time ago," Nicole said in dinosaur-ese. "I chase one who stole thing of mine. He and I go to pack and fight bad ones. I go, and now I come back to find friends. You know where friends are?"

"Names?" the pterosaur asked.

Nicole thought hard for the Struthiomimus' name, then said it.

The Pterodactylus' eyes immediately widened. It echoed the name, then said, "He is dead! Died almost four Turns ago. Wait, did he steal the *Intimidator*?"

Pete and Mark didn't understand a single syllable except the 'Intimidator,' which was said in English. "The *Intimidator*?" Mark said. "Where is it?"

Nicole translated Mark's words.

The pterosaur narrowed its eyes at it thought. "The *Intimidator* was given to a young. . ." *grunt growl* ". . . and she fought very hard against the great evil that came over us. The evil is gone now, but she and many, many others are wasting away because of the lack of food."

"You take us to her?" Nicole queried eagerly.

"Yes," was the immediate reply. "But we will wait until daylight. Until then, may I have more of that meat?"

CHAPCER CHIRCY ONE

As the grayscale of daylight returned, the humans began tearing down their campsite. After that, the pterosaur led them through the ashen forest to a rocky mountain pass. Halfway up the pass, the lava's edge finally ebbed and revealed the natural unevenness of the untouched ground. But even the ground was lifeless; any vegetation had been burned to a crisp.

"Looks like the lava flow ended here," Beatrice stated as she snapped several pictures.

Nicole looked up at the pterosaur, which had flown ahead and was now beginning to circle back. "Beatrice, finish up. We need to keep moving."

"We've been walking all day," Mikaela said. "The sky's going to get darker any moment now."

"The further we go before nightfall, the better," Samuel said curtly to Mikaela.

They kept on walking. It wasn't long before the mountain pass ended and revealed a barren forest. The Pterodactylus glided amongst the trees, lazily weaving through them. Nicole hurried at a fast walk, not wanting to lose sight of the pterosaur. Her comrades also picked up their pace.

Nicole heard someone coming up behind her. Turning, she saw Mikaela drawing alongside her.

"Yes?" Nicole asked.

Mikaela was frowning, occasionally looking between her mini-datapad and the Pterodactylus. "That pterosaur shouldn't be here," she said.

Nicole raised a questioning eyebrow.

"Pterodactylus don't live in North America! They're Europe-an pterosaurs."

"They could've migrated."

"All the way across the Atlantic?" Mikaela asked dubiously.

"Well, I can always ask it." And Nicole did.

The Pterodactylus alighted on a branch and looked down at them. "My family and I fly where the water leads us. I grew up in. . . *Europe*, but have been on the move my whole life. We had just come across the great lake when the volcano blew."

Nicole translated and shrugged. "Maybe their bones weren't fossilized."

"It's not natural," Mikaela grumbled, tapping on her mini-datapad. "Things should stay where they were born."

"So, you're grouping humans into that statement, too?" Pete said, making Nicole jump. *When had he walked up?* "You're saying that people should stay where they're born, too? Where would we be if the Pilgrims hadn't packed up and left for America? Cortez? Captain Cook?"

Mikaela mildly glared and began using a stylus to write on her 'pad. The conversation was dropped, and the Pterodactylus continued escorting them.

Darkness was just beginning to fall when the pterosaur screeched at Nicole; "Stop!"

Nicole froze in the middle of a step, her leading foot hanging motionless in midair. "What?" she asked in English, too startled to speak in dinosaur-ese.

The pterosaur dived down toward the ground. Nicole's eyes widened, expecting the pterosaur to crash headlong into the ash-covered ground, but the pterosaur seemed to vanish into the dead grass and dry dirt. It was a few seconds before it seemed to fly up from the ground again.

With a theory forming, Nicole cautiously lowered her foot but did not put an ounce of weight onto it. Where the stiff dead blades of brownish gray grass were just two feet before her, her foot went through them and kept going into thin air.

Nicole put her foot down beside her other one and leaned forward. A ridge of tall grasses and the skeletons of shrubs lined what appeared to be a pit in the ground. There were a few dead saplings at the bottom, a small pond which obviously used to be about twice as large, and a cave in one wall of the pit.

"Why'd you stop, Nikki?" Pete asked, striding forward.

"Don't take a step past me!" Nicole warned, throwing out her arm. "There's a pit here. It's maybe two meters between here and the bottom."

Pete immediately became more unsure in his movements as he moved forward to examine the pit. "Maybe more. That's the first source of water we've seen yet."

"There used to be a huge lake in the center of the valley," Nicole stated sadly. "The lava must've displaced it." She knelt down and looked closely at the steep walls of the pit. "How do we go down?" she asked the pterosaur in dinosaur-ese.

The pterosaur chirped and flew a short distance away. It landed next to a small outcrop of rocks that laid next to the pit. Nicole followed it and saw that there was a thin path of dirt and stone going down into the pit.

"Thank you," Nicole said.

"Well, let's get down there," Samuel said. "That dinosaur the pterosaur mentioned must be in that cave."

"I think so, too," Nicole said. "Okay, people, leave the heavy gear up here. I don't think anyone would find anything useful in them." As the others moved to obey, she began going down the path.

Once she got down to the bottom, she walked toward the cave. The daylight wasn't nearly strong enough to show what was past the first few inches into the darkness. She pulled her pistol from its holster and held it ready. Kneeling down, she turned on her penlight.

The white beam of light instantly landed on a tawny yellow hide that was stretched over a mess of bones and waning muscles. Nicole moved the light up the body until it got to the head. The head of the dinosaur, apparently some sort of raptor, was blunt-nosed with a ridge going over each eye, sort of like natural parasols. The eyes were closed.

I've seen this kind of raptor before, Nicole thought. She moved her light again so that it illuminated the limp magenta fringe that lined the entire length of the neck. *Wait, that fringe. . . it's an Utahraptor!*

Nicole gasped as the light hit the shiny *Intimidator* that was mounted on the Utahraptor's back. The *Intimidator* was slightly scratched up and far dirter than when she had last seen it. But, it appeared to be in good shape.

"What's in there, Nicole?" Mikaela called, kneeling at the entrance of the cave.

"An Utahraptor," Nicole replied over her shoulder. She shined her penlight around the dinosaur's battered body. "Heavily injured. It's fortunate that those wounds aren't infected by now."

"What kind of wounds?" Mikaela asked as she entered the cave.

"Burns and cuts, mostly."

Mikaela moved to crouch at Nicole's left. "Is it dead?" Using her flashlight, she began to inspect the wounds.

Nicole wasn't sure. She focused her light on the Utahraptor's abdomen and kept a close eye on the skin there. After a long minute, she saw the area slowly inflate, then equally slowly deflate.

"It's alive!" Nicole said. "It needs to get something to eat quickly, or else it'll starve to death. Mikaela, have one of the boys get some water and meat and throw it in here. I'll wake it up and feed it. Go."

"Going," Mikaela murmured as she moved away.

Nicole was a step away from being able to touch the Utahraptor. She took the step and reached out her arm. Her fingers lightly brushed the bridge of the dinosaur's nose. The hide was smooth, the flat scaly skin letting her fingers easily glide over them. It felt like snake skin.

"What happened to you?" she muttered.

The Utahraptor took a shuddering breath and let it out, startling Nicole enough for her to level her pistol at the dinosaur. The eyelids twitched but didn't open. As she lowered her pistol, Nicole hoped that it wasn't in a coma from the injuries and lack of sustenance.

Footsteps at the cave's opening caused Nicole to turn her head. Mikaela was there and throwing in several packages of hot dogs and a water bottle. Nicole nodded her thanks.

"You handle the meat," Nicole said. "I'll wake it up."

Mikaela nodded.

Nicole leaned forward and gently shook the Utahraptor. When she got no response, she did it again, slightly harder. This time, the dinosaur made a soft groan but still didn't awaken. Nicole shook it even harder as she shouted in dinosaur-ese, "Up, you! Up!"

The Utahraptor's eyes flew open as it made a startled yelp. It hurriedly attempted to get onto its feet, but the leg muscles were weak and it couldn't rise. The dinosaur looked at the two humans and made a quiet growling sound.

Mikaela quickly scrambled away, leaving Nicole alone with the raptor. Nicole grabbed a package of the hot dogs and ripped it open. The Utahraptor's nostrils flared as it focused its gaze on the meat.

"Food for you," Nicole said in dinosaur-ese. "I help you. Eat?"

The Utahraptor flicked its eyes back to meet Nicole's. "You are not going to hurt me?" it rasped.

"No," Nicole affirmed. "I help you." She pulled a hot dog from the package and held it out.

The Utahraptor didn't raise its head from its resting spot on the floor as it sniffed the wiener. After a moment, it opened its jaw, revealing its sharp teeth. Nicole tossed the meat onto its tongue, and the dinosaur quickly chewed the meat a few times before swallowing.

"More?" the Utahraptor asked. "Water?"

Nicole obliged, pouring a little water into its mouth. Once it swallowed, she added several wieners. "You name?" Nicole asked in dinosaur-ese.

The Utahraptor swallowed the hot dogs currently in its mouth before making a sharp grunt. "And yours?" it asked.

"Nicole."

The Utahraptor gave her a heavy stare. "Nicole?" it echoed. "*The* Nicole?"

Nicole blinked. "You know me?"

The Utahraptor nodded, a semi-startling familiar gesture. "My leader once told stories of you and. . ." It said the Struthiomimus' name.

"You know. . ." Nicole started in dinosaur-ese, then added the Struthiomimus' name.

"Not personally," the Utahraptor said with a small shake of its head. "He died a long time ago."

"Oh," Nicole said with a sigh. "You get up?"

The Utahraptor shifted a little, then bit its bottom lip as it whimpered. "I hurt all over."

Nicole glanced at the wounds. "I get things to help that."

"You can heal injuries?" the Utahraptor said in amazement.

Nicole nodded. "I come back," she said before moving out of the cave.

"Is it awake?" Mikaela asked as Nicole emerged into the open.

"Yes, and thank you *so much* for that show of superb bravery in there," Nicole replied sarcastically. "Mark, please bring your medical kit."

Mark nodded and sprinted for the path.

While Mark was gone, Nicole looked up at the clouded sky. "Beatrice, do those clouds show any signs of leaving anytime soon?"

Beatrice shook her head. "Unless the volcano stops fueling 'em, this whole land will stay in darkness. The clouds are made of ash. If it ever rains, it'll be an acid rain."

Samuel frowned. "Without sunlight or rain, the plants will die."

"And then that causes the herbivores to starve," Mikaela jutted in, looking down at the ground as she thought. "When the herbivores are dead, the carnivores have nothing to eat, so *they* starve. This volcanic eruption must've been what wiped out the dinosaurs! It starved them to death, and those that survived must've only lasted a short while before dying of something else."

"We're witnessing the beginnings of extinction," Pete uttered forlornly.

Nicole stared absent-mindedly into the flames of the bonfire that Samuel had erected an hour earlier. Her cooking stick with a hot dog stuck on the end hung limply from her arms. The meat wasn't cooking at all, as it was too far away from the heat.

The Utahraptor was bandaged and back on its way to health. After Mark had finished applying the first aid, the team had managed to bring it out of the cave and near the bonfire. It was staring into the flames with an expression of nostalgia.

The Pterodactylus had flown off to no one knew where.

Everyone else was sitting around the bonfire, eating their hot dogs. Other than the sounds of fire crackling and chewing, there was silence.

"How'd the dinosaur get so beat up?" Pete finally said.

Nicole glanced at Pete, then translated his query into dino-saur-ese.

The Utahraptor rumbled deep from within its throat before replying, "I was in a great battle with an evil. . ." *growl, hiss* ". . . who had taken over the valley using the *Annihilator*."

"The *Annihilator*?" Mark repeated, his eyes wide. "Nicole, what'd it say about the prototype?"

"It said that some really evil dinosaur had the *Annihilator* and used it to take over the valley," Nicole translated. She turned to the dinosaur and said, "Why you fight?"

"For free. . ." *rumble.*

Nicole frowned as she mentally ran through the Utahrap-tor's reply. It had said 'free' with a rumbling noise at the end. Was it trying to say 'freedom?' She assumed so and applied it to her mental dictionary.

"Freedom," Nicole finally translated. "It was fighting for freedom."

"Maybe that's what we should call the Utahraptor," Mikaela said. "We just can't go around calling it a nameless 'it' all the time."

"We shouldn't even be calling the dinosaur an 'it' at all," Nicole said. "Girl, boy?" she asked in dinosaur-ese.

"Girl," the Utahraptor instantly answered.

"She's a girl," Nicole said to the others. "Freedom the female Utahraptor." She turned to the newly dubbed Freedom. "We call you Freedom," she said in dinosaur-ese.

Freedom nodded. "Fine with me. Nicole, teach me your words. I do not like this constant translating."

Nicole nodded. "When day come," she said.

Freedom nodded again.

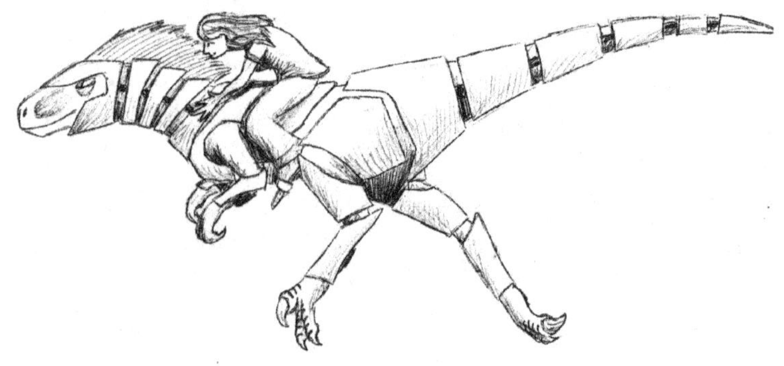

chapter thirty two

Nicole was dreaming about riding a dinosaur. The dinosaur had a saddle and seemed to be wearing some sort of armor. She couldn't tell what kind of dinosaur it was under the armor. They were running across a wide field at a high speed.

"Nicole! Nikki, wake up!"

Shaken back into the realm of the awake, Nicole cracked open her eyes and glared at the person who had awakened her. "What's wrong?" she asked.

"You'd really want to see this," Pete said. "Mikaela's going shutter-happy."

If Mikaela was being crazy with a camera, then dinosaurs had to be involved. With more than a smidgeon of curiosity arising, Nicole shimmied out of her sleeping bag and stretched. She got to her feet and followed Pete toward the path that led out of the pit.

"What's going on?" Nicole asked as she combed her hair with her fingers.

"You'll never guess what our little Pterodactylus friend was doing," Pete said as he trod up the path.

"Don't tell me that it was gathering together everyone it could find and sending them to us with the promise of free food."

Pete made a choked humming noise and looked down.

Nicole's eyes shot to their widest limit. "I was joking! Surely, that's not true!"

"See for yourself," Pete said as they reached the top of the path.

The second Nicole could see over the rim of the pit, she froze. There were dinosaurs all over the place, ranging from Ankylosaurus to Troodons and practically everything else in between. They must've been peaceful despite their hunger, because Mikaela was dancing through them snapping pictures like she had stumbled upon a gold mine.

"Have they been fed yet?" Nicole asked Pete.

He shook his head. "Not yet, but thankfully they haven't eaten Mikaela yet."

Nicole groaned and held the bridge of her nose. "How much

food do we have?"

"We've got the apples, carrots, celery, and corn, but those are bound to go bad in a few days, so it's not like we're going to be missing them. The canned tuna and chicken can go to the carnivores. . ."

"Stop, Pete," Nicole said with a groan, holding up a hand. "Let's empty our food bags, see what can be eaten by dinosaurs and what can be left for us. How many dinosaurs are here?"

"Well, they started coming as soon as daylight started, and they keep trickling in. I'd say about 20 so far."

"Have the others grab the bags and dump them out in the pit."

Several minutes later, the humans were bent over a large heap of cans, fruit, vegetables, freeze-dried food, and bottles of water. Nicole sectioned her comrades to separate the food into two classifications. While they worked, Nicole took it upon herself to teach Freedom English by pointing at the foods and saying their names.

Once the food was divided, Nicole asked a nearby pterosaur to get the dinosaurs into sections by herbivore and carnivore. The pterosaur, in turn, called upon its friends and began screeching at the rest.

"They're organized!" Beatrice called down into the pit a short while later.

"How long could this much food feed more than 20 dinosaurs?" Samuel asked Mikaela.

Mikaela snorted. "This will last them one meal, and *we* get at least a week's worth if we really ration."

"Let's feed them," Nicole said. "After at least the carnivores are sated, we can argue about how much food we've got left. Now, who's going to help me carry this stuff out of the pit?"

Nicole and Samuel took the meat up top. The carnivores eagerly awaited, shifting their bodies impatiently from side to side.

"Wait," Nicole said in dinosaur-ese as some Troodons began advancing eagerly. When the Troodons hesitantly stopped, she continued, "All have some. I give out."

She dumped her load onto the ground, then used her hands to scatter the meat out so that the carnivores wouldn't be crowding around one area. As she did this, the carnivores grew more and more restless. A few were darting forward a few steps before stopping.

A minute later, Nicole took several steps back and nodded to the carnivores.

They rushed forward as one and surrounded the meat strewn on the ground. Nicole watched them eat for a moment before turning to see how her comrades were faring with the herbivores.

Mikaela looked like she was about to faint from happiness as a Corythosaurus ate some leafy greens from her hand. A smaller Corythosaurus joined the other one. As for the others, they were throwing the food at the ground and trying not to get trampled, speared, or bashed by hunger-mad herbivores that were much larger than they were.

Separating from the carnivores, a small Utahraptor approached the ramp of the pit and started down it. He carried a small rodent in his mouth. Nicole almost went over to stop it, but Freedom made a happy screech. The other Utahraptor replied in kind, albeit muffled, and dropped the rodent before Freedom. Nicole watched as they ate the rodent together. They were obviously very close.

"Who is this?" Nicole asked in dinosaur-ese as she entered the pit.

Freedom swallowed and smiled. "Brother." She grunted to the other Utahraptor.

Nicole looked over the Utahraptor as he did the same to her. He was smaller than Freedom, and had a very pale gray splotch covering most of his head.

"Nice to meet you," Nicole said. "What's your name?"

The Utahraptor said something close to 'pale.'

Pale. Pale. . . "Pale?" Nicole repeated.

Both Utahraptors shook their heads. "Not quite, but close enough," Freedom said.

Nicole nodded and strode over to what food was left over for the humans to eat. Freedom left Pale and stood over the remaining food, sniffing it.

Freedom looked up at Nicole. "You don't have enough food to last you long."

"I know," Nicole replied. "One of us need go back and get

more."

"It must be soon," Freedom said. "You gave out all of the meat you had. You're fortunate that your kind wasn't mauled when you arrived."

Nicole frowned and held the bridge of her nose. "I send some back for more food."

Freedom shook her head. "You'll have the same problem again later on."

A proverbial lightbulb flashed on over Nicole's head. *What if I take the dinosaurs to the food?* she wondered. "You know one who got others here?" Nicole asked Freedom, referring to the Pterodactylus.

"Yes."

"Call for more. We save all we can."

"How?" Freedom asked with a tilt of her head.

Nicole grinned. "You all go back with us humans."

"Are you insane?" Mark yelped.

Nicole had waited until nightfall to tell her comrades her idea. When all of them were settled around another bonfire eating freeze-dried food, Nicole told them. It apparently hadn't gone over well.

"This could be the only way to save the dinosaurs," Nicole

said. "We can't just make steady trips to the future and back. The dinosaurs *have* no future here. They can survive back in our time."

"Nicole, there's a *war* going on out there!" Beatrice said. "There's rumors of the Unison Order using long range weapons to attack us past the front lines. The dinosaurs would be at risk even if they stayed an enormous distance away."

Nicole scowled. "From what you're saying, it's either a slow starvation here, or death by missile there. Personally, I think that they'd fare better where there's still grass, trees, and squirrels!"

"What about their privacy?" Mikaela said. "From what we've all seen, dinosaurs are sentient, or *really* close to it. The press will have a field day and swarm them, and they'll get disgruntled and maybe attack. Have you *seen* how huge these dinosaurs are? What am I saying, of course you have. Humans are toast if they attack us."

"Well, what would you choose if you were faced with extinction?" Nicole said. "Constant media coverage or death? You're trying to think up reasons why the dinosaurs can't go through the portal when all that awaits them here is starvation!"

A tense quiet settled over the pit. Freedom, who had been standing a short distance away, limped closer. Nicole glanced at the Utahraptor.

Freedom's fringe twitched upward as she took a shaky step closer. She made a crooning sound to draw the others' attentions. "Nicole right," Freedom said in raspy English for the first time. "Death here."

Nicole was impressed by how much English Freedom had managed to grasp at in less than 24 hours. Everyone else was shocked to hear a dinosaur coherently speaking a human language.

It was like hearing a parrot talking, but it was known that the parrot was only mimicking and repeating without knowing what was actually being said. With Freedom, it was obvious that she knew exactly what was going on and was giving her input.

"Is this settled, then?" Nicole said.

Pete gave a slow nod. "In the morning, I can go back through the portal and alert the authorities. It's one phone call. It shouldn't take too long, even with this passage of time difference."

"You're not going alone," Samuel said to Pete. "The word of one without backup won't be believed as readily as the word of two."

"And proof?" Beatrice asked. "What about proof?"

"The media covered us going through the portal and it closing behind us," Mikaela said. "Isn't that proof enough?"

"Just in case that's not, we'd better take one of the dinosaurs with us," Pete said. "One of the smaller ones, so that anyone we meet won't immediately cower."

"I go," Freedom said in English.

"You've barely healed enough to walk without severely limping!" Nicole said. "No, you're staying here. We'll just have to find someone else."

"How about one of the pterosaurs?" Beatrice said.

"It could fly away and we'd have a really hard time getting it back," Mark said. "It has to be at least one of the herbivores."

"But all of them are huge!" Samuel said. "There's no such

thing as 'small' with them. Just 'big' and 'bigger.'"

"Wait," Nicole said. "When I was with the Struthiomimus, he had a Microvenator with him. We can check up there to see if there are any Microvenators. They're small."

"That could work," Pete said. "Before we leave tomorrow, we'll scan the group up top."

"So, now this is all settled?" Nicole said. When she saw heads bob up and down, she smiled. "Good. Rest up people, we have a big day tomorrow."

CHAPCER CHIRCY CHREE

"Nicole! We could use some assistance over here!"

With a quiet sound of disruption, Nicole looked up from where she was working. After carefully putting her work away in her satchel, she went to see who had called her.

Pete and Beatrice helplessly stood near a milling bunch of small dinosaurs. Nicole strode closer, eyeing them curiously.

"What's wrong?" she asked.

One of the dinosaurs screeched, a high pitched sound that made the humans cover their ears. The others began making panicky noises, looking around frantically.

"That," Beatrice said.

"I didn't hear anything like that earlier," Nicole stated, rubbing at her ear in an effort to rid it of a ringing.

"The screech was new," Pete amended. "They were running around like chickens. None of them seem to like humans at all."

"I simply can't think of a reason why," Beatrice added. "Unless there are other humans here, they shouldn't be able to know to fear us."

"Why do birds and deer flee in terror when we come near?" Nicole asked wryly. "Let me try and get them to calm down."

Pete and Beatrice moved to stand further away while Nicole took a few steps closer to the small dinosaurs. The beasts chirped warily as they kept their gazes on Nicole.

"What wrong?" she asked them in dinosaur-ese. While the dinosaurs uncertainly glanced at each other, she took the chance to discern what breeds they were. There were a few Microvenators, what looked to be a teeny tiny Utahraptors, but obviously full grown (she thought them to be Hesperonychus), and a few Bambiraptors.

One of the Hesperonychus hissed at her, its frill stiffly standing erect. The sight of a dinosaur smaller than a house cat making such a noise was more humorous than alarming.

Nicole frowned. "What wrong?" she repeated. "I no harm you."

A Microvenator butted one of the others to the side and came several steps closer to Nicole. It seemed to search her face, the eyes squinting and the lips clenched.

It was with a start, Nicole recognized the diminutive dinosaur. "Spines?" she said in English.

The Microvenator jumped back a little, its eyes widening. "Nicole?" it replied, also in English.

"Spines!" Nicole exclaimed, this time in dinosaur-ese. "It you." She picked up the Microvenator and held it to her chest. "I miss you much! You heal, too. I scared you be killed in attack!"

"You are alive, as well!" Spines said in its own language. "You can understand me now?"

"Yes," Nicole replied.

"You've gotten better. Who's been teaching you?"

Nicole said the Utahraptor's name.

Spines' eyes widened. "She is here, alive? What good news this is! We've been hoping that she had survived the mountain. Where is she?"

With a gesture to the pit, Nicole said, "Down."

Spines squirmed out of Nicole's arms. "Could you take me to her? It's very important that I speak to her."

"Nicole?" Beatrice asked. "What's it saying? *Who* is it? You're wholly familiar with the little bloke."

"It's Spines, a Microvenator that was friends with the Struthiomimus. I've told you my abrupt excursion. And to answer your first query, she's wanting to see Freedom."

Spines began taking long strides toward the pit, and Nicole followed after. She wanted to see what the Microvenator had to say to the Utahraptor.

Mark and Samuel glanced up from where they were working as Spines and Nicole stepped foot on the floor of the pit. A short distance away, by the ash-contaminated pond, Freedom looked up as well. Her expression was intrigued as Spines approached. Nicole stopped a respectful distance away.

Freedom's eyes widened as Spines suddenly dropped its head and lowered its torso into a bow.

"Why do you do that?" Freedom asked in dinosaur-ese.

Spines briefly glanced up at the Utahraptor. "You have defeated. . ." Nicole heard a growl, which she could only assume was a name.

Freedom shook her head. "I didn't do it. A rock killed him. Don't bow to me."

After a long moment, Spines straightened from its stance. "But what do we do now? We can't possibly go back to the life we once lived. There could be another one, one even more ruthless than him! We need a guardian."

Eyes widening, Freedom made a squealing noise of disbelief; another word that Nicole couldn't understand. "I'm not suited for such a thing! If asked, I refuse."

"You are the only one who could handle another. . ." A growl. Spines gestured to the *Intimidator*.

Freedom twisted her neck around so she could see the shining machinery fastened to her back. Turning back to the Microvenator, she said, "It's empty. Nothing inside. It's useless, and I'm now nothing more than a normal. . ." *Grunt-growl.* Nicole was beginning to think that was what 'Utahraptor' was in dinosaur-ese.

"Then who will lead us?" Spines said plaintively. "We need someone to look to with the land like this."

A small smile graced Freedom's mouth then. "We are not staying here. Nicole has offered us a new home back in her time. There is the sun and lots of food. A guardian won't be needed, since there will only be so many of us."

Spines was silent, eyes flickering across the ground. After a moment, it nodded. "I defer to you."

Freedom grimaced. "Please, I beg you, treat me like I'm ordinary."

With a small nod, Spines started to bow again but caught itself just in time. The Microvenator gave a little smile to Freedom before walking away.

Nicole glanced at Samuel. He and Pete would be going back through the portal, and they needed one of the smaller dinosaurs as proof. To her, Spines would be the best candidate, not only having a rather level temperament, but because of its familiarity with humanity. Taking a breath, Nicole moved toward the Microvenator.

"Spines, I need you help," Nicole said in dinosaur-ese. "My friends go for my time soon. You want go?"

The Microvenator pursed its lips. After a few seconds, it nodded. "I will go," it said.

Nicole beamed. "Thank you, Spines."

What's taking them so long? Nicole mentally groaned.

It had been three days. Three entire days since Pete, Samuel, and Spines had travelled through the portal. The Microvenator had promised to be careful and keep an eye on the two humans with her. Laughing and ignoring Samuel's pleas for a translation, Nicole had given the diamond and the Portal Ore to Pete so that they could reopen the portal after they had called the authorities and verified their claims.

Their job was one that should've taken at most five hours. But there *was* the time discrepancy.

Nicole felt like her stomach was trying to digest itself in desperation. Despite earlier estimated, the freeze-dried food had run out just that morning, leaving herself, Beatrice, Mark, and Mikaela with nothing but the last five bottled waters.

There was something that she had said in her youth to her mother when she was hungry. *What was it? Oh yes, 'Mom, my digestive system is going to get lazy because it has nothing to do. . .'* She had no idea if the digestive system *could* get lazy, but she was definitely testing that out.

Nicole was lying on her back on top of her sleeping bag, staring at the dark and dismal ash clouds above. A few pterosaurs glided across her field of vision, little more than mere silhouettes against the clouds. She idly wondered how long it would take her eyes to adjust to the sun once she got back to the future.

"What are you doing?"

It wasn't hard to identify the voice. Freedom's English had gotten far better over the past three days, and the Utahraptor, in return, was helping Nicole's grasp on dinosaur-ese. According to Freedom, she no longer sounded like a hatchling trying to say its first words.

"Nothing much," Nicole replied in English, watching Freedom settle down beside her out of the corner of her eyes. "Just thinking about random things. You?"

Freedom looked up toward the sky. "I'm trying not to think about food. I've lasted longer, but if none of us carnivores eat within the week, we're going to attack the closest source of meat we see. I cannot promise your safety then."

Nicole shivered. "Let's hope that Pete and Samuel come back before then."

"I have some pterosaurs keeping watch for the portal," Freedom said with a reassuring tone. "If it opens, they will screech."

"Good to know. Want to lie down on your back with me?"

Freedom gave Nicole a sidelong look. "I would, but not many of us are as comfortable showing our soft underbellies as you humans are. Not only that, but the *Intimidator* wouldn't allow me to lay down on my back."

Nicole glanced at the silver metal weapon fixated on Freedom's back. "Oh. Right."

"Did you forget that I wear it?" Freedom asked with a wry smile.

"I guess so. Just got so used to seeing you with it I forgot."

Freedom made a soft rumbling noise not unlike a guttural chuckle.

Nicole averted her gaze from the sky and looked at Freedom. She just couldn't get over how flexible and impressionable the dinosaurs' faces were. They seemed to be able to show the same amount of different expressions as humans could, although the crests that lined the tops of their eyes were stiff and they couldn't use the differing eyebrow expressions.

There were dinosaurs speaking up top. Nicole tried to listen in, but she could just barely catch a few words. Freedom, however, apparently could hear them quite well because her expression began to look more dismal.

"Something wrong?" Nicole asked.

Freedom gave a slow nod. "The Troodons came back from their hunt. They could only find a few mammals. Not nearly enough to feed all of us."

Nicole frowned. The dinosaur population around the pit had exploded ever since she had had the Pterodactylus round up as many as it could find. Instead of around 20, there seemed to be well over a 100. Nicole was astonished by how many there were, but Freedom had said that a hundred was a pitiful fraction of how many dinosaurs had once populated the valley and the surrounding lands.

Pete and Samuel need to hurry back, Nicole thought in worry.

Something furry fell next to Nicole and she yelped in surprise. She looked down at the furry thing and saw that it was a rodent-esque creature a bit smaller than a groundhog. Nicole looked up and saw Pale gazing down.

"I can't take this," Nicole muttered, picking up the mammal and preparing to toss it up.

"He gave it to you," Freedom interjected. "It's more for you, the other humans, and me. We need food just as much as they do."

"We humans can last three weeks without food," Nicole said, holding the mammal out to Freedom. "Our water, hopefully, will last us for the next couple of days. From what you told me, you can only last a week and a half before you turn feral. You need this mammal more than we do."

Freedom eyed the mammal. "But what about the other humans?"

"They'll understand," Nicole said, hoping that they wouldn't be too mad at her for giving up some food.

With a hungry growl, Freedom wrapped her teeth around the mammal and jerked it out of Nicole's grip. Freedom carried it a few steps away before she dropped it on the ground between her and Pale. She placed a foot on top to keep it still, then they began tearing out chunks of the mammal.

As they finished devouring it, a shrill screeching ripped the air.

"Are those the pterosaurs?" Nicole asked excitedly.

"Yes," Freedom said.

Nicole scrambled for the path, then jogged along it until she reached the top. She quickly looked around for the portal, and spotted it a short distance away. The dinosaurs next to it were trying to move away, sometimes even forcing their retreat through other dinosaurs. Nicole weaved through the masses as Pete and Samuel appeared. A moment after they came through, the portal collapsed.

"How long were we gone?" Samuel asked as Nicole approached.

"Three days," she immediately replied. "What took so long?"

Pete and Samuel shared a glance. "We were only there for a couple hours," Pete said.

Nicole sighed, then nodded. "So, what happened?"

"We called the local animal control, then alerted the police," Pete said. "They're both going to make sure that the dinosaurs stay in line. The police are arranging for a place for all these dinosaurs to stay."

"That's good," Nicole said. "I'll have Freedom help me get the dinosaurs together and in line. Why don't you two get Beatrice, Mikaela, and Mark packing up?"

The two men nodded and walked to the pit. Nicole trailed after them and called for Freedom to come up. The Utahraptor limped up the path and to Nicole.

"I could use your help in getting the dinosaurs together," Nicole said to Freedom. "We're about to go to the future."

Freedom's eyes widened. "For real?" she breathed.

Nicole nodded.

The Utahraptor grinned, showing her razor-sharp and thin teeth. She turned to face the dinosaur masses and roared. Their heads rotated to face her, and Freedom ordered them to collect in herds and packs according to their breed.

As the dinosaurs moved to obey, Nicole descended down the path. At the bottom of the pit, her fellow humans were gathering together the last of their supplies and bundling them all up. Nicole pitched in and started taking down the tents.

After several minutes, a small Pterodactylus glided down and alighted on Nicole's shoulder. "Is it true?" it chirped in dinosaur-ese. "We're really going to a place of plenty?"

"Yes," Nicole replied in kind with a smile. "Go get with your friends. We leave soon."

The pterosaur's beak opened in a vague grin and it flew off.

"Samuel, Pete," Nicole said, "what was on the other side of the portal when you went through? Where were you?"

"On the outskirts of the city," Samuel answered. "The portal opened near the middle of a cornfield. The city's about five miles away."

Nicole nodded. "Well, the herbivores will have plenty to eat. Did you warn the farmer?"

"The police are," Pete interjected. "We did have the animal control get about seven hundred pounds of meat. When they asked why, Sammy and I told them that if they wanted several dozen starving carnivores to keep going hungry, go right ahead and leave the meat behind!"

Nicole snickered, shaking her head. "They're bringing the meat?"

"They're bringing the meat," Pete affirmed.

It was a little while later before the humans were packed up and ready to go. After the team hefting everything out of the pit, they cleared a wide area. Pete handed the rocks to Nicole. She took the diamond in her left hand and the Portal Ore in her right.

Nicole faced the middle of the open area and paused with her arms held out to her sides and level with her shoulders. Looking around, she saw that all of the dinosaurs were watching her intently. Many of them were restlessly shifting their weight from leg to leg.

There was no sense in making them wait. Nicole took a breath, then struck the two rocks together. Green sparks flew from the point of impact and landed on the ashy ground. From where the sparks landed, the air above crackled, snapped, and then the portal appeared.

Freedom gazed at the portal with awe for a moment before turning to a herd of Ankylosaurus. "Go through!" she ordered them in dinosaur-ese.

The Ankylosaurus belied their weight and weakness from hunger as they cantered forward. Their clubbed tails swung wildly from side to side as they moved. Mikaela slipped through the portal with the Ankylosaurus. Nicole knew that Mikaela was going to make sure that the dinosaurs didn't go too far on the other side. And then the Ankylosaurus vanished into the portal.

The portal began to quiver, but Nicole collided the rocks in the hopes that they would continue to fuel it. The portal shook once more before returning to its perfectly circular shape.

"Keep moving!" Freedom said in dinosaur-ese.

The herbivores went through the portal in alphabetical order; Ankylosaurus, Corythosaurus, and Edmontonia. Nicole had to continually reignite the portal because it lasted only about thirty seconds before beginning to close. After the herbivores went the carnivores; Albertosaurus, the pterosaurs, Stygimolochs, Troodons, the tiny raptors, and even a few other Utahraptors.

When the last tail had vanished from sight, the portal closed completely. Nicole turned to Freedom, who was the only remaining dinosaur in the area.

Freedom's eyes were closed and had her muzzle raised toward the dark sky. She was inhaling deeply, as if she was relishing the scent of the ashen and volcano-hinted air. There was something glistening in the one eye Nicole could see. It took a moment for Nicole to realize that Freedom was on the verge of shedding tears.

"Is something wrong?" Nicole asked in dinosaur-ese.

Freedom didn't open her eyes, but she did lower her head. "I'm fine," she replied in kind. "I am just lamenting that those who didn't make it here in time to be rescued are going to meet a terrible fate."

Nicole gave the Utahraptor a sad smile. "But at least some of you are saved from death. Come on, let's go."

Opening her eyes, Freedom limped over to Nicole's side. Nicole took a moment to gaze at the battered dinosaur. Despite all of her bandages and wounds, Freedom seemed to carry herself with honor and radiated an ambience of courage. The *Intimidator* suddenly seemed cleaner, as if it shined in the rays of an invisible sun.

Nicole took a breath and struck the rocks together. From where the resulting sparks landed, the portal rose into existence. Freedom began limping forward, Nicole striding at her side.

Once they went through, the portal collapsed. The pit and shriveled forest were eerily silent and empty once more.

Nicole held back a pained yelp as searing bright sunlight hit her sensitive eyes. It took her a short while before she could see again, and the sight was breathtaking. Nicole stopped suddenly, and Freedom made a small squeak.

Dinosaurs were all over the field of corn that Pete and Samuel had mentioned. The herbivores were wolfing down the stalks of corn as fast as they could, while the carnivores gorged themselves on a downright *gigantic* pile of raw meat. Humans dressed in authority clothing milled around, and scattered among them were a few media crews. The police were keeping a safe distance away, holding their standard-issue pistols in their hands but pointed at the ground. The animal control were getting close to the dinosaurs but nowhere near the point where they could touch them.

"It's so warm," Freedom breathed in dinosaur-ese.

"Of course it is," Nicole replied with a smile in kind. "The sun is out today and the Earth is being warmed."

A couple of Troodons left the veritable mountain of meat and trotted toward one of the animal control members. "Hey, you look like that other person that has the rocks!" one of them said.

The animal control member in question froze as he saw the Troodons coming closer. He didn't understand a word they said, of course, because all of the dinosaurs except Freedom spoke only their own language of dinosaur-ese. The member began to look more and more apprehensive and nervous the closer the curious Troodons came.

Nicole shook her head in humor and called out in English, "Troodons!"

The Troodons stopped and turned to look at her. One of them made a shrill chirp and cocked its head.

"Don't scare him," Nicole said in dinosaur-ese. "He's never seen anything like any of you before."

The Troodons glanced at the animal control member, then nodded. They chirruped at the man before jogging away.

The animal control member stared at Nicole. "What was *that?*" he said.

"What was what?" Nicole replied in kind.

"Those growling sounds you made! What did you do?"

"The dinosaurs have their own language," Nicole said. "I call it dinosaur-ese, and I speak it quite well."

The animal control member gaped. "The dinosaurs have a language?"

Nicole nodded. "Some of them have even learned English." She made a gesture toward Freedom.

Freedom gave the animal control member a toothy smile. "Nicole is right, but I'm sad to say that I'm the only dinosaur here that can actually speak English."

Now the animal control member was now trembling. Nicole worried if he'd faint from shock.

While he attempted to recover, Nicole turned to Freedom. "Why don't you go and stuff yourself?" she suggested. "You're little more than skin and bones! I'm astonished that you can move around at all."

Freedom looked at the meat and began to drool. "I'll see you later," she said before limping off as fast as she could toward the mountain of meat. A couple of Albertosaurus spotted her coming and moved aside so Freedom had a clear path straight to the food.

Nicole chuckled and leaned so that her weight was mostly on one of her legs. She placed her opposite arm on her hip and let the other one dangle limply from its socket. There was a sense of excitement and happiness filling the air, and Nicole was absorbing it with relish. It was a joyous atmosphere.

"Miss Nicole Nike!"

She blinked and looked around for the person who had called her name. After a second, she saw a well-dressed man striding toward her with two people flanking him on the left and right.

"Governor Pierce!" Nicole said, straightening her stance. "It's an honor, sir."

Pierce gave Nicole a small smile. "Welcome back from the wilderness. Did you find what you're looking for?"

"The *Annihilator* was irretrievable," Nicole said. "But the *Intimidator* is being well taken care of. It just needs to be completely refueled, reloaded, and recharged."

"Wonderful. It's nice to know that over a year of your hard work wasn't all for naught," the governor said with a smile. He looked around. "So, where's the *Intimidator*?"

Nicole pointed to Freedom. "On her back, sir."

The smile slightly dropped from Pierce's face. "The dinosaur is linked to it?"

"From what she told me, her mentor hid it from a couple evil dinosaurs, one of whom was linked to the *Annihilator*, then she found it and used it to defeat their leader."

Pierce humphed. "Well, it would be in your research's best interests to have it unattached and studied. It had a splendid field test, impromptu as it was. Anyway, Miss Nike, I came here to inform you that these dinosaurs have been given permission to live in the state forest reserve a couple miles from here. There are trucks at the end of the field, ready to be loaded to take them here."

"All due respect, Governor," Nicole said, "but dinosaurs aren't like cattle. They have complex personalities, mayhap even sentience. They won't like being tightly packed into a dark truck. If they could rest here in the field for the night, I can have them marching to the reserve in the morning."

The governor hummed. "You're going to have to get permission from the farmer for them to stay the night. He's *already* complaining that the dinosaurs are eating his cash crops."

"Could you point him out to me?" Nicole asked.

Pierce glanced around, then pointed to a man talking to a

policewoman. "That's him. His name's Methuselah Berth."

"Looks like a happy fellow," Nicole remarked, watching Berth's face contort angrily as he spoke.

"Good luck," Pierce said before striding off.

Even from a good 20 yards away, Nicole could see that Berth was just a tad mad; the man was just short of physically assaulting an officer of the law. The policewoman was looking ready to handcuff Berth, so Nicole wasted no time in walking over.

"Methuselah Berth?" Nicole said to the farmer.

The policewoman appeared a tad relieved as Berth turned around to face Nicole. "What do you want?" he asked gruffly.

"I'm Nicole Nike, one of the leading members of the recent expedition that resulted in all of these dinosaurs appearing here."

Berth glowered. "So *you're* the one who's at blame for the all the money being eaten as we speak?" He turned completely away from the policewoman so that his body directly faced Nicole.

"It has been brought to my attention that there are trucks waiting by the road to take them away. . ."

"Good riddance."

"I wasn't done, Mr. Berth! These dinosaurs won't allow themselves to be packed into a truck like cattle. They're hungry, tired, and all they want to do is bask in some sun and enjoy the stars of the night. Can't you let them stay here overnight? Come morning, I *promise,* you'll be rid of them."

Berth stroked his bearded chin. "But I have to allow them to eat as much of my crop as they please."

"They're literally starving."

"What, they had no trees back in that prehistoric age?"

"A super volcano erupted. Their forests are dead."

Berth set his jaw. "So, I let them eat all they want of my corn. I expect to be reimbursed for my losses!"

"I can't help you in that regard," Nicole said. "You'll have to consult the authorities for a compensation. So, can they stay the night?"

With a distressed growl, Berth nodded. "Fine," he spat.

Nicole sighed in relief. "Thank you."

Berth grumbled incoherently and stalked off.

Nicole ran her hand through her hair and tilted her face toward the sky. A small weight lifted off of her chest, knowing that the dinosaurs would be sated, and they would be relocated to a stable home within 24 hours.

"Miss Nike!"

There was a news reporter with a camera crew coming her way. The camera was already trained on Nicole's face, the guy was holding the boom mic in a ready position, and the reporter was looking eager.

"Can I help you?" Nicole asked.

"I'm Cassandra Khan with Channel 11 news," the reporter said in an enthusiastic tone. "You've brought back all of these dinosaurs from the past. What happens now?"

Nicole put on a half smile. "Well, arrangements have been made for them to spend the night here before they're permanently moved to another area."

"Can you let us know where?" Cassandra asked.

Nicole shook her head. "I'm not at liberty to discuss the location over national media. Perhaps you could talk to the police force, or Governor Pierce, for more information. Now, if you'll excuse me, I need to make sure that the carnivores don't decide to go on a rampage." From what she could see, the carnivores were either eating or taking naps in the warm sunlight, but the Channel 11 crew didn't need to know that nothing was amiss.

A few of the Stygimolochs heard her coming and glanced at her. They gave her a few greetings before returning back to eating from the now well diminished mountain of meat. Nicole smiled, happy to know that a creature her size was on good terms with her.

Of course, I'm the one who led them to a veritable Heaven on earth from a volcanic wasteland, Nicole thought with a mental shrug. *Anyone would be grateful to whomever saved them.*

Nicole found Freedom resting a short distance from the meat. The Utahraptor's eyes were closed, but from the rate she was breathing it was apparent that she was still awake. Nicole knelt down by Freedom's head and stroked the soft domed nose.

"Tomorrow morning I'm leading you all to your new home," Nicole said softly in English. "It's a state forest reserve not far from here. About a full day's walk. There's plenty of food, a couple streams and ponds. Maybe all of you will like it there."

"After back there?" Freedom murmured in dinosaur-ese. "I'll be happy anywhere. Thank you, Nicole."

"You're welcome, Freedom," Nicole replied with a huge smile.

CHAPTER THIRTY FOUR

"Is this necessary?" Freedom inquired, eyeing the horse trailer.

Nicole held in a sigh. "It's a long drive back to the city, and my job requires that we access the *Intimidator*'s microchip to see how it performed."

"I could tell you all you'd need to know."

"But we need to access the microchip. Your word, I'm sorry to say, won't be good enough. *Please,* Freedom, get into the trailer."

The Utahraptor took a wary sniff of the interior of the trailer, then took several steps back. "It smells terrible! I'm not getting in that."

"You'll get used to it."

"What are horses, anyway? Are they edible?"

"Don't stall. Get. In. The. Trailer."

A muffled woof came from the jeep Nicole was using to tow the trailer. Translucent smears were left on the windows thanks to a curious black nose. Freedom's head whirled to face the vehicle, the dinosaur's eyes showing caution.

A sinister idea came to Nicole's head right then. "Have you ever heard of a dog, Freedom?"

The Utahraptor slowly shook her head, not looking away from the jeep.

"They're one of the most dangerous creatures of this time. Thanks to hard work and a terrible amount of trial and error, the dog has been given the name Man's Best Friend. Would you like to know *why* they are so dangerous?"

Freedom glanced at Nicole, swallowing nervously. She nodded slowly.

Trying to keep from showing the sadism she was feeling (and kind of feeling bad about it), Nicole continued, "They have a bite that is so venomous, it could kill a Corythosaurus in minutes. You would not believe the death count amassed over the centuries to domesticate dogs."

Freedom's goldenrod eyes were wide.

"My dog is trying to get out. He is hungry. I suggest that you get in the trailer before he finds out where the door handle is and how it works."

The horse trailer's doors were wide open in a blatant invitation. Nicole knew that the tight enclosure was probably becoming more and more tempting to Freedom by the moment. After a few seconds of staring at the jeep, the Utahraptor took a breath and walked up the ramp and into the trailer. The shocks dipped sharply before stabilizing.

Nicole folded up the ramp and closed the two doors. As she latched them securely, she said loud enough for the dinosaur to hear, "Sorry, Freedom, but this was the only thing I could think of to get you inside!"

There was a moment of silence. Then, an earsplitting shriek of frustration rendered the air, and Nicole winced from the volume.

"It's not a long drive. I swear, I'll let you out when we get there."

Freedom's head appeared by one of the barred windows. Her eyes narrowing threateningly, she said, "You'd better."

Recoiling from the angry glare, Nicole hurried to the jeep and hopped into the driver's seat. Compeer bounded into her lap, licking at her face with much fervor.

"Down, boy," Nicole said, pushing him off so she could start the engine. "You'd better not be this hyper when we reach the vet's. Ugh! And you desperately need that dental check. That breath of yours. . . !"

With a hard twist of the key, the engine roared to life like the angry dinosaur in the horse trailer. Dirt flew out from under the jeep's wheels as Nicole stepped on the gas pedal. The horse trailer bounced on bumps and ruts as Nicole headed for the city.

Compeer yipped excitedly, placing his front paws on the dash. Every jolt threatened to send him careening to the floorboards, but to him that was part of the thrill. Nicole ordered him to sit down. With a whine, the golden Lab dropped to all fours. One of his paws brushed the dashboard on his way down, accidentally flipping on the radio.

Nicole let out a startled yell as hard metal music blasted out of the speakers. Struggling to keep her eyes on the road, she fumbled for the volume dial and the station switch. Lowering the volume to a barely audible level, she then flipped through radio stations until she found a just news station. She turned the volume a little higher so she could hear the hosts.

By the time she turned onto a paved road around half an hour later, Nicole was unquestionably depressed.

With a sigh, she reached over and flipped the station to a decent music one. A hard bass beat filled the jeep, and Nicole grinned, dialing up the volume to the point where she could feel the beat. She tried to sing along, but the voices were just at the right pitch where she was either singing too high or too low for her comfort. She settled for humming off-key.

Another half hour passed, and by then the jeep was just entering the main part of the city. Low houses and small businesses gave way to huge skyscrapers, monorails that trailed high above, and a drastic decrease in shrubbery. Nicole got onto on off-ramp and drove for a few more minutes before pulling into a parking lot. Managing to find two spaces directly across from each other, she parked.

"Behave," she warned her dog as she fastened a leash to his collar.

Compeer gazed up at her with wide brown eyes. "Who, me?" he seemed to say.

Nicole opened the door and slid out, Compeer jumping down behind her. She slammed the door shut and locked the jeep.

"Are we there yet? Let me out!"

"Sorry, Freedom!" Nicole said. "Just a quick stop. We'll be back on the road soon."

"Hurry up! This trailer stinks!"

Telling Compeer to heel, Nicole strode through the doors of the clinic. The receptionist looked up as they approached, then woke up the computer.

"Name?" the receptionist asked, hands on the keyboard at the ready.

"Nicole Nike with Compeer."

The receptionist's hands flew across the keyboard. "Yes, you are leaving your dog here for a complete checkup?"

Nicole nodded.

"Our holding pen is just down that hallway. Please clip this tag to his collar, and take this card. When you come back to pick him up, show the card for identification. Have a nice day, miss."

Several minutes later, Nicole unlocked the jeep and threw

the empty leash onto the passenger seat. Less than a minute later, the vehicle was back on the highway.

The horse trailer's door unfastened with a loud clanging, and the ramp noisily slammed down on the asphalt. Nicole winced as her ears rang from the clamor.

"It's about time," Freedom grumped, her fringe twitching irritably. She stalked down the ramp, saying, "The ride was terrible. It was bumpy and I'm positive that I'm sporting a few new bruises. You are a cruel human, Nicole, to use that dog trick."

"It got you into the trailer, didn't it?" Nicole said, shutting up the trailer. "You're going to need to follow me. This is my workplace, and, please, try not to scare the other workers. Not many people are used to close contact with dinosaurs. Most of them wanted me to take the *Intimidator* off of you."

"I'll keep that in mind," the Utahraptor said offhandedly.

With a sigh, Nicole strode to the entranceway and palmed the door open. She held it open so Freedom could pass through before letting it go.

The receptionist was filing her nails as Nicole and Freedom neared, on their way to the freight elevator. Freedom sped up a bit.

The receptionist barely glanced up as they passed. "Hey, Nicole," she said. She held up a hand for self-appraisal. "Welcome back. Have any fun?"

"Plenty," Nicole said.

Freedom, silent as a silk blanket over a hardwood floor, stalked around the reception desk just out of the receptionist's peripheral sight. Nicole wilted a little as the Utahraptor came up behind the receptionist's chair and peered over her shoulder.

"Why do you trim your nails?" Freedom asked, squinting.

"To make them pretty. It's a girl thing."

"Mine are. . . pretty, and I've never done such a thing to them."

"Really? Let me see."

Mouth arched into a grin, Freedom extended an arm for the receptionist to see.

The receptionist did a double take, her eyes widening to the limit. She whirled around to see the full body of an adult raptor standing behind her. Her mouth opened, but it was obvious that the scream was caught in the throat.

"Freedom!" Nicole said with an exasperated sigh. "What did I say about scaring the workers?"

"To not to," the Utahraptor replied, slinking away from the receptionist and standing by Nicole.

"I'm sorry about her," Nicole said to the receptionist. "She hasn't learned any politeness yet. Fresh out of the Cretaceous, you see."

Before the receptionist could get over her shock, Nicole herded Freedom into the freight elevator.

As it descended, Freedom said, "Her expression was, as you humans say, priceless."

"I'm not talking to you right now."

Freedom snorted. "You have no sense of humor."

"You have no sense of politeness."

"I thought that you weren't talking to me."

"I wasn't. I was merely correcting you."

"You are directing your words at me. You are talking to me."

Nicole pursed her lips and sent a moderate glare at the wall. She felt as if she was bickering inanely with a sibling, something that she would normally consider immature. And yet, she was giving the dinosaur a childish silent treatment. Inwardly, she sighed and externally smoothed her expression.

When the elevator doors opened, Nicole led the way down the hall and to Room 7. The guards stared at Freedom as Nicole swiped her security card through the scanner.

Freedom gave the guards a playful growl, but the guards only heard a threat. Their hands twitched over their guns while their eyes darted Nicole's way.

Nicole subtly kicked Freedom's leg.

The door opened with a pneumatic hiss, and the odd twosome went through. Nicole stowed away her card.

Pete was the first one to greet them. "We're ready for the

procedure," he said. "Mark has the computer. Mark, bring up File: Alpha Vega and enter the code."

Mark did so, then projected the monitor's image on the wall. The code was entered, the combination masked by asterisks, and a cross-section of the *Intimidator* was displayed. Alongside the diagram was a long chronological list and a miniature map of the city and the surrounding suburbs.

One of the scientists stepped closer to the projection, carefully avoiding interrupting it. "The *Intimidator* started re-cording the moment the Struthiomimus exited the portal. It spent approximately two days apparently in this very room before slowly making its way to the countryside; another three days. It stayed in the countryside for a little over two years before briefly moving to another section of the country for roughly three days. This is when the entirety of its weapons and fuel were consumed. Then it went almost all the way to Sybre Town. Right along the edge of Berth's farm, it seems."

Nicole slowly nodded, sneaking glances at Freedom. The Utahraptor was paying close attention.

"Bring up the weaponry and fuel logs," Pete said. "Let's see how they performed."

Mark obeyed.

Nicole frowned a little as she quickly read over the display. "Freedom, the fuel was used up incredibly quickly. Can you further speculate?"

Freedom nodded. "I think most of it was used bringing me out of a free fall. Then it lasted for about two. . . minutes, was it, in your time measurements? Then I had to either land or crash."

"The *Intimidator* was designed to carry only two hundred and fifty pounds, maximum," Mark said. "You weigh, what, fifteen hundred pounds, perhaps more? No wonder the fuel was consumed so rapidly."

"We'd need to alter it, then, to make it more efficient," Nicole mused. "Allow it to bear at least half that fifteen hundred for at least ten minutes."

"We can't tweak the *Intimidator* now," a scientist said. "It's linked to the dinosaur."

"The *Intimidator* is a prototype," Nicole replied. "We learn, then make a new one with upgrades."

Mark stared at the projection for a moment before saying, "I believe that's all we can learn from the *Intimidator* and its host. Nicole, you can carry Freedom back to the dinosaur home now."

"Am I not getting restocked?" Freedom asked. "New exploding black things, the light, and the fuel?"

"They're called missiles, a laser, and jet fuel," Nicole explained. "The laser is recharged by your movements, as you may have noticed. But we're not restocking the missiles or refueling. Why would you need them? But should you need to fight again, we will restock the *Intimidator*. Now, let's get you home. I also need to pick up Compeer on the way."

"Not the dog. Can't the dog stay behind until I'm dropped off?"

"No."

EPILOGUE

It was a gorgeous spring day with a shining sun that was miraculously unhidden by war-produced haze. It had been a dry but cold winter, but with the spring had come abundant rain, which lad finally cleared the war haze. The songbirds were constantly filling the air with beautiful chirps. The sun shined. Squirrels chattered. Flowers bloomed. Trees budded.

Nicole stopped in her walk when she spotted a small herd of deer up ahead. There were a couple of does, a buck with a gorgeous 10-point rack, and several fawns with their light brown fur that looked like someone had flicked a dripping white paintbrush over them. They had heard her coming, and their heads were facing her. Nicole stayed perfectly still for a long moment before slowly gripping the camera dangling from her neck and snapping a few pictures.

Suddenly, an Utahraptor leapt out from behind a bush and took down the buck. The does and fawns scattered as the raptor feasted.

"Well," Nicole murmured, taking several steps backward. "How Bambi meets Godzilla."

She left the scene. With each stride, her camera and her badge bounced against her chest. Nicole glanced down at the badge but didn't read it; she knew by heart what it said. 'Nicole Nike, CEO and Senior Overseer of the Dinosaur Reserve.' She had started the Dinosaur Reserve almost as soon as the dinosaurs began to settle into their new home. Her business was funded entirely on donations and out of her own pocket. Volunteers that ranged from the teens to retirees helped her take pictures, write documents on how the dinosaurs were coping, and develop a website that could let even more people know dinosaur facts that were straight from the Utahraptor's mouth. She was also writing an audial language book she planned on calling *Dinosaur-ese; the Translation to English.*

Nicole hadn't dropped her weapons development work though, so she was juggling both.

About a mile further along the path, Nicole pulled her phone from her pocket and checked the compass. *I'm going the right way, and I'm about six miles from the Jeep. So, where are they?*

Nicole glanced upward so that she could see the sunlight coming in through the tree canopies. It was still near the beginning of the morning, so she had plenty of time for a visit before she had to get back to the Jeep by nightfall.

It was time to announce her presence. Besides, not many of

them liked sudden surprises; if she came out of nowhere screaming, most would probably attack her before they could recognize her. War would do that to someone. Surprises took on a very negative meaning in wartime.

"Hello!" Nicole yelled in dinosaur-ese. "Is anyone out here?"

She held her breath and listened for a reply. It took a minute, but she finally heard an answering screech. "Who's there?"

"Nicole!" she shouted back.

There was silence for a moment, and then she heard leaves crunching underfoot. A Corythosaurus appeared through the trees. In its arms it carried a bundle of tall grasses. It blinked at her, then smiled as best as it could with a very stiff beak.

"Hi," Nicole said in dinosaur-ese. "Which way are the others?"

"We moved over the winter to a place with a larger body of water," the Corythosaurus stated. "Turn a little to your left, then walk until you reach them."

"Thank you," Nicole said with a grateful smile. "Why are you collecting grass, if I may ask?"

"For my mate. She can't leave the nest."

"Nest?" This was news to her.

The Corythosaurus nodded. "You will understand better when you get there. Farewell." It trod off again, presumably to gather more grass.

"Careful now!" Nicole called out after it. "You're getting close to the boundaries!"

The Corythosaurus gave an acknowledging trumpet.

Nicole hummed thoughtfully, then turned as directed and continued her trek. It took about twenty minutes before she began to catch the familiar sounds of dinosaurs talking and moving up ahead. She sped up her pace from a walk to a jog, then felt her backpack begin smacking the small of her back with each stride she took. She broke through a line of trees and emerged into a large clearing.

Her jaw dropped. Dozens upon dozens of holes were dug in the ground, ranging in size according to the species of dinosaur. At least one dinosaur hovered around a certain hole. Nicole took a few steps further into the clearing and peered into one of the holes. At the bottom were five light green eggs about the size of a football.

"Back off!" an Edmontonia snarled, bursting into Nicole's peripheral vision. As Nicole stumbled backward with a surprised yelp, the Edmontonia blinked and lowered its head. "Oh, it's only you, Nicole! I'm sorry for the shout, it's just that you got a little too close to my eggs."

"It's quite all right," Nicole said, holding a hand to her chest. She could feel her heart beating her ribs like a drum. "No harm done. Just scared me a little."

The Edmontonia turned around and laid down next to its nest. It paid no more attention to Nicole, who was looking around for any Utahraptors. From what she could tell, the dinosaurs had their nests in little groups according to the breed of dinosaur; for instance, all of the Ankylosaurus were together in one area with all of the Albertosaurus in another area. It only left to logic that the Utahraptors would be together. It was only a matter of finding *where*.

It took a minute before Nicole finally spotted an Utahraptor sitting next to a nest. Nicole weaved toward the Utahraptor area, careful not to arouse a protective parent as she passed by.

From there, it was easy to distinguish who Freedom was, as she was the only one who had a vibrant magenta fringe, not to mention the shiny *Intimidator*. She was gently nosing some eggs in her own nest as Nicole approached.

"Freedom?" Nicole said in English.

The magenta-fringed Utahraptor looked up. "Nicole!" she exclaimed happily in kind, striding toward the human and momentarily resting her chin on Nicole's shoulder. "What brings you here?"

"I missed you," Nicole said. "Besides, this was your first winter here, and I wanted to see how you all fared. Anyone die?"

"No, thank goodness. Our numbers are small enough already. We managed to find enough mammals to sustain us."

Nicole looked down into the nest. There were six black eggs inside, a little smaller than a volleyball with the shape of an ostrich egg. "Are these yours?"

Freedom beamed. "Yes. I found a mate at the end of autumn. He's away right now, hunting. The eggs are due to hatch at any time."

"Congratulations," Nicole said. "So, what's your beau's name?"

"Beau?" Freedom mimicked with a frown.

"Mate."

"Oh. Well, translated, his name would be some sort of marine plant. You'd have to give him an English name."

"Well, then I'll name him when I see him. Do you mind if I snap some pictures of your eggs? I need to document this."

"Go right ahead."

Nicole took several pictures of the black eggs, then twirled on her heel and snapped even more of the entire clearing. "I'll need a picture of each dinosaur egg so I can match it to the breed of the parents."

"I'm sure that no one else will mind either, just as long as you don't get too close to the nests."

With a cheerful demeanor, Nicole went around shooting pictures of the nests. She made sure to take a picture of a type of egg and then have an immediately following picture of the dinosaur breed that laid the egg. It took a while to get all of the pictures she wanted, and when she was done, she meandered back to Freedom's nest while she flipped through the pictures she had taken.

Freedom arched her neck so that she could peer over Nicole's shoulder. "You can copy your sight of an area and freeze it for looking at later?"

"Something like that," Nicole muttered. "It's called a camera. It basically does what you just said."

There was a screech from the trees. Freedom was the only

one who looked toward the sound. She crooned happily, then screeched back. A second later, a large Utahraptor emerged from the forest with a dead badger in its mouth. It trotted to Freedom and dropped the badger at her feet.

"Who's this?" the newcomer asked.

"Nicole," Freedom said. She rumbled something in dinosaur-ese to the Utahraptor, then continued in the same language, "She will give you an English name."

"Hello," the Utahraptor, a he, said in dinosaur-ese with a curt nod to Nicole. "So, what is my English name?"

Nicole hummed thoughtfully as she looked the Utahraptor over. He towered a good foot over Freedom when both were standing straight. His hide was a lovely sunset yellow color, with a very pale brown underbelly and a greenish yellow fringe. He had light blue eyes.

Freedom said that his name would equal some sort of marine plant in English. With those colors, it's either Algae or Kelp. Since Algae doesn't sound like a name I'd give my kid. . . "Kelp." Nicole finally said.

The male Utahraptor repeated his name, then gave Nicole a tight smile. "Thank you, Nicole," he said. "I shall be called Kelp in English."

Nicole smiled, happy to know that Kelp didn't mind his translated name.

Freedom suddenly gasped and whacked Kelp with her tail. Both of them gazed into their nest. Nicole looked at the black eggs and saw that they were beginning to twitch and rock. Nicole's breath caught in her throat as the three of them edged over, closer to the hatching eggs.

One of the eggs developed a crack that snaked over the shell like a lightning bolt. The crack widened, and then a piece of shell popped off, big enough for a tiny Utahraptor hatchling to tumble out through. The hatchling blinked hard in the sunlight, its eyes cross-eyed.

"Congratulations," Nicole breathed.

Freedom lowered her head and nudged one of the hatchlings. The hatchling looked up at its mother and chirruped softly. Freedom crooned, and the hatchling giggled. Nicole felt little tears bud in her eyes as she took a few pictures of the hatchlings.

The rest of the hatchlings emerged from their own eggs. It didn't take very long for the hatchlings to visibly bond with their parents. Once the bonding was done, Kelp began ripping off slivers of badger meat and dropping them in front of the hatchlings. The hatchlings hungrily wolfed down the slivers of meat. Freedom helped Kelp feed their offspring. The hatchlings were only able to take a few slivers before their teeny tiny stomachs filled. One of them burped and fell backward onto its back.

Freedom looked at Nicole, catching her eye. "Do you want to hold them?" Freedom asked gently.

Nicole blinked in shock. "What?"

Kelp eyed Freedom, then Nicole, but said nothing. His fringe flattened a bit, however.

Nicole edged forward until she was at the very rim of the nest. One of the hatchlings, a light golden one with a blue fringe, noticed her and toddled closer. Nicole slowly extended her hands, palms up and fingers curled, toward the hatchling. The hatchling froze as her fingers neared, but it must've deemed them unthreatening and waddled onto her palms. Nicole slowly pulled back her hands and brought the hatchling closer to her face.

The hatchling chirped, staring. Nicole could almost see what it was thinking; *What is this strange looking creature? It has no scales, just those weird stringy thingies. I hope it's nice.*

"Hey, little one," Nicole cooed with a puckered smile. "I'm Nicole. You probably don't understand me, but don't worry! I'll teach you and your siblings English when you're older."

The hatchling was silent and still for a moment, eyes staring, before bursting out into giggling chirrups. It fell over onto its side as its stubby little tail waved through the air.

Nicole grinned as she gently placed the hatchling back into the nest. "Thanks," she said to Freedom.

Freedom said nothing, but the erect fringe and the huge fond smile carried the meaning clear as spring water.

As the two adult Utahraptors shifted their attentions back to their children, Nicole sensed that it was time to leave. She snapped a few more pictures before checking her compass and heading toward where she had left her Jeep. The dinosaurs she passed by gave her nothing more than a glance or a grunt of farewell.

Nicole entered the trees, and it wasn't long before the clearing was lost to sight. She took a deep breath and looked up to the sky. It was a gorgeous spring day, perfect for the first generation of dinosaurs to come forth unto the earth.

GLOSSARY

Age

> *Hatchling* - A newly hatched dinosaur
> *Youngling* - A dinosaur one year old
> *Adult* - A mature dinosaur. Age range between youngling
> and adulthood varies with the species.

Luna

> The dinosaurian term for the moon.

Pace

> The dinosaurs' term of measurement. Roughly
> equivalent to a meter.

Seasons

> *Green* - Spring
> *Hot* - Summer
> *Colors* - Autumn
> *White* - Winter

Squama

> What the dinosaurs collectively call themselves.

Turn

> The dinosaurian term for a year.

DINOCTIONARY

ACROCANTHOSAURUS

Pronounced: ak-ro-KANTH-uh-sawr-us
Diet: Ground-dwelling carnivore
Home: USA
Weight: 3.5 - 5 tons
Height: 16 feet
Length: 40 feet
Name Means: "High-Spined Lizard"

ALBERTOSAURUS

Pronounced: al-BERT-oh-sawr-us
Diet: Ground-dwelling carnivore
Home: Canada, Mexico, USA
Weight: 2.5 tons
Height: 10 feet
Length: 28 feet
Name Means: "Alberta Lizard"

ALLOSAURUS

Pronounced: AL-oh-sawr-us
Diet: Ground-dwelling carnivore
Home: Canada, Mexico, USA
Weight: 1 - 5 tons
Height: 14 feet
Length: 32 feet
Name Means: "Different Lizard"

ANKYLOSAURUS

Pronounced: an-KIE-loh-sawr-us
Diet: Ground-dwelling herbivore
Home: Canada, USA
Weight: 4 tons
Height: 5 feet
Length: 22 feet
Name Means: "Stiff Joint Lizard"

APPALACHIOSAURUS

Pronounced: ah-pah-LAY-chee-oh-sawr-us
Diet: Ground-dwelling carnivore
Home: USA
Weight: 2 tons
Height: 9 feet
Length: 25 feet
Name Means: "Appalachian Lizard from
        Montgomery"

BAMBIRAPTOR

Pronounced: BAM-bee-rap-tor
Diet: Ground-dwelling carnivore
Home: USA
Weight: 7 pounds
Height: 1 foot
Length: 3 feet
Name Means: "Baby Raider"

BRACHiOSAURUS

Pronounced: BRA-key-oh-sawr-us
Diet: Ground-dwelling herbivore
Home: Tanzania, USA, Zimbabwe
Weight: 60 tons
Height: 40 feet
Length: 80 feet
Name Means: "High Chested Arm Lizard"

COELURUS

Pronounced: see-LURE-us
Diet: Ground-dwelling carnivore
Home: USA
Weight: 40 pounds
Height: 2.5 feet
Length: 5 feet
Name Means: "Hollow Tail"

CORYTHOSAURUS

Pronounced: kore-ITH-oh-sawr-us
Diet: Ground-dwelling herbivore
Home: Canada, USA
Weight: 3.5 tons
Height: 14 feet
Length: 33 feet
Name Means: "Corinthian Lizard"

DEINONYCHUS

Pronounced: die-NON-ih-kiss
Diet: Ground-dwelling carnivore
Home: USA
Weight: 110 pounds
Height: 4 feet
Length: 10 feet
Name Means: "Terrible Claw"

DILOPHOSAURUS

Pronounced: die-LOAF-oh-sawr-us
Diet: Ground-dwelling carnivore
Home: China, India, Usa
Weight: .5 tons
Height: 10 feet
Length: 22 feet
Name Means: "Double Crested Lizard"

EDMONTONIA

Pr
Diet: Ground-dwelling herbivore
Home: Canada, USA
Weight: 4 tons
Height: 9 feet
Length: 22 feet
Name Means: "Of Edmonton"

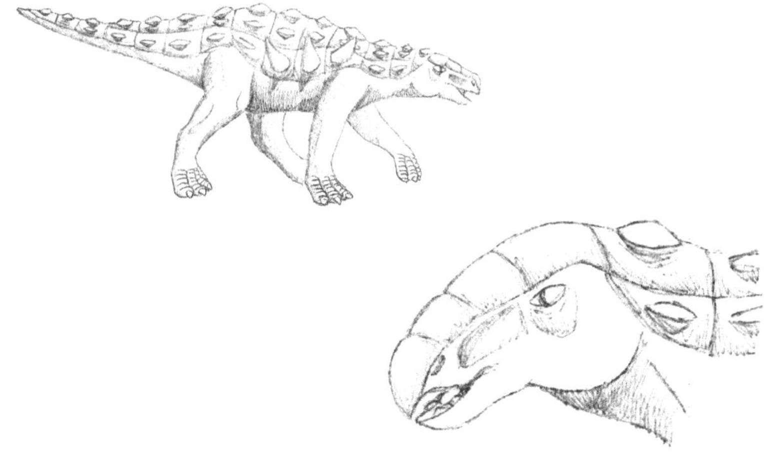

hesperonychus

Pronounced: HESS-peh-RON-ih-cuss
Diet: Ground-dwelling insectivore
Home: Canada
Weight: 4 pounds
Height: 1.5 feet
Length: 3 feet
Name Means: "Western Claw"

MICROVENATOR

Pronounced: MI-crow-VEN-ah-tor
Diet: Ground-dwelling carnivore
Home: USA
Weight: 7 pounds
Height: 2 feet
Length: 4 feet
Name Means: "Small Hunter"

QUETZALCOATLUS

Pronounced: KEWT-zal-co-AT-lus
Diet: Aerial carnivore
Home: USA
Weight: 55 pounds
Wingspan: 30 feet
Length: 29 feet
Name Means: "Feathered Serpent"

PTERODACTYLUS

Pronounced: TEH-roe-DACK-till-us
Diet: Aerial carnivore
Home: UK, France, Germany, Portugal
Weight: 10 pounds
Wingspan: 11 feet
Length: 6 feet
Name Means: "Wing Finger"

STRUTHIOMIMUS

Pronounced: STRUE-thee-oh-MI-mus
Diet: Ground-dwelling omnivore
Home: Canada, USA
Weight: 330 pounds
Height: 6 feet
Length: 10 feet
Name Means: "Ostrich Mimic"

STYGIMOLOCH

Diet: Ground-dwelling omnivore
Home: Canada, USA
Weight: 440 pounds
Height: 5 feet
Length: 10 feet
Name Means: "Styx Molcoch"

TRICERATOPS

Pronounced: try-SARE-oh-tops
Diet: Ground-dwelling herbivore
Home: Canada, Mexico, USA
Weight: 7 tons
Height: 8 feet
Length: 28 feet
Name Means: "Three Horn Face"

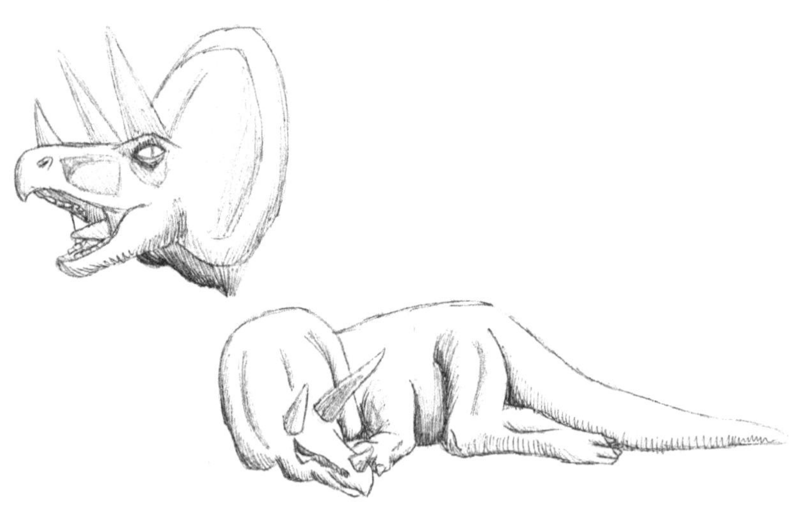

TROODON

Pronounced: TRUE-don
Diet: Ground-dwelling carnivore
Home: Canada, USA
Weight: 110 pounds
Height: 2 feet
Length: 6 feet
Name Means: "Tooth That Wounds"

TYRANNOSAURUS REX

Pronounced: tie-RAN-oh-sawr-us rex
Diet: Ground-dwelling carnivore
Home: Canada, Mexico, USA
Weight: 6 tons
Height: 16 feet
Length: 40 feet
Name Means: "Tyrant Lizard King"

UTAHRAPTOR

Pronounced: YOO-taw-rap-tor
Diet: Ground-dwelling carnivore
Home: USA
Weight: 1 ton
Height: 8 feet
Length: 23 feet
Name Means: "Utah Robber"